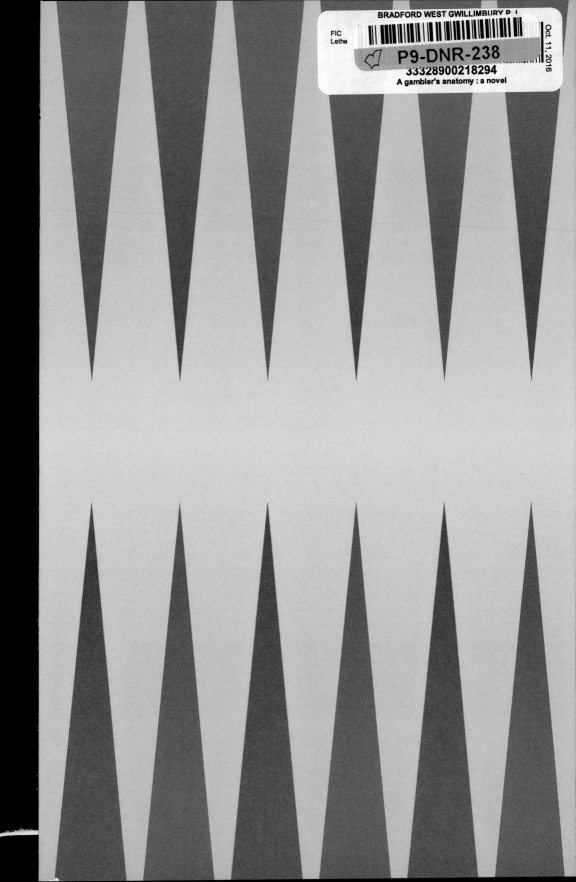

A
GAMBLER'S
ANATOMY

Also by Jonathan Lethem

A
GAMBLER'S
ANATOMY

a novel

Jonathan Lethem

Doubleday

New York   London   Toronto
Sydney   Auckland

Copyright © 2016 by Jonathan Lethem

All rights reserved. Published in the United States by Doubleday, a division of Penguin Random House LLC, New York, and distributed in Canada by Random House of Canada, a division of Penguin Random House Canada Limited, Toronto.

www.doubleday.com

DOUBLEDAY and the portrayal of an anchor with a dolphin are registered trademarks of Penguin Random House LLC.

Book design by Michael Collica
Jacket design by gray318

Library of Congress Cataloging-in-Publication Data
Names: Lethem, Jonathan, author.
Title: A gambler's anatomy / by Jonathan Lethem.
Description: First edition. | New York : Doubleday, 2016.
Identifiers: LCCN 2016006646 | ISBN 9780385539906 (hardcover) |
ISBN 9780385539913 (ebook)
Classification: LCC PS3562.E8544 G36 2016 | DDC 813/.54—dc23
LC record available at http://lccn.loc.gov/2016006646

MANUFACTURED IN THE UNITED STATES OF AMERICA

1 3 5 7 9 10 8 6 4 2

First Edition

for Bill Thomas

Contents

Sixteen

Thirty-Two

Book Three
Sixty-Four

Gammon

Backgammon

BOOK ONE

One

I

It was there when he woke up. Presumably also when he slept. The blot. Standing alone at the back of the sparsely populated ferry to Kladow, mercifully sheltered behind safety glass against the chill of the lake at evening, Alexander Bruno could no longer deny the blot that had swollen in his vision and was with him always, the vacancy now deforming his view of the receding shore. It forced him to peer around its edges for glimpses of the mansions and biergartens, the strip of sand at the century-old lido, the tarpaulined sailboats. He'd come to Berlin, half the circumference of the world, two weeks ago, whether to elude his fate or to embrace it he couldn't know.

He'd been biding his time in Charlottenburg, breakfasting at the quiet cafés, watching the days grow steadily longer, overhearing more spoken English than he'd have preferred, running through his last funds. His tuxedo had remained in its hanging bag, his backgammon case latched. All the while the blot had been with him, unacknowledged. Bruno its carrier, its host. He'd passed through customs with the innocence of the accidental smuggler: *Nothing to declare.* It was only after having at last called the number provided him by Edgar Falk and consenting to visit the rich man's house in Kladow, only upon his waking, this very day on which he'd dusted off tuxedo and backgammon case, that the blot had insisted he grant its existence. An old friend he'd never met but recognized nevertheless.

Why get too fancy about it? He might be dying.

Under the circumstances of Bruno's dread, the slide of the S-Bahn through the endless roster of stations from Westend to Wannsee had seemed as long as his voyage from Singapore to Berlin. The German

3

city, with its graffiti and construction sites, its desultory strips of park-land and naked pink water pipes, had its own sprawl and circumfer-ence. Berlin wended through time. On the S-Bahn toward Wannsee the tall girls in black leggings with bicycles and earbuds, so prevalent in Charlottenburg and Mitte, had thinned out, replaced by dour Prus-sian businessmen and staring grandmother types, slouching home with briefcases and shopping bags. By the time of the ferry there was little to defeat the irresistible illusion that the city was newly van-quished and carved into sectors, that the prevailing silence and gloom derived from remorse and privations not seventy years past but fresh as smoldering rubble.

When Bruno had called to ask his host for directions to Kladow, the rich man told him that the ferry across the lake at evening was an experience he shouldn't miss. Bruno, the German had said, should keep his eye out on the right for the famous Strandbad Wannsee, Berlin's traditional resort beach, and, on the left, for the Wannsee-Konferenz villa. The site of the Final Solution's planning, though Bruno had needed this legacy explained by his hotel's concierge. Of course, scanning for it now, Bruno had no way of distinguishing the site from other mansions arrayed on the western shore, each of which heaved into the void at the center of his sight.

For how long had Bruno considered the blot nothing but a retinal floater grown mad or the looming ghost of his inattention? Only a fool wouldn't connect it to the perennial headache that had caused him, as he'd walked from the Wannsee S-Bahnhof through the steep park leading to the boarding dock, to shuffle his fingers into his tuxedo jacket's interior pocket in search of his packet of paracetamol, that incomparable British aspirin on which he'd grown dependent. Then to gulp down two pills, with only the shimmering lake before him for water. He'd accept the verdict of fool if it meant the paracetamol repaired his sight. Made a full cake of that which was presently a doughnut: the world. He raised his hand. The blot obscured his palm as it had the shore. Bruno noticed he'd lost a cuff link.

"Excuse me," he said. He said it to a tall girl in black tights, one of those who'd journeyed in his car of the S-Bahn, all the way from the fashionable Mitte, to board the ferry. She'd maneuvered her bicycle into the ferry's rack before joining him at the back windows. Bruno spoke to excuse crouching at her knees to feel on the floor, on the chance that the cuff link had only tumbled down at his feet. A hopeless impulse, like the drunkard in the joke who, wandering at night on a side street, and discovering he has lost his key, searches not in the place he believes it was lost but instead beneath a lamppost, simply because the light is better there.

The joke came to mind because the girl crouched to help, without knowing what she was looking for. In the joke, the drunk was aided by a policeman, who searches for a while beneath the streetlamp too. Now, as she bent to join him, Bruno saw that *girl* wasn't actually the right word. Her lined face was both severe and attractive. So many women in Berlin, athletically slim, dressed in a universal costume and couldn't be judged for age by their outlines.

"*Kontaktlinsen?*"

"No . . . no . . ." The Berliners all spoke English, and even when they didn't, the meanings bled through. In Singapore the alien tongues of Mandarin, Malay, and Tamil had left him happily sealed in his cone of incomprehension. Did she guess that the problem was with his eyes because he groped like a blind man?

"*Kuffenlinksen . . .*" he bluffed, pinching his loose sleeve. He doubted it was a word in any language. *Additionally I am probably also soon losing my life,* he added in pidgin telepathy, just to see if she was listening.

She showed no sign of having read his thoughts. He was relieved. Alexander Bruno had forsaken thought transference years ago, at the start of puberty. Yet he remained vigilant.

"English?" she asked.

Bruno enjoyed being mistaken for British. With his height and high cheekbones, he'd been told he resembled Roger Moore, or the bass player from Duran Duran. More likely, however, she only meant the English language.

"Yes," he said. "I've dropped a piece of jewelry. I'm sorry, I don't know the word in German. Man jewelry." He displayed his cuff, which was slightly foxed, scorched by hotel-room ironings. Let her see it. Bruno was aware that his appeal was that of a ruined glamour. His neck and jaw, considered in the mirror lately, were those of the father he'd never known. The flesh only tightened over Bruno's chin in the old familiar way if he thrust his jaw forward and tilted his head back slightly, a pose he'd recognized as definitive of middle-aged vanity. He caught himself at it frequently.

Now he looked not into the mirror but into the face of the would-be rescuer of his nonexistent contact lens. White hair interspersed with the blond. Enticing lips framed by deep lines—to Bruno, expressive, though they must have bothered her. Two humans beyond their prime, but hanging in. He had to deflect his glance in order to see her at all, likely making him appear more bashful than he felt. "Never mind," he told her. "I'm sure I lost it on the train."

Flirtation, so effortlessly accomplished. Mention of the train had done it. Train unspecified; they both knew which. They'd ridden together and now shared the ferry, and though a thousand identical to her might have strolled past his Charlottenburg café window in two weeks, the shared destination worked its paltry magic. And both tall. This little was enough to excuse lust as destiny.

Bruno had imagined a day when he'd outgrow distractibility. Instead, approaching fifty, the window of his interest had widened. Women once invisible to his younger self were now etched in flame in his imagination. This wasn't erotic propriety. Bruno was still capable of desiring the younger women who no longer—mostly—returned his glances. But those his own age, their continuing fitness for the animal game newly visible to him, these he found more arresting, for their air of either desperation or total denial. Would he eventually crave the grandmothers too? Perhaps by that time the blot in his sight would have expanded to a general blindness, and so have freed him.

They stood. "I'm Alexander," he said, and offered his hand. She took it.

"Madchen."

The question was in what language they'd extend their special destiny. English, or . . . ? Not German, since Bruno had none. English or the language of no language, which he preferred. He began slowly and deliberately, but with care not to suggest idiocy on either of their parts. "I have an appointment in Kladow. It is at a private home. I am expected alone, but it would surely delight my host if I arrived with you as a guest."

"I'm sorry?" She smiled. "You would like—?"

"I'm hoping you'll join me, Madchen."

"To a dinner, *ja*? Sorry for my not-good English."

"I should be the one to apologize. I'm the visitor in your country. It's not a dinner exactly. An . . . appointment." He raised his back-gammon case slightly. If she took it for a briefcase, she wasn't precisely wrong. The tools of his trade. "But there's sure to be something to eat, if you're hungry. Or we can go out after."

I will never lie to you, he promised silently, again just in case she could hear. Bruno had only encountered a small scattering of those in whom he observed the gift of telepathy he himself had renounced. But you never knew.

"It is very nice, what you ask, but I think I can't."

"You'd be completely welcome."

"If it is your work?"

"I'm a gambler," he said. "You would be my good-luck charm." Steadiness and poise, these were Bruno's old methods. He wasn't going to let the blot make him squirrelly.

She didn't speak but smiled again, confused.

"You're beautiful," he said.

They should have had a bar on this ferry, and an ocean for the ferry to cross. Instead the voyage was concluding. The boat had curled around a small island, into the landing at Kladow. The passengers bunched at the doors.

"Or, afterward," he conceded. "I could call you when I'm finished." He gestured at the twilit town beyond the ferry dock. "Have you a favorite place for a late drink?"

"In Kladow?" Madchen seemed to find this funny. She raised her bicycle's front wheel to free it from the rack.

He drew his phone from his tux's interior breast pocket. "Will you give me your number?"

She raised her eyebrows, glanced to one side. Then took his phone from him and, scowling intently, keyed a string of numbers into the device and returned it to him. The ferry emptied quickly. They brought up the rear, shuffling out along the short pier where others now queued for the return crossing. Under the Kladow docks, a family of swans bobbed together. Farther from the boats, he saw a diving cormorant. The bird called Bruno to some memory he couldn't quite retrieve . . .

He scanned the near shore for the car the rich man had promised to send. The view confirmed the ferry's power as a time machine, one which had transported them from the fashionable Mitte, the urbane international Berlin of present reputation. Alt-Kladow stood clustered uphill, a sleepy nineteenth-century village. Perhaps it was here German life truly resided, fires banked against history. Bruno might understand Madchen's amusement at the suggestion of a late drink now. Though the shorefront was strewn with cozy biergartens, he'd be surprised if they remained open much past sundown on a Wednesday. The crowd from the ferry lowered their heads and trudged past the biergartens' wooden-bower entrances, hell-bent for domestic finish lines.

"Do you live here?" he asked.

She shook her head. "I come to do . . . *kindersitting.* For my sister's girl."

"Your niece."

"Yes."

They crossed the street, Madchen wheeling her bicycle by her side. They passed a workman who knelt in a scattering of loose squarish stones, which he pounded with a large block hammer into the familiar grid pattern that made up Berlin's sidewalks. Bruno had never seen the stones dislodged from the ground until now. They seemed a reminder to him of his trade, his purpose here. Berlin was paved with unnumbered dice, smashed flush to the ground with wooden mallets.

As the few vehicles meeting the ferry departed, and the crowd of walkers filtered up the hill, Bruno spotted the car he'd expected, the car the rich man had sent for him. A Mercedes-Benz, two decades old but impeccable. Another output of the time machine. The driver, crew cut and thick of neck, examined Bruno, who would have fit the description he'd provided the rich man, except for the presence of his companion. Bruno held up one finger, and the driver nodded and rolled up his window. Madchen followed his glance.

"Madchen—" He took the tip of her chin gently between his thumb and forefinger, as if adjusting a framed picture slightly skewed on a wall. The nearer he brought her face to his, the less the blot mattered. As if he'd invited her in, behind its curtain. "One kiss, for luck."

Her eyes closed as he leaned in and brushed her lips with his. Bruno felt a surprising numbness in his lips. He hadn't noticed feeling cold. *You have been kissed, Madchen, by a vision in a tuxedo.* Albeit one not so well preserved as the car that had come to collect him.

"I'll call when I'm done." He thought of his earlier promise. One enforced the other.

Madchen drew back and shed a last curious smile, then slid onto her bicycle and was gone, into the center of his blot and up the hill. By the time Bruno entered the backseat of the waiting car, she wasn't to be seen. He glanced once more shoreward, at the jostling swans, the bobbing fearless cormorant, then nodded to the driver. The Benz crawled up the same road she'd taken, the only route into Alt-Kladow.

II

Wolf-Dirk Köhler, the rich man, opened the door to his study himself. The driver of the car had led Alexander Bruno inside, to the plush darkened foyer, and rapped lightly on the door that now opened, casting out light and warmth and wood smoke. Flames lapped in the fireplace.

Köhler, advertised by Edgar Falk as "a potentially historic whale," barely came up to Bruno's chin. Nothing could have surprised Bruno. Marks, hemophiliac free spenders, gamblers of miscalibrated vanity: These appeared before him in an assortment of human containers. A whale might resemble a whale, or a minnow. Köhler's big swank house was his true body. His money his true clothes. Bruno was here to bare him of what he could in an evening. Money ennobled nothing, except when you needed to have it. After what had happened in Singapore, and his flight to this city of dubious refuge, Bruno needed it very badly.

"Edgar's man of mystery," said Köhler in perfect English. He held out his hand and grinned, a balding sprite in a blue velvet dinner jacket. "How I've been wishing to meet you. The veritable prince of the checkers, Edgar told me. Please come in."

"Luck is the prince," said Bruno. "I am its servant." It wasn't the first time he'd used the line, or some variant: luck the *master,* luck the *sorcerer,* luck the *caliph* or *samurai* or *Brahmin,* Bruno merely *footman, apprentice, pilgrim* . . .

"Hah! Very *good*! You have just won a first point, I think. Come in, come in."

The room was insulated with leather volumes, plush furniture, oak paneling, all burnished in age and redolent of cigar. A pewter tray atop a wheeled cart displayed crystal decanters of amber drink, glasses, a bowl of ice. Bruno's glance went to the table, where a felt-and-leather backgammon set lay open between two comfortable chairs.

"You brought your set," said Köhler, arching his eyebrows. "How charming."

"I carry it. You never know. I'm happy to use yours."

"To insist on your own, *that* would be superstitious indeed!"

"It would be useless," said Bruno ambivalently. He did prefer his set, its smoothly inlaid points, its simple wood checkers, stained light and dark. No ivory or porcelain, no stitched felt or leather points to cushion the play in false glamour or comfort. The clacking of the checkers on the hardwood points was the music of honest thought, resounding in silence as it navigated the fortunes told by the pips on the dice. Bruno had for his entire life associated backgammon with candor, the dice not determining fate so much as revealing character.

Bruno's wooden set was the baseline, the pure enclosure. Any other, like the German businessman's felt-muffled luxury item, was a euphemism for the true reality. Having his own in the room with him was touchstone enough.

"I can no longer get into a game with any of my acquaintances," said Köhler. His voice was lascivious. It was this greed that would kill him tonight. "Not for stakes—and yet we all quickly lose interest in their absence."

"Yes, I understand," said Bruno, as if in sympathy. "This is typically when my services are needed." He failed to add that he'd known several gentlemen of leisure who, on blundering into the gulf between the level of play they'd attained in topping their club companions and that required to persist through an evening with a player like Alexander Bruno, quit backgammon entirely. Relieving such men of their pretensions: Those were Bruno's services.

At Köhler's predictability, Bruno's confidence grew. Never mind the blot. "What stakes interest you?" Bruno spoke in a humdrum way. It was his own fervor he had to keep in check, the smell of blood.

"Shall we begin at one hundred euros a point?"

Bruno had no bankroll, less than sixty in his pocket. He'd need to win the first game in any event, and on from there. "Better a thousand, if you don't mind." Stakes to sting the rich man, if not bleed him, not yet.

"You are in a hurry!" But Köhler was only delighted. "Would you care for a drink? I can pour you one of several excellent scotches, or you may prepare your own."

"What you're having will be fine."

"Sit, then." Köhler indicated the chair facing the fire. So, Köhler preferred the black checkers, moving clockwise. Every such preference was another vulnerability revealed. Apart from his wooden set, which he placed on the floor to one side of his chair, Bruno was careful to have no preferences at all.

The scotch was good. Bruno nursed it, not asking its name or year. He won the first three games leaning back from the board, letting the hearth's flames caress the edges of his vision's blot, watching them gleam off the shined curve of his opponent's bent head. Bruno mostly blitzed, making points with no concern for building primes, and beat the rich man three times in a row not on the board itself but with the doubling cube. Bruno offered increased stakes when his own position looked least promising, and "beavered"—instantly redoubling, to seize control—each time Köhler dared touch the cube himself.

Köhler was a "pure player." He slotted checkers and tried to cover them, working to build primes with the monolithic purposefulness afflicting those who believe they've discovered a system or cracked a code. Bruno might have guessed this from the air of ritual and fetish in the rich man's study, books pedantically flush to each shelf's lip, dustless crystal decanters of ancient scotches, heavy curtains making the room a womb of comfort. He might even have guessed it from Köhler's automobile, if he'd been paying attention instead of trying to catch one last glimpse of his ferry companion.

The pure style had peaked sometime in the 1970s. Bruno relinquished it himself at seventeen. Maybe pure play was good enough for Köhler to routinely fleece his wealthy compatriots at club evenings fogged by cigars and scotch. Perhaps in this very room. Bruno would be surprised, but he'd been surprised before. The level of play in Berlin might not be equal to that in Singapore, or London, or Dubai, though Bruno couldn't imagine a reason why that should be so. Possibly Köhler had stupid compatriots, or had seized up at the prospect of sitting across from a player like Bruno. Possibly Köhler was a masochist. To this point, anyway, he played like a fish. Bruno didn't have enough of Köhler in his pocket yet to declare the German a whale.

"The boys!" Köhler chortled, when he rolled double sixes, though in fact they'd come for him at an inopportune time. Then, "The girls!" when it was double fives. "I'm dancing," he said sadly, when he failed to reenter his checker from the bar. The rich man was a fiend for jargon; he must have been, to know it all in English as well as German. He jabbered through the first two games. He knew the difference between a "back game," with multiple points covered in the opponent's inner board, and a "holding game," which spread the held points into the outfield—not that this knowledge had gained him anything against Bruno. An unprotected checker, sitting singly on a point, Köhler called a "blot." The term was universal in backgammon, and Bruno had heard it spoken by sheikhs and Panamanian *capos de la droga,* by men who didn't know the English term for "thank you" or "motherfucker." Of course, for Bruno, *blot* had taken on a new meaning. Bruno, for his part, never decorated his play with either tournament or club argot. The game's language had, with the advent of online gambling sites, become common coin. It told you nothing about the real experience of the player before you.

By the end of the third game, in any case, the German had fallen silent. In the fourth, he disconcerted Bruno by refusing logical surrender. Bruno doubled him up to eight on the cube, then played it out, the rich man apparently believing he was in a legitimate race to bear his checkers off. He wasn't within reach. Either Köhler was praying for a run of doubles to validate his decision, or he simply wasn't good at counting pips on the dice. Not that Bruno counted pips anymore. A glance was enough. Still, after Köhler's acceptance of the redouble, Bruno had to turn his head from side to side slightly, to examine the whole board around the blot. He needed to be certain he hadn't missed something, so poor was Köhler's decision. He'd missed nothing.

As Bruno threw the numbers that bore off the last of his men—of course *he'd* drawn the doubles, his opponent's misplay earning its typical reward—Köhler grunted and abruptly stood. His small head almost seemed too narrow, as if in a vise at the temples. "How much do I owe to you now?"

"Twenty-eight thousand euros." Bruno knew better than to insult him by softening the blow. "Edgar mentioned, I hope, that I need to have cash tonight. I'm only in Berlin briefly." Bruno had in fact no idea where he'd travel next, or how soon. "I'd prefer not to have to cash a large check."

"I cover my losses."

"I'm sorry to mention it."

"Oh, no!" said Köhler, in another of his bursts of exultation. "You have me in a pretty spot! Let's find out what we can do about it!" He poured himself another scotch and topped Bruno's glass. "Would you mind music?" The German stepped over to an ornate cabinet and lifted its top, revealing an antique phonograph.

"Not at all."

"Shellac 78s," said Köhler. "I collect them. Nothing sounds the same."

"Any type of music in particular? Or just shellac 78s?"

"It is my belief that jazz died with Charlie Parker. He was a revolutionary whose innovations ought to have been firmly refused."

"Where would that leave us?"

"Ah! A believer in progress!"

Bruno had only been flippant. He had no knowledge of how Charlie Parker had changed jazz, nor any interest in learning. If Köhler had proposed the music as a stratagem, intending it, with the scotch, as a distraction to his opponent's play, Bruno was indifferent. Since his discovery of backgammon at age sixteen, the game had acted as a funnel on Bruno's attention, excluding the bafflement and seduction of a universe beyond the checkers and points. More likely, anyway, playing the record was for Köhler another expression, like the scotch, the whiskey, and the jargon, of his preference for a thickened atmosphere.

Bruno sought to lose the next game. It served two purposes: to delay while he determined how far he wanted to push Köhler, and to soften the German up for the push when it came. Bruno played a reckless trapping game, his preferred form of intentional error. Tonight, however, he was luck's prince. The dice simply disfavored Köhler, and he missed every one of Bruno's naked checkers, his *blots*. Soon enough Bruno had three of Köhler's checkers on the bar and had built a prime. The doubling cube had lain untouched during Bruno's blitz, and now Bruno offered it, intending a merciful finish. But Köhler accepted and played on.

Bruno's next roll, double fours, closed the last point on his inner board. To decline doing so would have been conspicuous, a display of something much worse than pity. Contempt. Bruno brought in half his men before opening an escape for Köhler's captured checker. The jazz had long since squealed to its conclusion, the 78 clicking and popping under the needle at its inner groove. Against that backdrop Köhler's grunts were audible each time he rolled his dice, waiting for the miracle. None came. Bruno finished bearing off before Köhler's last man limped into his home board.

I am aware I have been playing like a complete asshole. Bruno beamed this thought at Köhler, though there was no less likely candidate for susceptibility to Bruno's old telepathic gift, which was anyhow abandoned. Köhler was immaculate in his shrine of self. *In fact, I tried to throw the game your way. The dice wouldn't permit it. They don't like you very much.*

The gammon brought Köhler's debt to thirty-six thousand. Bruno didn't imagine he'd inflicted hurt. He wouldn't have been surprised to learn that prize items in Köhler's shellac 78 collection had cost the German half that sum. Still, it made Bruno's first good night in two months. If he walked out now he'd be in a position to repair his debt to Edgar Falk and pay his hotel bill. Enough would remain for Bruno to ponder his next move, and the prospects for true independence from Falk, at leisure.

The result was too good—too much too soon. For the price he'd extract here tonight he owed Köhler an evening's entertainment, some back and forth, a shred of hope, not this catastrophe. The situation exposed Bruno's least favorite aspect of his profession. At such times he became a courtesan of sorts. A geisha boy massaging the customer's vanity until he could make off with the loot. Backgammon's beauty was its candidness. In contrast to poker, there were no hidden cards, no bluff. Yet because of the dice, it was also unlike chess: No genius could foresee twelve or thirty moves in advance. Each backgammon position was its own absolute and present circumstance, fated to be revised, impossible to falsify. Each roll of the dice created a new such circumstance. The game's only true gambling device, the doubling cube, served an expression of pure will. Yet now, having to pull the German businessman back into the game to protract the evening, Bruno would be required to make a piece of theater.

"You've lost a cuff link!" said Köhler.

"I dropped it on the ferry . . . or the train . . ."

Bruno felt overwhelming weariness. He'd arrived with what should have been sufficient handicaps: losing streak, near-empty pockets, an occlusion to his vision like a tunnel of dark he approached and might soon enter. What more must he offer in order to throw the rich man a game? Play with his eyes closed? If he could only throw the dice in his sleep, Bruno would have gladly let his head slump on the chair's high cushioned back. Winning again, after passing through the vale of misfortune in Singapore, ought to revive him. Instead it seemed to have released Bruno into the clutches of a fatigue that resembled despair. He took a drink, fantasizing that the scotch could enter his head and dissolve the blot, like a solvent for stains on furniture.

"Fletcher Henderson," said Köhler, his back to Bruno as he changed the record.

"Uh-huh." Bruno pushed the checkers back onto their starting points.

"Should we raise the stakes?"

Bruno shrugged, covering surprise. He shouldn't be so naïve. If the German truly wasn't feeling any pain yet, it was only a reminder that real money, the kind Bruno would never know, was bottomless. Since Bruno couldn't excuse himself from this room, he could perhaps at least wake himself up by seeking out Köhler's threshold, to wipe away the rich man's tiny lizard smile.

"Two? Three?"

"Five."

Bruno nodded. At that, the air in the room was slightly electrified.

"Mr. Köhler, may I ask your business? Edgar didn't mention it when he sent me to you." Bruno guessed that old money, at least some element of family fortune, lay behind the combination of splendor, complacency, and passivity on display. Entirely self-made fortunes were typically compiled by aggressive men, even feral ones. Not that Bruno expected a confession. Old fortunes were usually given some industrious-sounding veneer.

"Call me Dirk, please. And may I call you . . ."

"Alexander."

"Alexander. Were you watching on television in 1989, when the Antifaschistischer Schutzwall was breached?"

"I'm sorry?"

"The Berliner Mauer," said Köhler, showing his teeth to his bottom gums. "The Wall."

"Oh, sure."

"Well, you should not feel embarrassed, those Germans who were not in the streets with a pickax or a blowtorch were also sitting watching on television, apart from me. I was on the telephone." Köhler reseated himself and rolled his single die, to win the opening with a six-four. He began as usual, dropping builders into his outer board. "I was part of a consortium of interests that had been for some time acquiring what many believed entirely without value—the land deeds beneath various parts of the Wall."

"Real estate. You're a developer." Bruno rolled his dice, missing Köhler's exposed checkers. He split his own back men, figuring to run for a change. Perhaps this was the game to lose, though conceding the first contest at the raised stakes would be irritating.

"A developer of sorts."

"So you built a lot of, what, really thin apartment buildings?"

"Funny! But between the eastern perimeter and the famous Wall of the Western imagination, covered with graffiti and celebrants, lay thousands of square meters."

Bruno had intended a mild flattery, inviting Köhler to talk about himself and about his money, of which he'd concede some share tonight. Köhler seemed reanimated, however. He soliloquized as if from some interior script. "These blasted lands consisted of demolished buildings and filled-in canals, laid with traps, watched over by guard towers—the so-called no-man's-land. All on the eastern side, of course, and claimed by that government for the People. But in the background lurked various private owners, families not even any longer in Berlin, quite willing to sell . . . we required the services of a great many lawyers! I built nothing myself, I haven't the appetite for it, but anyone who tried was forced eventually to negotiate with me and my partners."

"A onetime killing, then."

"The Wall? Yes. How dare I hope for a second such windfall? But I find ways to carry on. This city puts a great emphasis on the rights of tenants and squatters, and on the privilege of sites to remain in a state of commemorative ruin. Few have the patience for the art of speculation, it is a very slow game. But you know, even the graves themselves must eventually give way . . ."

"Urban renewal."

"Yes, you Americans have this admirable name for it. Urban renewal. Everything in its right place!" Köhler rolled a six-four a second time, and closed a three-prime in front of Bruno's split runners. After Bruno's next roll didn't clear this hurdle, the German reached for the doubling cube.

Bruno accepted, putting them in a ten-thousand-euro game, one in which Bruno controlled the cube. He'd break Köhler badly now, or let him come back, then settle in for the longer and likely bigger kill. Let the dice decide. Bruno would run his back checkers unless the pips commanded otherwise.

But first, Köhler rolled to hit Bruno's two unprotected checkers, and Bruno found himself unable to reenter from the bar.

"You're dancing now!" said Köhler, childishly. "Have I got you in a spot?"

Bruno, annoyed, replied with the doubling cube. Twenty thousand. Losing, he'd cough up half his winning streak, a phenomenon he knew better than to credit exclusively to talent. Bruno'd had the dice on his side to this point. No matter. Köhler had proved himself beatable. Bruno rotated his head to study the entire position. *Leave the blot alone,* he counseled himself, as if like a pimple or a wart he could worry at the thing with his fingertips. Really, the blot was less important even than a pimple, since no one could see it beyond Bruno himself.

"Speaking of appetite," said Köhler, "I've asked my kitchen to prepare some delicious dinner sandwiches. We'll have them brought in, so as not to interrupt our wonderful game."

"Thank you."

"Alexander, do you like women?"

"Yes."

"Then I have another delightful surprise prepared for you!"

It's your turn. Köhler annoyed Bruno now by not playing. At the current price, Bruno wanted to climb back in. It would be a matter of orchestrating a dogged holding game, and he wanted to get on with it. Or had he blundered? Köhler reached not for his dice but for the cube. A blunder, yes. Bruno conceded, reminding himself he'd intended to bring the German back, though that had presupposed the rich man needed encouragement to continue playing; Köhler now seemed more than game. Bruno's bigger kill felt remoter than he preferred. His temples throbbed.

They were halfway into Bruno's second defeat when the woman entered the study. She wore a trim leather mask, with tight-stitched apertures for her eyes and nostrils, and an impassive zipper muting her lips. Otherwise, a black shirt, a man's collared shirt, buttoned to the top, and nothing on beneath it apart from low black heels. Her legs were elegantly long and smooth, twitching through the gloom as though spotlit. The hair between her legs was fawn-colored, trimmed close. As the woman lowered a silver tray heaped with tiny sandwiches to the level of the board, Bruno glimpsed the hearth's orange glow between her knees. Thanks to the blot, his gaze averted itself.

Two of Bruno's checkers sat on the bar, a gamble annihilated. "After you," said Köhler. Bruno's host held the dice, keeping the game hostage in favor of his splendid presentation.

Bruno lifted a triangle from the tray. Tiny shrimp curled in cream, and lettuce, on crustless toast. "Thank you," he said to no one in particular, splitting the difference between addressing the midsection of the woman who'd served him and the rich man's grin. His own backgammon set caught his attention, where it leaned untouched against a chair's leg. He bit a corner of the sandwich, tasting not the shrimp but the tart cream. He pushed the remainder into his mouth and rinsed it down with the scotch. His lips were again strangely numb, though the room was hot.

"You see, it is a question of where one's attention falls," said Köhler.

"Excuse me?"

The rich man gestured at the woman, unabashed. "With the face and the breasts concealed, there is nowhere else to look. The astounding mystery is right before you."

Bruno believed he understood. If Köhler could have had the woman's body borne in headless on a silver tray, the German might have done so. Bruno wondered if it qualified as an act of solidarity to look upward instead, to try and make contact with the tall woman's eyes through her mask, or whether this would only add to her shame. There was nothing Bruno could look at directly anyhow. The headache that had begun in his temples now pulsed precisely between his eyebrows, as if a third eye—one capable, as the others were not, of penetrating to the reality behind the blot—sought to force itself to the surface.

"You may touch her, if you like."

"I'll keep it in mind," said Bruno.

"Yes, yes, there's no hurry . . ."

"Are we playing?" Bruno asked with irritation. Köhler had risen to the phonograph again, and he dropped the needle now on an even scratchier recording. The woman stood silent to one side, the tray dividing her at the waist, the shirttail concealing nothing. In his mind Bruno rearranged the silver platter into a game board, the triangular sandwiches into points. There was no appeal in any of Köhler's offerings, Bruno wished only to play, to return to the points and checkers, his urgent business. This was ungracious, he knew. Köhler was providing for his own evening's entertainment, in order that Bruno could be relieved of any duty except taking the German's money. Yet the night was going wrong.

The jazz shrieked and cackled. Köhler dived in like a fiend and grabbed the dice, shook them excessively, and rolled double sixes. His checkers swept past Bruno's feeble broken prime. When Köhler offered a double, Bruno conceded.

"Bix Beiderbecke!" Köhler shouted, the rich man apparently reverting to some arcane taunt in his mother tongue.

"Play again," muttered Bruno.

"Of course," said Köhler. Bizarrely, he stood and placed the needle at the record's start, leaving Bruno to sort the checkers onto their points. The woman stood with her tray, legs goose-pimpled as the flames waned to orange shards of coal. Though Bruno felt warm. Köhler returned, threw a die to open the game, and then called to her: "Come closer!"

She stepped up again, her puzzle of sandwiches intact apart from the sole triangle Bruno had lifted out. Bruno felt he could retch it out exactly into position if she brought the scent of dill any nearer. He won the opening with a weak four-one and used it to split his runners. Köhler began immediately to smash at them with an anarchic blitzing game. His and Bruno's positions were reversed now. Köhler had become unpredictable.

Bruno, not even conscious he'd turned to look, was suddenly aware of the woman's lips moving beneath the tight-zipped leather. Was Bruno supposed to be able to lip-read under these conditions? A cry for help? No. He shouldn't be naïve, she was a professional, as much as

Bruno. This was Berlin. Traditions existed which Bruno ought to be able to take for granted. A warning, then? His host still hadn't reached for one of the sandwiches. Had Bruno been poisoned?

Köhler gammoned. It was Bruno's luck that had been poisoned. His money, which had never been his, and had never been money, was gone. He owed some amount, was losing track. It was only numbers in his head, not so much as a dime had been laid on the table. A gentlemanly game, on friendly terms Bruno knew well: one shark, one whale. Bruno would have to steel himself, play it out. This couldn't be Singapore, he couldn't allow it. He'd rebelled against Falk, run to Europe, and now he had to make it good, had to persist with the evening, build his bankroll again. At such stakes it shouldn't take long. He rolled a single die to start the game and turned his head to read it: three.

Köhler reached out, as if for a sandwich, but bypassed the tray. He rubbed his palm talismanically on the server's buttocks and scatted along with the trumpeter's hectic solo. Then he threw a four to win the opening and dropped his builders. Bruno, snakebit, failed to hit. Köhler cocked his head as Bruno faltered at choosing a play for his roll, a useless four-one. Was the German about to reach for the doubling cube again? Was he turning bully?

Instead, Köhler asked, "Alexander, are you completely well?"

"Why?"

"I wondered if something was wrong with your eyesight."

"No."

"You appear to be . . . *listening* to the actions of the backgammon pieces. Perhaps it is common among players of your caliber? I admit the method is unfamiliar."

Bruno caught himself. His head was inches from the board. He'd imagined that his tilt, if it had been noticed at all, would be taken for leering. Stolen glances at that cosmic mystery between the masked woman's legs. Now, understanding fell on him: his denial of the blot. For how many weeks had he been managing this affliction? It had been with him in Singapore as well, even if it was worse now. It was certainly worse now.

Bruno had been giving lessons without knowing. If a fish like the German could absorb and mimic Bruno's practice by studying him, what might the sharper gamblers in Singapore have taken away? Though perhaps Köhler wasn't so daft. He was looking sharkish, for a whale. Bruno had lost everything, including the stake he didn't have in his pocket when he entered the room. He tried to tally his debt here and in Singapore cumulatively, but couldn't. But, Bruno reminded himself, Falk had promised to make his stain in Singapore evaporate; tonight was all that mattered.

"When I listen to them I can hear the sea," said Bruno flippantly. *If you'd just turn down this damn music.*

"Ich habe die Meerjungfrauen einander zusingen hören," said Köhler. He turned his wrist, dropped a perfect number. The German closed his primes like clockwork now.

"Sorry?" said Bruno. He answered with another calamitous roll. A universe of misfortune was at Bruno's fingertips, he only had to touch the dice. Usually just single games of backgammon were prone to such abrupt reversal. Here the whole evening had hinged irreversibly, into defeat.

"The mermaids singing, one after the next, of course. T. S. Eliot!" And now the German proffered the doubling cube.

"Each to each," Bruno corrected, the line recalled from some memory swamp. He waved off the double, having had enough. A further five thousand down, but it expunged the game in favor of a fresh one. Bruno reached into his tuxedo's inner breast pocket, hooked another paracetamol with a finger, and pushed it quietly into his mouth. To swig it down he gulped scotch across his numb tongue. "Another game."

The woman in the mask had turned to Bruno. She rubbed one finger above her zipper, beneath her cipher nostrils. A further signal? Or was she about to sneeze? How would that work, behind the mask? In place of either beauty or a hideous disfigurement beneath the leather disguise, Bruno now conjured eyes grown puffy and watery, sinuses draining down the throat, a coughing spasm suppressed. The life of a professional half-nude masked housemaid; just another day at the office.

But no. The issue wasn't the woman's nose, but Bruno's own. He sensed the trickle, the coolness across his lip, at the exact moment Köhler spoke.

"Your nose, Alexander. It is bleeding."

"It's nothing," Bruno said, his fingers trailing away crimson. There was the problem of where to wipe them. Then, without transition, Bruno found himself looking at Köhler and the masked woman from below, from the carpet. He raised himself on his elbows—where was his chair? Gone. Some interval had passed, and when his elbows failed to support him he discovered that a large cushion waited beneath his head. Köhler stood above, holding a smartphone. The phonograph was mercifully silenced. Instead, Köhler and the woman spoke German, in tones of argument—or was it only that German always sounded argumentative?

"Ich kenne ihn. Ich kann ihm helfen."

"Halt dich zurück, Schlampe. Bitte!"

"Lass mich ihm doch—"

"Ich lass ihn in die Charité einweisen. Da wird man sich um ihn kümmern."

"Ich fahre mit ihm—"

"Das wirst du nicht tun! Ich werde mich nicht noch einmal wiederholen."

The blood on Bruno's fingers had crusted. When he touched them to his nose again it was repainted fresh. The blood had stained his white shirt, perhaps also the black tuxedo, though that had been laid open and so possibly spared. The woman stood quite near, all legs and mystery. She should have seemed absurd now, but what embarrassed Bruno most was her lack of embarrassment, as though his nosebleed had unmanned him.

Noticing Bruno lifting his head again from the cushion, Köhler knelt and spoke to him in painstaking English.

"Listen, Alexander. You've suffered some kind of seizure. Do you remember where you are?"

"Yes."

"The same driver who fetched you at the ferry is bringing the car around."

"I'll be fine—we can play again—" *It was only that music,* he wanted to say.

Köhler ignored him. "He'll bring you to the emergency room, at this time of night the journey by car won't be at all long. The hospital is called Charité, there you'll be cared for—"

"I'm not some charity case."

"No, no, that's only its name. Charité is one of the most important hospitals in Europe."

By all means, then, thought Bruno in his despair. Nothing less than an important hospital.

.

Through blinding confusion Bruno nevertheless grasped that he'd been returned to the backseat of the limousine and was being driven the long way off Kladow, in avoidance of the ferry. Light flashed across the car's interior roof as he lay on the seat. It was then that he recognized the tug of memory represented by the shorebird, the cormorant.

At age six Bruno had moved, with his mother, June, from her guru's cultish compound in Marin County to Berkeley. He remembered little before Berkeley, which suited his preference—if he could, he'd forget Berkeley too, all his California life. The commune itself, in San Rafael, he recalled only in flashes of gabbling confusion, hippies at vast smoky spaghetti dinners, their voices and wide-open minds seeming to overrun his boundaries, and communal outdoor showers where women other than his mother herded him with gangs of muddy children for scrubbing. Bruno's clearest recollection, before June had rescued him from that place, was of a visit he'd taken alone, with his mother's bearded guru, to Stinson Beach on a cold morning when they had it to themselves. If there had been an explanation or reason for this special attention it was never offered, then or after.

There in Köhler's car, Bruno remembered it: The guru had pointed out the cormorants, where the rocky cliffs met the infinite basin of the Pacific.

"You're some kind of a kid, Alexander," the guru had said to him, trying to lock on his gaze while Bruno remained focused on the water's lapping, and the black diving crow-ducks that rode the waves. "I can see you watching June, I see you watching everyone. You're deep."

I don't want to be deep, the child had thought. *I want to quiet the voices, the crazy shrieking voices of all of you, June included. I want to be like that bird.*

III

Long past his fifth, then sixth hour in the emergency-room waiting area, seated clutching his wooden backgammon set to his dried-bloody shirtfront, head against the chair's stiff, sleep-defeating back, Alexander Bruno had been reduced to wondering: What were the red footprints for? These were painted, or stickered, across the floor. He sat contemplating them, under garish fluorescents, at a Formica table, in a room of false-wood paneling, beneath a flat-screen flaring muted German newscasts, with the unused trauma doors to his back. Minutes died serially into hours.

Bruno shared this zone, for whatever reason, primarily with not quite elderly women, four or five at a given time. He should have been able to tabulate their comings and goings, to fathom who among them was sick and who waited on some other family member's sickness, to discern fine differences, but no. They melted into a drab resemblance: *Older Woman in Waiting Room*, a series. The blot didn't help, of course, remaining centered in his vision, obliterating their faces.

For brief variation, a young couple with a shrouded baby had appeared and been ushered inside, not to return. One or two policemen had ambled through, and plenty of weary orderlies, but never with any urgency, never appearing less than explicitly bored. They merely paced out the night's smallest hours. No one in Berlin, apparently, was ever shot or stabbed or crushed in a vehicle. Or at least not tonight. Bruno's bloodstain was anomalous. If he'd memorized one useful phrase in German, which of course he hadn't, it should have been, *It's only a nosebleed.*

Bruno's quarantine from the intrusion of human language was as total as he could ever have wished. No one spoke. When they did, it was inaudible. When audible, it was German. Bruno'd had his flash in the pan of relevance here, but it seemed years ago. They'd been excited about him, once; he clung to the memory. When Köhler's driver had dropped him off, they thought he'd had a stroke. The triage nurse had shown him to a doctor, and the doctor had spoken to him in coldly accented English, with simple questions, ones Bruno could answer with relative confidence. The blot itself had caused the excitement—that and his brief passage of unconsciousness or seizure. Though of course Bruno had only Köhler's testimony to suggest a seizure. The rich man wasn't available now to explain, and when they asked Bruno what he meant by the word he realized he had no idea.

The doctor tested his visual field. What had been Bruno's private meditation upon the blot, his own small esoteric mystery, was now common currency—but at least it was currency. In everything else, he felt he'd only disappointed the doctor. Numbness or tingling in his limbs? No. Difficulties recalling words? Sorry, no. Inability performing a series of routine movements, walking, raising his arms, following the doctor's commands? No. Bruno was, sadly, capable of performing each simple action. As he performed them, giving the doctor little or nothing to inscribe on his clipboard chart, Bruno felt the energy drain from the examination room. He further disappointed by confessing to the headache, the drinking of undiluted scotch, and the use—overuse, frankly—of paracetamol. At the last moment, before dismissal, Bruno mentioned the sensation of numbness in his lips. The doctor raised one eyebrow. Nearly of interest but, alas, no. Bruno fulfilled far too few of the assessment criteria for stroke, and so it was as if he did not exist. He'd been returned to the waiting area.

The question of how to interpret the trail of red footprints—which ran from the entry doors through the waiting area and down one corridor of the hospital—was now Bruno's sole preoccupation and solace. He had nothing else to contemplate. Nothing, that was, apart from the blot, or the course his evening at Köhler's home had taken—the result, even if the reasons remained puzzling.

The sudden change of fortunes, timed to Köhler's raising the stakes:

Could Köhler have hustled Bruno? It should be impossible. Yet Bruno was haunted by the irrational certainty that Köhler had been the shark. He wondered now if the German had come to the encounter with as little ready cash in his pocket as had Bruno. Perhaps the mansion in Kladow wasn't really even Köhler's. Perhaps the person Bruno had met wasn't named Köhler. It was madness, thinking this way; better to consider the red footprints. The waiting-room floor featured yellow footprints too, actually, leading in another direction. Bruno would get to the bottom of it. Why not? He had time enough, and the talent, apparently, for finding the bottom of any circumstance, of his own life.

The ER entrance doors lay under a pedestrian bridge, and little natural light reached the antiseptic purgatory of the waiting room. Still, signs of dawn crept in. The clock read 4:45. If Bruno strained, he thought he heard a bird twittering. The older women were unmoving, though they'd slept as little as Bruno. When a young doctor in mint-green scrubs emerged and stood with a clipboard in front of his chair, it took Bruno a long moment to understand he'd been drawn back into the realm of the visible. The young man was skinny, with blond curls. He appeared untroubled by the long night, perhaps had just signed in or woken from a refreshing nap on a surgical table. Did the word *intern* apply in Germany? Bruno couldn't know.

"Mr. Bruno?" The doctor held out his hand.

"Yes."

"I'm sorry you had to wait so long. It might have been preferable to dismiss you."

"Are you—American?"

The young doctor smiled. "No, I'm German, but thank you. I studied in Columbus, Ohio, and for a while in Scotland."

"Ah." Looking up from his seat, Bruno's blot made the young doctor with the perfect English a faceless Aryan angel, his curls a blond halo.

"You must be exhausted. Let's talk about your results so you can go—I see you've listed a hotel."

"Yes."

The doctor sat across the circular Formica table and lifted the clipboard's covering sheet. Nothing he saw there required more than a glance. "Your blood glucose levels are normal. The examining doctor was confident in ruling out stroke."

"Yes . . ." he said.

"And no history of migraine with visual field distortion?"

"I've never been diagnosed. I have been suffering from headaches."

"Migraine onset can be possible in later life."

Later life—so that was what had come to Bruno. Next, a discount on movie tickets.

"Okay, but also, the visual disturbance you detailed, there is a chance of temporal arteritis—an inflammation of small vessels of the eye. However, this would be premature. I've prepared information on two specialists you might wish to visit immediately, an *Augenarzt*—an eye doctor. And as well a neurologist."

"But . . . I did suffer the seizure."

"So, but, reflex analysis indicates not." The doctor glanced again at the page. "Is this correct, that you fainted upon sight of the blood from your nose?"

"Yes."

"And not again after?"

"No . . . no."

"I see a suggestion from the doctor you saw: vasovagal syncope response. Did he discuss this with you?"

"No."

"Are you familiar with this term?"

"I'm sorry, no."

"Ah. With vasovagal, one loses consciousness at the sight of one's own blood. An autonomic response, impossible to regulate with the will. It can be highly inconvenient for routine procedures—we are often having patients fall unconscious upon having their blood drawn, for instance. But it is a silly abnormality, of no consequence."

A silly abnormality? Bruno would trade it for a death sentence. The young doctor's smile was evident, even at the edges of the blot. Was his unusual kindness merely an impression given by his unaccented English? Possibly Bruno's spell here had softened him up, like Patty Hearst in her closet.

"Please don't misunderstand. The migraine diagnosis is a speculation, we really recommend you visit the specialists noted here, okay?
But—headache and nosebleed, a single episode of fainting. One thing
is clear, you needn't be here any longer."

"Okay."

"You're a visitor to Germany, Mr. Bruno?"

"Yes."

"You have no insurance of any kind?"

"No."

"Please do not let that keep you from making these appointments.
Or if you are leaving, see your doctor in the States."

"I . . . have no plan to return." Bruno was self-conscious again of
his worn tuxedo, his brown-crusted shirtfront, his lost cuff link, and
the mysterious wooden case he still clutched, white-knuckled, in his
lap. If only it contained radioactive isotopes or microfilm. Or stacks
of cold currency, unmarked. He'd purchased the inlaid wooden set
at a games shop in Zurich, with a fresh check for thirteen thousand
Swiss francs in his breast pocket. From Bruno's present juncture, such
triumph seemed as exotic as microfilm or isotopes.

"Do you know the way home from here to your hotel?" Perhaps the
angelic doctor had been inspecting Bruno too. After all, they'd tested
his blood and had surely noted the presence of paracetamol and Wolf-
Dirk Köhler's scotch. The intern's diagnosis, unspoken behind *vasovagal* and *migraine,* might have simply been *alcoholic bender.* Given the
plentiful men wandering Berlin's streets at midday with unconcealed
liters of beer, the emergency room likely knew this type of patient.

"If you can direct me to the S-Bahn, I'll be okay."

"We're just across the river here from the Hauptbanhof. It's a very
pleasant walk across the old section of the hospital—come, I'll point
you in the right direction." Another angelic service? Perhaps the young
doctor wished to observe Bruno placing one foot in front of the other
before releasing him to his fate. Moving together to the sliding entry
doors, they stepped across the red footprints.

"What are these for?"

"Excuse me?"

Bruno pointed. "They seem to lead nowhere."

"Oh, those! The red lead to the red zone, the yellow to the yellow zone. For when it is needed."

"I don't understand." Outdoors, Bruno was overwhelmed by the world's resumption: the smell of exhaust and rotting grass clippings, the angled light, humans with a purpose on earth, with paper cups of coffee in their hands. He and the doctor walked together across the endless cobblestones, the cobble-dice, and out from under the pedestrian bridge.

"Yes, it's odd, but no one ever thinks of it. It's a plan for some catastrophe greater than the system can handle. The footpaths show where the more badly injured should congregate, as opposed to those with minor injuries." Under the effort of this explanation, the young doctor's accent began to revert. "There's a green zone too, for those not requiring a doctor, but who have come to the hospital because of losing their homes, or to donate blood, or so forth."

They'd crossed out of the grimly utilitarian modern complex into another, more serene century. The old hospital was a grassy campus of red-brick buildings, each with Shakespearean alcoves and porticoes. Dawn had broken out on the wide paths, a pale-pink sky visible through the greenery, and impossible numbers of birds twittering overhead. But when Bruno raised his eyes to the branches, the blot intruded. It dominated the upper half of his field of vision more than the lower. No wonder he'd become so concerned with what lay underfoot.

His escort had stopped on the path, to fish in his scrubs and come out with a pack of smokes, likely his real motive for stepping outside the ER. "You're well on your way," the young doctor said, lighting a cigarette. "Just follow the main road here through the old Charité, and you'll hit the river. You'll then see the train station. Just cross the river and you're there."

"How charming it is here."

"Charité was first built as a plague sanitarium, so it's a city within the city."

"It makes a pleasant sort of preserve."

"Yes," said the doctor, assuming a wry look, "with a great number of buildings and streets named for famous Nazi physicians."

Berlin, tomb city. Everywhere you walked on graves or bunkers, or the ghostly signature of the Wall. And so the red footprints: Why shouldn't future catastrophes be legible too, trudging columns of dirty-bomb refugees or zombie-plague survivors traced in advance? Between cigarette and cheap Teutonic irony, the blond doctor had surrendered his angelic aspect, but no matter. He'd delivered Bruno from the terminal sector to this little paradise of birdsong. Bruno was ready to part with him.

"I'll be fine."

"I'm sure you will."

Alone, Bruno settled into a false exultation. His condition could as easily have been the result of an all-night fleecing of some puffed-up financial wizard or real-estate baron much like Wolf-Dirk Köhler (who Bruno now understood could only have been sincere in his pomposity and his fortune, and the beneficiary of an ordinary lucky streak). It wouldn't make the first time he'd wandered the dawn streets of a foreign town looking like a daylight vampire. The only difference was the absence of the money he should have had to show for it. And what was money?

Bruno smiled greetings in passing, swinging his backgammon case as he walked. The medical students, one younger than the next, answered with their eyebrows, beguiled from their Prussian reserve. One or two even gave forth with an awkward *"Morgen!"* Armed with a fresh shirt and a double espresso Bruno might not even need sleep, though nothing stood between him and eight or fifteen hours dozing in a curtained room except the brief journey back to Charlottenburg and his hotel. He might even sleep away the blot, he felt now. Why not? Though he had no way of paying the bill, he assumed the keycard in his pocket still worked.

Crossing out of Charité and over the river, the Hauptbanhof in sight, Bruno's spirit only soared higher. Berlin's sprawling indifference, its ungainly, crane-pierced grandeur, liberated him. Perhaps he'd only needed to blow the Kladow opportunity Edgar Falk had flung his way, and his subsequent vigil in the ER, to understand. He'd wanted to dissolve his tie to Falk, not reconstitute it. Let the whole absurd episode—his being gammoned, his nosebleed—be taken as a depart-ing fuck-you.

As he slid into the morning crowds approaching the sun-twinkling central glass atrium at the Hauptbanhof—the train station another city unto itself, more chilly and anonymous than the medieval campus of Charité but also, therefore, more familiar, with its Sushi Express and Burger King and international newsstand, its dozens of tracks leading anywhere he might wish to escape to—Bruno had in his giddy escapes from death and from his former profession concluded he needed only a new name. *Mr. Blot. Blotstein. Blottenburg.* It was there he fell. Not across the Hauptbanhof's threshold but before it, just past a construc-tion barricade at the river side of the station entrance.

He fell into a shallow rupture in the walkway, a section where the cobblestones had been disrupted, the earth below laid bare. A small pile of the granite paving cubes lay to one side, at a point now level to his view. Bruno's legs had gone. He didn't try to stand again. The blot made everything confusing. His backgammon set was clutched to his chest still, or again. He saw the station looming, a Zeno's paradox target now. He'd been nearer to it standing on the other side of the river. The front of his face bled again. He moved his legs now, but only swam in the dirt and the rubble of stones. No one paid attention. He smelled dust, mud, sunlight, and grilling sausages, nauseating so early in the morning.

If only he had a wooden mallet, Bruno could pretend to be work-ing. Did a vast supply of older cobblestones circulate throughout Ber-lin, endlessly repurposed, or did fresh ones need to be quarried and shaped? What would happen if he kidnapped a stone, took it out of circulation? Would the system collapse? Bruno could enjoy contem-plating the rough cubes forever, now that they'd captivated his imagi-nation, if he weren't lying sideways, watching blood from his nose drip into the dusty soil, if he weren't embarrassed to be seen here. *Forever* had become a squishy concept, anyway. Time slipped from him in blacked-out instants, like a film in which one blotted passerby was replaced by the next—a jump cut. How ironic, he thought, that behind him, across the river, on the idyllic campus, a crumpled figure would surely find himself swarmed by compassionate attention, the medical students competing to show off their training. On this side of the bridge, below the edifice of the Hauptbanhof, he lay beneath consideration, resembling as he did the contemptible derelicts and drifters accumulating at major train stations all over the universe.

He'd met a just reward for flirtation with the wish to disappear.

For amusement, Bruno reached out for one of the squarish stones. The result was more than he could have hoped for. He'd unknowingly been touching at his nose or lip; the fingers that seized up the stone dotted it with brash bloody fingerprints. Three fingertip prints on one face of the stone, a thumbprint on another. Three-one, always a pleasant roll at the start of a game. Just close up the so-called *golden point* on one's own inner board, though this term had later been disputed, once computer algorithms confirmed it wasn't as valuable as the bar-point. But Bruno had decided to give up backgammon, so never mind. He brought the bloodstained cobblestone nearer. Touching his nose again—there was plenty of blood!—he carefully daubed the remaining faces, making a two, a four, a five, and a six. Between glaring sun and absorbent stone, the dots of fresh blood dried almost instantly. The challenge was to keep from staining it further. Bruno wiped his fingers on his shirt, which had been sacrificed hours ago. The task was amusing enough to distract him from the matter of the opinions of passersby, or even whether they glanced his way or not. When the rough granite die was complete, he rotated it in all directions to confirm, around the obstacle of the blot, that he'd made no error. No. It was perfect. Bruno grunted in satisfaction. Then he opened his set, which was itself printed with flurries of reddish fingerprints. There, to accompany the two sets of wooden dice, the blond and the ebony, and his doubling cube, he pushed the giant die inside. He was just able to clasp the set around it, then let the entirety slip from his arms, into the sidewalk's seam, into the dust. That the blunt object would damage the smooth inlaid wood of his board, Bruno was certain. He didn't care. The cobblestone die might be the most valuable thing he owned. It was proof, at least, of what Berlin otherwise denied: that he existed, here, now.

IV

Bruno awakened inside the hospital. He needed to be roused intermittently for the X-rays, the CT scan, and the MRI, so woke to discover himself an object in custody of German orderlies and technicians scarcely interested in consoling him in English, or even explaining their purposes in composing this escalating series of deep inner portraits of Bruno's face and head. In between, he slumbered, slurped broth and tested bites of flavorless meat and vegetables on bedside trays whose arrival and departure usually eluded him, and learned to use the bedpan.

Had he succumbed to a sleeping sickness or been tranquilized? He supposed he was exhausted by his ordeal, his all-nighter. In fact the illusion of days slipping past was only that, an illusion, brought on by the timeless vacuity of the windowless room, and by the frequent wakings by nurses to check his vital signs, a routine punctuated by those more dramatic sequences when he was wheeled up to and engulfed by the gigantic thrumming machines.

When Bruno recovered consciousness more completely, only a day and a night had passed. His backgammon case had been placed into the cabinet section of his bedside table. He opened it to discover the blood-dotted cobblestone. It took this evidence to persuade him he'd ever departed the hospital, so nearly had his brief sojourn across the river resembled a dream or hallucination. He found his wallet and passport in the table's drawer, along with his cell phone, gone dead. Its battery life had been a shrinking hourglass, one he should have heeded. Also in the drawer, the slip of paper naming the two specialists he'd been commended to visit. Bruno showed this to the doctor on rounds, but he seemed unimpressed. Bruno's emergency-room diagnosis might only have been a poor hasty guess, the bum's rush. He'd entered some other situation entirely, he only didn't know what it was.

This second, more lucid phase of his hospitalization had begun on a Thursday evening. Bruno was informed it would be Monday morning before he was visited by *der Onkologe*—the oncologist. He had a week-end to kill. The second bed in the room remained, mercifully, empty. Bruno asked the nurses to switch off the babbling German television, the soap operas and soccer, the dubbed Mel Gibson revenge stories. The barrage of incomprehension seemed to taunt him; Bruno wanted only silence. He took the cobblestone into his sheets, nestling it under his right hand, refusing all petition of the nurses to take it away and wash it for him.

The blot was with him, invisible to others. Or not: Maybe the machines had taken its portrait from the inside. Bruno waited to know. In the meantime, the stone was its crooked, obtrusive twin. With these sole companions, Bruno spent two days contemplating the mystery of his changed relationship to luck. From the vantage of a hospital ward the lows of Singapore and Kladow were magnificent attainments, sacred stations of a vanished existence. He'd gladly lose a thousand games to Köhler, gladly go back and spend an eternity prone on Köhler's carpet, even, basking in hideous jazz on crackly records. If granted an eternity, Bruno might spend it regretting he'd failed to caress the bottom of the masked woman, a chance that had at the time seemed squalid and negligible but now might be a shrine he'd failed to honor. He should have eaten his share of shrimp and dill sandwiches, manna beside the hospital fare. It was as though Bruno had rolled a die and revealed some previously unknown face: zero. Perhaps that was the cobblestone's significance. *In Germany, dice roll you!*

•

Was it only Bruno's imagination that the nurses put an extra effort into neatening him up, tightening the sheets of his bed, straightening his little tabletop's possessions, like realtors prepping a house? No accident, anyway, that they wheeled him to a sink with a mirror low enough so he could shave, and provided a clean disposable razor. The nurses wished to sell him to the oncologist. For his part, Bruno eschewed the bedpan, insisted on his own toilet. At this minor attainment, his own sense of excitement was wakened. In this slough of time, everything ached for some major happening, even if it was death. Perhaps the nurses were more like nuns, then, preparing themselves or him to see God.

At midmorning his visitor was ready. In fact it was two visitors. *Der Onkologe,* Dr. Scheel, was attractive, tense-jawed, with salt-and-pepper brush-cut hair but younger than Bruno, and impatient from the moment he came through the door. His suit, three-piece brown flannel, was the nicest thing Bruno had laid eyes on since entering the hospital. He carried a large flat envelope. Its contents, perhaps, Bruno's fate.

Dr. Scheel possessed, or anyway revealed, no English. To translate on his behalf had come Bruno's second bedside visitor, Claudia Benedict. She was older, quite tall, with owlish glasses beneath her platinum bangs, and craggy, sunken cheeks, severe in aspect. Yet she offered Bruno the solace of his mother tongue. "Dr. Scheel asked me to be present to avoid any potential misunderstandings," she explained. "I'm an Englishwoman actually, though I've been in Berlin for more than twenty years."

"I'm awfully glad to meet you, Dr. Benedict," said Bruno. Dr. Scheel, for his part, had shaken Bruno's hand, then stood aside, waiting for the cessation of niceties. "Pardon my appearance. These hospital pajamas aren't too flattering." Bruno gestured at the narrow wardrobe closet, behind which hung his tuxedo, invoking other options. He'd checked: The shirt had been laundered. He supposed the hospital had a special aptitude for bloodstains.

"I actually am a physician," said Benedict, "though I've never been licensed here in Germany. Please understand that I'm not your doctor."

Then can you be my mommy? Bruno beamed at her, his rote test. If Claudia Benedict read his thoughts, she didn't show it, in either warmth or disdain.

"Dr. Scheel wants you to understand that he's examined your case carefully, and he regards it as a highly serious one. I've made myself familiar with his written reports, and I'll try to answer any questions you may have, but I'm primarily here to function as a translator." Was Benedict's slightly shocked look that of meeting a dead man who didn't know it? She turned now to Scheel. The oncologist nodded brusquely, and they conducted a rapid exchange in German.

"... *Frag ihn, ob er die radiologischen Befunde selbst sehen möchte, oder ob die mündliche Diagnose ausreicht. In solchen Fällen irritieren die Aufnahmen einen Patienten oft ...*" At these words from Scheel, Benedict paused, then turned back to Bruno.

"Yes, um, Dr. Scheel asks whether you would like to see the images yourself, or only have the situation described. He's afraid you may be disturbed by them."

"You mean . . . all the CAT scans and so forth?"

"Yes."

He smiled in a way he hoped was courageous. "I'm ready for my close-up, Mr. DeMille."

The joke was lost on her, and on the German. It occurred to Bruno that he was being readied for that moment when anything endearing about you was revealed as etched in dust, then swept over a cliff. This would be doubly true if one were without family or other social bonds—if one were largely endeared only by, and to, oneself.

Dr. Scheel slid the transparencies from the folder and laid them out over Bruno's bedsheeted knees. Bruno saw amorphous ghostly gray-and-black mud puddles, veins of white mineral running through a rock, nothing he'd identify with himself or any other human being. The images were peppered with tiny arrows and brackets and miniature handwriting in red ballpoint. While Bruno avoided seeing more, Scheel spoke softly and steadily in German, then waited for Benedict to render the sentences in English.

"Dr. Scheel believes you are suffering from a meningioma—a tumor of the central nervous system. Are you at all familiar with that term?"

"No."

"Meningiomas are commonly associated with the brain, but not exclusively, they're—excuse me, this is far from my specialty. They frequently occur along the central brain stem, intracranially, I mean, *inside.*" She put a knuckle to her forehead. "Yours is in an unusual but not unknown position, an anterior cranial fossa filling the olfactory groove. It has also inserted itself . . . behind your eyes, the cause of the optical dysfunction you've reported."

"The blot."

"Yes—excuse me." She turned and resumed in rapid-fire German. Then back. "He says it's likely you've also lost your sense of smell, though patients are frequently unaware of this until it's pointed out to them."

"Tell him he's wrong. I smell things especially vividly, in fact. For instance, the lunch they're preparing for us now—I can tell they're grilling sausages."

Benedict and Scheel exchanged a look, and then another string of irritated-sounding phrases. "Neither of us smells sausages grilling, I'm afraid."

"Well, there you go!" said Bruno. "My groove is wide open and ready for business." It was as if he'd disproved the new word, *meningioma,* without having even once said it aloud.

"Olfactory hallucinations are not excluded," said Benedict, with as much sympathy as could be imparted to these words. "Though such presentations are a great deal less common . . ."

At this Benedict stalled. Scheel had stepped nearer to the bed and was putting his finger to one of the transparencies, meanwhile filling her ear with German that might be industrial or military jargon. The oncologist tapped again at the page, never glancing, however, at Bruno himself. Having the benefit of a translator, Scheel appeared to feel no need to grant Bruno's existence. This affair was strictly between Scheel and blot.

"He's keen that you understand the severity of your case," said Benedict, when she was allowed to resume. "Many such growths are nonmalignant and respond to resection—to surgical removal. Dr. Scheel regrets to say that the placement and size are in your case utterly prohibitive. He says it's extraordinary to discover one so developed. He's surprised you've reported no symptoms before now."

"Let me get this straight," said Bruno. Giddiness overtook him, unleashed by this triangular arrangement and the prospect of death by blot. "I've been neglecting to apprise Dr. Scheel of the symptoms of my giant fucking outlandish and unprecedented nose cancer, is that right?"

"Mr. Bruno."

"Pardon my awkwardness with the medical terminology, but that's what I've got, yes?"

"Herr Bruno!" It was Scheel this time.

"Because, tell fucking Dr. Scheel I'm sorry I didn't notice, it's just that I've never had a giant nose cancer before, so I didn't recognize the symptoms."

"Herr Bruno." Scheel stepped between Benedict and the bed, and tapped with the point of his pen at the images strewn across Bruno's knees. "It is not that I cannot understand English at all," Scheel said.

"Ah!" said Bruno, unashamed. The nurses had vaporized. Bruno felt their absence as a pulsation. They might have fled the ward, the entire hospital building.

"You are misinformed when you say nose," said Scheel. "Nose is incorrect."

"You're saying it's not my nose but some other olfactory part of me."

"*Nein.* Here. You asked to look, but you have not chosen to see." With the plastic cap of his pen, Scheel circled again and again the black blotch dominating one of the images. "Here, *bitte.* You see this shape?"

"Paging Dr. Rorschach! It looks like a horseshoe crab. Is that the right answer?"

"It is not your nose. It is between the casing of your brain, you see, and your face. It is pressuring behind your face, from underneath. Behind your eyes and the flesh of your entire *Antlitz*—your countenance."

"How unfortunate."

"Very much so."

"Because if it were just a fucking nose cancer, you could probably just take off my nose and be done with it, but this, it's not so simple."

"*Nein,* it is not simple at all."

Scheel appeared suddenly to tire, as if it had cost him too much, after all, to meet Bruno's outburst in its own tongue. He muttered in German. *"Er kann den Rat eines Chirurgen einholen, wenn er möchte, aber das ändert auch nichts. Es gibt jedoch verschiedene Palliativtherapien, die unmittelbaren Symptome lindern können . . ."*

Benedict spoke again, without moving nearer to the bed this time, as if Scheel's role here needed to be honored by her deference. Her voice was muted and distant, like that of a translator on a radio broadcast, flattening the rhetoric of some terrorist or despot. "Dr. Scheel wishes you to know you have the option of meeting with a surgeon, but he doubts anyone would seriously consider such a procedure. His recommendation is for . . . palliative care. He believes your immediate symptoms can be managed, at least for the time being." She paused. When she spoke again, it was clearly on her own behalf, or of that humane part of herself that had been present when she'd first entered the room. "I understand you have no insurance, Mr. Bruno. Nor relatives in Germany."

"No."

"Do you have friends here?"

He thought of the woman on the ferry. *Hello, Madchen, I have cancer.* "Not apart from you beautiful people right in front of me."

Scheel forced more English out of himself. "What is the reason?"

The question was bewildering. The reason for cancer? "I'm sorry?"

"The reason that are you here. Was it business that brought you?"

"It was this that brought me!" Bruno pulled the stone die from beneath his sheets and thrust it at Scheel. Letting evidence of the open gravesite that was Berlin be his reply to the martinet doctor. Now, as if according to some prearranged signal, the nurses flooded back in. Bruno was wrong, they'd been close by, concealed just outside his door, waiting to reclaim command of his temperature and blood pressure, to resume plying him with regular and unexplained medications. Probably they'd try again to take his stone from him and wash it, too.

Scheel, in his distaste, was the one who was a million miles away, even before he'd passed through the door. He spoke only through

Benedict, who absorbed the brunt of his crisp German, then turned to Bruno and said, "Your attending physician will be given Dr. Scheel's recommendations. The treatment is in any event quite minimal, since it seeks merely to . . . abate your discomfort. He says he's sorry." Scheel gave Benedict a glance of reproach, as if she'd improvised this flourish.

"May I keep these?" asked Bruno, placing his free hand on the printed-out images scattered over his legs.

"*Ja.*" Scheel moved his hand dismissively. Of course they had their proof locked deep in the machines, engraved on hard drives . . .

Bruno shoved the pages, with the stone, into the drawer of his bed-side table.

At that, Scheel was gone. Bruno found himself ministered by three sets of hands, as the nurses performed their trick of changing the sheets beneath him without moving him from the bed. They'd enfeebled him by design, it was a lie, he could still walk, talk, probably fuck. He receded behind the blot, into his sorrow. Claudia Benedict spoke some slight words of departure herself, took his hand for an instant, and then she too vanished into the corridor.

He refused lunch and possibly dozed. Before long the nurses brought the artificial night, which might have no relation to the world beyond these walls. He sought consolation in the idea that he would die within the ancient preserve of Charité, the plague asylum, but in this antiseptic modern wing it was no good. Perhaps they would release him to the streets, and he could expire on the lawn before some nineteenth-century brickwork renamed for a Nazi doctor, or atop a cairn of paving stones. He wanted to imagine that Berlin had cast him as Hamlet, vital in the dirt, contemplating skulls, but it was the other way. He'd be Yorick, tossed aside.

•

The next morning, Claudia Benedict reappeared. She was alone.

"Mr. Bruno, I wonder if I could have a word with you?"

"I thought you weren't a doctor here, only a ventriloquist's dummy." He was startled by his own uncontrollable bitterness.

"It's true that I have no jurisdiction in this hospital. I only thought I might offer you some advice."

"Things to do in Berlin before you're dead?"

"I'm not certain you should stay in Berlin."

So this was the reward for his imperial stubbornness in not attempting to speak German. A higher class of pity was the best he could expect now. Maybe she'd glimpsed the pressed tuxedo in the wardrobe and been somehow impressed, poor old bird. Maybe she was lonely. "See the world?" he said. "No, Berlin seems like a good place to die."

"Mr. Bruno, you've lived a long while with this disease to this point, and you might live a while yet. I spent last night browsing the current research on meningiomas, and speaking with a surgeon I know in London."

"He'll take my case?"

"No. But there is someone who might, who would at least be worth your meeting." She unfolded from her jacket pocket a medical article, "A Surgical Approach to Complex Intraorbital Meningioma," five or six stapled pages printed from a PDF copy of *The Journal of Head and Neck Surgery,* volume XXI, April 2011. Beyond the title page lay columns of dull text ruptured by black-and-white surgery photos so much worse, so much more literal than the modernist scans of his blot that Bruno had to flip the pages shut.

Benedict pointed to the name at the top, Noah R. Behringer, MD, FACS. "He's a senior fellow in surgery at a hospital on the West Coast of America, a very long way from here. I'd never heard his name, but he's created a bit of a stir with several quite radical resections in deep areas of the face. I think there's a chance you'd be able to interest him in your situation, precisely for the reasons most other doctors, like Scheel here, will regard you as beyond surgical treatment."

"The West Coast?"

"A very fine hospital in San Francisco. I've never been there myself."

Northern California, where Bruno least wished to return. He gave no indication it had special importance. "Does Charité have a working relationship with this hospital?"

"Charité isn't likely to be tremendously helpful to you, Mr. Bruno. You're an American, and, excuse me for this, but, unless I'm mistaken, an impoverished one. A derelict."

"I prefer the terms *lush* or *rake*."

She arched an eyebrow. "Berlin is tolerant of the tide of young expatriates and backpackers arriving here on a daily basis, but they're relied upon to tend to themselves."

"I'm almost fifty."

"Your behavior yesterday morning didn't reflect it. The attitude of the oncologist will not have been a unique one, I'm afraid. Have you heard of the German concept of *therapie hoheit*—therapeutic sovereignty?"

"No."

"Essentially, the physician's right to be unquestioned. You'll not find anyone here necessarily keen to defer to a California surgeon, especially one with a beard and ponytail."

"Can you help me?"

"Apart from the fact that I'm overstepping my bounds even now, I think a . . . personal appeal to your countryman would be better, frankly."

"Throw my derelict American self on the mercy of Dr. Beardinger, you mean."

She carried on as if he hadn't spoken. "May I suggest one more thing? If you are discharged from here, be certain you request a CD with a full set of your radiological images. They can't deny you that in any event, but it may be subject to certain bureaucratic delays if you don't leave here with it on your person."

Bruno experienced a flood of mute feeling toward Benedict, precisely at the instant she was bound to refuse him anything further. He'd been ungrateful. But he'd been speaking as a dead man. Now she'd enriched and burdened him with the return of his human hopes, his credentials for species participation. Benedict had no way of knowing how little he'd tended to these before his death sentence.

"Thank you," he said. "I'll do that."

"If I may say, it's perfectly human to look for someone to blame, or

45

to blame yourself—essentially, to make a story, or a moral, out of what has befallen you."

"I . . . wouldn't. I won't."

"The temptation will be strong, but far better if you accept that it is quite random."

"Yes. Of course."

"Mr. Bruno, I'll leave you now. Do you possess means for traveling to America?"

"I'll manage."

"Is there someone who might assist you on your return? Have you friends in the San Francisco area?"

For decades now, Bruno would have replied, *I've made certain not to.* That was before Singapore.

Two

I

He'd recognized Keith Stolarsky, but not before thinking, *How could they let that bum in here?* Casual Western dress wasn't frowned on in Singapore, so long as that meant appalling tourist pastels, striped Lacoste polo shirts, and rack-fresh sports or hip-hop gear, Juicy Couture, and so forth. And that was what you saw. Not this. The American, who had a posture like a question mark, was dressed in layers of baggy, unwashed black polyester, too tight on his paunch, and a windbreaker over black jeans and worn running shoes—a costume exhumed from some *Dungeons & Dragons* basement. His hair, greasy over his ears, had been combed back from a widow's peak that revealed an unhealthy scalp; his shave looked five days old. Of course, that Bruno found this presentation arresting was perhaps a sign, one among many, that he'd been in Singapore too long. The man would be invisible in America, unless he buttonholed you for a handout.

Then the man's features, and general comportment, his warped grin and pigeon walk, resolved into those of Bruno's boyhood acquaintance Keith Stolarsky. Throughout the next days, which he would spend partly in Stolarksy's company, Bruno was made to marvel at the treacherous intensity of restored memory. Until the man walked into the Smoker's Club, Bruno never would have believed that he recalled the child, or young teenager, named Keith Stolarsky. Indeed, Stolarsky had been purposely forgotten, with so much else. Yet in his presence, each lost gesture and intonation of Stolarsky's lined up on the front shelf of Bruno's awareness, waiting to be retrieved. By this process, Stolarsky was magically doubled in Bruno's gaze. He was simultaneously a forty-seven-year-old wreck—Stolarsky had been a year behind Bruno at Berkeley High, as Bruno now easily remembered—and a frisky, provocative thirteen- or fourteen-year-old, late to mature physically but with an insinuating, gremlin wit.

"Someone you know?" asked Edgar Falk, at the instant Bruno suffered this first recognition. Nothing escaped Falk. Anyhow, there was nothing to hide.

"Yes," said Bruno. "From long ago."

"A gambler?"

"I have no idea."

Falk's question, though, was really no different from Bruno's: What was a man looking like Keith Stolarsky doing here? The Smoker's Club wasn't merely a VIP lounge; it was a secret one, unlisted in guidebooks or in the Marina Bay Sands Casino's own brochures. One didn't merely wander in. One learned of the place in an aside or whisper, and was invited. The club eschewed the sterile gloss of the complex's malls, hotel, and casino in favor of a suggestion of old-worldly glamour: burnished wood panels, brass fixtures, beveled mirrors. A cloud of cigar fume marked an alcove featuring a never-ending poker game, in which men worked to fulfill the fantasy by loosening their ties and draping jackets over the backs of chairs, revealing suspenders, even sweat-patchy shirts, the sleeves of which they rolled to mid-forearm, framing Swiss watches. In another quadrant a snooker table was more lightly employed by a couple of chubby Englishmen indulging their own quaint fetish with pints of ale. Yet the club was no less antiseptic, finally, than the casino. Tricky up-lighting at the tables made faces appear like roast meat laid out at a swank buffet.

In Falk and Bruno's case, they'd come to the Smoker's Club to meet Billy Yik Tho Lim, the former director of the ISD, Singapore's secret police. Yik Tho Lim had gotten involved in a long-term investment of Falk's, the fixing of a Korean football match—a matter outside Bruno's scope of involvement. But in the process, the former director had told Falk that he hoped to test himself against the backgammon wizard Falk had been bragging of.

This assignation, Falk had been engineering for weeks. It wasn't Falk's first visit to the suite, nor Bruno's; he'd played in these rooms, and in fact had his backgammon set on the chair beside him, though serious contests were ordinarily taken elsewhere. He doubted a man like Yik Tho Lim would play in view of gawkers and bystanders. An apparition like Keith Stolarsky might spook him completely.

Stolarsky hadn't come in alone. He was accompanied by a woman, dark-haired and robustly handsome, at least forty when you examined the lines around her mouth, but healthier than Stolarsky by a mile. The woman was dressed in black too, only to a different effect. A tight sweater and pegged jeans gave the appearance of a film actress dressed slightly down for a part as a jazz musician's or Beat poet's girlfriend. The sweater was tucked above a wide, silver-buckled belt; the refusal to conceal her thick waist was itself brazenly attractive. Her expression both quizzical and commanding, Stolarsky's companion made the best evidence that Bruno's old acquaintance wasn't a street person.

"Invite them over," suggested Falk.

"Why should I do that?"

"For amusement."

"He doesn't recognize me. He probably won't remember me."

"I doubt that."

"I haven't seen him since we were children." Bruno knew it was the wrong word for who he'd been when he last saw Stolarsky, at the point when he'd departed Berkeley for good. As if catching this thought, Falk said, with luxuriant irony, "You were never a child." Then he added, "That fellow recognizes you, he just hasn't noticed it yet."

Possibly this was what had first made Bruno comfortable in Edgar Falk's company: Falk read all minds, not Bruno's in particular. He made it unimportant, a prerequisite to deeper pursuits. The nature of Falk's deeper pursuits, however, remained after much time permanently opaque.

Bruno's decision was made for him. He and Falk sat near enough to the path between the entrance and the bar that Keith Stolarsky and his companion passed their table.

"No fucking way."

"Hello, Keith," said Bruno, as airily as he could manage.

"Alexander Bruno," said Stolarsky. "Figures you'd turn up in a place like this." Stolarsky turned to the woman. "I once told you about this guy, we were eating at Chez Panisse, remember? That there was a kid in my high school who worked as a waiter there, who all the moms were in love with? Then he just floated away? *This is that guy.*"

"I'm Edgar Falk," said Falk, holding out his hand. Stolarsky gazed at it for a crucial second, as if unsure. His hands had been shoved into his pockets, and he drew out just one. Though it was Falk who took it, Bruno at that moment recalled the creepy, ratlike feebleness of Stolarsky's clasp.

"Keith," he said. "This is Tira."

She stuck out her own hand, and Bruno stood a little in accepting it, warm and strong, into his. "Tira Harpaz," she said. Was adding her last name a rebuke to Stolarsky's manners?

If so, Stolarsky wasn't chastened. "What a fucking scenario this is, huh?" he said to Bruno.

"The Smoker's Club?"

"Sure, and Marina Bay Sands, and Singapore, the whole kit and caboodle."

"I suppose so." Bruno released Tira Harpaz's hand, even as he came fully up from his chair. "Please sit. What would you like to drink?" He was conscious of wishing to live up to any legend he'd left in his wake at Berkeley High. Stolarsky and Falk were witnesses, at either end, of the construction of Bruno's sole life accomplishment: his personality. There was nothing to threaten him in any comparison of notes between them, since he'd been perfectly consistent. It was the woman for whom Bruno would perform, a new, blank screen onto which he'd project himself.

"Nah, you sit, let me buy you a round. I want to take a look at this joint. What are you having?"

"Another of these—a Tiger Beer, it's called. But I'll go to the bar with you. Ms. Harpaz, please . . ." Bruno pulled out a chair.

Falk waved his hand across the top of his glass, which Bruno knew contained only cranberry juice and soda.

"I'll have a Tiger Beer too," said Tira Harpaz, slipping into the seat.

"Are you staying at the Sands?" Bruno asked, applying mild pressure on Stolarsky and the woman to clarify their relation. If there was daylight between them, they might reveal it in their response. *I remember the man you are with before he could grow hair anywhere but on his head,* he told Tira Harpaz with his eyes. *I'd wager he's grown it in far too many places now.*

"Not a fucking chance," said Stolarsky. "I'd feel like a rat in a psych experiment." At the word *rat,* Bruno stiffened. Was Stolarsky reading Bruno's thoughts? Stolarsky went on, apparently oblivious. "We're at Raffles. After some of the joints in Thailand and Sri Lanka we were ready for a little five-star action. The place is a trip, it's got that total Kipling vibe."

"Naturally," said Falk. "He lodged there."

Again, Stolarsky paused, to measure Falk. Bruno could sympathize. He recalled his first impression of Falk, at White's, in London. Bruno had been there at the whim of an English peer from whom he'd removed upward of thirty thousand pounds, and who plainly regarded seeing Bruno do similarly to a number of his friends as adequate compensation for his losses. To the great amusement of the callow swells in the peer's circle, Falk had been presented to Bruno as "the other American." With his dyed, seemingly lacquered hair and rouged cheeks, Falk had first struck Bruno as much older than sixty, an aging queen with everything to conceal.

Now, a decade later, Falk looked not a day older. Bruno understood Falk's Kabuki mask as his true face, and never sought a glimpse underneath. The longer Bruno knew Falk, the less the first impression mattered: Falk seemingly wasn't aging, might not be a queen. Yet Bruno knew Falk struck others this way. Falk relied upon it.

"Yeah, naturally," said Stolarsky. He seemed to swallow another thought. Instead, he and Bruno went to the bar, leaving Falk and Tira Harpaz at the glowing table.

"Shit, that's no better than a Budweiser," said Stolarsky, when he'd slurped off the top inch of Tira Harpaz's Tiger. He'd done it right at the bar, without regard for how it affronted the bartender, and showing no signs of hurry to deliver his companion or girlfriend her drink.

He'd ordered a Grey Goose Magnum, a double, for himself, and now he winced down a mouthful, chasing off his disappointment in the beer, which had left a foam trace on his grizzled upper lip.

"Every nation needs its Budweiser," said Bruno.

"Okay, okay, but listen now, Flashman," said Stolarsky. He spoke as if they'd been delaying some negotiation for long enough already, for years. "We're gonna have to fill in some missing chapters here."

"Flashman?"

"Don't pretend you don't remember you put me on to those books in high school. George MacDonald Fraser? Flashman the coward, the asshole, the heel? You've obviously based your whole life on him. Hell, it was obvious by eleventh grade."

Bruno remembered the books, barely. He was more interested, however, that this shambles, this heap of a man, appeared so immune to embarrassment.

"I've got the whole sequence in first editions, man. I think of you every time I open one. So who'd you murder for that tuxedo, Alex? Please don't tell me you're that old weirdo's significant other."

"Sorry?"

"Should I translate? His, whatchamacallit, his *catamite,* Alex."

"What a word!"

"Give it over, yes or no: Are you or are you not Liberace's protégé?"

"No," said Bruno, without any shame of his own. It was hardly the first time it had been suggested. If Stolarsky didn't believe him it wouldn't be the first time for that, either.

"So he's your CIA handler? Are you about to bust in on some big operation here?" Stolarsky's tone was sardonic, but it wanted an answer. It had been sardonic, but urgent too, when at twelve or thirteen a virginal Stolarsky had interrogated Bruno on Bruno's experiences with girls. In this manner, by a series of associations, these ruins that called themselves Keith Stolarsky leveraged Bruno back into the unwelcome past.

Still, there was something beguiling in Stolarsky's attentions, which made Bruno willing to carry on teasing him. "No," Bruno said. "Not that, either."

"I get it, I'm blowing your cover, huh?"

"Impossible to do, since I'm utterly uncovered."

"Just our man in a tux in a secret club in the Singapore Sands? Did you know this pile of gleaming shit and infinity waterfalls is human history's most expensive building?"

"I hadn't heard."

"If you're not sick of me guessing I can try to come up with more insults. You're the waiter, right? Nah, you're the janitor."

"I do clean up from time to time."

"Fuck you. You're a gigolo, obviously. I could buy you for Tira for five hundred of these Singapore dollars, right? You're holding up okay. You're no Dorian Gray, but you're not quite the portrait, either. It's been a good life, and so long as you've still got your hair you can run out the string a while longer. You work hard for the money. Just like this building, you put every fucking cent on the screen."

"You think you've guessed it this time?"

"Sure, of course I did. I even guessed your nickname in the trade. They call you Infinity Pool. Because a woman can gaze into your eyes and feel like she's drowning, plus you're really fucking expensive."

"Would you really buy me for Tira?"

"Sure, but I'd have to be allowed to watch. She gets whatever she wants."

"Like that beer?"

"I'm glad to know you'll be working that Goofus and Gallant routine into the grave, I'd be disappointed if you dropped it. But you've got a point, let's go. I bet she's pumped that old character actor for your vital statistics, probably got your social security number and passwords while I'm still here trying to get in the door, conversational-wise."

"Are you telling me the two of you are some sort of grifters?" At this, the balance turned. Bruno laughed in his heart, though his face was still. Stolarsky had no power over him. Bruno's high-school acquaintance was a barely viable man who'd saved his entire life for Southeast Asia on a package tour, likely not even a competent sex tourist but a wannabe, a talker, who'd blundered his way into this room by the act of overtipping some concierge.

"Yeah, sure, Alex, that's great, Boris and Natasha Badenov, you caught me."

"I doubt she'll find my associate an easy mark."

"Your *associate*? You're fucking killing me."

"I'm a professional gambler, Keith. I relieve wealthy men of the delusion that they're any good at backgammon."

"You hustle *board games*? For real?"

"For real." It was suddenly possible, Bruno felt, to speak to Stolarsky not merely as though he were still the pesky, craven, retarded adolescent Bruno recalled but as if to a child. "Now, let's bring Tira her indigenous Budweiser, and let's enjoy ourselves conversational-wise for a minute or two, and then I'd appreciate it if you'd make yourselves scarce." Bruno had realized he simply wasn't interested in spending time watching Stolarsky and Falk try to fathom each other, or listening to them comparing fatuous characterizations of Bruno's temperament.

He remained curious about Tira Harpaz, but that could wait.

"You're blowing me off?"

"Go play poker, or do whatever you were hoping to do in this place. You see, I wasn't being completely truthful when I said you couldn't blow my cover. In fact, my associate has arranged a meeting with a very dangerous and corrupt public official, one with an appetite for expensive contests of chance. He's a rare quarry, and I don't want to scare him off."

"Holy fuck, Flashman, you're the complete package."

"Then, if you like, I'll pick you and Tira up at your hotel tomorrow at noon, and show you some parts of Singapore that are a little more— textural. And then you'll tell me what you've been doing with yourself."

"Because you really don't give a shit."

"On the contrary, I'm dying to know."

"Riiiight."

II

As he came in out of the glare off Beach Road into the Raffles lobby, Bruno didn't know if he was in the mood for more of Keith Stolarsky's banter or not. He'd suspended judgment, waiting to let the sight of Stolarsky decide for him. The morning after, his schoolmate's presence at the Smoker's Club seemed apparitional; Bruno had kept the promise to visit Stolarsky at his hotel as much to confirm its reality as out of any desire for Stolarsky and his girlfriend's company, or for any other.

Since the apparition declined to reappear, Bruno was left to wonder. Tira Harpaz came alone, hailing Bruno where he'd been corralled by a female butler. He was stuck on the far side of the "residents only" barrier, despite having been careful to wear a jacket to meet the hotel's dress code, despite the day's heat. Raffles exemplified the dull rigidity of Singapore's old colonial fantasies about itself. He wondered how the staff felt about Stolarsky's disheveled presence, but of course Stolarsky must have applied the universal solvent of money to the problem.

Tira Harpaz had prepared for the noonday sun in a suitably wide-brimmed straw hat, so Bruno led her out onto the avenue rather than suggesting the hotel's restaurant or bar, or a cab. It seemed to be what she wanted, anyhow. He himself wore a Borsalino, shade enough, though he already felt humidity cleaving shirt to ribs beneath the unnecessary jacket. When Bruno offered an inquiring glance back at the hotel's upper stories, she shrugged. "My cell works here," she said. "Keith'll find us, if he ever wakes up . . ."

"Fair enough. We can easily walk to Lau Pa Sat for some food from the market stalls. Or in the other direction, to Orchard Road, if you like."

55

"He said you'd promised the underground tour, whatever that consists of."

"I hope I wasn't misleading. To be blunt, by comparison to Thailand and Sri Lanka, you'll be awfully unimpressed with the underground scene here."

"No dens of iniquity?" she teased. "Chewing-gum orgies, nothing?"

"Orchard Plaza does feature one very brightly colored condom store. We've got the usual massage parlors, but you can't have come all this distance just for a happy ending now, can you?"

"Hey, who doesn't like a happy ending?" Her tone was cryptic, but cheery.

Bruno again twitched his head behind them, at Raffles. "Late night?"

"He moaned something about seeing the sun come up and stuck the pillow over his head."

"So you got started on the dens of iniquity without me, then? Or Keith did."

"It's not like you think. He spent all night drinking Red Bulls from the minibar. He went online and started playing backgammon against machines and people, and then arguing strategy on these forums with all these international night-owl backgammon assholes. He, like, built this whole new backgammon persona for himself in eight or nine hours, which, if you know Keith, is weirdly typical. He woke me up at two and tried to get me to play him, said he'd figured it all out. Of course I told him to fuck off. He's hoping to pit himself against you, obviously."

"You can learn everything about backgammon online in eight or nine hours, with the precise exception of how to beat someone like me."

"He'll be eager to hear it."

"I don't sit down for less than five hundred Singapore dollars a point." Bruno wasn't sure why he'd exaggerated. He'd been in games for lower stakes recently enough. Five hundred, it occurred to him, was the price Stolarsky had suggested it would take to purchase Bruno for Tira Harpaz for the night.

"Yeah, well, he can afford you." Now she was sardonic—toward whom, Bruno wasn't sure. "Is that what you played for last night? Keith said you had a date with the Asian J. Edgar Hoover?"

"My game last night didn't materialize." Whether spooked by sight of the anomalous Americans, or for some other, unknown reason, Yik Tho Lim had sent an emissary with an apology to Falk, deferring the contest.

"Sorry to hear it. Christ, this heat. This is, like, our fifteenth country, and I've pretty well exhausted my curiosity for meandering around in the blazing sunlight. I'd love some iced coffee, though."

He'd read her wrong, despite her eagerness to put the hotel behind her. Perhaps she'd expected him to have come in a car. "We'll jump in a taxi," he said. "I'll take you to the market, if only just to look." They'd crossed Bras Basah Road, but other hotels approached and finding a taxicab wouldn't be difficult.

"I imagine I might work up some appetite once I'm sitting in the shade. No offense, but if I didn't know any better, I'd imagine I was walking in LA, you know?" She waved at the toy-skyscraper skyline and, nearer, at the narrow, empty pavement, with its inadequate cover of trees.

"None taken." He recalled what Los Angeles signified, if you lived in Northern California: the contemptible height of vacuity and poor taste, where only Mexican cleaning women were ever sighted on the sidewalks. Partisans of the Bay Area were so certain they had it better. To Bruno the two ends of the state might nearly be identical. "I've no stake in your opinion of Singapore. I don't think much of it myself."

"So what's the appeal, just 'the women are cheap and the boys are cheaper'?"

"I wouldn't know the price of either. What I like about Singapore is how little it asks of me. It brags three or four native languages, a mélange of cultural styles and so forth, but in truth it's perfectly flavorless."

"Would you like some ABC gum?"

"Gum?" He actually did feel an irrational and disproportionate surge of panic, as though Keith Stolarsky and Tira Harpaz had been sent to him in some obscure sting operation.

"ABC gum. Already Been Chewed. Sorry, just free-associating. I read in the guidebook about the prohibition on chewing gum, and then you reminded me of this joke from Plantation Farm Summer Camp, in Sonoma, circa 1988."

"Ah, flavorless because chewed, I understand."

"Are you hiding?"

"Only in plain sight."

"What keeps you here, then?"

"Nothing does. You find me here because nothing keeps me elsewhere."

"My native tour is looking really promising at this point," she said, with mock exasperation.

"We can sit and talk. I'd like that." He surprised himself. He turned his body, just enough to guide her to the left, toward the entrance to the Swissôtel. "Here, they'll summon a cab for us in the lobby."

"Fuck it. Let's check out their bar. I don't need texture, I need air-conditioning."

Inside, they plumped themselves in a vacant corner of the Swissôtel's modern lounge and ordered iced coffees from the disinterested waitress. Opaque conversation droned from the only other occupied booth, salaryman Japanese. Tira texted Stolarsky their location, then placed her smartphone on the table between them, but it lay dark. Bruno eased himself back in the booth, pleasantly abstracted, faintly turned on, hovering in a benign cloud of non-urgencies.

Tira said, "Look at this." She tugged at her neckline to show a fresh stripe of sunburn between her collar and where she bulged from her red brassiere. "I walked out yesterday in a new shirt, without any sunblock. I've been using it pretty religiously, but I figured I could afford fifteen minutes—guess again. The advertising campaign for this place should be: Too impatient to wait another hundred years for global-warming apocalypse? Try Singapore!"

"You don't feature a lot of natural defense."

"No. Me and my girlfriends used to walk around Goth for a while, they'd go in for dye jobs and then spend half an hour at the mirror doing the whole ghoul-white powder application. Whereas with this black hair and white skin, all I had to do was pretty much slash on the bloodred lipstick, et voilà."

People delivered themselves, helplessly, if you gave them the chance. It was to Bruno a matter of permanent wonder, though he seldom knew whether to be bored or enthralled. Tira proved herself an extreme case. "I'm sure you were a fright," he said.

"You should have seen me before this tan. The men in Thailand stared like I was radioactive. I guess that must be what blondes feel like everywhere they go."

And yet she never quite got to the point. Few did, without help. "Are you two really sex tourists?" Bruno asked. "Or some kind of swingers?" It would be blunt, if Keith Stolarsky and Tira Harpaz hadn't dropped what seemed like a hundred hints.

"Har!" Her laugh was a seal bark.

"What?" To himself, he already sounded defensive.

"It's just that where I come from, by which I mean the Bay Area and the twentieth century, or I guess this is the twenty-first now, we use the term *open relationship*. Which, if you'd asked me in so many words, I'd have had to say, *Sure, maybe sometimes, I guess.* Keith does pretty much what he wants, which I deal with in my various and sundry ways. But I'm certainly no swinger, Alexander. I'm not sure I've ever even met a certified authentic swinger, not by that name. Christ, this stuff is like maple syrup." Tira had swigged half of an iced coffee, plumped down by the waitress during the course of her monologue.

"They don't know any other way," he said. "And no offense intended."

She barked again. "It's cool, Keith has been accused of plenty worse than sex tourism! So have I, just for being in his general range of operations."

Operations? It struck Bruno as an odd word. "What's the source of all this money?"

"Are you pulling my leg? When did you last see each other?"

"Not since high school."

"But you must have come back through Berkeley in the last, uh, thirty or so years, right?"

"Not once." It was probably as near to a distinctive accomplishment as he could claim in his life. A slow-forming, barely perceived performance-art piece: *Alexander Unreturning* (1981–Present, Found Materials).

"I guess that's what it would take not to know. Keith owns about half of Telegraph Avenue. You know Zodiac Media, right?"

"No."

"The superstore? Electronics, games, T-shirts, all that garbage? Or Zombie Burger?"

"No. Neither."

"Well, those are his stores. The source of the dough, since you asked. Keith's empire takes up a block of what used to be, you know, head shops and used-book stores and Afghan tabbouleh joints, all that good old Berkeley shit. They call it the Death Star. Keith's viewed as kind of like Darth Vader in your hometown, Alexander, that's why I figured you must know the score."

Bruno shrugged. She looked at him oddly.

"I'm not confused—you did grow up there, right?"

"I moved to Berkeley with my mother when I was six. We'd lived in Marin County before that."

"So . . ."

He was free to decant himself as readily as any other person. Tira's question was obvious, even if she couldn't put it in words. It was Bruno's to answer or duck. He tried to recall the last time he'd chosen to go at it directly.

"I don't know whether June is alive or dead," he said. "Though I'd be surprised if there's much left of her. She fled the affections of her guru in San Rafael, as I said, when I was six. Her idea was to lay low in Berkeley, let the drugs wear off over time, but she was in poor shape already. I mean, mentally. We lived in a shabby apartment in the flats, and she worked making custom architectural plasterwork, on San Pablo Avenue. I wonder if the place is still there." Bruno didn't bother describing the two chubby, imperious gay men who'd run the storefront workshop, where they produced concrete pediments and decorative plaster scrollwork for restored Victorian ceilings. The Italian and the American, with their beards and bottomless supply of marijuana, which they'd made too available to June, not helping a bit, and how they'd bully June to tears when she cracked some fabulous plaster construction coming out of the mold, spoiling a day's effort. "When I was in the seventh grade I started washing dishes at Spenger's Fish Grotto, and then they let me bus tables, but I really had my eye on the Gourmet Ghetto—do they still call it that?"

"Sure." Tira's eyes were wide. "The Cheese Board, right? And Keith said you worked at Chez Panisse? When you were in high school?"

"Yes."

"Then you just, what, ran away from home?"

"I wasn't living at home. June couldn't maintain a home or anything else. She was in a city shelter, except I'd see her quite a bit at People's Park, too, living in a rather . . . feral manner." June's street boyfriend was a man with a shopping cart and a distinctive rasp that seemed to resound through a megaphone buried in his chest. Bruno had some- times heard it outside the classroom windows of Berkeley High as the man gleaned the school grounds for recyclables, between recess and the lunch hour.

"I'm sorry."

"I don't think of it that way."

"You lived at the shelter?"

"I'd farmed myself out to some friends' extra rooms, a thing you could do in Berkeley back then. Maybe you still can."

"Wow. Did you stay at *Keith's?*"

"By friends I don't mean at school. I mean restaurant people, waiters and so forth."

"So you were, like, the most legendary teenager ever. I can't believe Keith never told me that part."

"Keith wouldn't have had even the slightest suspicion."

"Because you were, what—already too cool for school, nobody's fool, and dressing like Peter O'Toole? I'm writing a poem about you, if you hadn't noticed."

He waved it off. "Keith, remember, was in a lower grade. I'd learned to keep June out of my life with other . . . children . . . long before then."

Tira's phone pulsed on the glass tabletop. She grabbed it and read. "Here he comes now. Will he ever be pissed he missed out on your confession."

It was absurd that the risk of Keith Stolarsky's learning about June, at this late date, a century and continent distant from Berkeley, should feel somehow like a noose tightening. "You can give him a paraphrase," said Bruno to Tira now. "Just don't make me sit and listen while you do it. And please, let him think there was some cost, that it didn't come spilling out so easily. I have a reputation to uphold." The room seemed suddenly smaller. Even the Mandarin-speaking businessmen appeared to be listening to him.

"Maybe I waterboarded you? Or—" Tira put fist to lips and tongue-ballooned her cheek from within, miming fellatio.

"Watch yourself," said Bruno, trying to cover his surprise. "That type of sign language might be illegal in Singapore."

"What's a horny deaf girl to do? I was going to suggest *chew gum*, but then I remembered." Tira had hit the accelerator, as if frantic, at the prospect of Keith's arrival, to confirm her mastery of innuendo.

"She could always write her proposal down on a piece of paper."

"What if she's illiterate too, poor thing?"

Bruno was as exhausted by the banter as he was dazzled, or titillated. "I should have at least questioned you in return," Bruno said. "Instead I learned next to nothing, outside your sinister background as a Goth."

"I'm pretty much what I look like. Just your typical Israeli-born, St. Louis–raised, academic-brat Berkeley Rhetoric Department all-but-dissertation recovering-Goth sex tourist."

"I had you pegged, then."

"Meet one, you've met them all."

Keith Stolarsky waddled across the lobby and joined them and the banter ended, as if dropped off a cliff. Along with it, the confessional atmosphere and the raw sexual taunting, each of which had floated just beneath the banter, fronds in a murky pool. Stolarsky seemed uninterested in what they might have done in his absence, as if confident it hadn't amounted to much. Maybe it hadn't. Nor did Stolarsky pursue the questions he'd claimed such interest in, the evening before, at the Smoker's Club.

"Okay, you fucker, I'm going to eat your lunch."

"You want lunch?" asked Bruno.

"Sure, but that's not what I'm talking about. We're gonna play backgammon tonight, or this afternoon, as soon as you're ready. I want to see if you can surprise me."

"I play for money."

Stolarsky just smacked his lips and rolled his eyes.

"Fair enough, we'll plan to sit down," said Bruno. He'd seen men pronounce themselves instantaneous players before, gripped by a fever upon discovering that high-stakes backgammon existed, and captured by the romance Bruno represented, wishing to climb into his skin. That it should happen to Stolarsky wasn't so distinctive, no matter the odd circumstances. "Would you still like a go at the food stalls at Lau Pa Sat?"

"Sure. Look at him, cool as a cucumber. Lead on, Flashman." But Tira said nothing. She'd receded joylessly behind him, a moon.

"I'll ask for a cab," Bruno said. "The sun's only getting hotter."

Really, Stolarsky's arrival in the Swissôtel bar described the sharpest possible U-turn in Bruno's encounter with Tira. Not just at that moment but for the remainder of Tira's and Stolarsky's sojourn in Singapore. Bruno couldn't make contact again. Where there'd been double entendres, exposed cleavage, and doggerel about Peter O'Toole, now—nothing. Bruno had realized the startling sweetness of their exchange at the last instant, like the condensed milk at the bottom of his glass, which crept between his lips only after he'd drained the black coffee above.

"You an adherent of Paul Magriel?" Stolarsky was saying as they entered the shady courts that housed the vendors' stalls. "I mean, I gather he's like the J. D. Salinger of backgammon, right? But then again a lot of that shit seems out-of-date now since the computers came along, huh?"

"Tournament play may have changed somewhat. A serious money game, less so."

63

"You played the top programs? Jellyfish, Snowie?"

"No."

"You ever play against *Magriel*?"

"Never had the chance." Stolarsky had peppered Bruno with lore through the cab ride and while they began browsing the stalls. Whether Stolarsky was a quick study or merely a magpie for jargon remained to be seen. The two weren't mutually exclusive, anyhow. Both traits would be congruent with the adolescent gadfly Bruno recalled from Berkeley.

"Wow, this whole place is pretty slick. You could make something like this fly on Telegraph, pull a bunch of grunky street merchants under one roof, legitimate 'em, and take a flat skim off the top. Call it the People's Park Atrium, hah!" Stolarsky looked to Tira. She only half grunted in reply.

"Of course, you wouldn't have the benefit of a really hard-ass police state to keep it all so spanking clean. More's the pity, eh, Flashman?"

Under Bruno's gentle stewardship they sampled char kway tweo and sambal stingray, rinsing the spice with cold pale beer. Pulut hitam— black rice pudding—for dessert. Bruno couldn't discern a hint of real delight in Tira Harpaz at the exotic food, or his company, or anything else. In Stolarsky's presence she only seemed numbed, enduring. Had the arrangement between these two soured just lately, perhaps in a hotel in Cambodia or Hanoi? Was the erotic animus they'd each revealed a brandishing of some fresh wound, a Band-Aid on recent betrayal? Or were they bound in slow-cooking love-hate, a folie à deux obscure to anyone outside their secret system? Bruno knew just enough not to imagine he could tell the difference.

III

Bruno stopped by Edgar Falk's rooms for a drink at nine, before making his second visit to Raffles.

Bruno had spent the afternoon in his own hotel in a deep slumber, after the heavy meal and the unsatisfying encounter with Tira and Stolarsky. He'd slept dreamlessly but woke into melancholy. A nap ending precisely at sunset, with its undead overtones, was rarely a good idea. In fact, Bruno realized as he waited for the butler to open the door to Falk's rooms, he *had* dreamed, not of a situation, nor of a lost person or place, but merely of an image. Bruno had dreamed a reverse sunset, a black sunset.

The black sun had been sinking against a field of yellow. This sun was haloed in electric purple, a purple unstable like a pattern of interference or static. In Bruno's dream he'd watched this black-purple apparition sinking below its yellow horizon, only to abruptly re-center in his vision's field and begin its lonely plummet again. It was this that had brought the profound melancholy upon him, and this that, when he awoke and moved the curtain aside, had made the orange half orb on Singapore's harbor appear so dire and alien.

Later he'd recall this as his first conscious apprehension of the blot.

Falk's Singapore "butler" was a houseboy, really, supplied at first by the hotel but soon usurped to Falk's local purposes. For the hundredth time, Bruno had forgotten his name. The houseboy served Falk with a deference suggesting a wholesale blindness to vice, and was present for any number of untaxed transfers of gross amounts of Singapore dollars, among other dubiously legal exhibitions. Bruno would hardly be surprised to learn he also reported routinely to unseen authorities, who'd then contact Falk for their touch. Falk conducted an invisible orchestra of graft; his mantra was "price of doing business." In Southeast Asia, particularly, Falk held off the incursion of officials and mobsters on Bruno's delicate operations, such as closing maneuvers on a drunken rich man, after a night of letting him win just enough to risk a double-or-nothing match on a debt that had grown outrageous. Then, while Bruno departed his hotel to the airport, to evaporate into a new locale, Falk stayed behind to settle affairs and collect debts. Falk always collected debts. Bruno supposed it was here the routine investments in policemen became essential. No doubt Falk had spared Bruno jail a few times, too, without Bruno ever knowing of it.

"Mister Edgar is massage."

"He asked me to come by. I can wait, or come back—"

"No, he want you come in."

Of course he did. Falk seemed to relish exposure of his nudity to Bruno, and to others who came in range, in steam rooms or at private swimming pools, anywhere such a display could be managed. Exposing his crumbling flesh, Falk appropriated time's power to his own, needling younger men with what they must inevitably become. *If I can take it, you'd better.* Bruno stepped past the butler and entered Falk's dimmed bedroom. Bruno smelled saffron—possibly some tinctured oil or incense. A towel lay draped to conceal Falk's sallow buttocks, as he stretched facedown on the table. Possibly it would find a way to come off before the interview was finished. A Malay masseuse kneaded the loose, brown-flecked, papery skin covering Falk's shoulder blades. She lowered her eyes from Bruno's.

"Alexander." Falk didn't raise his head. His groan rose sepulchrally from within the cushioned doughnut concealing his face. Like putting your head in a toilet seat, it struck Bruno now.

"Yes."

"I had coffee with Billy Lim. He apologized for last night. He said he'd been . . . unavoidably detained." Falk's tone savored this received unit of non-explanation as though it suited his own sense of decorum. No doubt Falk and Yik Tho Lim had been talking over their pet project, the fixed soccer match. But Falk wouldn't mention that.

"Elusive fellow."

"Worth indulging, I think. We've made an arrangement for Friday night. He'd like to hold a small party at a certain restaurant."

"Back room?"

"I think he's reserved the entire establishment."

"Sounds serious."

"I hope so. He told me he once won a Bengal tiger in a poker game with the director of the Singapore Zoo."

"Travels everywhere with him now, this tiger?"

"Billy ate him, for strength." Falk murmured this enigma around a sigh, as if the massage had eased the words from him. The masseuse had slung Falk's elbow over her shoulder, exposing his white-sprigged underarm as she mashed her thumbs deep into the sockets of his shoulder.

Bruno, idling in the saffron gloom, was left no clue whether the eaten tiger was a garish boast or a witticism of Yik Tho Lim's—or a witticism of Falk's, at Lim's expense. But, accustomed to Falk's obscurantist passages, Bruno didn't seek clarification. It was time, anyhow, to quit stalling. "Listen, Edgar, I've had no chance to tell you. Much to my own surprise, I'm actually in a game *tonight* with that American who wandered in—" It was for this that Bruno would be returning to Raffles. Keith Stolarsky had arranged a separate room for what he'd proposed, at parting, as "an epic all-night throwdown."

"Your ancestral friend. Yes, I know."

So Falk had heard. The butler? The masseuse? He likely knew it from a dozen sources. Stolarsky wouldn't have taken any care to hide his preparations, nor would such an attempt have added up to much, not in this town.

"It's a good thing Billy Lim didn't want to play tonight, isn't it?"

"I wasn't concealing it from you."

"I know."

"It came as a surprise." Bruno was repeating himself.

"I'm sure it did. Action?"

"I think there'll be action. He doesn't look it, but he's a rich man, apparently."

"Retail, I gather." Now the masseuse applied a dust or powder of some sort to Falk's limbs. Sure enough, the towel was removed for full access. Could it possibly be curry, the smell now mixing with that of saffron? Was she preparing Falk for a tandoori oven? Everywhere lately, Bruno smelled meat.

"Yes. He sells cell phones, I guess, or video games, to college kids."

"You'd rather I wasn't there."

"It wouldn't matter one way or another, to me, Edgar. But I don't think it's what Keith has in mind. You're cut in, of course—"

"Say nothing more."

Bruno had been dismissed. To underline it, Falk farted and exhaled wheezily, like a body slackening in death. Bruno felt Falk's disappointment in him, a general condition and nothing new. Whatever bound them—it included affection—had long since outworn the illusions of pride. The old jackal faced the young one in a merciless mirror. And Bruno had fewer tricks at his disposal than he should have; he'd relied too long on Falk's. If so much as a single member of the Raffles staff was present in the room Keith Stolarsky had arranged, Falk would know every word of what passed there. Perhaps Bruno would ask Stolarsky to banish any, for this reason. But then, Bruno might find himself the one to give a full report afterward—he'd always done so before. His resentments were those of a slave. Was it time to break away?

When Bruno found himself eye to eye with the butler on his way to the door, neither spoke.

•

An hour later Bruno appeared at Raffles. He'd dressed informally, in a white suit appropriate to the hot night, and carried his backgammon set under his arm. The staff welcomed him now, their wheels greased. They directed him to the door of the Straits Settlement Suite.

"Yeah, I got Tira another room for the night. She doesn't need three fucking TVs and a safe-deposit box just to sack out." Stolarsky was in grotty black lounge shorts and a San Francisco 49ers jersey, its red-and-gold emblem laminated, not stitched. His white robe and slippers were presumably courtesy of Raffles. Despite the slick, fussy Victorian decor of Raffles, Bruno was startled by the degree to which Stolarsky's presence reduced the suite to a bug's lair, as if by opening the door Bruno had lifted a rock. The act of entering, which Bruno did now, became that of shrinking oneself to size, of joining the flea circus. The rooms had only superficially been neatened up, the lamps illuminating little piles of travel receipts, wadded-up currency, other detritus. The door to the bedroom was closed. "Figured we'd put it to better use," Stolarsky was saying. "After all I paid for the goddamned thing."

"She's sleeping already?"

"Nah, she's out trolling around with this bored Kansas City housewife she met at the bar, I guess it's a Missouri thing. Told me to tell you she'd come by at some point, but I think she's kinda pissed off I'm not dedicating our last night to showing her the nightlife, what there is to speak of. Cool, you brought your set, I asked the concierge if he could get one for me and he looked pretty dubious. We'll see if one shows up. I been doing nothing but playing online, I feel like someone poured Drano in my eye sockets."

"Your last night?"

"Yeah, we moved up our ticket. Got sick of this shit in a hurry. I don't know how you stand it."

"It's the same to me as any other place."

"Okay, Magister Ludi, I read you. You see nothing beyond the horizon of the board. Now I'm going to clamber into your minimalist Zen-master rock garden and we'll see if I can muss your hair a little."

"I really have no idea what you're talking about. May I fix myself a drink?"

"Your secret garden, your enclosure of enigma. The arena in which you pilot your fickle finger of backgammon fate. I'm calling your bluff, old sport, old *pip,* old *cock.* Make me one of those while you're at it."

Bruno splashed Macallan into two tumblers and said, "Backgammon isn't a bluffing game."

"Hey, leave room for ice. What about the doubling cube? You're just softening me up, you fucking hustler."

"I wouldn't ice this. Doubling isn't the same as bluffing—both players can see the entire board."

"Right, you wouldn't ice good scotch, of course not. So probably you don't want a splash of Dr Pepper either, huh? I'm kidding. Anyhow, I don't mean bluffing about shit hidden on the board, Alexander. I mean bluffing about what's in your *mind*."

Bruno just stared. He tested for any intrusion of Stolarsky's thoughts. None came. He handed Stolarsky the tumbler of scotch. Had Bruno ever discussed telepathy with Keith Stolarsky in high school? It would have been a remarkable lapse. Stolarsky's provocations were too scattershot, and inane, for Bruno to concern himself with.

Stolarsky grinned and raised the scotch in a silent toast.

"I'm an open book," said Bruno, opting for the blasé. "If you find anything in my mind that can alter the facts on the board, you're welcome to it. Shall we get started?"

By the time of the first interruption, Bruno had concluded that Stolarsky's game, cobbled though it might be from Internet research and contests with programs, or with players hidden behind their own screens who were themselves schooled in contests with programs, was not too shabby. Stolarsky displayed a spongy intelligence and wasn't stuck on one or another principle of play at the expense of what the dice commanded. Still, Bruno won five of the seven games, and he amused himself by never touching the cube himself, to Stolarsky's bedevilment. It denied Stolarsky any cue as to when he ought to resign.

"I don't get it, why don't you double me?" Stolarsky said during the eighth game, when put on the bar. Stolarsky had already doubled, as on two previous occasions. Bruno was resolved to accept any of Stolarsky's doubles as a matter of policy, for the time being. It was a way to needle the new player, to learn what he was made of. Bruno had insisted they begin at stakes of one hundred per point, in direct contradiction of his claim to Tira Harpaz. They could build from there, or not. He was up eight hundred as it was.

In answer now, Bruno just shrugged.

"Are you saying I've still got a shot here? I don't see it."

"One always has a shot."

"You're toying with me again."

"Resign if you like."

"Chuck you, Farley." Stolarsky rolled. As if the dice had conspired with Bruno, to educate Stolarsky in the caprice of their possibilities, Stolarsky reentered from the bar on his first try, and also hit Bruno's sole uncovered checker.

"There you go," said Bruno.

"Guess you saw that coming." Stolarsky meant it sarcastically, but he was unable to hide his satisfaction at the turn of his luck, a loser's hunger for the flavor denied him.

"No, but I've seen it happen before."

It was then that the suite's doorbell chimed. A member of the staff, chaperoning a delivery boy with a steaming bag of food. Was this Edgar Falk's spy? Possibly, though Stolarsky took credit for placing the order. He tipped the kid and placed the unopened package on the countertop. Bruno and Stolarsky were left alone.

"What is it?" asked Bruno.

"A big pile of Omakase burgers. I heard they were the real deal around here, hope I wasn't misinformed."

"Not at all."

"Dynamite. Fuel for the long haul. But I'm not letting you off the hook, Flashman. Roll."

Bruno managed to lose, though not before accepting a double from Stolarsky, which he beavered, pointlessly. The result brought them close to equilibrium, Bruno just four hundred up after an hour of play. A gentleman's game, therefore a total snooze. Stolarsky's monomaniacal focus on the checkers had drained off the chaotic intensity of his other behaviors. With them evaporated the flow of peculiar memories overtaking Bruno. He wondered if he could find an occasion to wander into the closed bedroom. Examining Tira Harpaz's private belongings might give a further clue—but to what? Would Bruno even want to know? It diverted him, at least, that he felt the urge.

Stolarsky arranged two of the takeout burgers on the table, between himself and the board. Bruno helped himself to one as well, barely a dent in the large supply, but he'd only eaten half before Stolarsky had devoured his own pair. Stolarsky burped, sighed, and smacked his lips, stretching in his chair to relieve the pressure at his waist, within a growing halo of crumpled wrappers and balled-up napkins.

"All right, all right, you ready?"

Bruno nodded his assent at the dice.

"I'm not really interesting you, am I?" Stolarsky swirled a mouthful of Macallan as if it were mouthwash, then grimaced, and worked his bared teeth with the tip of his tongue.

"Not enormously."

"Ah, most delicately put. What would float your boat, Mr. Enormously? What qualifies as enormous to a size queen like yourself? Just be warned, I plan to maneuver it up your rear passage."

"Five hundred a point might keep me from falling asleep."

"That's the spirit, and if falling asleep is an issue, there's more than one approach to that problem." Stolarsky threw a die to open the game.

"A pot of coffee?"

"Fuck coffee. I got something better, which I need to use up before the plane anyhow."

They sniffed the cocaine off a marble side table, after moving lamp and telephone to the carpet below. The lowered lamp, its shade ajar, threw goonish shadows, revealing the room's massing chaos—crumpled wrappers joined now by wrinkled foil and a spilled arc of white powder, Stolarsky's shed robe flung across the sofa's arm, spilled ice cubes melting on the countertop. Stolarsky, despite the Raffles's mellow AC, seemed to face some kind of internal thermostatic crisis; crouching and grumbling over the dice and checkers, he mopped sweat from temples and brow with his sleeves. It might not have helped that he'd sprung himself at a third Omakase burger, wolfing deep into the thick center, leaving a peripheral crust behind as if it had been a slice of pizza. At five hundred a point the battle was properly joined. Stolarsky won twice before Bruno cracked him again, the sweating man playing at the very edge of his capacity, a capacity expanding before Bruno's eyes. Bruno doubled Stolarsky out of the next few games, but not before Stolarsky miscalculated, doubling back foolishly, to a penalty of four thousand dollars.

"All right all right all right," Stolarsky incanted, shoving the checkers back to their starting points.

"There's no hurry."

"Oh, there's a hurry. You keeping count of all the dough I'm losing to you?"

"I won't lose track."

"Thattaboy, Flash. I'm sure you're just as diligent a counter when you're losing."

"I suppose I might be, I wouldn't know."

"Roll, fucker."

Bruno had gone back for another line. The cocaine stretched the parameters of the room, and also Bruno's skull. A chasm had revealed itself, between his eyes and the board, and between his brain and eyes. Bruno felt the desire to shovel more of the amazing clean powder into the new available spaces. Stolarsky had unveiled what seemed at first a stunning amount. Now Bruno wondered if it would be enough.

"Why . . . the . . . fuck . . . would . . . you . . . hit . . . me . . . there?"

Either Stolarsky's voice had slowed or Bruno's attentions were revving. Stolarsky's inquiry wasn't totally naïve: Bruno had hit a lone back checker on the one-point, with nothing but his five-point covered. Only double sixes would keep Stolarsky out—on any other number he'd either hit Bruno in return, or gain ground.

"I'm not your tutor, I'm you're opponent—"

"Uuuup . . . youuuurs . . ."

"—but, as I was about to say, has no one in your online support group mentioned 'tempo play'?"

"See, now that's a question I wanted to ask you: Why does all backgammon nomenclature sound like *The Kama Sutra*? 'A stripped and cramped position on your inner beaver,' all that shit."

"What you just said makes no sense whatsoever."

"Yeah, but you know what I'm saying, it's like sex code."

"The explanation is obvious. Intercourse was invented one day by a couple of bored backgammon players. They simply used the language that was available to them."

"You got a weird sense of humor, Flashman. Goddamn it, I'm going to lose this race, aren't I?"

Bruno shrugged. "Roll your dice and see." He did wonder a little, at the strange expansion his personality underwent in Stolarsky's presence. Bruno would credit it to the drugs, except he'd felt it the evening before, something new in the foreground of his attentions—a block or diversion, an obstinacy—that he needed to go around, to ignore. Yet so long as he kept winning games, Bruno remained himself. Little matter what idiotic banter Stolarsky drew from him. Bruno bore off the first of his checkers and Stolarsky threw up his hands in disgust.

"You should double me so I can resign."

"I choose not to."

"I resign anyway."

"Why not race?"

"Because I fucking lost."

The women came through the door. Tira Harpaz and Cynthia Jalter, that was the name she gave, the couples therapist from Kansas City who'd attended not the same high school as Tira, no, but whose school had played field hockey against hers and the women were pretty certain they remembered each other from one of the always surprisingly ruthless and bloody extramural battles, all these well-bred suburban girls elbowing and strangling one another into Ace bandages and flexible casts and weeks of physical therapy, and wasn't it funny, here they were, the four of them not *exactly* but *almost* two pairs of high-school friends, in a palatial hotel in Singapore, while Cynthia Jalter's husband, Richard, a probate lawyer and a cold fish—Cynthia Jalter could use some couples therapy herself!—snoozed downstairs. Tira and Cynthia enjoyed some cocaine—Bruno was of two minds, seeing so much of it disappear up these new noses—and all this information came tumbling out.

"So have you fleeced Keith for, like, six months of your usual salary? Do you own one of his stores already?" Tira seemed to make the men equally the target of her jocular scorn, but her mood was lightened in contrast to when Bruno had seen her last.

"I don't draw a salary."

"You just split the take with your parole officer, or whatever he was, huh?"

"Sure."

"So how bad is it going to get? Keith gonna have to sell the Jag?" The women snorted and giggled together, rolling on the couch in hilarity. Maybe Cynthia's presence brought out the garrulous Midwesterner in Tira, or Tira was drunk—well, she was—or drunk on the conviviality with a woman. Bruno didn't know Tira so well that he could say, never mind how he'd been consorting with her in his thoughts.

Stolarsky awaited Bruno's verdict without comment. Was Stolarsky cowed by the last loss? It couldn't be the money. He crouched over the glass table to lay out more lines of the drug and do some himself, before the women sucked it all up, but not before pushing the checkers back into position for another game.

"He's a decent player," Bruno said. "We're still just feeling each other out." He opted for a dignified tone, reeling himself in, somewhat, now that Tira and her newfound long-lost friend had filled the suite with hilarity. Weary dignity might be the first impression Bruno needed to make, anywhere.

"Oh, fucking fantastic, you're *feeling each other out*! You find anything . . . hard?" Now the women screeched. "'Cause we've been out feeling around for that ourselves, but *no cigar* is sometimes just *no cigar*—"

Tira launched herself from the couch in an attempt to perch in Stolarsky's lap, in doing so jarring the board, as she pushed herself between it and Stolarsky. Checkers were sent clattering—fortunately not a position in progress, only a game set to play. Stolarsky widened his knees and let her tumble to the carpet.

"Hey!"

"Chill out."

"Oh, I get it, you wanted me *down here*." She knelt between Stolarsky's knees and tugged at the waistband of his lounge shorts. He clapped his hand over hers.

"Quit, Tira."

"I'm just *feeling you out*."

"You guys can watch, if you want—"

"Watch *what*?"

Cynthia Jalter draped her arms over Bruno's shoulders, from behind. "She told me you looked like James Bond, but I didn't believe it," she stage-whispered.

"Now, see, that's just *outstandingly* stupid," said Stolarsky. He brushed Tira's hands from him and began restoring the checkers to their right points. "Because James Bond has been played by, like, twelve different actors by this point, so he doesn't look like anything at all, except, like, the *default masculine blur*. Which I guess is pretty much what you're getting with Alexander here, so you may have a point, but then again it's on top of your head."

Nothing made enough sense to matter. Bruno was made aware, though, of his prudishness in fearing that Tira might succeed in pulling off Stolarsky's shorts—he dreaded beholding the man's underwear, if he wore underwear—and his surprise at Stolarsky's insulting a woman he'd met moments before. Very much on the other hand, and though he'd found her peroxided hair and jowly, excessively rouged face decidedly unattractive when faced with her, Cynthia Jalter's arms, and her heavy chest, didn't feel in any way terrible against Bruno's shoulders. He marveled at his twenty-four-hour descent, from that first disquieting glance of Stolarsky in the Smoker's Club to this homely immersion into Americana-style cocktail-hour debauchery. Bruno had never visited Missouri, but he felt he might be there now.

They were seven or ten moves into a game to which he'd barely attended when he found himself with three of Stolarsky's men on the bar and his tongue down Cynthia Jalter's throat. At that proximity he could see nothing at all wrong with her face, though she seemed a risk for suctioning his tongue from its root.

"You're patronizing me," said Stolarsky. "Take my fucking money when it's there on the table."

"I'm a little distracted—"

"Here, I'll put the doubling cube down her fucking shirt where you can find it."

"Mmmmghh-um—" Cynthia Jalter unpeeled her face from his long enough to say, "Take his money, baby, it's what we're all here to see. I'm not going aaanywhere." To prove this, she bent and began addressing his neck with a blunt force that suggested she might be a trumpet or French horn aficionado.

"Yeah, Alexander," added Tira, "for fuck's sake, put him out of his misery."

Bruno felt reasonably certain Cynthia Jalter wasn't Edgar Falk's mole, but he wasn't taking anything for granted. "Okay, I double you."

"And I accept. Roll the dice."

"Why why why would you do that?" said Tira.

"It's called *recirculation,* sweetheart, it's called a *back game,* so keep your kibitzing to yourself."

"It wouldn't be kibitzing if I did."

"Back game?" gasped Cynthia Jalter, coming up for air. "I haven't gotten into one of those in a long time. Maybe tonight'll be the night."

"You play backgammon?" said Bruno.

The others all found this hilarious.

IV

In the taxicab en route to Billy Yik Tho Lim's residence in Sentosa Cove, a passing car flooded their backseat with light and Edgar Falk leaned in and scrutinized Bruno's neck.

"Driver, would you give us the light?" said Falk.

"What?" said Bruno, rubbing at the spot. "A mosquito bite?" Then it occurred to him he knew what had drawn Falk's attention.

"A blemish. Keep still." Falk reached into his interior jacket pocket and produced a small vial, which he opened to reveal a chamois pad drenched in greasy, flesh-colored powder.

"You're putting makeup on my *neck*?"

"That I am doing, yes."

"I can't believe you even carry that around with you."

"You'll find yourself wanting to be prepared sooner or later, Alexander. It's a situation that comes with age." If Falk recognized that the bluish mark on Bruno's throat was a hickey—he did, of course—he said nothing. Instead he gazed out the window. "I am getting older, you know."

"Yes."

"I could retire here," Falk mused. "I like it. Sentosa Cove in particular."

"Now?"

Falk didn't speak.

In the end, Bruno's and Cynthia Jalter's clothes had stayed on. She'd merely barnacled to his neck and gripped his cock through his pants while he lost the last six games in a row to Keith Stolarsky, either willfully or not, Bruno couldn't tell, but he let Stolarsky double him out of each of them and as a result gave back many thousands of the Singapore dollars he'd won, and with relief. Bruno didn't want to take

Stolarsky for too much, he couldn't say why. He'd lost the last six and then begged off. The cocaine was gone, leaving a hole in the center of his attention, of his sight. There, with Stolarsky, had come the official start of the losing streak, unrecognized by Bruno, along with his early gleanings of the blot.

Bruno had gotten out without looking Tira Harpaz in the eye, and that, in the end, was what had seemed to matter most.

At the Sentosa Cove beach house it wasn't until nearly one in the morning, when Bruno was already more than a hundred thousand in the hole, that Billy Yik Tho Lim said anything about the mark on Bruno's neck. Either Bruno had sweated off the makeup Falk had applied or he'd rubbed at the mark in some unconscious nervous action. Or, perhaps, Yik Tho Lim had spied it from the start but delayed mentioning what he saw. Yik Tho Lim wore a pistol he never removed, which made two in the room, or two visible, since his bodyguard wore one as well. The beach house was among mansions that crowded the beach and wasn't particularly well appointed or charming, though it was close enough to hear the surf crashing beneath the covered rooftop deck when the sliding doors were opened. Bruno imagined how human screams could be covered by the surf's roar and then decided he was being silly. Yik Tho Lim was retired, this was his pleasure house, however spartan, and the former director's current occupations were more along the lines of fixing football matches.

"Your luck is no good," Yik Tho Lim had said at first, making no direct reference to the hickey. The former director's English was governmentally genteel, but with a blunt overtone.

"Not at the moment," admitted Bruno.

"You shouldn't have played tonight," said Yik Tho Lim, grinning. "You been kissed by an octopus." It was then he pointed at Bruno's neck.

Two hours later, after too few good turns and very many worse ones, Edgar Falk's entire stake was gone.

A week after that, Bruno was on an airplane to Berlin.

Four

I

Now, departing Berlin by the portal through which he'd entered it, Bruno had only the contents of his hospital room to his name. Wallet, passport, battery-null phone, backgammon case with its secret bloodied stone. All else, abandoned to his Charlottenburg hotel in lieu of payment. The orderlies had washed and returned his tuxedo, which he wore, with its bleached shirt beneath, as he moved through Tegel's Terminal E for the short jump to Amsterdam.

From Amsterdam, there to continue on to San Francisco. Keith Stolarsky had booked the ticket, and paid as well, when Bruno had called him from the hospital. Stolarsky was to meet him at the airport and had promised to provide him a bed too, in Berkeley. Bruno's last-chance credit card, which had in the past been guaranteed by one of Edgar Falk's accounts, was dead. Bruno had asked the hospital accountant who'd established its uselessness to scissor the card into fragments and dispose of them. It was the last string to his old life, to Singapore—if Falk were even still in Singapore.

Though the hospital's crude, starchy laundering should if anything have shrunk the tuxedo, it hung too loosely on Bruno, and too heavily. Without radiation or chemotherapy he'd achieved the cancer patient's ghastly pallor, and seemingly the weight loss as well. Or was it that the hospital gowns had conditioned him to feel his clothing as feeble cover, on a form eligible to be stripped and washed at any instant? Shifting through the terminal's crowds in the tux, even as he absorbed the attentions of those who seemed to find him amusingly sinister or odd, or of women who persisted in finding him something more than sinister or odd—he'd shaved that morning, preparing for his discharge

80

from Charité, and discovered the bones of his glamour still lurking beneath the week's beard—he was unable to avoid the sensation that his pants were open at the ass.

At check-in he turned his head to meet the representative's gaze around the blot.

"Bags to check?"

"Just carry-on."

She'd seen it all. He felt ethereal, a vision who might float across the ocean with no need of an airplane. Even at security, he met only slight resistance. He placed his shoes and the inert phone into a plastic bin, along with the CD of medical scans, which he'd requested just as Claudia Benedict had suggested he do. Then he laid the backgammon case on the belt.

"Open duh computer."

Germans ought to farm out all positions of petty authority. The accent remained too full of implication.

"It's not a computer."

"Open, please."

Travelers stacked wearily behind Bruno as he displayed the wooden set and the square painted stone that was steadily degrading its interior.

He braced for further inquiry, but no. The security man merely gestured to show that Bruno could close the set and send it through. It's a computer for fates, Bruno wanted to say. The stone is a virus.

I am a tumor that might infect the plane.

He wasn't dangerous, and they knew it. He retied his shoelaces. There was nothing needed of Bruno but to wait, to be passive and orderly, and in this regard, the airport was at last no more than an elaboration of the hospital. Charité's nurses had trained him well. He could shuffle in the manner of a patient through corridors of the sky, unprotesting, in pursuit of mercy. He shouldn't mistake that it would be found here. He took a seat near the gate and folded his hands in the lap of his tux.

The novelty of his restored anonymity, moving through international airspace, could be enough to keep Bruno content to Amsterdam. Except he was hungry. With nothing in his pocket, he decided to wait for a meal over the Atlantic. Maybe after, he'd sleep. The others waiting to board his plane all stared at live screens, deepening Bruno's apartness. Yet he couldn't imagine he was any lonelier than they appeared, seeking into their void reflections. Then he noticed a chubby college girl tethered to a tree of outlets, gathering electricity.

"Excuse me, could I possibly?" Bruno raised up his phone, identical to hers. "I've died completely. My cable is in my checked luggage." Never mind that none existed. Should she be booked with him all the way through to San Francisco, he'd be discredited at the carousel. But what odds?

She stared.

"If I could connect for just a moment, and see my messages—"

"Suuuure." She measured him with the syllable. He smiled into the gray pudding of the blot and let his tuxedo beguile or baffle her from her distrust. *My lies are harmless,* he added, in the event she could peer into his thoughts.

"Uh, just a minute."

"Take your time."

The girl handed him the bare end of the cable just as boarding began. His phone wouldn't even glimmer, at first. Then it managed an icon of a sickened battery, warning not to disconnect. "I should go," the girl said.

"Just another moment—" He'd begun to beg.

She glared while he drew another minute of charge into the device, then stuffed the cable into her knapsack. Bruno let her proceed before him, to the dwindling line for departure. He'd no need to compete for an overhead bin, might just as well be the last on the plane.

He nearly was. The girl with the charger wasn't to be seen. Bruno smiled tepidly as he moved down the aisle, past those now free to examine him brazenly, bolstered by the slight but unmistakable moral advantage of having seated themselves first. The plane smelled of charred meat, which made no sense—what could they serve during the brief hop to Amsterdam? Bruno settled into a window seat, tucking his backgammon case at his feet, then examined the phone. Nothing from Falk, but three missed from the same unknown caller. The enfeebled battery allowed him to hear the sole voice mail.

"Alexander, I leave you a message this time." A woman's voice, German-accented, and with some urgency. A nurse? Or the front desk of his hotel, in hot pursuit? Had he been so foolish as to give out the number? "I was trying to reach you at the hospital, but I'm not knowing your family name." Then as if answering his unspoken question: "It is Madchen. I hope you don't mind I call."

The bicyclist on the ferry, a thousand years ago.

"I was present when you became ill, but I could say nothing," she continued. The meaning here was unclear, perhaps a failing of her English. Yet the reference to illness confused him. Unless she'd visited the hospital, present when or how?

At an instant's contemplation, the puzzle collapsed. Madchen had ferried to Kladow for nothing to do with babysitting anyone's niece. She'd crossed the Wannsee for a gig, as Wolf-Dirk Köhler's bottomless masked server. At that, the flight attendant leaned in, rendering Madchen's last words inaudible, to request that Bruno switch off and stow the phone.

As they bent toward Schiphol, the suburbs of Amsterdam hovering into view, Bruno played his customary landing game, a secret matter between him and himself: to spot a human form before the plane berthed at its Jetway. Evidence of human life, to prove the world in which the plane arrived hadn't been vacated during the flight's duration. Difficult in the best of circumstances, never mind the blot. To see a distant truck in motion, on a lane between two furrowed fields, this wasn't rare but didn't count—what evidence the truck wasn't an automated thing?

Human beings, it turned out, were scarce and largely remained indoors: Flip the rock of the world, and the ants declined to appear. More landings than not, Bruno lost his game. Today, at the last possible second, just beyond the fence marking the edge of the landing field, at the loading dock of some vast warehouse that suckled a hundred trucks, a shadow stepped into the light. A man, perhaps lighting a cigarette? Bruno leaned to the window, turned his head, navigating his blot.

The man looked up as the plane's shadow crossed the lot before him. He was tall and wore a tuxedo. Was it possible?

Yes, Bruno admitted to his double on the warehouse dock. *I am here only to change planes. I am exiting the wider world, to return to my homeland of bullying, psychosis, and bad taste.*

Forgive me. It is a medical matter.

Once on the tarmac, when permission was granted and a hundred cell phones were hustled from stowage and powered up, Bruno tried to listen again to the German prostitute's message, but by that time his battery was drained.

II

Bruno crossed the ocean in a middle seat. He'd fallen asleep with his shoes on and clutching the backgammon case to his chest under crossed arms, never waking long enough to solve the conundrum of how best, in the crowded row, to shift it to a position beneath the seat in front of him. A savage weariness had overtaken him, some bill come due. He missed the meal. Whatever meat they'd been roasting for hours—they appeared to have carried it through the Dutch airport as well, and shifted it from the European flight to the transatlantic one—he tasted only in his dreams.

When the flight attendant shook him awake the plane had emptied. He might have been twitching continuously over the ocean. More drool soaked his chin and collar than remained in his mouth; his lips and eyelids seemed pasted together. The airplane might have passed through several nights' worth of dark, but now the lifted shades bled scalpel-sharp California daylight. The flight attendant tucked an arrival card between his sleeve and the case, though basic behaviors might already have discredited him for arrival in this or any other city.

Last in the line for mild interrogation by border agents, Bruno filled out the landing card with a borrowed pen, meanwhile licked his cracked lips, tried to swallow off the knot in his throat. The array of posted warnings and admonitions surpassed any European port of call, or Singapore's, or Abu Dhabi's. He tried to recall whether the United States had worn its police-state ambitions so brazenly at his last return, but it was too long ago. No one, in any event, paid him notice. The tuxedo might represent a guarantee of irrelevancy—who'd travel on a mission of deceit in such an eccentric costume? Or perhaps his blot had swollen into a field, an aura, within which he traveled unseen.

"Tira and I thumb-wrestled to see who'd get to pick you up, and I won." Keith Stolarsky waited outside customs, where Bruno emerged swinging his backgammon case amid the travelers wheeling trains of luggage. "I figured she'd probably discreetly pack a bag and whisk you down the coast to Big Sur, check in at Esalen, and rape you in a hot tub, and I'd never hear from either of you again." Stolarsky, in black cargo pants and a zipped windbreaker, his hair greasy, looked as exposed in the airport as in the Singapore casino: a figure exhumed from night into day. He reached up to pluck at Bruno's collar, as if discovering a thread of lint there. "Look at you, dressed to sweep her off like Cary goddamn Grant, which leaves me grasping the Ralph Bellamy end of the stick. You're confirming all my worst suspicions."

Was Stolarsky trying to kid him out of his condition? Irradiate his tumor with crass hysterics? Bruno's appointment to meet the famous and iconoclastic surgeon was two days from now. Until then, at least, Stolarsky was Bruno's sole patron.

"Where's your bags? You got nada?"

"Everything was left at the hotel." Bruno's voice emerged as a croak.

"You should've told me. I'd have paid it off, have the stuff sent."

"You still could."

Stolarsky poked at the backgammon case. "Just your lucky box of kryptonite for the whole fucking universe, huh? What were you, working the plane? Gammon your way up to first class?"

"I slept." *Or died and was only quarter-resurrected.*

"Of course you did."

The sarcastic, grubby entrepreneur, who'd agreed to pretend to a long history of friendship with Bruno based on a trifling familiarity, and then paid for Bruno's ticket out of pity, had nonetheless no pity in him, or no language with which to let it out. So he'd picked up where he'd left off, treating Bruno as he had in Singapore. But now he said, "You must be starved. Let's get you a meal."

"Yes, please."

"We got a table waiting for us at Zuni."

Plainly Bruno was expected to recognize the name. The land of his homecoming was an island shrouded in its distinct code and idiom, as much as Zurich or Marrakech. This realm, like those, he'd navigate by ear. "Lovely," he said.

Stolarsky's car was a Jaguar, an older model, bronze paint worn to a matte finish. Its floors, Bruno discovered when he slid inside, were covered with candy wrappers and crushed soda cups. Stolarsky yammered into Bruno's insensate ears as they carved their way up the peninsula, through hills littered with pastel cigar-box homes and incoherent billboards for Backblaze and DuckDuckGo and Bitcoin. The sales pitches converged, in Bruno's bafflement and dismay, with Stolarsky's attempts at small talk. Bruno's brain might have parachuted somewhere over the Atlantic.

"What do you love?" said Stolarsky, breaking through his haze.

"Sorry?"

"What do you love, you stupid motherfucker? Because we're gonna get you some of that."

"At the restaurant?"

"In life."

"Let me think about it."

"You do that, Godot, you puzzle on that real good."

Zuni occupied a storefront formed of two corner stories of a triangular block of Market Street, the restaurant a glass prow of street views and exposed laminated beams, struck open by the blazing flat sunshine. There was nowhere to hide, no trace of discretion or shame in the arrangement of tables or their visibility to the street. And no one inside seemed leery of the beetle-like man in his homeless garb or his companion in the hospital-starched tuxedo. Indeed, Stolarsky drew immediate fawning attention, was obviously a regular here, if he wasn't in fact a part owner. Having communicated with the maître d' only in grunts, when the waitress arrived Stolarsky preempted the menu, ordering prosecco and oysters and roast chicken for two.

"The German ambassador hasn't eaten in two days," he told the waitress, who wore a white button shirt with sleeves rolled to unveil forearms entirely blued with floral tattoos.

"The roast chicken might take twenty-five—"

"Right, so be like the little fucking engine that could."

The fizz of the prosecco stung Bruno's nostrils and made his eyes water. He blinked against the tears and sun, his lids heavy. Could he possibly want to sleep again? His words came slow, as though the thing pressing against his eyes lay against the root of his tongue as well.

"You're known here."

"The opposite, actually. I come to San Francisco to go incognito. Dunno if Tira told you, I can't go around in Berzerkeley anymore for risk of being lynched by my enemies, from the fields of both real estate and proletarian revolution."

"Darth Vader, she called you."

"Heh."

They slurped oysters from icy shells and tore apart roast chicken while Bruno considered the life moving beneath the tilted city's glare, bike messengers with padlock necklaces, bald-shaved business-suited men on long skateboards, Amazonian transsexuals who might not be transsexuals. He imagined for an instant he'd spotted the man from the Amsterdam loading dock, the tuxedoed watcher of airplanes, but it was a trick of Zuni's plate glass, his own reflection. He nudged his backgammon case with his toe to be certain it was where he'd placed it. The Berlin paving stone was within it, hidden like the thing in his face.

"You know, Alexander, I like eating with you just fine, it's only that you're a little retarded on conversation."

"Sorry."

"Fuck it, you got depths, that's what I like about you."

"Thank you."

"Listen, I made a plan. There's a vacant apartment in this building I own on Haste. I got a key for you."

Bruno was surprised. They'd specified nothing, when he'd reached Stolarsky on the telephone from the hospital, but Bruno had imagined himself a houseguest. He couldn't decide whether to be disappointed or relieved. "That's generous."

"Forget it. We'll snag you some clothes, a toothbrush and shampoo and some stuff like that, then you can go to sleep for a million years."

"That's actually what I'm hoping to avoid."

"I didn't mean anything you couldn't wake up from."

"I'm sure you didn't."

In Stolarsky's Jag they crossed the Bay Bridge, its futuristic new length from Treasure Island like a bridge soaring between planets. Yet the new span was still shadowed by its decaying industrial twin, which Bruno supposed would have to be bombed by drones to collapse it into the water. On Shattuck Avenue, a block or two from their old high school, they parked in front of a CVS. Nothing was familiar. After Europe, Berkeley appeared flattened by sunlight, made of stacked concrete slabs and received cultural notions, a font squeezed out of a computer printer five minutes earlier. Stolarsky gave him three twenties and waited in the car while Bruno went inside to walk the aisles and round up the designated items, toothpaste and brush, soap for his body and hair, and a bottle of Tylenol—the nearest thing, he hoped, to his late lamented paracetamol. He swallowed a handful of pills without water before leaving the store.

Returned to the car, he shoved the plastic bags down at his feet, a shame creeping over him at his pitiable new dependency. Stolarsky possibly sensed this and grew sparing in his remarks. Something had damped in the retailer, anyway, as they crossed the bridge, into what was ostensibly Stolarsky's domain. He edged around the campus and up Channing Way, onto Telegraph, then slid the Jaguar into an illegal spot at the curb in front of Zodiac Media. Stolarsky's emporium was three stories high, a shadowed edifice of neon and glass. It was as if Zuni had been intended to sound the architectural note, a glass box's false modesty, here carried to ponderous extremes. Instead of transparency, though, Zodiac's facade mirrored glints of the street, their car, the smaller, more traditional storefronts—a tattoo parlor, leather goods, a head shop—in the brash flat sunlight behind them.

If Zodiac was a kaleidoscope, Zombie Burger, farther down the block, was a rusted meteorite crashed to earth. Or a giant turd, with signage. The restaurant was made of hammered, irregular steel corroded to earthy brown. Its surface was impaled everywhere, like a whale laden with harpoons, by flagpoles, many flying only the letter

Z in bloody red on black. The building sucked light toward itself. It seemed calculated to animate hatred.

"Your fiefdom," said Bruno.

"Yeah. Half the street. Real estate falls on me like rain falls on other guys." Stolarsky sounded unimpressed with himself. "I got the building I'm putting you in as a throw-in when I did a back-taxes deal on a condemned warehouse. Nobody knows what anything is worth."

"Except you."

"Not even me. Here's the keys." Stolarsky plopped a simple key ring with a pair of new-cut keys into Bruno's palm. "The building's around the corner, 2400 Haste. It's called the Jack London Apartments, you know, like White frigging Fang, you'll see it painted in gold above the door. Number 25 is yours." He sounded tired, suddenly. "You can grab some clothes at Zodiac first. Here." He followed the keys by shoving a handful of twenties at Bruno.

"For the clothes?"

"Nah, you take what you want, complimentary. Ask for Beth Dennis at the front counter, the floor manager. She's expecting you—I called while you were in the drugstore. You got the run of the place. This is just walking-around money."

"Is the apartment—furnished?"

"There's a Murphy bed. Tira took care of sheets and some other crap." Stolarsky failed to conceal his impatience, his stare verging on hostile now. He'd hunkered into the Jaguar's bucket seat, a turtle with an overlarge shell. Bruno folded the money into the tux's interior breast pocket. He didn't bother asking whether the proprietor meant to enter his own store.

"Thanks for everything, then—"

"Don't go sincere on me, Flashman. You lose your irony, the terrorists win."

With that, Bruno stepped from the car to the curb, and Stolarsky was gone.

Bruno crossed to the entrance of Zodiac Media through a small, desolate mob of curb-sitting, punked-out runaways, impossibly young, impossibly filthy. Despite the begging appeals on their hand-lettered signs they seemed enclosed in a bubble immune to his concern, cooing to puppies leashed with strings, speaking among themselves in a family tongue that might no longer consist of English. When Bruno departed California he would have searched such faces for members of his Berkeley High cohort, the druggier, tie-dyed sort that had never attended class, had been an inch from dereliction even at thirteen, even while their parents still made their beds after rousing them off to the school grounds on Grove Street. Now Bruno could be the parent. He'd as soon lead one of the teenagers by a string leashed to its neck as try to engage in conversation.

Inside, a sleepy-eyed security guard gave Bruno something short of the once-over but required him to check his backgammon case. The guard placed it in a warren of cubicles empty apart from three or four backpacks, in exchange handing Bruno a playing card, the six of spades. At two in the afternoon the ground-level electronics showroom was occupied by just a scattering of clientele, if that was the right name for the slack-eyed undergraduates testing themselves on the newest flat and folding screens. Some might have been staff, in fact, playing games or checking Twitter on the blinking devices. Bruno wandered upstairs. The glass tower's second story was filled with racks of flannel and spandex and T-shirts, much of it blue and gold and emblazoned with the University of California logo. Bruno found a lone employee leaning on one elbow at the register. It was a tomb, despite the pulsing dance music. The Death Star slumbered.

Stolarksy's clerk was a small, nattily dressed woman with short dark Brylcreemed hair and heavy black glasses frames.

"Pardon me, are you Beth?"

"You're Keith's old friend, right?"

"Yes."

"Well, go crazy." Beth spread her hands wide. "*Mi* boss's *casa es su casa,* apparently."

"Excuse me?"

Now she looked him over, adjusted her glasses. "Take free clothes."

"Yes, I was told to do that."

"I can give you some shopping bags. I just have to scan it all first. We don't have, uh, the kind of stuff you're wearing."

"I wasn't expecting so. Is there more upstairs?"

"Nah. Upstairs is games, comics, figurines, that kind of stuff. The basement is Blu-Rays and audio. This is all the clothes."

"Thank you."

At the rack nearest the window, where he browsed the darkest, least athletic-looking black polyester lounge wear—the pants eschewed a stripe, but a cursive *Golden State Warriors* still ran up the leg—Bruno gained a view up Telegraph, toward Sather Gate, with a glimpse of the campanile and the scrubby yellow-earth hills. Farther, beyond sight, lay Northside, Euclid Avenue, the Gourmet Ghetto. Memories might be strewn in this landscape, early cigarettes and blow jobs, if he troubled to collect them. Yet all sealed, pleasantly enough for the moment, behind glass. More immediate, this side of the pane, the horrendous clothes and vapid music, the monotonous oppressions of the present life, the fact that not only was Bruno surely dying but he might have to do so in a flamingo pink or lime green T-shirt reading *Marilize Legijuana* or *All Aboard The Hot Mess Express!*

Was there authentic heartsickness for Bruno here? He doubted it. The nemesis growing inside his face eclipsed such vanity. So what if he didn't like it here? Nothing in Stolarsky's shop should be any more an affront to him than what he'd encounter flipping through a hotel television's thousand channels. Zodiac Media made no particular incursion on any special Berkeley of the soul, for Bruno had no such thing. Telegraph Avenue was the same as it had always been, muddled, obscene, in an endless fall from a distant glory Bruno hadn't known and wouldn't have enjoyed in the first place.

He found a T-shirt he actually liked, for its coal-gray shade, and for the enigma of its logo, silk-screened in white, red, and bronze. The shirt depicted a middle-aged man, bearded, with soulful brow and bemused mouth, above the single word *ABIDE*. The letters looked engraved, like those on U.S. currency. In the middle of racks of fluorescent pastels screaming inanities and insults, or Cal sports affiliation, the *ABIDE* T-shirt seemed to be espousing its own method of survival. Bruno preferred it so completely to anything else in Stolarsky's inventory that he gathered up the whole supply: four large, two medium. To that he added one zippered Cal sweatshirt with a hood, though he could hardly afford sacrifices in peripheral vision at the moment.

"You like this one, huh?" said Beth, as she scanned and bagged the six T-shirts, along with the sweatshirt and the lounge pants and crew socks and Jockey shorts he'd chosen for himself. The girl obviously found Bruno an amusing pendant on her loathsome employer. Stolarsky's decision not to accompany Bruno into the shop now seemed merciful.

"I do." Bruno hid the young lesbian behind the blot and pretended to smile along with her condescension, scouring up what dignity was available. *Beth, the day will come where you too shall be called upon to abide.* But she either failed his mind-reading test or couldn't be troubled in his case.

"One further thing," he asked her. "Is there any chance this shop has a charger for this phone?"

"Accessories, downstairs. It's a separate register. I'll page the front and tell 'em to comp you."

"Thank you."

The Jack London Apartments was a building he'd likely walked past a hundred times in his prehistoric Berkeley life but never taken note of, a prewar with brown inlaid panels and a wooden elevator in the lobby. He chose instead wide creaking stairs to the second floor, there to find the empty number 25, a one-room studio with cool hardwood floors and the promised Murphy bed levered into the wall. Bruno placed his backgammon case and the lurid Zodiac Media shopping bag just inside the door. He removed only the charger, which he cracked from its plastic shell, then laced between his phone and a wall socket. He couldn't face his new clothes, not yet.

The Murphy bed, too, he left stowed for the moment, as it promised to fill half the room's space. He went instead to the windows, which opened to the placid interior courtyard, the backyards beyond, no hint of Telegraph's atmosphere, though he was barely half a block away. Another mercy. Bruno might be drowning in them. Distantly he smelled jasmine or honeysuckle, and cooking meat. He withdrew his head, electing not to foul the yard. In the bathroom someone—Tira Harpaz, that was—had placed a neat stack of white sheets, a pillow, and two towels on the toilet lid, the studio's only elevated surface apart from the kitchen counter. Bruno shifted them to the floor and raised the lid and his stomach erupted, as it had threatened to ever since he'd woken on the airplane, loosing an oil-spill rainbow slurry of oysters, roast chicken, and prosecco.

III

He had no way of knowing the hour when he woke in terror, having dreamed that a person had entered the room. He might still be in the ward at Charité. But no. The airplane, San Francisco, the Jack London Apartments; all trickled back in, much as light leaked through the unshaded window to outline the barrenness of the radiator and floor, his legs under the sheet. He'd pulled open the Murphy bed and collapsed on it, late afternoon, he supposed, and night had come. The terror dream had been inchoate at first, without logical boundary, then drawn itself to a point of focus, a visceral panic: the presence of an intruder. He touched his face, his eyelids. The blot was a piece of night he couldn't rub away. At that instant he detected the intake of breath that precedes speech, a living body apart from his own. No dream, someone had entered the room. A woman's voice spoke his name, *Alexander.* She stood by the door. It was Tira Harpaz.

"I let myself in."

"Why?"

"I thought you were out. I brought you some groceries."

"What time is it?"

"Almost ten."

"Will you excuse me?"

"Should I leave?"

"No, stay. I'll shower." Wrapping the sheet around himself, he gathered the shopping bag into the bathroom and switched on the bare bulb inside, leaving her behind, in darkness. The water brought him out of the dream. When he opened the door, wearing his fresh strange clothes from Stolarsky's store, sweatshirt zipped over the *ABIDE* T-shirt

95

to warm him, he found her in the kitchen, leaning against the counter, where the courtyard's light was strongest.

"I packed it in the fridge," she said. "Just yogurt and bread and cold cuts and some other crapola. Orange juice. There's nowhere to shop around Telegraph."

He opened the refrigerator door. "Doughnut holes," he said, squinting into its light. Beads of water from his hair dotted his fresh white socks.

"Yeah," she said apologetically. "Real health food. I don't know what you like. I'm not much of a shopper."

"I appreciate it."

"I didn't mean to bother you . . ." She fell silent, in shyness, he supposed. The silence in the empty apartment was overwhelming; Bruno might have wished for a window on the street now. The only contents of the single room was a bed, so they clung to the kitchen. Bruno felt absurdly grateful for his illness, which substituted its clarity for the ambiguity pooling everywhere around him, for his pointless desire for Keith Stolarksy's middle-aged girlfriend, for his presence in Berkeley to begin with. Perhaps his tumor had arisen from a need to insist form upon the formlessness of his life. In the greater scheme, what Bruno did until the appointment with the miracle surgeon in San Francisco probably didn't matter at all.

"Is the apartment okay for you?" she asked.

"Of course." He was touched. She clung to some notion of splendor on his behalf, though he stood before her in mismatched CAL sportswear.

"It smells like puke."

"A little, yes." The shower's steam had conveyed out some essence from before. He'd have to check the floor around the toilet.

"I thought Keith hired someone to clean these places out."

"The smell may be coming from the street."

She frowned. "Do you want to take a walk around the block?" They understood each other: The apartment had to be fled, if for no other reason than to circumvent the starkness of the bed.

Bruno had nothing but his dress shoes, Italian leather, absurd with the clothes. He put them on. He'd spend some of Stolarksy's "walking-around money" on some cheap tennis shoes tomorrow, to complete his transformation.

For the quiet of the inner courtyard, and his time-zone disenfranchisement, Bruno might have believed, despite Tira's claim to the contrary, that it was three in the morning. Now they exited the Jack London Apartments and turned the corner to find Telegraph alive in a way it had given no evidence of even being capable earlier, when he'd arrived. The street vendors had doubled, squeezing the sidewalks. Pods of students and slumming tourists navigated between the open shop doors and the homeless and runaways who staked claim to any congenial doorway or stairwell. As for Zodiac Media, it pulsed like a nightclub, its three glass levels no longer reflective, instead like a triple-level wide-screen display now, the clothing level startlingly full of browsers, as if they'd replaced the merchandise with something actually desirable during the hours he'd lay in a coma in the empty apartment.

Zombie Burger had come to life, too. The matte brown edifice was still like a thumb in the eye, a blot for anyone who lacked their own. But now the object bled laser-like beams of red light from various apertures that hadn't been discernible in daylight, as if the meteorite bulged with molten lava. It also boasted a rattail-like queue of chattering, cell-texting students, wending from the door and choking off another portion of sidewalk. Those streaming out, who'd taken their meals to go, chomped on the outlandishly huge and drippy burgers with their backs hunched, arms bowed as if they blew on tremendous meat harmonicas, in the attempt to protect their clothes.

Bruno had stopped on the sidewalk, without noticing. Following his gaze, Tira drew on his arm and said, "Promise me you'll never go inside."

"Please excuse me, but it looks like someone moved their bowels, I mean in an architectural way."

"It's supposed to be a burger, Alexander. Like, rare, with juice oozing out."

"Ah, not a bloody stool, then. I'm a bit slow. It's sort of like a Hieronymus Bosch painting, isn't it?"

"You hit the nail on the head. *Hooters in Hell,* that's Keith's own words."

"I'm sorry, what's . . . Hooters?"

"Lord, you really are a big dumb delicate flower, aren't you?"

"Just explain."

"Keith doesn't hire anyone but girls with really big tits, *comprende?*"

"Be kind to me, I'm not from this planet. Is that legal?"

"It's not any kind of public policy, and you're right, it wouldn't be legal if it was, but anyone who goes in gets the point pretty quickly. The place is lit with only red bulbs except for these black lights and they all wear bright white T-shirts and so it's like this hellish cavern of glistening red burgers with this big white tit show floating around everywhere, okay?"

"And this bothers you?"

"Some days it does, yeah. Today, for instance. See, Keith once told me he picked them to look like me, fifteen years ago, when he first met me. Dark hair, a little small, except for, you know, in the chest. I looked like that once. Just tell me you won't go in." They were past the entrance now, yet she clung harder, her grip on his bicep a plea. What did Bruno mean to her? Was she so afraid he'd rate her against those teenage body doubles? He crooked his arm, linking with Tira's to convert their touch into something more formal, as much to relieve himself of her lopsided neediness as from any gallantry. "You have my word."

"Don't even look."

"The burgers must be good, though, judging from the line. I remember Keith in Singapore, sizing up the international competition."

"The opposite: They're total garbage. The students will eat anything, so long as it's huge and costs four dollars. It's like this slag of bun and processed cheese and unripe supermarket tomato. It looks big, but Keith has the cooks smash the patty flat on the grill so it's all spread out and burned as hell. Keith wouldn't eat there if you paid him."

"He only eats burgers abroad?" They walked arm in arm, more relaxed now as they crossed Channing Way, the Death Star behind them. The sidewalks were no more navigable, but Bruno and Tira proceeded like a bubble through a tube, sealed from what surrounded them.

"There's a place on Durant, almost to Bowditch Street, Kropotkin's Sliders, you know it? It's like the punk-rock alternative to Zombie. That's where Keith eats, the hypocrite. We can go if you want."

"Oh, no, I'm not hungry."

"Jet lag?"

"Several lags, I think. Jet might be the least of them."

"Are you . . . on medication?"

"Nothing important. Tylenol."

"I guess you have to be dying to get the really cool drugs."

"I promise when that happens, I'll share."

"When my father died I ended up with a whole bottle of Dilaudid. They'd refilled it just before he croaked. It was right when I met Keith, when I resembled the girls at Zombie. I was *like* a zombie, I think Keith had a nose for the land of the dead, for those of us with one foot in it, I mean. He took me in his convertible to Big Sur and we did a whole bunch of my father's pills and went to Esalen and fucked in the hot tub on the cliffs until they kicked us out. Even then we were laughing our asses off."

"Why are you telling me this?"

They'd turned up Channing, away from the avenue, into the eucalyptus cover. Now she turned to face him, without unhooking her arm from his. Hinged, they were drawn close.

"I was in grad school, right here, Alexander. This is my life you floated into, this stupid town. If you didn't want to meet me you shouldn't have come." Her reasoning was flawed; it wasn't even reasoning. They'd met in Singapore. He understood her well enough, though.

"I didn't choose to, not exactly." He kept his voice neutral, hoping it didn't sound unkind. He couldn't afford the story she seemed to wish to write for them, not just now.

"Why'd you call Keith, Alexander?"

"He didn't say?"

"Of course. You came to see a doctor."

"Yes."

"It just happens to be here."

"San Francisco. It's a very particular doctor."

"You could have stayed in San Francisco, then."

He would have rather done that, but manners prohibited saying so. They'd resumed walking, come out of the trees, to the corner of Bowditch, stopped again. If they turned the wrong way, People's Park lay in wait, that dusty no-man's-acre of rhetoric and human feces, of Bruno's bad last glimpses of June and her boyfriend, when he'd tried to make them understand that he was leaving. "Keith's paying," he said, by way of explanation. "For everything."

"He told me that and I didn't believe him."

"It's true."

"Look at you. Where do you come from? Are you even *real*?"

"Just barely." A figment, he thought. That was what he'd wish to be, a figment of her desire, one incapable of disappointing or being destroyed. He felt destined to both.

"Are you dying?"

"I'm in need of radical intervention."

"Are they going to cut you up?"

"The problem is inside, where it's difficult to reach."

She reached a finger up, to touch the tip of his nose, then lay it across his upper lip, as if silencing him. Doing so, she vanished her hand entirely into the blot. Bruno felt a sudden violent wish to confront her with the contents of the compact disc, hidden in the pocket of the tuxedo, which lay in a corner near the Murphy bed. In his rage he wanted Tira to be met with the self behind his nose, his upper lip. His true self now. Certainly it was the self that had driven him here to within a block of People's Park, the "People's Pissoir" as they'd called it at Chez Panisse, the squalid quadrant he'd achieved nothing in his life except to avoid. This comically garbed body which now squired Tira Harpaz through the cool night, through the fog of eucalyptus, urine, and clove cigarettes, none enough to disguise the hamburger exhaust from Stolarsky's dire meat factory, his black-light prison house of tits—Bruno's outer form was nothing but an envelope for delivery of the blot to its destination, its rendezvous with the remarkable doctor.

Stolarsky's money was the fluid medium in this intercontinental transaction, the fuel jetting the blot across the sea. Unless it was made clear that it was what Stolarsky had summoned him for, Bruno wouldn't dream of touching Tira Harpaz. Her own game wasn't clear, anyhow. It might not be clear to her. This was the most generous thing he could manage to believe.

"I have to sleep," he said.

"I'll walk you back."

"I know the way." He disguised his anger, or hoped he had. "Would you give me your copy of the key, please?" A guarantee of privacy wasn't too much to ask, even for a beggar. The Jack London Apartments weren't People's Park.

"What?"

"The key." She hadn't misunderstood, so it didn't really require explanation.

"Of course." Plainly she felt entitled to appear, to fill his refrigerator with doughnut holes at her whim. Her will was a function of Stolarsky's, however she might present herself as her lord's disgruntled peon. They were a power couple, into it.

If disease and abjection freed Bruno from anything, it began here. Seeming to understand, she worked the key off the ring and placed it in his hand.

"Good night," he said.

"Do you know how to reach me?" she asked, quietly.

"I have a phone." His pride was as cheap as the clothes he wore. He had no idea whether Edgar Falk would continue paying for the phone service. A small string connecting him to the larger world, enmeshing him in old obligations. Yet he hadn't glanced to see if Madchen had called. Perhaps even that should be left behind, with Europe. What freedom was desirable, in Bruno's situation? It wasn't clear. Only that tonight he should free himself of Tira Harpaz before he accepted her pity.

He pocketed the key. They stood in silence for a moment, until he said, "Should I walk you to your car?" Still a prisoner of chivalry.

But now it was her turn to grow brusque. "It's a block away."

"Of course."

At that, he retreated to the Jack London and fell almost instantly into thick and dreamless sleep.

•

He woke in darkness, the room lit only by the moon above the courtyard and the tepid glow of the cell phone, which delivered the unwholesome fact of the hour. From three to five he lay still on the Murphy bed, moving the blot along the wide blank ceiling experimentally. By six he had light, and resorted to orange juice and doughnut holes. At seven, he went downstairs and out, past a worker hosing the sidewalks in front of Amoeba Music, to find the Caffe Mediterraneum just opening its doors. From a heavy pint glass scored with what looked like decades of tiny scratches he gulped a latte, gratefully.

He helped himself to a paperback from a carton someone had placed at the door of a closed bookstore. A donation, so fair game. The book was a thriller. He walked to campus and read absently on a grassy hill, stopping frequently to watch the students, then lost interest and left the paperback on a low concrete wall. He crossed to the mouth of Northside, where Euclid curved into the hills, then returned, skirting the Gourmet Ghetto, choosing not to haunt there. In present form he made a better fit for Telegraph. At the edge of campus, to complete the picture, he bought fifteen-dollar sneakers and wore them out of the store, placing his shoes in a bag.

Telegraph was again innocuous, fangless, as when Stolarsky first deposited him at the curb in front of Zodiac. Birds whistled in the trees, the puppies on string leashes licked their owners' dirty fingernails for traces of hummus, or dozed. The gigantic stores were reduced in the daylight, Zombie no worse than an architectural goof without its lasers and queue. Still, he honored Tira's plea, despite his craving for the meat and smoke whose scent he'd been inhaling for what seemed an eternity now. At the very moment he acknowledged his hunger, Bruno found himself at the corner of Bowditch Street. A sign read KROPOTKIN'S SLIDERS.

The shop was a walk-in closet. Its surfaces—countertop, stools, the small shelf full of transparent pump bottles of ketchup, mustard, and yellow-green relish—were everywhere coated with greasy spatter and drips, though the flattop grill itself was set against the rear wall, which was backed with a mirror, also ages deep in the droplets of slime that danced from the broiling miniature burgers. The picture window that ought to have allowed light and a view of the street was instead layered on its interior with Scotch-taped flyers and broadsides, most hand-scrawled or typed on a misaligned manual, and badly photocopied, as if the originals had been unavailable. Bruno didn't trouble to read a word; the pages reeked of obsession and arcana.

The man tending the burgers presented his back and a completely bald head, shaved and shined, though surely nature had given him a head start. He wore a threadbare gray T-shirt, from which his elbows dangled skeletally. A white ribbon at both his neck and lower down, strung in a loose bow over his black jeans, indicated an apron. He didn't turn, but called out, "Cheese, or extra onions, and how many?" Presumably the counterman charted his clientele's arrival in the filthy mirror.

"What do you recommend?"

"I don't presume."

"What's most typical?"

"I'll make you two with extra onions. In a bag?"

"Mind if I eat them here?" At eleven thirty, the place was empty.

"Nobody's stopping you."

All this without turning. The counterman flapped his large spatula, shifting the disks of meat, which rode along the flat steaming surface on a carpet of onions, from the grill's cooler zone to the hot, to speed their finish. Then he delved with the spatula into the onions, mincing them rapidly with the utensil's bladed edge. The buns, too, were lifted from a steaming tray and separated with the spatula's edge, and given an instant to warm atop the finishing burgers. Bruno had nothing to do but be hypnotized by the actions, what he could make of them in the fogged mirror.

The man didn't turn until he presented the finished results, side by side on a paper plate. When Bruno looked up he discovered a face younger than he'd imagined, though burdened with thick-lensed browline eyeglasses, like a farmer's, making him appear ready for a retirement home. The man's nervous, undersize features clustered in the middle of his face. His gaze was an object closer than it appeared.

"Five bucks."

Bruno offered up the last of Stolarsky's twenties.

"Nothing smaller?"

"Sorry."

While the counterman made change, Bruno dug in the pockets of his new pants for coins to drop into a tip jar labeled, in black marker on translucent plastic, It Is Forbidden to Forbid. The counterman had already lifted his murderous-looking spatula and resumed sorting his burgers' placement, then turned the tool sideways to scrape char into the grill's gutter. Bruno moved with his paper plate to the condiment shelf and blurted pools of red and yellow onto his plate.

"Mad props to a dipper."

"Sorry?"

"I've got maximum respect for those who leave the goop to one side for a more controlled dispersal, one bite at a time. Nothing's irreversible, plus the bun doesn't sog out. The only higher state is eschewing the goop altogether."

"Eschewing the goop?" This, Bruno actually understood. He repeated it just to hear it repeated.

"You heard me."

"You feel the onions are enough?"

"Onions, plus copious salt and pepper, for those in the know." The counterman reached down and clapped twin shakers, glass with tin screw tops, like chess bishops, onto the counter.

"I thought you didn't presume."

"I take measure of who I'm dealing with."

"I'm honored." Bruno lifted back both of the miniature buns and salt-and-peppered his onion slush.

"You're staying at the Jack London, aren't you?"

The counterman, having surprised Bruno mid-bite, stood and

waited, his ferret-like attention concentrated by the thick lenses into something in the middle distance.

Bruno swallowed and spoke. "At the moment, yes. How did you know?"

"I live there. I saw you going out."

"Keith is loaning me one of the empty apartments."

"First-name basis, huh?"

"He's an old friend."

"A landlord and sharecropper."

"We were, uh, friends in high school."

"I'll have to treat you as a spy or a mole until demonstrated otherwise."

"Okay," said Bruno, exhausted suddenly. "You don't mind if I eat here?"

"Maximum freedom obtains within these four walls, my friend. Mutual aid, even for suspected spies and moles."

Bruno wolfed his burgers, dipping or not dipping in the yellow and red pools in a state of maximum insecurity. The counterman was a type, with his '50s glasses and bald head and bony elbows, with his absurdly demanding speech routines, but Bruno couldn't be troubled to put the elements together and give the type its name. The sliders were delicious notwithstanding, whether red-or-yellow-gooped, or gooped not at all. Bruno's physical appetites had landed belatedly, after a layover somewhere over the Atlantic. His hunger to live? Perhaps even that. If Tira Harpaz were in his room now, he'd have her immediately on the Murphy bed, not flee outside.

The counterman extended his dangerous spatula across the counter, balancing a third slider. He flipped it artfully onto Bruno's grease-soaked plate.

"I can't afford another."

"This one's on me, comrade. For an old friend of an enemy of the people."

IV

He'd arrived early for his appointment at the surgeon's office, in a drab cereal box of a building at the UCSF medical campus. Parnassus Avenue was a windy bridge of a street, vaulted by San Francisco's perverse topography into the fog and wind, and at least ten degrees chillier than Market Street, where he'd changed to the streetcar. The hospital buildings had the span to themselves, apart from a café or two and a florist. Coffee for the visitors, and petals to litter the patient's floor after the visitors had gone.

Shuddering in his insufficient layers, Bruno hurried inside.

The second-floor clinical wing seemed abandoned. Then, around a dusty corridor's elbow, he located a nurse receptionist who'd been given his name. Yes, Mr. Bruno was expected in less than an hour by Dr. Behringer and could stay until then in this room here—she indicated a glassed-in nook full of nothing but identical chairs, magazine-strewn side tables, and a water cooler. Her attitude, however, suggested it was a poor idea, one she couldn't recommend.

He sat. There were no people in this place, only *People*. Bruno tried to savor his boredom, an oasis in his journey into medical doom by way of BART and the streetcar from Market. San Francisco was a futuristic cartoon of the dozy, cozy city he recalled. The new place was alien, slick as Abu Dhabi in its top layer, with Bluetooth and Google Glass cyborgs strolling beneath glass towers. The underside was as gritty as Mumbai, with no one on the N-Judah streetcar except untouchables, Walker Evans photographs retouched with murky color. Bruno had likely descended to the status of untouchable himself.

He crept around the corner to see if the nurse had abandoned her post. She halted in her inaudible texting to catch him staring.

"Yes?"

"Nothing, just waiting."

"You were early. Now the doctor's late." Her disapproval covered patient and surgeon both. Yet at that moment the man appeared. Noah Behringer, shorter than Bruno and heavier, came bustling from the elevator with a knapsack and wearing jeans and sandals. His white hair was bundled in a braid, and his beard was dark, with barely a white thread, as though provinces of his head were different ages entirely. Behringer was not a handsome man. His eyes were deep-set, warm, and asymmetrical. Nothing but a white linen coat said he was entitled to entry of a medical building on any basis whatsoever, and the coat could have been acquired at a yard sale or Halloween shop.

"Alexander Bruno." The surgeon dropped his knapsack at his feet to clutch Bruno by both shoulders. His fingers were long, his grip persuasive. "You look nothing like your pictures. I've been living inside your face for the past few days. It's a strange way to get to know someone."

"I don't understand." Bruno had the CD full of imaging in the pocket of his lounge pants. He'd left his backgammon set and the bloodied paving stone behind, crossing the Bay with nothing but his mobile phone and the Charité scans.

"After we spoke, my assistant, Kate, located your German doctor, the oncologist, and we got hold of all your pictures. She's a genius, Kate, she can find anything." These words, once spoken, appeared to remind Behringer of something. He turned, releasing Bruno, to clasp the hand of the surprised receptionist-nurse in both of his. "Thanks for coming in and opening it up for me," he told her, then added, for Bruno's benefit, "I lost my key."

"That's perfectly fine, Doctor," said the nurse. Her tone contradicted the words, yet she regarded him with a certain helpless wonder. Bruno took solace in this. If his doctor was crazy but marvelous, perhaps this was what his marvelously crazy condition required.

"Come in, come in, I barely ever use this place, I'm sure it's a disaster area. I keep an office at home. Sit down." Bruno sat. The office was a mess, yes: thick dusty books slanted in postures of permanent damage to their spines, loose papers and file folders heaped on the desk. But Behringer's office wasn't thrillingly antic like Behringer, only desultory, in keeping with hospitals everywhere. The anomalous item, so far as Bruno could index anomaly here, was a framed Jimi Hendrix poster, with an autograph Bruno suspected might be real.

"I even spoke with the British lady, Benedict," said Behringer. "She's a good egg—get it? 'Eggs' Benedict, that would be a great nickname. And these pictures of yours are intense. The German machines are terrific. Of course ours are better."

"So you've . . . already seen?" Bruno felt shame at the uncontrolled circulation of the blot's mug shot, that Rorschach horseshoe crab squatting behind his eyes.

"Yes. I'll order up a whole new set, of course. Kate will contact you with appointments. You'll be swimming in appointments, she'll run your life like she runs mine."

"Is that Kate out there?"

"What, that unfriendly woman? I don't even know her name, she's just a nurse with a key to this door. Kate works exclusively on my caseload—she's *my* unfriendly woman."

"I see."

"You'll meet her soon enough. But meanwhile, listen, I've been on a fantastic voyage behind your nose and orbitals—your eyeballs. It's good to meet the outer surface. It's a fine-looking one, I'll take the utmost care of it. Did Eggs get a chance to explain my procedure?"

"Maybe you'd better."

"Think of your face as a door," said Behringer. "One that's never been opened." If doctors ordinarily snowed you with jargon, Behringer seemed to prefer to work by rebus, or mime. "We're going to open it, most gently. And then we'll take it off its hinges and lay it aside, whole and undamaged. Much better than drilling and sawing at the door itself, don't you think?" The surgeon talked with his hands, representing door, hinges, drill, and saw in the air with his curled, expressive fingers, the same that would attempt this carpentry on Bruno's head.

"My eyes?" asked Bruno. "Do you . . . take off my eyes?"

"Not unless you'd like to go blind. No, preservation of the optic nerves is an utmost priority. Of course we'll juggle them loose in their sockets to a degree, and flense some of their muscles temporarily, to retract them for entry—"

"Very well, thank you." It might be as well that Behringer didn't get any more evocative. "When do we take the cancer out?"

"There's no hurry. And, incidentally, you don't have cancer, not technically, or at least it's highly unlikely you do. We'll be more certain with tissue analysis, but my hunch is you're carrying an atypical meningioma."

If I'd known I was carrying it, I'd have gladly dropped it. This, Bruno floated toward Noah Behringer's thoughts to see if it might be taken up and answered, the usual test. Apparently not. "In what sense atypical?" asked Bruno instead.

"For meningioma, we'd need to see radical cell disruption, with metastases." Now, the delayed jargon. "We can't make any assumptions with a neoplasm of such radical extent, but it seems fairly well differentiated . . ." Bruno began to drift into passivity and inattention, as when, long ago, the women at the compound in Marin had insisted on giving him a reading with tarot cards or analyzing his astrological chart. The terminology seemed to detach him from himself.

"Differentiated," he managed. "Is that a good thing?"

"That's a very good thing. Atypical describes a region between cancer and not-cancer—you probably didn't even know there was such a region, did you?"

"No."

"Like a lot of things, cancer's actually a spectrum."

"Wow."

"You could even say we're all living there, in that place between cancer and not-cancer."

"Wow."

"You're just living there a little more urgently, that's all. But you've got plenty of company."

"But there's no hurry to get it out?"

"We'll operate soonish, sure. But this isn't going anywhere. The German pictures are great, but I want a better look. Think of it like this, Alexander, can I call you Alexander? Or Alex?"

"Anything." Though the surgeon wasn't so much older than Bruno, with his sandals and ponytail and Hendrix poster, he struck Bruno as essentially June's peer. In such, he evoked everything Bruno had fled California to avoid. Yet today Bruno saw him through his mother's eyes, as consolingly simpatico. Sandals, knapsack, beard, all inspired Bruno's fledgling love.

"Think of it like this. What's inside you, behind your face, it's been traveling for many years to this rendezvous with me. And all this time I was getting ready to be the one to meet it, inventing and perfecting my technique. I don't mean to sound like Dr. Frankenstein or something. But this is fateful!"

"Your technique of opening the door and . . . laying the face aside."

"That's right."

"Well, of course take the time you need, Doctor."

"Call me Noah."

"I'm only . . . at the moment I'm reliant on the generosity of a friend. Did Dr. Benedict explain—"

Behringer flapped his hand. "I'll waive my fee, which is all I'm in control of. I'm happy to do it. The hospital costs are something else, they can't be helped, and frankly, with a resection like we'll be doing, they're incredible. We'll have a team in there in shifts, we're looking at a twelve-, fourteen-hour procedure—"

"Fourteen hours? I'm sorry?"

"Yeah, at the least—"

"A team—doing what?"

"More or less taking your face off, like I said. So I can scoop it out with my copper spoons—you let me know when this is getting to be too much. Then we put you back together, which takes even longer. That's on top of surgical nurses, anesthesiologists, which I suspect you'll need three of, the whole deal. My residents do a lot of the cutting and arterial cauterization and so on, and they all go in and out and sleep and eat in shifts, but don't worry, I'll be running the whole show, I never budge."

"When do you eat and sleep?"

"Afterward. That's just me: I don't feel hunger or exhaustion until I'm done."

It was the first time Bruno suspected that Behringer wished to impress his patient. The boast inspired a first flare—perhaps it would be the only one—of professional kinship. Bruno had more than a few times gambled through a night and the whole day after without noticing his appetite, or desire for sleep, until he stepped out of the arena. He sometimes barely used the bathroom.

However, he'd heard just enough of arterial cauterization, even if he chose not to admit it. "So this little army of your helpers, mopping your brow and so forth, they all need to get paid."

"Through the hospital, but yeah. You're an expensive problem, man. I'd estimate it at, like, three or four thousand dollars an hour in there. And there's your recovery, immediate post-op you'll be in intensive care, that's costly stuff too. But your friend Keith was already in touch. He's covering it all, flat out. That's a pretty terrific friend you've got there, Alexander."

"Thank you. And please accept my apology for not paying your personal fee." *Thanks and sorry, thanks and sorry*—Bruno's new stance as a penitent stretched to the indefinite horizon.

"Listen, forget about it. Thank Christ you found me. Thank Eggs Benedict, I mean."

"I owe her a bouquet or a box of chocolates or something," said Bruno. "I'm a little short of cash at the moment." Though he'd readied himself for further help and interference, in fact there'd been no evidence of Keith Stolarsky or Tira Harpaz. He'd treated himself to another latte from the Caffe Mediterraneum before realizing he needed his last dollars for the BART fare to the consultation appointment with Behringer, so stuck to baloney-and-cheese sandwiches from the goods Tira had salted in his refrigerator.

"Do you need a loan?" Behringer dug in his front pocket and

flopped balled cash onto his desktop. Apparently he didn't use a wallet. "Here—" He sorted out three twenties, the exact amount Stolarsky had bestowed two days before. Sixty bucks, the handout you could apparently expect between mutually self-respecting acquaintances.

"I wasn't trying to touch you—"

"Please." The surgeon slapped at the bills and shoved them in Bruno's direction.

"Thank you, again." Bruno's shame dissolved in bitterness. The part of him that hated Noah Behringer like he hated any healthy person—it was not so different from hating the rich man across a backgammon board for having money when Bruno had none—freed him to claim the handout. He'd spend it in contempt, go for more Kropotkin's sliders, burned into cancer-encouraging cinders, and salt them with his own tears. Or blow the sixty bucks on a movie on Shattuck, on a bucket of fake-buttered popcorn and a shoe-box-size carton of Whoppers or Junior Mints. Cradling the bucket or carton he'd slip into the darkness, washed over by the phantasms of some sex comedy played by American actors a quarter-century younger than himself, who were meant to be taken for adults. This would make it permissible to die. Desirable, even.

"Listen, Alex, I grokked from Eggs that you're, well, not accustomed to, uh, institutional authority. She said you and the Kraut oncologist didn't exactly get along. She didn't think you'd been to see a doctor for a long time."

"That's true."

"I'm not here to judge you. Whatever you do, it's cool with me."

"I don't understand."

"You're a drug dealer, right?"

"No. I play backgammon. For money."

"Fantastic. That's just fantastic." Behringer appeared delighted, whether because he regarded this as an implausible truth or an audacious lie, Bruno couldn't guess. "Listen, you don't have to tell me a damn thing about what you do. People look at surgeons like they're some kind of gods, and a lot of surgeons play along. But I'm not an authority figure, I'm just here to fix your head, do you understand? You walk out that door and back into whatever life you want, I couldn't be happier."

Bruno apparently didn't need to wear his tuxedo to inspire fantasy. Thanks to Dr. Benedict, he'd crossed the Atlantic dressed in mystique; this might be his only real talent. So let the surgeon be drunk on whatever European whispers had come his way. It cost Bruno nothing and apparently secured him a surgery. Or was it the outlandishness of the blot itself that had done that?

In any case, Bruno couldn't sustain his hate for Behringer. He might be doomed instead to love him.

"Thank you."

"Sure, of course. Here's my card. Call this line tomorrow, I never answer, you'll get Kate, and she'll take care of your appointments. Now, listen, is there anything else I can help you with today, any questions I can answer?"

Bruno supposed he should want to know his odds. Or ask about his face, his appearance—what of it would remain? But his tongue felt numbed. He recalled a joke: A man walked into a bar with a frog on his head. When the bartender asked the man how long the disfigurement had been with him, the frog replied: *It started a year ago as a wart on my ass.* Even now the blot obscured Behringer's searching expression. Was it so simple, then, to be parted from it? What if the blot were Bruno's true self, or his unborn twin, or his talent for backgammon? What if it suppressed his unwished telepathy as it suppressed his sight? At its removal would the world explode in unwanted voices, worse even than the gabble in his childhood? Bruno was terrified the voices might come back. And yes, he was terrified for his face. Yet desperate to be shed of what lay behind it. Open it like a door, then! Unhinge and lay it aside! He sat in silence.

"Ask me anything," said Behringer. His compassion was immense, a flood pool in which Bruno might dissolve.

"I had been wondering, if you might know the answer—" Bruno touched his shirt: the bearded man, *ABIDE.*

"Yes?"

"Everywhere I go, people call me 'Dude,' or say 'the Dude.' I have been away from California for some time—" It had happened seven or eight times, at least, on Telegraph Avenue as he wandered alone the day before. This morning, crossing campus toward the BART station, three young men saluted him with the elongated syllable, as if mooing: *Duuuuuude.* Then once again, just before entering the hospital building, on Parnassus.

"Yes! Of course!" said Behringer. "There's a simple explanation for this."

"It's to do with this shirt, isn't it?"

"That's right. It's from a film, Alex. It's called *The Big Lebowski.* That man on your shirt, he's Lebowski. But he prefers to be called the Dude. He's very, uh, informal."

"Lebowski." Of course the surgeon had recognized the visage, one beard speaking to another.

"Yes. What were you thinking it meant?"

"The shirt? I liked the colors. And—'abide.'"

"It's a good word, a terrific word, in fact. Is there more I can help you with?"

"No," said Bruno. "I think that's fine. That's all for now."

•

Moving to the streetcar stop through a salt-tinged breeze, Bruno felt overtaken by a relief like jubilation. A sensation of beams of light squeezing through the chinks of his soul. He might be shedding beatitude. Once Noah Behringer opened his face and set it aside and then back into place Bruno would grow a beard, be like Behringer and Lebowski, whoever Lebowski was. He'd inhabit this dawning fate. He'd abide, not merely wear the shirt.

It might only be Bruno's face that had always set him apart. So his face had to be wrecked for him to be saved. His face was as much a burden as the blot behind it. This attitude was sudden and absurd and he embraced it. He'd become the Saint Francis of San Francisco—how had he never noticed the one hiding in the other until this moment? Saint Francisco, Saint Bay Area, he'd love all creatures, those wearing Google Glass and equally those booted to the curb and sorting deposit bottles from trash bins. The jocks and skate punks of Telegraph, the tattooed tribes of lower Haight, their lobes deformed with piercings. The BART or Muni riders slumped in bondage, lowly analog workers, handlers of waste and foodstuffs. Those he'd fled to Europe, fled into history, to avoid becoming, he'd embrace one and all. He'd even go to People's Park and seek June's traces. Maybe find June herself still alive, it wasn't impossible. In his beard, in the devastation to be wrought on his aging face, Bruno would resemble his own lost and unknown father, his unnamed father. June would gasp at this apparition, then Bruno would explain and they'd be reunited. The love he felt was boundless, idiotic.

As the N-Judah streetcar pulled in again to roll him down to Market Street, back to BART, Bruno's mobile rang. The surgeon's assistant, already? No, it wasn't possible. He glanced at the phone.

It was the prostitute from Berlin, from the Kladow ferry. Masked Madchen. Her fourth attempt, her calls were stacking up. No one else had rung his phone, which only made sense, since the instrument was a vestige of Falk's will, of Falk's purposes, and Falk seemed to be done with him. Yet Madchen's string of calls were like a pulse in an otherwise dead body. Europe hadn't forgotten him.

BOOK TWO

Eight

I

The resection of Alexander Bruno's meningioma began for Noah Behringer on a Monday in April, at four thirty in the morning, with a wake-up call from Kate, the surgical coordinator he'd corrupted into his own personal assistant, hobbling her career in the process.

"Hi, darling," he rasped when he lifted the phone, his land line, from the bedside table. Behringer had left a desk lamp on to make it possible to find the instrument, and prided himself on catching it before a third ring.

"Are you awake?" Kate asked. When he said, "Yes, I've been thinking about you all night," she hung up.

Behringer no longer troubled to set his own alarm clock, in fact no longer owned one. Kate had once surprised Behringer by saying the cell phone he carried could be used to set an alarm, but she hadn't meant he should try to do so. She was only teasing.

Behringer had been asleep, of course, but it was true that he had also been thinking of Kate. He'd masturbated to thoughts of his assistant in order to put himself to sleep. It was the only way he knew—masturbation, that was, not to Kate in particular—to divert his mind from the vast, scarab-shaped neoplasm behind the face of the gambler from Germany. Behringer had failed to grasp Bruno's nationality, and the question of his patient's unplaceable accent and odd manner had resolved, in this deficit, into an association with the notes and scans from Berlin. These lay strewn, with newer materials generated from the tests Kate had scheduled for Bruno over the past weeks, in heaps around Behringer's apartment, for study. Behringer didn't want to dream all night of the anatomy he'd be addressing in the surgical suite.

119

Worse yet, lie awake all night visualizing it. A sixteen-hour surgery was itself a waking dream. He'd have enough time to contemplate the backgammon hustler's tumor.

At Ninth and Judah he stopped at Donut World. The all-night shop was at this hour reliably bringing out trays of fresh, piping crullers. Behringer took a bag of them and a tall Styrofoam cup of black coffee. He ate a single cruller hurriedly in his parked car, then recrimped the bag and drove to the hospital. When he stowed his car behind the hospital's steam vents, at the base of the steep, pine- and mulch-smelling hill, his special spot, he carried only the coffee and the bag of crullers. All paperwork, all transparencies, all notes in preparation for the day's procedure were duplicated on the hospital's computers and in a sheaf of material printed out for him by Kate. She trusted, rightly, that Behringer's apartment was a black hole, from which nothing useful could be expected to return except the neurosurgeon himself.

A chief of neurosurgery at a major medical center such as this one—the career Noah Behringer had been on track for, had sacrificed everything for, had progressed diligently toward, until developing his fascination with untreatable tumors of the olfactory groove, intractable invasions of the paranasal and orbital region, patients more thoroughly doomed even than those his training had destined him to encounter—a chief of neurosurgery wouldn't be up at this hour, munching doughnuts in the dark. A chief of neurosurgery would be at home while the anesthesiologist put his patient out. He'd be asleep, or enjoying a long shower, a slow breakfast, while his residents cracked and drilled and flapped the skull, while they cauterized and clipped and retracted, those first hours of painstaking tedious craniotomy that made the interior arena of the skull ready for the big man to sweep in and do his work. The brain surgeons were cleanup hitters who sat in the clubhouse while the singles hitters and bunters made their occasions ready for them.

Behringer could have been one. A cleanup hitter, a star making cameo turns. Show up for a few hours in the middle, resect a tumor, clip a thorny multiple aneurism, reorganize a major draining artery. Or fuck up, slice through the major artery, explode the aneurism, maul the language and motor-control quadrants in overly robust pursuit of a fundamentally untreatable glioblastoma or astrocytoma. Casey hitting it out of the park or striking out. Either way, his day was finished. The interns closed up the skull and flap for you, whether the skull of a triumph, a solid bragging point, or that of a new-made human vegetable never again to breathe without a tube, or the skull of a bled-out corpse.

Kate met Behringer at the elevator. Riding with him, she freed his hands of the coffee and the paper bag containing the remnants—not many—of his crullers. For these, she exchanged a folder containing the scans and transparencies, as well as notations he'd dictated briefly to her on the phone. The stuff was redundant: not only were the best images to be readily called up on the in-surgery monitor but he'd barely glance at these once he'd plunged inside, by means of the binocular microscope. The map was not the territory, etc. The monitor was for the residents, so they could study Behringer's approach without crowding him, and to magnify artery and nerve bundles for more adept support work. Paperwork was afterthought now. From the first incision the matter was between Behringer and the flesh beneath his instruments.

For if all this was what Behringer could have spared himself—waking in the dark to be scrubbed and in among the residents for the very first incision—it was also where the distinction lay. In Behringer's procedures, nothing was routine. Entry to the domain of the tumor was itself the adventure, whose intricacies were personal to him each time. Not that he didn't have residents to assist. The younger men viewed their sporadic call to Behringer's procedures—well, who knew how they viewed it? The residents were themselves on track to become top-dog neurosurgeons, they featured all the characteristic monomaniacal disposition, and though they might indulge a fascination with Behringer's eccentric method, his reckless path through the face, they couldn't afford to sustain it.

In the passage to the lockers and washroom, in the windows lining the corridor, Behringer glimpsed the sunlight dawning now. The last he'd see until the following day. Not unless on some break he wandered into the corridor, but the cost of such wandering was to disinfect, change gowns, scrub in again. He rarely bothered. There was no sunlight in the surgical room, of course, nor in the lockers or washroom. It was enough to scrub in after the two or three bathroom voyages he'd need—he'd exaggerated during his consultant visit with Alexander Bruno—and after the meatball parmigiana sub Kate was deputized to retrieve from Molinari's in North Beach. By Behringer's dinner hour Alexander Bruno's nose and eye sockets and upper lip might hope to be in the early stages of a reunion with his head. As to this matter of eating during surgeries, Behringer had been entirely dishonest with his patient. He always was.

In terms of sheer imperial arrogance, Noah Behringer was actually typical of the neurosurgical caste. Yet many of his colleagues hated Behringer, not only for his eccentricities but for his audacity. These mostly short and Jewish men were meant to be the cowboys, the Clint Eastwoods in this landscape. The brain surgeons stood atop the heap, sneered and sighed and rolled their eyes at internists, at oncologists, at phlebotomists, at the neurologists. All other specialties lay beneath them in sheer balls—even the cardiac surgeons. Pop a heart out, put it on a plane, stick it in another body. Make a dozen mistakes—hell, you could *drop* a heart. Whereas one nick, one wrong turn, the brain died. A heart surgeon was Scotty in the engine room, sweating, up to his elbows in greasy parts. The brain surgeons were the Vulcans.

His comparisons, Behringer was aware, were forty years out-of-date. Scotty no longer ran the engine room. Most of those actors were probably dead. (It was a miracle he'd been able to identify the *Big Lebowski* T-shirt, entirely due to a girlfriend, whose favorite film it had been.) To be woefully out of touch with everything except medicine since the day you entered the machine was the price of doing business, of rising to this place, and Behringer's compensations were as pathetic as the next guy's, despite attempts to read the latest best seller, or to do more than trot his weekly *New Yorkers* from mailbox to recycling bin, having grasped nothing but the occasional article by Oliver Sacks or Atul Gawande, the rest an opaque hash of fashionable names, communiqués from a world that had left him behind. One morning *The New Yorker* had informed Behringer, while on the shitter, that Jerry Brown was governor again. Imagine! Which other bewilderments might be lost on him, who knew?

Behringer scrubbed now, honoring the ancient regimen, each arm treated elbow to fingertip, not the reverse, each finger to be treated as a four-sided object, scaled and buffed individually, fingernails a minimum of twenty-five times, contaminated soap sluiced downward yet while keeping elbows lower than fingertips, etc.

Behringer, who liked to speak of his "writing," had actually passed through his Oliver Sacks delusion long since. He was compassionate, sure, but a ponytail and beard didn't make him Sacks. Nerdy spectacles didn't make him A. R. Luria. Nor did his eccentricities render him a humanist, a soul surgeon; he'd abandoned the pretense. Behringer's minor flirtation with the brain-mind perplex had been satisfied by reading a few articles. Confronted with a book on the topic (there was a new one on a monthly basis), Behringer drifted. His interest in the fabulation known as human consciousness was bounded neatly inside its traditional container. He was interested in his own surgeries. He recognized himself in the word *solipsist*.

Behringer stepped inside the surgical room, no longer referred to as a theater. His anesthesiologist, McArdle, a jolly raffish Scottish lady he was always glad to see, had done her work; the German was out. She'd given way to the scrub nurses and technologist working to drape the man, to shave his eyebrows and position his limbs to endure the procedure. As usual for Behringer's marathons, a neurological technician would monitor the risk of "positioning effect," preventing nerve or tissue damage a body's length from the surgical area. Behringer couldn't recall the technician's title or name: another watcher-participant, another minor actor. Yet the surgical stage still wasn't a theater because there was no audience. The only non-player at Behringer's performance was guaranteed to miss it entirely: the German with his head now bolted in place, his body draped and insensate on the table. Breath flowed to the patient's lungs through a hose in his throat; Behringer needed to assault the oropharynx and the posterior nares and the sphenoidal sinuses with impunity, not be forced to work around tracheal intubation.

First, however, and feeling real excitement at the thought, the good burst of adrenaline at last, Behringer wanted to dismantle the sockets and loosen his patient's eyes.

Behringer didn't need it to be a theater, not for playing Hamlet or Macbeth or Godot or any other figure riddled with hesitation and remorse. He needed no witness, nor sidekick or foil, no Sancho Panza here. Thanks to the power of the binocular microscope, for Behringer the incision into the patient became a planetary landscape, cavernous, labyrinthine, enveloping. In that zone, everything was between Behringer and his fascination, between his hands and the meat. A hundred watchers couldn't drag him back to the human realm here, if he was honest.

His sole tether was the music. Now was the time. He nodded to Gonzales, the surgical technologist who knew him best. Gonzales tapped the iPod, mounted in a small speaker bay, and it started playing "Night Bird Flying" from *First Rays of the New Rising Sun,* as always. It was set at a volume that permitted work to be done, the instructions and observations to pass among the members of the team, but loud enough to cover the drone and whine of the motors driving the suction and drill, loud enough to matter.

With this, and after one last impatient glance at the 3-D scans on the screen and his own brisk notations, Behringer asked for the first instruments he'd need to carve his German's face apart.

If he was hated by the brain surgeons the real reason was here, in this ripple of disturbance—ambient, denied, intangible, but unmistakable—that Behringer triggered as he laid the honed blade to the backgammon player's forehead, along the line where eyebrows had been, and worked the incision down, around each eye socket, to the underside of the temple. Behringer was a heretic, an outlier. Nobody was supposed to delve farther for a tumor than into the braincase. That some other secret place resided so close, "hidden in plain sight," yet even more inaccessible to traditional treatments, freaked everyone out. The Bermuda Triangle of self. The brain surgeons were top dogs, Behringer a coyote. Specifically a coyote eating frontally, into the face. Nobody liked someone who came at the face. In surgeon's terms, the face was for the plastic guys, the sleazy, go-for-the-buck tit-lifters, who congregated down in the Southland. Behringer stunk of this impurity, he knew. It gave the neurosurgeons a way of feeling superior to him.

Really, they were afraid. The neurosurgeons draped the face, dehumanized it for their convenience, before cutting. They taped off a bald cranium to appear like an orb, a science-fiction egg. The unity of face and skull, if encountered suddenly, sickened even the most hardened among them. They defended themselves from this awareness. Snobs for depth, they slighted the surface and those who engaged with it.

In Behringer's view it was all meat, the surface and depth alike. Physicians were, each and every one of them, mechanics of the meat. The stuff of which dreams were made, sure. But not itself dreams, not ectoplasm or soul or spirit. Those eluded the knife. Instead, gum and glue, nerves and fat. Animals made in evocative and stirring shapes, out of a meat that sometimes tried to wreck itself with mutation. The brain surgeons were plastic surgeons; plastic surgeons were all there were.

II

Though he wasn't quite old enough to have seen Jimi Hendrix play live, in his younger days Noah Behringer had been a "rock doc," working the medical stations at festivals and backstage at Winterland and the Warfield, in exchange for free entrance. There, he'd dispense prescription medicine to touring musicians and roadies, while doling out ibuprofen and Gatorade to sunburned LSD overdoses and dehydration cases among those in the audience. Most who manned the tents were nurse practitioners or stoner family-practice types; Behringer was the only neurosurgeon among them. He'd begun during his internship, on a colleague's suggestion, at a string of Hot Tuna shows in the late '80s.

The music fans seemed to Behringer a population worthy of curious study, full of childlike adults presenting simple problems he could usually solve. The musicians? Strangely, they reminded him of surgeons. Professionally aloof and unreachable, until that moment when the lights went on and they became exacting technicians. They were interested only in the cleanest and most efficient amphetamine doses in Behringer's supply, and in B-vitamin shots. All of this seemed precisely arranged to say to Behringer: What are you doing here? Go back to what you're best at. To where *you're* the star. The music itself, for which he'd been hopeful, barely interested him. He got more from retracing, on headphones, Dave Gilmour's guitar solo on "Dogs" for the thousandth time than he did from anything in the events he now attended, with all the indignities of the rock-doc's role, his button shirts infused with clove, cannabis, and vomit.

Behringer's last show was at the Oakland Coliseum. The Who, or what survived of them. The venue had ordered up an excess of doctors, so Behringer snuck into the general-admission area on the Oakland A's ballpark grass, and during a rote rendition of "Pinball Wizard" filtered his way through the blankets and folding chairs of the infield until he found the mound, which sat bandaged in tight-pinned canvas. He stood on top, facing the stage, and pitched a no-hitter in an imaginary ball game. Behringer wasn't needed in this place. He left before the band's encores.

It was eight years later, while attending a surgical conference in Seattle, that he'd defected from the dull seminars to visit the garish new rock-'n'-roll museum, and wandered into the Jimi Hendrix exhibition. There, finding Hendrix's godlike youth frozen in commemoration, Behringer had reconnected with rock 'n' roll. In the gift shop he bought it all on CD, the reissues and posthumous albums, then reappointed his home with a top-line system for playing them. Later he indulged in memorabilia, a gold record, framed tickets, the autographed poster. Over his stereo hung a guitar, though not one of those Hendrix himself had actually touched, which were absurdly expensive. Forget the cost of those his hero had set aflame.

Behringer no longer needed to confront the decline or mortality of the aging bands. Hendrix's music didn't decline and wasn't mortal. Played in the surgery room, it made Behringer and the guitarist twins on a plane of pursuit that was esoteric to those at levels below. Did it cause certain of the older surgical nurses to vow never to work with him again? Fine, Behringer preferred younger ones. The music was something for the residents to roll their eyes over, while covertly digging it themselves. Standing in for his entire professional "personality"— *Crazy Behringer with his Hendrix!*—the music released him from the difficulty of formulating one.

Now Behringer's attention refastened to the present situation. The German gambler's face had been flapped downward, to lay on the tray mounted across his throat and chest. *Like a baby's bib!* it appeared suddenly to Behringer. A resident named Charles Kai, skilled in vascular microsurgery, had diligently stemmed and redirected major arterial flow, working under the binocular microscope, like a diamond cutter or watchmaker with his loupe, to accomplish stitches half the width of a human hair.

The German, had he known, should consider himself fortunate the young and eager residents carried out the more prosaic tasks. After Behringer's first bold violence, unlocking the patient's nose from the axis of the orbital bones, it was the residents who had teased free the exposed flesh to form the flap that hung from the German's chin like a beard of meat. Next the minor arteries had been individually cauterized, with a painstaking diligence Behringer could no longer be bothered to summon, he with his hundreds of entries behind him. A circular section of the bone comprising the upper sockets and lower brow had also been removed and set carefully aside, with bone chips from the saw blade conserved for eventual use in forming a reconstructive cement.

The cavern of the German's inmost face was now prepared for Behringer's spelunking. Copious irrigation on the part of the nurses had cleared his view, nerve bundles identified and tagged for preservation. The surrounding tissue appeared nicely relaxed. Before him now lay the entity the neurosurgeon had made this appointment to encounter. The meningioma, the flesh-crab that had squatted blackly in the scans, was revealed beneath the surgical lights as feeble-sickly pink. If was faintly veinous but, happily, not fed by any major branches of the sphenopalatine artery—not, in other words, a bag of hemorrhage-eager blood.

The tumor appeared soft, not especially firm. Behringer observed, even without magnification, some fibroid tissue, but not a troublesome extent. The central mass had undergone a measure of expansive deformation, relieved from containment behind the eyeballs and underneath the mask of bone. With mild probing it was evident that the tumor's adherence to surrounding tissues was minimal. They'd biopsy a portion for frozen-section diagnosis and learn for certain before Behringer had gone far with his cutting, but he felt zero doubt of the diagnosis.

No meningeal tumor, outgrowth of the brain's lining, could be one hundred percent removed. But the less sticky, the greater the percentage removed. Slow-growing, such an invader might reassert itself in ten or fifteen years. With vigilance, such a recurrence could be thwarted easily, with minimal invasiveness, by Gamma Knife. Such trite procedures interested Behringer not at all. Thousands were capable of them. Behringer's present task, which he now guessed might top out at five or six hours of steady debulking work, was his alone to accomplish. In fact, thanks to dawning innovations like the Gamma Knife, gene therapy, and the like, the medical world might never cultivate another explorer like Behringer. The German drug dealer was lucky his surgeon existed.

"Mr. Gonzales," he said without looking behind him.

"Yes."

" 'Red House.' The thirteen-minute version." The iPod contained nothing but Hendrix. It might hold in the neighborhood of ten versions of the song. But Gonzales, though he groaned at the crudity of the joke, knew which the neurosurgeon meant. This crude joke was a ritual one.

Jimi Hendrix played another role in Behringer's procedures, besides decorating the surgeon's personality. The dead genius also stood in for Behringer's patient. Delving hour after hour in the red interior, Behringer was prone to abstraction. Other surgeons learned some life facts to humanize their patient, to foreground those sweet stakes that dangled by a thread over the void, but this was not for Behringer. He had trouble recalling his patients' names. Nor was he keen on meeting with families (useless, anyhow, in the case of the German, who apart from his phantom sponsor seemed alone in the world). Behringer would meet if they desired it, but the petitions of families made no special impression.

No, to keep himself in mind of the stakes, Behringer relied on a stock fantasy. In this daydream Behringer was a rock doc, but at a level far above that of the internists handing out electrolytes and sunblock from a tent. In each and every procedure, the flesh beneath Behringer's Penfield was that of the epochal Negro guitarist, who'd been rushed in by paramedics, rather than left to expire in his bed of vomit, and required emergency resection of a neoplasm unapproachable by all but the most intrepid physician. Noah Behringer was, again and eternally, saving the life of Jimi Hendrix. The future of music depended on it.

III

Alexander Bruno's face, having surpassed its eighth hour as an open door, now crawled into its ninth.

The face was the subject of vast ministrations. Residents monitored the flapped lips and cheeks, the philtrum and the skin surface of the nose, attending to blood flow and temperature. Care was lavished on the retracted eyeballs, so easy to damage irreparably, and the hood of bone and cartilage that had been set aside to permit the neurosurgeon's entry.

The anesthesiologist, the Scottish woman McArdle, monitored the stabilized body. Alongside her was the surgical neurologist, who regularly tested and stimulated the patient's inert extremities. The two, McArdle and the neurologist, existed at a remove from the drama of the exploded face, below its horizon, and yet were as necessary in support of the adventure of the face as the invisible root system is necessary to the drama of the flowering tree.

Gonzales and the other surgical nurses attended diligently, around the circumference of the face, to irrigation, to tagging nerve bundles and cauterizing seeping veins, as these were exposed by the neurosurgeon's progress through the tumor's irregular mass.

At the center, Behringer.

If the disassembled face could have somehow beheld what craned down into its core, the binocular microscope might have appeared as a pair of mad enlarged pupils, bled in every direction to the periphery, so as to make a sky of eyeball—a skyball.

For hours Behringer had borne down, into the paranasal and maxillary trenches, the nasopharynx, the orbital cavities, and into the

131

tumor itself, the entrances he'd carved through its mass. His sense of scale was demolished. His tools and materials, the bipolar cautery and facial nerve stimulator, the tiny copper spoons and cup forceps and scissors, the neurosurgical Cottonoids, appeared like massive construction devices, excavators and steam shovels, brinked on shattered canyons of organ and tumor.

The Hendrix had played and played. Those in the room barely noticed it now apart from the transitions, the blips of silence between tracks, or at the start of a repeat—"Voodoo Child" or "Hear My Train A Comin'" for the fifth or twelfth time. Twice the neurosurgeon had startled them, calling out "Skip this one, Gonzales" for the "The Star-Spangled Banner" and "Room Full of Mirrors." This, the only proof Behringer offered that the music still mattered to him. Otherwise he'd mutter out for irrigation or a cleansed instrument. Their own chatter was deferentially minimal, though speech was hardly forbidden. Nor did they seek his permission to rotate out on breaks for rest or nourishment. He'd be unlikely to care who, at a given moment, made up this room's population.

In the tenth hour the neurosurgeon met a threshold; all sensed it. The air changed. Not a crisis (that being a thing for which his residents might subconsciously yearn, to bust into the tedium and test their untested courage), whatever shift had occurred might not even entail a change in the surgical routine. They'd likely remain in these postures for hours yet.

But Behringer fell back, slightly. What remained of the tumor were tendrils, requiring cauterization, not removal. Tendrils, and a neoplastic layer adherent to the arachnoid tissue, more than could be safely approached. For the neurosurgeon, reaching this juncture aroused senses both of fulfilled ambition and of thwarted perfectionism, each so familiar that he no longer distinguished the two. For all purposes, they were one sensation.

The face now began its slow journey to reassembly. The displaced parts clamored for it, in their voiceless fashion. Cellular degeneration, shrinkage, nerve damage, these accelerated beyond a certain hour, no matter the quality of maintenance. That hour was past. The neurosurgeon, answerable to the whole of the face, knew the clock dictated priorities: Some shit had to be left inside. This outcome was a given.

The German (Behringer now abandoned his fantasy, Jimi Hendrix's life had been saved, and he was also still dead, go figure) would or would not regrow his tumor incrementally, over decades; he'd die of something else before it mattered. What counted now was preservation of function—sight, skin sensitivity, swallowing, chewing. The patient would never know his face's interior as it had now been known by Behringer, never even glimpse or dream of such knowledge, let alone judge the compromises inherent in such a procedure. It was in terms of function that the patient would measure success.

Of course the German would never be the same in any event. The face had been an opened door, yes. But behind lay a battlefield. The door, reclosed, would give testimony to what had occurred there. Behringer hoped he'd been clear enough on that point.

"Somebody begin an anecdote with uncomfortable sexual content," commanded the neurosurgeon. "A compromising entanglement or position or proposal, something that once you hear it you can't get it out of your head."

He'd not lifted his face from the binocular microscope, allowing his staff to communicate behind his back—such that mute association of eyes over masks could communicate. Actually, you got good at this. The Behringer first-timers mimed helplessness to the Behringer veterans: Surely it couldn't be their place to speak first? The veterans silently replied, to say either that they were outright resisters, so look elsewhere, or else that Behringer had strip-mined their private lives at times previous, so the newbies should step up and take their turn. Gonzales and McArdle, knowing the neurosurgeon best, said with their gazes that it didn't matter who spoke, or whether anyone did. Behringer would find his way to turn the subject to himself, his own predilections, before long.

"Anyone been in an orgy?"

A rising scent of seared meat accompanied this query, as the cautery became Behringer's predominant instrument.

"C'mon, a threesome? Or ever walk in on one? Ever walk in on *any-thing*, your parents even?"

This was a shy group. One nurse exited the room, but then that was always occurring, it was unclear whether there was any special reason why.

"You people disappoint me. Last time there was that nurse, Gonzales, what was her name? Remember, with the story about the staircase?"

"I think it was Park."

"That's right, Korean girl, Park. Probably from an upright family, insane math scores, piano lessons, never in a million years. Remember her staircase thing, Gonzales?"

"I think so, yeah."

"Do I have to tell it myself?"

"Better you than me."

"She's in the stairwell of this sex party, I guess the whole scene was a disappointment, her girlfriend's still inside but she's ready to go, just having a cigarette on the staircase. But the guy she's gotten the cigarette from is super-handsome, a super-nice guy she'd want to date in ordinary circumstances, right? So they're talking, getting to know each other, soon they're kissing. Tender, slow, nothing salacious at this point, maybe they'll exchange phone numbers. I'm embellishing a little. At that point a guy comes out of the party and sees them on the stairs, this second guy's not attractive at all, sort of short and toad-like, but figure there's a perverse sexual charisma. Park didn't say this exactly but I'd assume he's one of those ugly-turn-on guys, women will admit to the existence of the category."

"Castles Made of Sand" had just ended, so these last remarks fell in a gap accompanied only by the hum and whine of machines, and the thickening smolder and perfume of cooked flesh. Then "Tears of Rage" filled the silence.

"And he sees them and goes down below where she's sitting—she's wearing a skirt, I should have explained—and puts his head up her skirt and just begins to go to work down there, while she and the attractive guy are still making out in a very chaste and affectionate way. Needless to say, like a lot of ugly guys he's pretty accomplished in certain techniques, a survival trait in his circumstances."

No acknowledgment came, only the hiss of the cautery. For an interlude they worked wordlessly toward the goal.

"See, now that's a story. But maybe we're setting an impossible standard, you're all intimidated."

Nothing. Hendrix.

"McArdle, you're from the United Kingdom, isn't that right? Scotland didn't vote itself out when it was given the chance."

"That's true so far as it goes, Doctor."

"Well, then, right, so maybe you can clarify something for me. A friend sent me an amusing thing in an e-mail: Apparently some people in England held a protest recently, where some British porn stars went to Parliament and demonstrated for their right to sit on people's faces. Have I got that right?"

"I couldn't say."

"I'm pretty sure of it. They were doing, like, a public sit-on-your-face-in. I just wondered if you knew what they were trying to establish, I mean, is it illegal in the United Kingdom to sit on someone's face?"

"Possibly, I don't myself know. I'll look into it if you want me to. Not right at the moment, of course."

"No, of course not. I just thought as the representative here you might have some angle on the whole deal." His tone flattened. "We're going to begin closing here, maybe as soon as half an hour." With this incidental remark everything and nothing was changed, the whole room put on standby. The long voyage of the face now sighted a distant shoreline, the variously tagged nerves and arteries soon to be recleaved to their estranged counterparts. The painstaking reassembly was itself a voyage, of course, of many hours, requiring as much or more diligence than had the creation of the flap and opening.

"Here's the thing that really nags at me. McArdle, are you listening?"

"Yes." If anyone here understood that Behringer's babble was the result of a comedown, his descent from the absolute promontory, it was the anesthesiologist.

"Do you think some of the appeal of having one's face sat on, or should I say sat *upon*—that's more properly British, isn't it? That some of the appeal has to do with oxygen restriction? Just lack of air, I mean. If so, it would put the whole exotic area of autoerotic asphyxiation in a different light, wouldn't it? Much closer to regular vanilla sex behavior, right? I mean, oral sex in general."

"I'd never given it a thought."

"Have you broken those particular laws yourself, McArdle? I mean, assuming we're guessing right about the whole protest."

"I've been known to in my time, Doctor."

"Not just here, but in the UK."

"Even there I've dared, yes, in fact."

"Well, there you go. So these people, these protestors, though you probably wouldn't be likely yourself to go down to Parliament and, you know, *do it on the sidewalk,* they were really speaking on your behalf, weren't they, McArdle?"

"I suppose I should be grateful to them."

"Yeah, you should, that's exactly what I was thinking."

"Would you like me to sit on your face, Doctor?"

The room's collective breath, held for nearly ten hours now, exploded in laughter, imperfectly suppressed beneath masks. Snorts through noses, subvocal hoots of incredulity, and so forth. McArdle was a sizable woman.

"I don't mean just now," she continued in her dry, even tone. "I can see you're occupied."

It silenced him, if only for the moment.

IV

After exiting the surgical room Behringer rested, on a gurney reserved for this purpose, in a disused office adjacent to the sixth-floor ICU. His residents concluded the closure regimen, disengagement of the patient's body from the apparatus that had immobilized it for fifteen hours, and the dressing of the incision wounds. Much care would be given now to the limbs, at risk for pooling of lymph fluids, and to the risk of surgical phlebitis or hematomas. These were concerns beyond Behringer's scope, were what specialization was for. The neurosurgeon slept.

More and more, lately, brain surgeons opted for swift awakening of the patient after craniotomy. Revival of function reassured the waiting family that the procedure had caused no neurological disasters, plus every hour shaved from anesthetic duration improved the pace of recovery. But Behringer still preferred, in his adventures into the face, to wait. Such patients were destined to be woken blind, with nothing to comfort them beyond a bedside voice. The German had no advocate present at the hospital. So Behringer had ordered six hours of instilled slumber, wanting to be present in person when his patient was revived. He'd instructed Kate to wake him after five.

She came in with a breakfast burrito and a tall coffee, his requirements, and a bottle of water, upon which she insisted. Behringer sat on the gurney's edge and prodded himself very slowly in the direction of the light, while Kate described, droningly, the patient's vital signs, and he ignored her. She'd placed the breakfast items on a Mayo stand, and Behringer began to reach for these, each in turn, while he let himself be soothed by her monotone recital. The room stank of Hibiclens, ChloraPrep, and furtive cigarettes.

"You're a magical specimen, too good for me by far, and yet here you stand. So close and out of reach at the same time." If his harassment the morning before had served to settle his nerves, this now was to prove that he still existed, to restore his contact with a world outside that of the gory cavity through which he'd plunged by binocular microscope. All during his uneasy five-hour sleep Behringer had dreamed of the inside of the German's face. "Someday I'll pull you into a broom closet. It would be today if I wasn't so damn wrung out."

Kate ignored him in turn. She'd had the benefit of the procedure's interval to sleep, to return to whatever she called a life—Behringer had no inkling, really—and to ready herself for presiding over the patient's first and most crucial forty-eight hours of recovery, here in the ICU. Kate never entered the surgical room during his procedures, which kept her sacrosanct, his alone, untainted by the collegiality of his residents and OR nursing staff.

"I feel like a boxer who's gone fifteen rounds," he said, yearning for her admiration and pity.

"Have you boxed?"

"The way I imagine a boxer would feel."

As much as he wished to molt the shell of the operating room, the spell of entrancement there, Behringer knew he clung to it too. Was reluctant to exit the drama of his centrality, that sphere of absorption and urgency. Until the final out he'd stood on the mound, pitching a no-hitter. Now he had to wander back into the prosaic days between such importances.

"Hurry up," said Kate.

"I don't have time for a shower and a dump?"

She shook her head. "Mr. Bruno woke early. They tried stepping him off by degrees, but he surprised them."

The German had needed to be restrained to prevent his struggling. He'd been trying to remove the IVs and breathing tube, the ICU nurse explained, and to examine by touch the bandages covering his eyes and the tracheotomy bandage at his throat. Now he lay, only moderately sedate, mostly helpless, surely confused. Where the patient's skin was visible it was deep gray.

Behringer touched the German's hand where it was strapped to the gurney and half covered with IV tape. Did he do this for Kate's sake, or the nurse's? No, nobody judged him. Behringer's gesture was sincere, even if he was self-conscious about it.

"They were thinking if we cut the steroids it might ease his belligerency," said Kate. "We could get him out of the restraints sooner."

"No, I want the steroid regimen. Give him morphine."

"Yes," said Kate, not quibbling.

"Did you reach his friend? The one who pays?"

"I spoke with him briefly."

"Good. I'll call him tomorrow." Behringer gave up stroking the pallid flesh, put his own hand in his pocket. Then he spoke for the sake of the unbandaged ears, whose function should not have been in any way impaired. "Mr. Bruno, this is Dr. Behringer. Your surgery was a success." The German would remember none of this, but it might soothe his sleep. "We removed your tumor. Now you have to rest."

You asked me to save you, Behringer thought. Though in fact the dissolute German had never used that word, not that Behringer recalled. *You asked me to save you, but to save you I had to destroy you. That is what I do.*

Sixteen

I

Alexander Bruno had been hospitalized in Oakland as a child, for burns. He'd spent almost a month there, including six days in intensive care.

Since that time, he'd never stayed overnight in a hospital, apart from his adventure at Charité. He'd barely entered a doctor's office. The helplessness he endured now, in recovery from his meningioma's resection, had formerly seemed to him purely a condition of childhood. It mingled in his imagination with his mother's reality zones— the Marin cult, his and June's tiny apartment in the Berkeley flats, the plaster-casting workshop on San Pablo Avenue, even the homeless shelter where he'd visited her after he'd begun living with the waiters at Chez Panisse. Now he seemed to have been force-shifted by sense memory back to that time.

Where was Bruno, now? The answer to his unasked question had come repeatedly, in voices bearing accents Filipino, Thai, and Mexican, voices now sympathetic, now impassive and hurried: "You're in the hospital, sweetie. Rest." The voices might add, "That's right, your face is covered, you're on a ventilator, but stop touching it or we'll have to tie you." Or: "You breathe good now. No need talk." He'd been informed of his status until he believed it and could recover the belief upon waking anew. It was then he began to knit it together with the memory of arriving at the hospital and placing himself in their care. The chubby, vivacious Scottish woman, who'd joked to him about offering him a cocktail as she plunged a syringe not into Bruno's flesh but into the tangle of plastic tubing taped across his hand.

What he couldn't conjugate was what he somehow recalled of the time between—between his intake, that was, and his immobilization now. Those events comprised a film reeling on a screen in the dark, glitchy with blood and feedback, from which he had to avert his awareness. And so, under the night of his bandages, seduced by the resemblance of one set of beeping, whining bedside machines to another, so long ago, and dislocated by blindness from any purchase in time and space, Bruno lapsed gratefully into a trance of memory.

•

He'd been burned by a pot of hot coffee. It had spilled on him while he sat at the breakfast nook of the apartment on Chestnut Street, the summer he turned eleven, just before the explosion of his puberty. Not coffee, actually, for the top of the Chemex was full of boiling water that hadn't trickled through the grounds and into the bottom of its hourglass form—it was the water that had seared him when the pot tipped.

June, who'd poured the kettle into the top of the coffeepot, was destined to award herself the guilt; who was there to contradict her? Bruno, however, blamed himself: The pot had been placed on a wooden trivet, shaped like a turtle, with four wooden balls for feet, one of which had come off. The trivet had been the product of a fifth-grade shop class. Once finished, it had struck Bruno as a gift his mother would cherish, despite the abject disinterest he'd felt in the tasks of cutting the turtle template, applying the feet, and a glossy laminate. He wasn't the sort of child to come home with stacks of drawings, parental valentines, glaze-globbed ashtrays. The turtle's foot had come off by virtue of Bruno's shitty gluing job—he'd done this to himself.

While the grounds belched harmlessly onto the plate of toast before him, the boiling water arced and splashed. It scalded Bruno along one bare forearm, his chest, stomach, and groin. It soaked into the Jockey underwear that had been his only sleeping costume the night before, in an apartment lacking air-conditioning. His mother, after one shocked interval of disbelief, had moved with swift efficiency, stripping off the underwear and plunging Bruno into a cold, shallow bathtub. Tatters of his skin floated gently free in bands at his inner thighs, where the underwear's thick seams had held the boiling water against him for crucial instants longer. These memories, and of her transportation of him to the emergency room, were kaleidoscopic, not sustained. Though Bruno must have been screaming, he recalled the sight of his own flesh unspooling from his body dispassionately, as if a page in a photo album. It was his weeks of recovery in Alta Bates hospital, laden with tedium and wonder, that had become a personal experience. He'd had his first orgasm there.

He'd been placed first in the ICU, under a sheet tented by an iron framework to prevent contact with his damaged skin. His burns were largely first- or second-degree, over half his skin surface. The third-degree burns were limited to those bands along his inner thighs and a small patch of his hairless pubis, where the underwear's fly had similarly trapped the boiling water. His penis had escaped damage—no miracle, since it was at this point barely larger than a hazelnut. At the start, though, the distinction between these burns and the others seemed moot, given how the second-degree wounds began peeling like accelerated sunburn. In the first twenty-four hours Bruno was in danger for his life, he understood later, from dehydration and the risk of uncontrollable infection across so much scalded flesh. Gloved hands smeared him nearly up to his neck in gel, while intravenous lines flooded his veins with nutrient fluid.

Bruno spent the next days under that tented sheet returning to himself. "Hospital" turned out to represent a punctuated tedium, the recurrence of blood pressure and temperature checks, the placement and emptying of bedpans and painful switching of IV lines from the crook of one elbow to the other, and the switching of nurses as day and night were destroyed and replaced with tripartite shifts. These women, mostly matronly blacks, treated the burned boy with affectionate exasperation, as an object blockading their efficiency and a confidant in their war on the obtuse and elusive doctors.

After a five-day stand in the ICU, his crisis passed, and Bruno had been moved to a quiet, ugly ward, into a room with an empty bed for a companion. The rate of attention slowed to a crawl, days yawning into chasms. Bruno succumbed to boredom, but there was something else as well. Though June appeared at his bedside, he was more often alone. His school friends weren't allowed to visit, if they'd even learned of his accident during summer break. The nurses weren't interested in him, and Bruno's burn injuries kept him bedridden, incapable of exploring the ward. Daytime television—soap operas, talk shows, game shows—was useless to fill the void. For the first time, it felt, Bruno was away from the babble of other children, or of June and her friends or boyfriends, who struck him suddenly as no different from children. With the toppling of the coffeepot he'd lucked out of his regular state, that of the intrusion of other voices into his mind.

By the accident of his injury, at eleven, Bruno had floated loose of the prison of his childhood, like an inmate of an open-roofed cell swimming to freedom in a flood.

He heard the talk the nurses conducted over his head, and the muttered remarks of the doctors as they glanced at the clipboard attached to the bed frame at his feet. None of it was directed at Bruno's attention, nor was it concealed. Bruno's invisibility at the center of this set of actions freed him to perceive his own outline, possibly for the first time. Emptied of his involuntary self, Bruno could refill the container with whatever interested him. He could manage the thoughts and feelings of others, those things that had formerly overridden his boundary, and manage which of his own thoughts and feelings leaked out for exhibition. He only had to understand his curse as a gift to control it. And, unlike a curse, a gift could be handed back or abandoned.

A nun came to his bedside. She seemed old to Bruno, at least by comparison to his mother, though the nun would probably only have been in her forties, he'd think later. She wore jeans and white tennis shoes and a cotton blouse with her brown-and-white habit, and a large pendant cross at her breasts. The nun wanted to know where his parents were, and Bruno explained that he had only a mother, and that she was "working"—he didn't know what June was doing with her days while he was in the hospital. Based on how she spent them in Bruno's company, no guess was safe.

The nun asked if she could sit and read to him, but when it turned out she had the Bible in mind, Bruno asked whether they could play cards instead. She located a deck and they played gin rummy. At first she let him win. He didn't guess this; he read her mind. Then he deliberately angered her by pointing it out, and she tried to win, and he beat her anyway. It was with the nun that Bruno first experimented with the control and limitation of his boundary. He'd detected the nun's conscious intentions, and also her helpless desires, the craven and keening portion of her brain, but now he simply shuttered those out. He only wanted to know what cards she held.

When he grew bored he let the nun win a game, then said he was tired.

The same method worked on June when she visited the hospital. At first, Bruno opened to her as always. His mother was typically hectic, fearful, preening. Flirtatious with the doctors and subservient even to the nurses, situating herself automatically on the lowest rung on any available ladder, arousing Bruno's contempt in the process. She asked repeatedly how long her son would have to remain hospitalized, and spoke openly of her fear of the mounting costs to attending doctors who even Bruno saw had no interest, nor the capacity to influence her situation. Anyway, she'd default on these bills, something Bruno knew already too—June might be the only person in the room with any doubt of it.

And then, as with the nun, Bruno simply retreated behind his own newly discovered boundary. He tuned June down, then out. In fact, he found once he had done so that it was difficult to tune her in again.

It was his encounter with the whirlpool attendant that sealed the transformation. In the last ten days of Bruno's hospital stay he'd begun to move gingerly to the bathroom by himself instead of using the bedpan. The majority of his burns had resolved into tender new flesh, and his treatment now centered on just the small areas of third-degree burns—his inner thighs and the patch above his penis. These areas remained raw and had to be salved against infection and to prevent scars. In this regimen, once a day an attendant ferried him, by wheelchair, to a strange, seemingly desolate wing of the third floor, into a room containing a large steel whirlpool. The hydrotherapy, a doctor explained, was believed to stimulate growth of new tissue and minimize scarring. There would be scarring, this doctor and others hastened to say, despite Bruno never having asked.

The whirlpool attendant was an angry black man with a salt-and-pepper beard and no bedside manner. His lack of solicitude was so total it was a kind of electricity, an assertion; this being Oakland, the man might have been a former or current Black Panther in his time away from the hospital. Each afternoon he delivered Bruno to this room, which was several degrees warmer than the rest of the hospital, and indistinct apart from the titanic whirlpool. The attendant then stripped Bruno of his gown and seated him in the water, on a steel bench bolted across the tub's center. Once the water was switched on, and a strong current swirled around Bruno's body where he sat on the bench, the attendant took a chair against the far wall to count the minutes. The metal tub vibrated steadily, its noise precluding talk. Afterward Bruno found himself lifted free and laid on a paper-covered table, and his wounds were regreased with a heavy yellow balm different from that which the nurses upstairs employed.

The second day, the attendant observed Bruno watching and volunteered a comparison.

"This stuff was used on napalm cases in Vietnam. I saw it done bunch of times myself."

He was a veteran. It wasn't a surprise. There were so many, both black and white, haunting Berkeley and Oakland, working as school custodians and liquor store clerks, or homeless in wheelchairs like the one in which this man pushed Bruno. Bruno had met them as a small child, too, at the guru's compound in San Rafael, men dressed as hippies who bragged of killing—a sniper's head count, or at close quarters, one swift punch to the throat. Like these men, the attendant's mind seethed with defiance, even as he preferred to imagine he eased through situations like a Buddha, or a jazz musician tempered to a different key and tempo than those around him. Enormous energy was involved in the man's not understanding how much he broadcast violence at a glance.

Bruno, fascinated and terrified, said nothing.

"They didn't use it on civilians back then, it was still an experimental thing," the veteran continued. "Tested on the *battlefield*." He then added, as kindly as might be possible for him, "It's good stuff. Do you good."

The attendant spoke as though he'd somehow prescribed this treatment himself, as a special favor to the boy. But no. Bruno knew no such prerogative existed. The connection of this medicine to whatever the man had witnessed during the war was either fantasy or happenstance.

Bruno, surprising himself, said, "I'm going to go there someday." He hadn't intended this as a provocation, let alone cruelly. He only felt that he craved destinations, anywhere far from where he was. To hear a place named was to have this desire given a focal point.

"What, Vietnam?"

"Yes."

"Don't know why anybody'd wanna do *that*."

In fact, Bruno was destined eventually to spend many months in Ho Chi Minh City and Vung Tau. For now, the remark returned the attendant to silence, though his mind still boiled in Bruno's direction.

Bruno's third time in the tub, the orgasm came unbidden. His erection had been trapped between his leg and the metal seat, which vibrated when the waters spun to their peak. He'd already accustomed himself to the dreamy, amorphous feeling the seat induced, when it culminated in a pitch of sensation he couldn't have known to bargain for. Then the magic vanished, to wonder at. Everything had happened, and nothing at all—nothing, Bruno imagined, that would have given him away, not over the grinding whir of the motorized pool. Yet when the attendant lifted Bruno free again, the man appeared to find something objectionable and applied the yellow gel roughly, with cavalier distaste.

Bruno didn't care. He simply ceased absorbing the veteran's surly charisma, that whole crude turmoil of envy and contempt. He blunted his own shame at exposure, or fear. Any deference toward blacks, inculcated by his mother and her circle, this he shed too. On his next visits to the whirlpool, Bruno walled himself in a silo of bliss. The game was solely between himself and the vibrating tub, while the attendant was quarantined to one side, as if sealed in plastic. Sensing his irrelevance, the man's fits of conversation ceased. The attendant was reduced to a function of the hospital, on a par with the wheelchair and elevator.

Alexander Bruno at eleven had become exquisite.

Still waiting to be proven was what he'd become exquisite for. To what purpose or for whom, beyond himself. Yet after discharge from the hospital, returned into June's care, to his mother's Berkeley, and to the schoolyard of Malcolm X Elementary, Bruno was no longer subject to the unwanted migration of thoughts or feeling across his boundary of self. His gift, once discarded, was a lost toy for which he barely troubled to search. What remained was the sporadic luxury of testing another, as he'd tested the nun. *Hello, can you hear me? No?* The absence of reply was only a relief.

One person in—what? ten million?—might spot him in his hiding place. Well, one had, eventually. Edgar Falk. This, Bruno, lying beneath his mask of bandages now, didn't want to think of. He thought of Falk too much. How often had Bruno rehearsed his trajectory from his exquisite isolation, the sultry implacable hauteur that had conveyed him to Chez Panisse and beyond, to his first passport and flight, to the first of so many private clubs and casino back rooms, to the night a decade ago, at White's in London, when he'd met Falk and become exquisitely enslaved?

No. Bruno, who usually preferred never to recollect at all, now languished in memory of the years after his burn injury. Sixth grade, seventh, Berkeley High. The reminiscences Stolarsky had tried to spur—now they came freely. The changes in his body, so soon after, the wild swift attainments of height and jawline. Hair covered his pubic scar, making it irrelevant. Girls, and women, when Bruno removed his underwear, never saw what he might have feared they'd recoil from. He'd need to point out the scars to have them noticed at all, and then they gained useful sympathy. *See,* he'd joke, *it's like I'm wearing phantom underwear!* Bruno's easy discovery of sex was only matched by the speed with which his teen conquests curdled into ennui. He needed games with a more definite score.

Flashman? Yes, he remembered the books now. And others, traded with boys like Stolarsky as talismans: *The Ginger Man, Fear and Loathing in Las Vegas,* Albert Camus's *The Stranger* and Colin Wilson's *The Outsider.* The books Bruno poached from the hippies' shelves, from the Soup Kitchen's free box, devastated every platitude the hippies claimed to exalt. Flashman had indeed been Bruno's idol, for an instant, sure. Except the point was that Bruno, like Flashman, was his own idol.

Bruno floated loose of June's orbit. The busboys and waiters he fell in with at Spenger's and then at Chez Panisse schooled him in what he'd pretended to know already, things he'd glimpsed in books and films and from Roxy Music and Robert Palmer on MTV. Matters concerning himself and the world and how one might be induced to glide along the surface of the other. The busboys and waiters introduced him to cocaine and to the after-hours life of dining staff, in bars that closed at five and six in the morning. It was there that he'd seen his first real gamblers. He spotted them at pool tables and card games, or at the bar, trading one-upmanship in sly or obvious anecdotes. For the time being Bruno couldn't sort the winners from the losers, and he left them alone. It occurred to him now that by present standards he'd have rated them losers, to a man.

Then again, lying here, how else to rate himself?

It was soon after escaping Spenger's, to the more rarified atmosphere of the Gourmet Ghetto, that Bruno had come under the tutelage of Konrad, a failed ballet dancer, a proud accentless Polish émigré and the café manager at the elite restaurant whose telephone he'd answer with the clearly enunciated words "Cheese Penis." Konrad's months-long siege on the sixteen-year-old Bruno's homosexual virginity was abandoned with the declaration that the boy's looks were a tragic waste; only afterward had Konrad's mentorship begun. Once Konrad showed Bruno how to dress and walk, Bruno didn't know how he'd managed either to that point. When, at an after-hours card game at a house perched on Wildcat Canyon, owned by a dissolute history professor who'd opened his hot tub and billiards room to the

Chez Panisse staff, Bruno had begun with regularity taking money off waiters five and ten years his senior, it was glowering Konrad who'd informed Bruno that poker wasn't a gentleman's game. And yes, it was Konrad who'd introduced him to backgammon. The café manager played the game with a severe focus, though he refused to gamble himself.

Konrad also taught lessons in behaviors others believed unconscious: the correct place in a room to rest one's gaze, and how to arrange one's limbs in parallel and turn one's hips in counterpoint, to make a pleasing, classical composition. Konrad wasn't so much feminizing Bruno—the impression Konrad himself conveyed wasn't feminine—only encouraging him to be aware of how he could make his newly strapping body both unthreatening and fascinating. In many ways it was as if Konrad were extending the principles Bruno had discovered in the hospital. Where Bruno had sealed himself within an internal distance, Konrad taught him that same distance could be externalized, worn as a cloak of unapproachability, rendering you hypnotic to others. The result was to induce the same longing you concealed.

The deeper magic was this: In the process of layering performance onto the outside of his container, Bruno could forget what the container disguised. All and anything was eligible for this amnesiac relief.

For years after Konrad had been dismissed from Chez Panisse, and departed Berkeley overnight, Bruno felt the café manager's tutorials as a somatic language rustling inside his body. Yet until this second recuperation, under the long night of gauze and bandages, he'd forgotten even Konrad's name. Now it was returned to him, like excavating a single jigsaw puzzle piece from beneath a sofa cushion. Could Konrad be found, Bruno wondered? Was he still alive, or an AIDS casualty? But no. The impulse was hopeless, sentimental. Bruno had done nothing more than regain a lost name. It meant nothing.

Why had Stolarsky wanted to save Bruno?

What was his life for?

Bruno had nothing but his questions. His chest shuddered. Air wheezed and whistled in the plastic tube and Bruno knew it was himself he heard, that beneath his bandages the numbed flesh of his face convulsed in sorrow. Whether his ducts could produce tears was anyone's guess. He wouldn't feel them if they could.

Yet all this, ancient formless memory and grief, was preferable to the alternative: remembering the surgery as if through Dr. Behringer's eyes.

II

Day and night, sleep and waking, past and present, all had lost their definition, until one morning Bruno was awakened by a Japanese nurse. He knew she was Japanese because she said, "My name is Nurse Oshiro, I'm from Japan"; he knew it was morning because she declared it so. She then removed his breathing tube and told him to swallow. With that, though his eyes remained bandaged, Bruno rose from his miasma. It was as if Oshiro had thrown a line into his well of dread and memory and drawn him up toward the light—though not so far that he could see.

Attempting speech, he produced a shredded whisper and a surfeit of pain.

"You want to write me a note?" asked Oshiro.

"Yes." The word came out wrecked. She understood nonetheless.

She brought him a small plastic slate and a blunt marker. "You write what you need to say. I'll wipe it clean."

WHERE IS MY DOCTOR?

"Your doctor's been here three times. He talked with you, you don't remember." He felt her seize the slate, and return it to him. He wrote again.

AM I DYING?

"It's a big success, everybody told you already. We told you lots of times. This time, you remember."

Oshiro's tone was ceaselessly chipper and admonitory. It gradually dawned on Bruno that she bore some special authority in his case. She'd been appointed his taskmaster, to teach him to swallow, to suck from a straw, and to cooperate with the management of his bedridden body, which, according to Oshiro, the nurses and orderlies were tired of negotiating during his long fugue. He must learn to help in their efforts to change his sheets and shift his bedpan.

"See," said Oshiro, "you're not too lazy!"

IT HURTS.

"You have to move, it's good for you. Soon you'll walk to the bathroom. Tomorrow you'll eat."

Next he endured Oshiro's removal of the heart monitoring stickers and redundant IV lines, the litter strewn everywhere on his body. Then, horribly, she dethreaded the catheter from his penis. Bruno's reward for answering Oshiro's beckoning him back to life was to undergo one painful and humbling effort after another.

Not that Bruno imagined he had any choice in the matter.

"Tomorrow we will change your bandage, too," she said, when he was exhausted.

MY EYES?

"Your eyes stay closed tomorrow, the gauze stays on. Doctor has to see your eyes."

AM I BLIND?

"I told you, Mr. Bruno, everything went good, you're very lucky. You should be happy."

I AM HAPPY.

"Good, now go to sleep."

III

Another day passed under the fresh bandage before Behringer came to examine Bruno's incisions and invite him to open his eyes.

This was a spell of wretched boredom. Bruno had started sitting in a chair beside his bed. After permitting himself to be guided to the bathroom once or twice, he'd begun shrugging off the attendants and nurses to grope his way there himself—it wasn't so far. His voice returned, a rasp but recognizable. He'd eaten, gelatin at first, and broth, then as swallowing grew less painful and he gained confidence in the disconcerted muscles of his face, soggy sandwiches and vegetables cooked to a paste. Nothing he ate, however, conveyed any taste at all, and Bruno made lavish complaints to whomever presented the portions of flavorless goo.

His irritation gave him courage. They switched on a television in his room, and Bruno demanded they switch it off. It was replaced by nothing, by the sounds of the machines and the nurses in the corridor and at the station at the end of the corridor, sometimes the sound of another patient's doctors in discussion with that patient's visitors. None of this diverted him, but neither did it bewilder him as the television had. For one thing, he could command they close his door and leave him alone; sometimes they complied. The other nurses had accepted his preference for Oshiro, and so they handled him lightly, with minimal talk, navigating his petulance as if he were a blind boorish lord, though no matter his complaints, they never apologized for anything. Increasingly they ignored him. For this, he began to abuse them under his breath, in arch tones, like a blind boorish lord. Of course it was Bruno who owed the apology; Oshiro informed him of this.

Night lasted forever. Bruno believed he never slept.

His second hospitalization revealed none of the mysterious depth or savor of his first. There were no whirlpool orgasms, no nuns to perplex. In these stark days, even his grasp of those recollections, which had overrun his first hours after the surgery, slipped away. What did such tatters of memory amount to? Now Bruno could picture the green, pocket-size paperback of Flashman that he'd carried in his trench-coat pocket—so what? He wouldn't stoop to retrieve it if he saw it on the street, so faint was his curiosity.

Oshiro prepared the patient, and his room, for Behringer's arrival. The ripple of quickened attention preceding a major doctor's entry to the ward had become familiar to Bruno.

"He's taking off your bandage today."

"Who, God?"

"You're a foolish man."

"He who shall not be named, but comes bearing scissors?"

"It's important to make the room dark, Mr. Bruno. Your eyes will be very sensitive."

"So you hope. Or not sensitive at all. I could be free to stare at the sun. Or sleep with the lights on."

"No, Mr. Bruno, they tested your eyes."

"That's good enough, then. I have eyes that pass tests. We can leave the bandages on." Bruno felt on the brink of being driven from a sanctuary, into the unknown.

"Tsk tsk." At her most censorious, Oshiro resorted to syllables, clicking sounds, as if she were scouring out a puppy's soiled crate.

At that moment Bruno felt the man enter the room—in fact, understood that the man had already entered, had indeed been listening to Bruno's moronic bantering for who knew how long.

"Sure, leave 'em on, if you want. But you'd be cheating us both of a gander at my masterpiece."

It was the voice of Bruno's champion and nemesis, the man who'd murdered his face. A man who addressed his quarry always in the superior and ebullient tone of a being utterly apart from his species. He *was* a god, perhaps, or at least a kind of medical Santa Claus. The air had dropped, seeming cooled and depressurized instantaneously, as if the room had been ejected like a capsule into space. Or possibly this was the air of the operating room; the neurosurgeon carried it around with him, a barometric and refrigerated wrongness.

"Did I frighten you?"

Bruno had raised his hands, involuntarily, lifting his IV tubing with them, his palms facing outward as if to fend off savagery from the direction of the voice.

"Frighten me? No . . . no. You surprised me."

"It's Noah Behringer."

"Of course."

"I heard you forgot my earlier visits."

"Yes."

"Well, the resection was a triumph. I can answer any questions if you like. We'll have a follow-up MRI, of course. But I took out your tumor, Alex."

"Nurse Oshiro explained it to me."

"I mean, I'm *thrilled* with what we did in there." The neurosurgeon seemed in search of adoration, a victory lap. Bruno couldn't be bothered. He rotated his raised hands slightly, miming an examination of them through the baffling thickness that bound his face, and which so far as he knew was all that was holding it together.

"What will I see when you remove the bandage?"

"Ha! Aside from me and your beautiful nurse, you mean? Who knows? Light sensitivity shouldn't bug you more than an hour or two. There could be some lingering fuzziness. My only concern is that the optic nerve may retain a phantom image of what you called your *blot*. Something like the visual-field equivalent of tinnitus. It may take some time for the receptors to reeducate themselves, now that they're relieved of the pressure, but they're adept little guys, receptors. Should we find out?"

Bruno soothed himself inside the blizzard of terminology and what passed for doctor wit. He lowered his hands and allowed Behringer to approach his face. Oshiro too. Her touch was known to Bruno, hands that worked with the same brisk chiding precision as her talk. Surgeon and nurse clipped and fussed at his edges, then levitated the weight of the bandages, like a clay mask, from the raw sealed mystery of what lay beneath. Bruno's eyelids remained shut beneath individual pads of gauze, around the periphery of which air now circulated, awakening the scourged contours of his former skin.

Behringer carried on intermittently jabbering—"You're healing beautifully," and so forth. Bruno barely heard. He felt himself rise through veils of stupefaction in the direction of a world vaster and more blazed by light than he'd recalled. He'd been a cave creature, sealed in mud and measuring distance in pebbles, in grains. The world was huge.

There remained some miles to cross to make contact with it. He still wasn't freed, Bruno now understood. The hands continued. Behringer merrily clipped and snipped, while Oshiro, teasing gauze membranes from beneath his eyes, opened him like a flower.

At the last layer it felt as if they'd lifted Bruno's nose and cheeks away to expose his uncooked skull. He felt no pain, though he was surely still dealt numbing medications through the vents of his inner elbows. Was this cultivating brutal addictions Bruno would need to sweat off later? He supposed he'd be grateful in any case.

Bruno thought of the coins placed on a dead man's eyes: The procedure was reversed now. Oshiro relieved his lids' burden, then told him to wait. She gently rinsed a superglue of sleep gunk from his lashes, painting saline with her cotton swabs downward across his cheeks as if bathing him in tears. He rolled them open.

Blurriness, yes, and double vision, until he could rein the split scene together, a mild muscular effort, still painless. He did retain a version of the blot, one which hovered translucently at the center of sight, a thing seen but not seen. Glitches peeled at the rim of his vision's field, too—as if the blot had been shattered, then swept to the far horizon of his gaze. Yet none of this was impairment enough to prevent the ruin of his romance with the formerly unseen world. Bruno's sight worked well enough—too well—to deny the crushing fact that there was nothing worth seeing.

God? Not even Santa Claus. Bruno had been mutilated by a pompous hippie in a corduroy suit. Oshiro was round-faced, short, pleasant, and a totally inadequate harbor for erotic fantasies Bruno had no clue he'd constructed until the instant they collapsed. The two figures stood in a room the size and vitality of a faded Polaroid. Bruno had been laboriously revived into a world unworthy of the name. If it were a page in a magazine, he'd have turned it.

"Don't touch," commanded Oshiro. Bruno's intubated hands had again drifted up, near his face.

"So, your eyes work," said Behringer. "I can see you're tracking."

"Tracking?"

"Be patient if there's some overlay, or floaters."

"Can I define you as a floater?"

"That depends. How many noses do I have?"

"The same number as you have beards, and half the number of your eyes." Bruno was tired already.

"He's joking! And he looks great, doesn't he?" Behringer's heartiness seemed not so much false as slipshod. And irrelevant. The surgeon had no purpose here. He'd had his way with Bruno and could muster nothing better than boorish gloating.

"I can just imagine," said Bruno. "My mouth feels like you sewed it on upside down."

"Ah, well, heh, we didn't actually *remove* your entire mouth. Sure, you've got some healing to do, but the latest stitching techniques are miraculous. The nurse is going to show you how to maintain the incisions to minimize scarring, you can do it yourself—"

"Does it involve a whirlpool?"

"Sorry?"

Bruno waved his hand, without shifting it from where it lay on his gown-clad thigh. He didn't wish to be corrected again.

"Do you want to use a mirror?" Behringer spoke gently for the first time. Bruno suspected this meant it was a bad idea. He'd already glanced into the rounded black eye of the TV mounted high in the corner, which displayed the same dire Polaroid, only reversed: two solicitous pygmies before an elongated straw man, one who lay vein-sucked by an array of devices. The features topping the straw man's withered form, too minuscule to examine in the screen's reflection, were easily imagined. A former face, crazy-quilted into a semblance.

"No, thank you," Bruno said to the offer of the mirror. His jigsawed exterior was the least of his problems. The vision he'd suppressed came to claim him now: his memory of his surgery as he'd suffered it through the anesthesia. Bruno had seen his own face converted into a flesh culvert, the root-gully voided by a toppled tree. He'd undergone a dream-voyage between two milky planets he was fairly positive had been his own unhinged eyeballs.

How to explain this to Behringer? "There's something I need to tell you," Bruno began.

"Of course."

"I can . . . read minds . . . again. I can read yours."

"That's terrific. How about scent? Can you read smells?"

"Sorry? Smells? No, nothing."

"See, I heard you were complaining about the food—that's less a tongue thing than a nose thing. Not that with the food here you're missing much."

"It mostly tastes like rubber or shit."

"It mostly is! No more phantom barbecue odors? You were babbling about pork ribs before you went in."

"No . . . no."

"We didn't damage the olfactory nerve, I don't think. The 'old factory,' I call it. Sometimes it takes a while, like a system reboot—"

"You don't understand. I watched you operate."

"Well, that would be impossible, but anesthesia can provoke some wild hallucinations."

"I saw the whole thing."

"Your eyes were, uh, let me just suggest they were securely out of commission."

"I didn't need my eyes. I saw it through yours." Bruno couldn't stop himself. He'd grown more certain of his miracle and catastrophe, and the need to make Behringer grasp it. No matter how flippantly he spoke, the surgeon was party to Bruno's disjointing.

"Nurse, will you excuse us? Mr. Bruno and I should talk alone, I think."

It seemed absurd to require Oshiro to leave the room, she was already so diminished. But so was Behringer and the room. Doctor and nurse, a pair of canceled postage stamps on a scrap of envelope. Had Bruno grown enormous, or was the hospital so small? He observed that though the surgeon had relied upon Oshiro to rehabilitate his victim, Behringer couldn't recall her name. Bruno, for his part, wanted to object that Oshiro should be allowed to stay, but couldn't find the strength. He watched her go, the only witness to what the bearded imp had done to him and still might do.

But no, Behringer was a reputed famous healer, he'd operated out of charity, munificently. He and Bruno were meant to be on the same team. These detrimental effects were wholly unintended. Bruno only needed to explain.

"When I was a child . . ." he began, slowly. Each word dredged from the past should be essential. What had happened was so strange. He'd have to forgo irony and indirection completely. "When I was five, I lived with my mother in an encampment in San Rafael—"

"I see."

"The adults around me . . . this was, you know, the seventies . . ." No, this wasn't the approach, he saw he'd lose his audience. A surgeon after all, not a priest or shrink, not a confessor. A surgeon's million-dollar minutes, ticking away. "But that isn't important. There used to not be any boundary, between myself and other people—"

"Yes?"

"You've probably heard this kind of thing before. I could read minds."

"Oh, sure."

"I mean, it wasn't a pleasant thing."

"I imagine it would be sheer hell."

This was easier than Bruno had bargained. "Well, yes, actually. I developed some defenses—"

"Who wouldn't?"

"Dr. Behringer, did you . . . keep what you took from me?"

"Keep?"

"The thing."

"Oh, huh, it doesn't really come out in one coherent piece. The opposite, actually. But for biopsy, sure, we kept segments."

"Right, well, I ask because, when I speak of my defenses, it appears you took one out. The blot. I know you meant well."

"I'm not following you."

"I developed the blot as a barricade. When you said it was pressing on things, deforming their function—apparently it was meant to restrict the kind of thought leakage that I suffered during the surgery."

Behringer retreated from the bedside. Brow furrowed, he clamped his hand over his lips and beard. The postage stamp now was a commemorative one, a depiction of Sigmund Freud in slippers, pacing in his study.

"I need it back," said Bruno, wishing to be absolutely clear.

"Yes, we've seen more of this," said Behringer, as if talking to himself. "It's the power of suggestion, of course. The notion of intraoperative consciousness has pervaded the popular imagination in the form of horror movies and television talk shows, but as with so many popular nightmares, it's much rarer than anyone realizes."

"I had it when I was a child," said Bruno.

"Intraoperative consciousness?"

"Mind reading."

"Ah. But, Alex, in a procedure like yours, we monitored your nervous activity by means of what's called 'evoked potentials'—that's what the surgical neurologist was there to do. We *know* whether you were in or out. You were out. Zonked, more dead than alive. In fact, it's the intensity of the anesthetic fugue that explains your bewilderment and paranoia—that, and the steroidal regimen, which I'm going to restrict for you now, beginning immediately."

"You listened to Jimi Hendrix."

Behringer looked at him sharply, then issued a single laugh, one so abrupt and bitter in tone that it was nearly a shout of rebuke. "Very good! You saw the poster in my consulting office."

"I need back what you took from me."

"It isn't there to give back. And I wouldn't—put it back. I can't believe I'm even answering these questions of yours, Alex. You're suffering from a marvelous delusion. Unprecedented, actually, in my experience."

"Listen, Doctor. Will you just do one thing for me?"

"That depends what you mean."

"My things. When I was admitted for surgery, the nurses gathered up my clothes and possessions. I was told they'd travel with me to my recovery room—"

"Yes," said Behringer. "Of course! That's so." He seemed unnaturally delighted by this prospect. "Let's find them!" The surgeon moved to the narrow closet beside the bathroom. In Bruno's unsteady passages in and out of the toilet, wheeling his tubes on a metal stand, it hadn't occurred to him to try the closet's handle. He lacked the energy to spare.

"Well, look at that," said Behringer. The closet revealed Bruno's clothes, neatly folded onto shelves, apart from the sweatshirt, which hung, falsely formal. On the highest shelf, his cell phone and charger, his wooden backgammon set, a ziplock baggie containing balled dollar bills, change, and the keys to the apartment at the Jack London Apartments, and a twice-folded *San Francisco Chronicle* he'd been reading in the surgery intake waiting room, a week or a lifetime earlier. Behringer treated this dreary cache as a revelation. "That's the ticket! You need to get up and out of this place. You'll feel more like your old self in your own clothes—"

"Those aren't my clothes."

"You don't recognize them?" The surgeon sounded giddy and panicked at once.

"No, I was wearing them, they're just not really my clothes."

Behringer presented Bruno's phone as if it were a prize in a game show. "You want to call your friends?"

"I don't have any."

"Your pal in Berkeley—"

"Not right now. There, you see that wooden case?"

"This?"

"Thank you." Bruno took it between his trembling hands, rattled it slightly, confirming its contents. He unclasped the top.

"Are we going to play a game?"

The Sigmund Freud figure standing before Bruno was ersatz. Nevertheless, he was all Bruno had to work with. Bruno concentrated himself on the fact that it was this toy person who had split him open, that indeed, he'd been sent across the ocean to meet the one man capable of that act, and therefore also capable of reversing it. Everything was circular. In much the same way, it was in Bruno's childhood hospitalization that he'd obviously gained the protection of the blot—though how it had been induced in him, by salve or whirlpool or orgasm, presently mystified him—and now it was in his second that he'd been robbed of it! But Bruno couldn't afford to dwell long on the perversities of his fate.

He widened the case just enough to draw out the Berlin paving stone. The daubs indicating the pips of the die had blackened and flaked. He doubted Behringer would notice them, and just as well, since the surgeon might be concerned about biological contamination. Then again, it was Bruno's own blood, in fact had seeped from his nose and so would be restored to its right place, in his head. But this was all too much to explain.

Bruno held the cobblestone out to Behringer. "Use this."

"What is it?"

"That isn't important." Bruno spoke carefully. "Use it to replace what you took."

"What I took?"

"Put it here." Bruno lifted his tubes, to draw a finger just short of contact with the bridge of his nose, or whatever disaster now dwelled instead between his eyes. "I want it put back."

"Put back? That was never in you!"

"It's the right size. It's the right . . . thing." *Re-install Berlin,* he wished to say, but he couldn't risk confusing the neurosurgeon.

"Remarkable," muttered Behringer.

"It was a simple mistake," said Bruno. "I don't hold it against you."

"We'll have to continue this conversation another time," said Behringer weakly.

"When?" Bruno felt no hope of seeing the pixilated clown-doctor regain his stature, let alone reclaim the wild confidence that had allowed him to inside-out Bruno's head in the first place. Bruno wondered if he'd erred mentioning Jimi Hendrix, the evidence of Bruno's mind reading which had seemingly left the neurosurgeon irreversibly rattled.

"When you're feeling more like yourself."

"That's the whole point. I feel too much like myself."

"Time is the great healer," said Behringer, in a tone suggesting he knew he'd offered up the greatest lie ever told.

"Please—" said Bruno.

But the rapidly diminishing figure opened what appeared to be a tiny flap in the corner of the Polaroid—Bruno supposed it was actually the door of the hospital room—and wordlessly exited the picture.

IV

The face—you'd call it a face, certainly—wasn't bad. It wasn't Alexander Bruno as he'd been before, and it wasn't not-Bruno, either, but a fascinating amalgam, flesh turned dough, swollen and mottled, here and there puffy or sagging, in other cases lightly flaking, and everywhere joined in sections to adhere to his skeleton's contour. This puzzle-putty grew increasingly sensible, alert to the fiery caterpillar of the incision knitting it together, and operable by his old and instinctive muscular reactions. He could make the face smile, for instance, without much pain. Oshiro, who used a six-inch cotton swab to stripe Neosporin along the length of the seams, encouraged it. Bruno smiled for her at least daily.

He used a mirror to examine the face until he grew bored with the effects. When surveyed up close, these approximated NASA stills of a blasted moonscape. Meanwhile, if he allowed Oshiro to hold the mirror at a certain distance the reflection offered a bleary approximate self, a stand-in he found barely worth the effort. There was no right proximity for his self-seeing. Any close-up was all useless turmoil, while the wide shots were too generic to tell him anything at all.

Should he mourn his beauty? Bruno found it difficult to bother. He'd never doubted his looks nor their effect on others, yet a life spent hanging on the fall of a die or the turn of a card had inured him to the abrupt loss of what was never earned in the first place. The thing that mattered, enduring such disaster, was one's comportment: not what lay on the table between yourself and another player, but one's inner mask. If he followed this logic to its conclusion, Bruno might be waiting for a new deal, another pair of numbers, a next face. What he glimpsed in Oshiro's mirror was just a bad roll. He might have to pay now for a run of facial luck that had gone decades. If it was the gambler's fallacy that luck could be cumulative—well, he was a gambler.

Or again, Bruno might be dead already and not know it. If he was dead, he could live with that.

If only Behringer had found a way to mutilate his name as well as his features, Bruno could pass from the small purgatory of his recovery anonymous, broke, yet by the logic of his destruction indebted to no one, including and perhaps most crucially his former self. Bruno's expectations that Behringer could do anything for him besides save his life—a paltry gesture, it turned out!—had collapsed. This freed Bruno from contrasts of before and after. Where he presently dwelled, this archipelago of bathroom, television, and gurney, notions of fortune or beauty seemed fatally preposterous. When Oshiro had trained him to apply his own balms, and to massage the anesthesia cramps from his own thighs and calves, when he'd been weaned from his last tube and his digestion could tolerate any old garbage, not just hospital garbage, Bruno felt ready to slink off ungratefully into the faceless crowd. He wouldn't beg another plane ticket, in fact wouldn't accept one if offered. He might live under a bridge.

On Bruno's tenth day in the hospital, Oshiro began preparing him for something, though she wouldn't say what. Behringer, perhaps spooked by their last encounter, hadn't visited again. Could anyone besides the neurosurgeon sign his discharge? Oshiro wouldn't say. Yet she was shooing Bruno like a cat to the door.

"I'm not ready," he told her, when she insisted he dress in his street clothes and visit the dayroom, a dry run for expulsion. "I'm still sick."

"No, the doctor fixed you, Mr. Bruno."

"People stay in the hospital for weeks or months after a surgery like mine."

She shook her head. "That's the old way. You'll recover better at home. You stayed too long already."

"I have no home." This was a simple enough declaration. In another life Bruno might have uttered it across a backgammon board, with brittle vanity, to the envy of a club man who'd only dream of saying the same.

"With your friends."

A shudder went through him. "What friends?"

"A mister and missus. They've been looking after you. The missus was here while you were sleeping."

"Miss Harpaz?"

"Yes, that's the one. Nice lady. They're taking you home tomorrow."

With that his despondency collapsed on itself, a dead star turning black hole. He'd been kidding himself. His ruined face, his shredded costume of defenses, these were sufficient only to this poor room. Sufficient only to the witness of Oshiro. Bruno had standards, after all. He was a terrible snob. His hands flew to his face, as if to contain what had ruptured. His hands weren't enough. He felt the grease of his jigsaw-stitchery imprint to his palms.

"I . . . can't be seen."

"Don't be foolish, Mr. Bruno. You look good."

"Never. I won't even go to the dayroom."

"You must do this, please. Your discharge is tomorrow. Your friend will come."

"I forbid her to." Bruno's claim of authority was surely absurd. He had none. Hearing Tira Harpaz's name introduced into the pale void of his recovery made Bruno realize he'd been working to forget it—Tira's name, and Keith Stolarsky's, and the conundrums that lay behind them. Why was Tira coming, and not Stolarsky, if Stolarsky was supposed to be his friend? What was Stolarsky's motive in paying for the surgery? Only amusement? Did Stolarsky have such surplus lying around? It was possible. It was always possible. Money pointlessly pooled, to extents few believed, few who'd never been in the practice, as Bruno had, of siphoning the pools. Yet if Stolarsky was so wealthy, why was he so juvenile, so squalid, so unrenovated? Where was his entourage? Money magnetized flattery and avarice, drew to itself toadies, under names like *adviser* or *secretary*, those who'd stalk the perimeter, jealous of the incursion of others like themselves. What was Keith Stolarsky's stake in Alexander Bruno? And why had he been jovially shoving his girlfriend into Bruno's lap?

Perhaps Bruno would find out. With the blot obliterated, his childhood porousness restored, Bruno might find Stolarsky's motives naked to him. Yet Bruno could only think of how he'd be naked to Stolarsky in turn.

"I need a mask," he said to Oshiro, in terror.

"What?"

"For my face. For my head, a covering of some kind. I won't see anyone, or leave this room, until I'm protected somehow."

Oshiro stood and stared, a rare heartbeat of stillness in her campaign forever to be adjusting, cleaning, or correcting some part of Bruno's setup. *Her* face, round and smooth, was a sort of mask. Sadly plain, forgettable, the wrong sex, yet Bruno could envy its impassivity. Could Oshiro imagine how it felt to gaze out through his own detonated minefield?

Her indefatigable pragmatism cut in. "Would you like to try a post-surgical mask?"

"There is such a thing?"

"Certainly. They call this a compression garment. It's made of fabric that can breathe, a very good device. You see this mostly with plastic surgery patients."

"Do they . . . cover the whole face?"

"With holes for your eyes and mouth, nostrils. You don't want that, we can't help you. Then you better hide your head under a blanket, Mr. Bruno."

"No, no, I want that, very much."

"I have to get a referral from the attending doctor, but it shouldn't be a problem."

"Please."

"I'll bring a selection. Will you promise to visit the dayroom?"

"I promise."

He felt her relief. Bruno had absolved Oshiro of his existential conundrum, in favor of a task to accomplish. The patient wants masking? Let him be masked. In this, the nurse's impulse wasn't so different from Behringer's: to hustle Bruno into street clothes and be shed of him. Bruno had to grow accustomed to his new role as an unwelcome guest. It mirrored his earlier life, in which he'd made his living as a form of human decoration, a perfume or mood to amplify an evening. Now he had the power to improve a scene by exiting it.

Oshiro, wizard of competence, cleared any paperwork hurdles at the nursing station, and within the hour returned to present him with a small array of the masks. These resembled Mexican wrestlers' costumes, or items from a masochist's toy kit, only purged of florid decoration in favor of the uniform sallow color of a Band-Aid, with neatly tailored Velcro fasteners for ease of removal. They roused some feeling of solace in Bruno. He allowed himself to touch them, the fine antibacterial mesh, both grainy and smooth, and warming to the touch, like the skin of a robot designed to soothe the elderly or dying.

While he browsed options Oshiro lay his folded clothes and sweatshirt across his knees, and placed his crappy sneakers at the bed's side, insisting in her quiet way on his keeping his promise of a dress rehearsal. She also withdrew his cell phone and charger, plugging it in within reach at his bedside table, and moved his backgammon set and the folded *Chronicle* to the shelf beneath the drawer there, to join the paving stone. Everything he'd brought to the hospital, a kit for reentry to a world in which he possessed barely more. In Berkeley, in the apartment he'd been loaned out of pity, there waited his shoes and tuxedo, and a few spare *ABIDE* shirts.

"This one." He found the mask with the narrowest eyeholes. The gaps at the bridge of his nose would reveal only glimpses of a jigsaw-self.

Oshiro had learned when best to goose Bruno and when to revert to the solemnity of ceremony. She silently guided his hands to fasten the mask, aiding and instructing him simultaneously—everything was homework for Bruno's next phase, in which he'd be nursing himself. She drew him to the mirror, placing his clothes in his hands as she did and shutting him into the small bathroom to change. Awarding him the dignity of modesty was another milestone—days earlier, Oshiro had bathed him neck to toe with a rough white washcloth.

Seeing himself in the mirror, Bruno realized why the mask had offered consolation: It recalled Madchen, her mute mouth behind zippered leather. He slipped into his T-shirt and began immediately to abide. Madchen had been the counterforce, the angel who'd attempted to intervene on the Kladow ferry, if it hadn't been in fact too late. Every person he'd encountered since then had conspired to hurl him into this dungeon, beginning with the monstrous jazz-loving German real-estate speculator, his opponent the night he'd gone to Charité—what was his name? At first Bruno could only think of Bix Beiderbecke.

Wolf-Dirk Köhler, of course. How could he forget? The mask, in containing and hiding Bruno, also restored his memories. And Köhler had been another pygmy. For that was part of being reminded of Madchen, in the mirror—the mask sat atop a full-size human. Straightening his shoulders, Bruno towered in the little restroom, as the bottomless girl in the mask had made a homunculus of her supposed enslaver. Behind the closed door Bruno could hear Oshiro scurrying, preparing his room, moving like a rat in a box. Readying him to be discharged by the rat-pygmy Behringer, into the care of the rat-pygmies Stolarsky and Harpaz. Never trust anyone shorter than 160 centimeters; if the axiom hadn't existed before now, Bruno had just coined it. What a relief to be thinking clearly again. The cell phone was charged. He'd return Madchen's calls. Not here, though. Not in this place.

The mask was good, but it wasn't enough. In the hard overhead light he made out too much, at the eyeholes and around the rim of his mouth. His ears, too, though they hadn't been carved up and reassembled, looked doofy jutting from the mask. A halo in his visual field, that phantom-limb version of the blot, only heightened the effect. He opened the door, just slightly.

"My sweatshirt, please."

"Are you cold?"

"No."

The nurse handed over the sweatshirt and he closed the door again. "Are you okay?" Her voice was anxious and he understood that the balance had shifted once he'd donned his clothes. He had leverage. In fact, Oshiro was the penitent now.

"Please intercept my friend, I don't want to see her today. No visitors."

"If you wish, Mr. Bruno."

"And tomorrow, I'll meet her downstairs. I don't want her coming up to the room, do you understand?"

"Yes."

Bruno had always found the gamblers who veiled themselves behind mirrored shades and sweatshirt hoods laughable. Their feeble armor a kind of fundamental tell. Unabombers, that was Edgar Falk's derisive nickname. Now, however, the hood cloaked Bruno's ears and put the rest in shadow, shrouding the pale mask as though in fog and distance. It changed, from something baldly medical, to an apparition. When he stepped from the bathroom, Oshiro stepped back.

Behringer had been right, in fact. These *were* his clothes.

•

The neurosurgeon made one final appearance, at the last possible moment. He signed Bruno's discharge—though, as Oshiro had indicated, any attending physician could have done it. Indeed, Behringer left it to a younger doctor to ask Bruno to remove his mask, to make a final examination of his incisions, and to test certain muscular actions, the rotation of the eyes as they followed a penlight through the air, the mime show of chewing and swallowing Bruno had by this time performed a dozen times before.

Behringer presented himself only when Bruno was dressed again and remasked, with his tiny stash of possessions bagged on the bed. A wheelchair had materialized in the corridor outside the room. Bruno knew Oshiro would insist on wheeling him into the elevator and to the curb, where Tira Harpaz waited for him; it might even be required in the hospital's protocols. It was Oshiro's last moment, and Bruno had no motivation to deny it to her. She'd moved to the door, and out, when Behringer entered the room.

"I couldn't be happier," said Behringer, his tone suggesting the precise opposite.

"To wash your hands of me?"

Behringer ignored him. "Your recovery is exemplary. In my notes I'm chalking up any stray delusional episode to a derangement associated with abreaction to the steroid regimen. Post-anesthetic trauma is a very real thing. But everything in the nurse's observations suggests a nice turnaround. I've no doubt you'll thrive in an outpatient recovery. Is the mask a comfort?"

"I require it."

"You don't! But wear it if it makes you feel better. You'll freak out cats and children. You're freaking me out right now."

"I didn't have a delusional episode."

"No?" Behringer's tone was falsely merry. In fact he seemed on the verge of crisis, as if any interruption to his filibuster would be fatal.

"You couldn't remember my name."

"It's right here on the chart! Alexander Bruno."

"In the midst of the procedure, I meant."

"Your hostility fascinates me. Who knows, it might seem entirely reasonable from your perspective. Still, no matter what you say, I'm going to claim you as one of my triumphs, Mr. Bruno. I'm one hundred percent delighted with what happened in there."

Bruno saw that Behringer had nowhere better to be, or he'd have been there. For all the deference the nurses and younger doctors gave the neurosurgeon, this maestro of disaster was otherwise essentially a thumb-twiddler, helpless to occupy himself until a next disaster strolled through his door. He'd come here killing time, neither concerned for Bruno nor seriously engaged with the puzzle his patient had presented when they last spoke. Still, for reasons of his own, Bruno wished to put Behringer in mind of it again.

"You imagined yourself as a baseball pitcher."

"Sorry?"

"On the mound at the Oakland Coliseum. Pitching a no-hitter. I don't know what it meant to you."

"Perhaps you're right," said Behringer, after a moment. "That sounds like me. But I suggest we discuss it in a few weeks. Kate'll call you to schedule a follow-up."

Behringer held out his hand. From appearances, he'd made himself impervious again. This was obviously a generic capacity, drawn out of the doctor's kit bag. Bruno, weary of probing fissures in the surgeon's vanity, accepted his hand clasp.

"I'll look forward to that," Bruno said. In fact he never saw Noah Behringer again.

Thirty-Two

I

Crossing the refurbished bridge for a second time, in Tira Harpaz's Volvo, Bruno saw he'd been wrong. The redundant span was already spidered with cranes, paused in the act of unmaking the gray steel armature. Since that day, weeks ago now, when Bruno was first retrieved from the airport, the demolition crews had severed the abandoned portion at both ends from the land. The pilings nearest Treasure Island and Oakland were reduced to bare pillars, sentinels in the water. The span that remained was unreachable unless by helicopter or parachute.

It was an error of sight. He'd been working around the blot, in denial, guessing. Now the former blot was flooded with light and information, his interior eyelid stripped away. Journeying from the hospital, Bruno found himself in the grip of a world both riotous and raw. The morning's light danced on the spine of the new bridge, which towered like the guts of a cosmic piano. The same light that agitated the picture windows of the gaudy homes tumbled so recklessly into the seams of the Oakland hills.

The hospital dayroom, the afternoon before, hadn't confronted him with such marvels.

It might be a rebus of Bruno's cleaved self. His obliterated past, charismatic and pitiable, an island at sea. Unreachable. Bruno had been turned from Tira to study the bridge; she might think he was ignoring her. But driver and passenger proceeded in silence, reaching the long eastern causeway before she finally spoke.

"Tell me something," she said.

"Tell you what?"

"Am I dreaming?"

"I might not be qualified to say."

"Because this all feels like the weirdest fucking dream I ever had. No offense, but I just wonder if you realize, Alexander, how it feels from my side. I dropped off a *person,* a new friend, someone at least I felt I could *talk to* for a change, a sort of weird sad gorgeous man who supposedly hung out with Keith when they were kids, though I can't really tell if you *like* Keith, or ever did, actually. So, anyway, I dropped this guy off at the hospital for some kind of life-saving operation that I don't understand *at all.* And I don't mind saying I've been thinking about you a lot. And now the day comes and I've picked up some—I don't know, what are you, like, the Ghost Rider or something? What are you hiding in there?"

"The Ghost Rider?"

"You know, a flaming skull, that type of thing."

"I don't have a flaming skull."

"I know that, for God's sake. It was just a figure of speech."

" 'Have you or haven't you got a flaming skull' isn't a figure of speech I happen to be familiar with, pardon me, I've been abroad and I missed a certain amount of—"

"Shut up, Alexander. Why didn't you let me visit you yesterday?"

"You've done enough."

It wasn't impossible to bruise her. Her tone showed evidence of it now. "I was in San Francisco for some other stuff."

"Good, I'd hate to waste your time."

"Fuck off. You want to get high?" As if oblivious to their presence in five lanes of zooming traffic along Berkeley's waterfront, Tira fished in her purse, which lay sagged on the cup holders between them, and pulled out a fat joint. Driving with one hand, she fished again for a lighter, then made several angry, failed attempts, the joint braced in scowl-tightened lips, to spark the tip. Bruno took it from her hand and steadied the flame to the paper for ignition.

"Have some."

"I doubt I have a choice." The car's airspace had filled instantly.

She drew again, then passed it to him.

"I'm probably on enough drugs as it is," he said. Oshiro had filled his prescriptions at the hospital's in-house pharmacy. They sat bagged in Tira's backseat, with a package of the long swabs, gauze, and ointment for incision self-care; a baggie containing balled-up paper money, coins, and keys; Bruno's backgammon set and, hidden inside, his stone die. The drugs had been courtesy, once more, of Stolarsky's largesse—Stolarsky, who couldn't be bothered to retrieve Bruno from the hospital.

"Well, put that out, then," Tira was saying. "Stuff nowadays gets you too fucked up to put two words together, if you take more than a couple of tokes."

"Why didn't Keith come?" Bruno snuffed the lit end between his fingertips, a teenage practice he'd never shed. Painful then, and painful now. He'd adopted it from a certain Spenger's dishwasher with an El Cerrito white-trash allure—these uncorked Berkeley memories had Bruno at their mercy, apparently.

"Chuck it anywhere," said Tira. Only at this did Bruno notice how five or six half-smoked, stubbed-out joints were littered underfoot. He glanced into the open mouth of the purse and saw a dozen identical joints piled there, each rolled with professional rigor. It figured that even in the unkempt and depressed mien of Tira's decade-old Volvo—nothing so ostentatious as Stolarksy's Jaguar—she'd find a way to underline the gratuitous waste that extended from Stolarsky's fortune.

Tira caught Bruno's glance. "Help yourself, if you want something for your wine cellar, so to speak."

He ignored her, to persist with his question. "Where's Keith? Why didn't he come to the hospital?"

"I have no idea where he fucking is, okay? Quit asking. You made your point: I'm not good enough, even for the man in the Styrofoam mask."

"You're not . . . in touch?"

"Actually, I do know where he is, or most likely. He owns a winery in Glen Ellen and he's been known to just take off up there and get shitfaced for days in the loft above the barrel room, like some kind of mad monk. Or not a monk, judging from the one time he dragged me along. We're not in touch, no, not strictly speaking."

"He knows you're picking me up."

"I'm sure he figures I'm picking you up, probably figures I appeared at the hospital nude under a trench coat, and that's what he's off getting drunk and jerking himself or getting blown by a hooker about." Her voice had closed, as though she might be near tears, but her face remained fierce, her position at the steering wheel windward-leaning and vigilant, as if outracing a field of pursuers. At the first red light she repeated the farce with her purse, a fresh joint, and the lighter. This time she got it sparked herself.

"Seems like you're on a bit of a binge yourself."

"Cat's away, et cetera."

They came up Ashby Avenue to Shattuck and coursed around the BART pavilion. He should have ridden the underground train and stayed innocent of the soap operatics in which Tira Harpaz seemed bound to enmesh him.

"Keith believes he's purchased the rights to me," said Bruno.

"If you say so."

"And he's ceded me to you."

"You've got us all figured out, so could we quit talking? I'll take you to the Jack London and you'll be a free operator, Alexander. I won't even get out of the car, just drop you at the curb."

"If you roll down the window just the right amount I'll be able to float up to the second floor on a gust of fumes."

"Now you're trying to make me laugh, which I guess has some potential in that getup, like a total deadpan thing. There was that *Gong Show* guy, right—the Unknown Comic?"

"I could be billed as the Unknown Tragic," he suggested. Their banter flowed, despite himself. His capacity for enjoyment of Tira: If he wasn't careful, Bruno might be forced to admit it. The situation between them was hopeless, but that traditionally was the point at which Bruno liked women best.

"Sounds like Henry James."

"I'll take your word for it."

"Oh, yeah, I forgot, you don't read or watch TV or listen to contemporary popular music, blah blah blah. Well, Henry James is a gangsta-rap star, he's pretty much the biggest thing out there. Here's your stop." They'd slid toward the nightmare bleeding patty of Zombie Burger, dull and anodyne in the morning light, also the glistening face of Zodiac Media, its windows like teeth with braces. Then turned the corner of Haste Street, into the shade. Now Tira double-parked at the door of the Jack London Apartments. She turned to arch an eyebrow at Bruno's jumble of possessions, while stubbing her second joint on the scarred dashboard then adding it to the mess on the floor.

"I guess you don't need help with your luggage," she said.

"No." Bruno reached to collect his paltry props, humiliated. The key to the apartment, in its baggie—that was his salvation. He only needed to retreat behind the sealed door of number 25 to end the farce for now. Never mind whose auspices that sanctuary placed him under.

"Is Keith really gone?" he asked, cradling the baggie, the paper sack of swabs and prescription drugs, the backgammon case with its secret rider.

"Gone today, here tomorrow, don't let it trouble you, sweetie. We're all Unknown Tragics on this bus."

"What happens if he doesn't come back?"

"I should be so lucky. In the will, I get the Evil Empire." She waved, indicating the apartment building and, beyond, the grotesque cash-factories of Zombie and Zodiac.

"Why does Keith need a will? Is he sick?" What if Stolarsky's generosity, then subsequent total avoidance of the hospital, and all his nihilistic benders, too, were the behaviors of a doomed man, with one eye on the hourglass?

"He's not sick, except in the soul."

"Why, then?"

"Because he's rich and paranoid. Also because, you know, just because you're paranoid doesn't mean somebody isn't out to get you. In fact, maybe I'll concoct the perfect murder. I've got a job opening for an accomplice, give me a shout if you're interested in the position. All this could be yours. Or half yours, at least until the day *you* murder *me*. Now get the fuck out of my car, masked man."

II

He was his own Oshiro now. There lay the man on the unfolded Murphy bed: wan, abstracted, waiting for the indirect sunlight and the faint sounds and scents of street life trickling through the apartment's cracked-open windows to seduce him to vitality, and finding that they did not. From another vantage, he regarded the figure on the bed with pity and became the attendant, moving to the sink for a glass of cold water, allocating a handful of pills to swallow, stripping off a foul T-shirt or sweatpants in favor of another less foul, widening or narrowing the open windows to regulate the temperature, and applying antibiotic ointment to the long ridged incisions that covered the patient's face. Then, rounds accomplished, he slipped back into the body helpless on the bed. In this state he passed two or three days. Each might have been a week except for night's failure to come and close the deal.

When darkness did fall he lay awake or slept and had no way of knowing the difference. If Bruno played possum, less sick than he pretended, he had only himself to persuade. The nylon mask barred him from what seemed a world grown remote, but the same was true of the hot, tightening mask of his flesh. He'd wake unsure of whether he wore the mask or not. Within the apartment it didn't matter, since there was no one to see him. He used the mirror only long enough to salve the wounds.

Eventually he had to eat.

The answer was nearer than he'd imagined. When Bruno opened his door into the Jack London's corridor he found someone had leaned a titanic yellow box of Cheerios and a quart carton of milk there. Both

179

toppled at his feet. He looked both ways, as if for a ring-and-run artist, though of course there had only been silence, and in fact the milk was tepid, droplets of sweat from its cooling soaking the carton's footprint into the hallway carpet.

Hidden, tucked behind the cereal and milk, came further tribute, an unmarked envelope full of twenties. Another Stolarsky stipend. Though delivered, Bruno guessed, by Tira Harpaz. He brought it all inside. Opening the carton, Bruno found the milk was sour, likely placed there days ago. Standing at the kitchen counter, he pushed a few dry handfuls of Cheerios through the slot of his mask, washing them down, like his morning's array of tablets and capsules, with tap water. With the dollars he could of course buy fresh milk or something else entirely.

Telegraph Avenue didn't flinch at Bruno's mask, if it was even noticed beneath the sweatshirt hood. Probably it wasn't. Though the sun had found a route over the low rooftops, the avenue, set to a student's clock, was slow to wake. At ten thirty it still had a breakfasty, groggy vibe, vendors setting up, shopping-cart rangers poking through the previous night's recyclables, café tables full of cooling lattes and broken scones. Berkeley had no eye for a lone eccentric strolling. By local standards for eccentricity, anyway, Bruno still fell short.

Kropotkin's Sliders was just waking too, readying for a lunch-hour rush, a pyramid of tiny raw burgers massed in abeyance on a cool sideboard, flame heating as the bald counterman scraped the broad flat grill.

"First of the day," said the counterman, not glancing inside Bruno's hood to find his mask. "Two with onions?"

"Same as last time, yes."

"Do I know you?" The strange, fist-like face now queried Bruno's through the retro glasses, its magnified eyes resembling oysters.

"We met before. You gave me a third on the house."

"Always brings 'em back around."

"A kindness, but if I want another this time I can pay for it."

"You're flush, eh? Oh, Pig Stolarsky's ward, I recognize you even in the spooky getup." The counterman's large bladed spatula flashed out, at the end of his gangly arm, and deposited two patties onto the onion carpet. "You get your special-delivery Cheerios?"

"I did."

"I don't mean to make you feel under surveillance. Though we're all embraced in the panopticon these days, huh? You're my next-door neighbor."

"I remember."

"You fortifying yourself to rob a bank today?" The counterman spoke breezily, while prepping onion slush on a cooler quadrant of the vast grill.

"I had surgery."

"Witness protection, I get it. Need a new face. Corporate criminal operator of some type, I'm sure—I had you made the first time you came in here. But don't worry, I'm unusually expert in these things, nobody else would see past that getup. Berzerkeley's the last place anyone would look, it's a brilliant destination."

Berzerkeley? Stolarsky had used the same joke. Bruno didn't point it out. "I'm not a corporate operator," he said instead.

"Pig Stolarsky's personal Swiss banker?"

"Really, just a high-school friend." Even this was more than Bruno cared to claim. "Does Keith really require a Swiss banker? Why do you keep calling him that?"

"You think he sinks it all into hamburgers and crumbling apartment buildings? Nah, he's gotta be shifting the skim offshore. I call him that to provoke you, comrade."

"Yet you inhabit his crumbling apartment building yourself."

"There's two principles embodied. The true anarchist in an oligarchical society lives as an unembarrassed, even brazen parasite on the corpus of wealth. The second is likelier to be familiar to you: *Keep your enemies close.*"

"That could be Keith's reasoning as much as yours. If he even knows how you despise him."

"Oh, he knows. He just hasn't figured out what to do about it."

"Everybody despises him in this town, from what I hear. Do you present him with some direct challenge that I'm not seeing?"

"No more than the cancer of bad conscience should present to the whole rotten system. I don't actually blame Stolarsky personally. His corruption isn't exceptional, it's just in the foreground of the local picture. Berkeley needs a face to hate, Stolarsky provides one. They should raise their sights."

"The word is he likes your burgers better than his own."

"Hah!"

The counterman's chaotic nerviness was wearing on Bruno. "Could you make those to go this time?"

"Eh?"

"In a bag."

"What about that third you're expecting to want?"

"My stomach's shrunken, thanks. Two should be about right."

"If you say so." Was the Kropotkin's counterman really hurt? He must have his conversational gambits walked out on a hundred times a day. Yet he sulked as he prepared the burgers for takeout.

"Listen," said the counterman as he handed over Bruno's change, though not before frowning at the bank-crispness of the twenty-dollar bill, "my door's open. In the Jack London, I mean."

Bruno's surprise went undisclosed. He couldn't arch an eyebrow that anyone would know of. But he widened his aggrieved sockets under the mask.

"Folks come around, you should drop in if you want, there's often something stewing in the pot." The slider cook's awkwardness made this attempt pathetic. He still hadn't given Bruno his name.

What kind of stew would be found in the counterman's pot? Bruno couldn't think. At the smell of the burgers his hunger was like a dog howling in a pit. "Thank you," he said impassively.

"*De nada.*"

Then, while Bruno passed onto the noon sidewalk, the counterman flung, with heavy sarcasm, "Don't forget to 'Like' us on Facebook!"

•

Bruno avoided the Jack London for a few hours. He gobbled the sliders on foot, strolling up to College Avenue, then above campus, toward the Greek Theatre, through groves of crisp-fallen eucalyptus. The aroma rising from the dusty ground was full of hints, inchoate memoranda Bruno ignored. Scuffing back down into the city, he found a men's bathroom in the low murmuring corridor of a campus building. His mask went unnoticed.

At the Jack London's door he puzzled at the tattered resident nameplates. *Next-door neighbor* put the slider cook on the building's second floor. Three apartments: "O. Hill," "G. Plybon," or another that had been defaced with a key's tip. But even the legible names might be generations out-of-date, evidence of nothing. Bruno went upstairs.

He'd exhausted himself walking and was barely aware of putting himself into the Murphy bed. He woke hours later, with a start, to the acrid scent of the soured milk he'd neglected to pour out earlier. He staggered into the kitchen and dispensed with it now. Then, with a cool glass of water, he gobbled a palmful of the new medications, with no regard for the timetables on their labels, which he couldn't read in the dark anyway. As the scent of the milk dissolved from the kitchen, another reached him, roiling his appetite. The stew in the Kropotkin's counterman's pot, planted like a hypnotic suggestion, now wafting down the corridor.

Bruno stepped through his door before he'd even cleared his head. His old colleagues, espresso and paracetamol, had deserted him. He likely stank, sleeping in his sweatpants and *ABIDE* shirt; he'd need to spend some of the twenties on new clothes, or do laundry. His mask, too, was grubby with ointment and sweat. None of this troubled Bruno now, as he moved in the corridor. He felt willing to become a monster, something enticed from a swamp by the hubbub and savor of human activity. The cooking smells were intense enough to be another hallucination. Bruno was willing to concede this to Behringer, that he'd conjured the seared meat that had enticed or repulsed him all the way from Berlin to San Francisco.

But no. Bruno creaked open the door to the counterman's studio apartment, which lay ajar as promised. Number 28, facing the block's interior courtyard. Though layered with bookshelves and posters, the apartment's dimensions mirrored Bruno's, the Murphy bed propped up to make room for the three figures squatted on cushions on the floor, crouching as if at a hearth around bowls of soup and a board with torn chunks of bread and smeared crusts of cheese. Squawking jazz sprang from an actual turntable resting on boards and cinder blocks beneath the window.

"We have the temerity to declare that all have a right to bread, that there is bread enough for all, and that with this watchword of *Bread for All,* the revolution will triumph." The counterman grinned beneath his bald dome and goggle-glasses, and raised a mason jar half full of red wine. "Come in, comrade."

"I didn't mean to interrupt."

"Interrupt what? This party is for you."

Bruno stepped inside. He recognized one woman, seated beside the counterman and in black glasses frames that seemed intended to match his. Beth, the floor manager at Zodiac Media, she who'd handed over the clothes Bruno now wore. Her short black hair was still slicked back, and her white shirt buttoned to the neck. The nerdiest man's outfit made for the most stylish lesbians. A sturdily attractive black woman sat cross-legged to Beth's left, likely Beth's girlfriend.

Neither woman seemed in any way surprised by the appearance of this masked petitioner who'd come begging a bowl of whatever the cooking pot contained. Though they didn't bother rising from their cushions, they scooted to widen their circle, and together patted an empty spot between them, as though to encourage a shy housecat. Perhaps the gathering really had been conceived in Bruno's honor. At least the Kropotkin's patty-flipper must have spoken of Bruno, to inoculate the women against reacting with surprise to his eerie mask.

"I'm Beth, we met before."

"Of course. Coincidentally, I was just thinking I ought to visit again for more of your wonderful T-shirts."

"Hell, I can bring you a dozen if you want, you don't have to darken the door of that shithole."

"That would be kind."

"This is my partner, Alicia." The black woman nodded hello, and

Bruno took her hand for a moment. "I'm Alexander. I will sit, if you really don't mind—"

"Sit, Alexander," said Alicia. Her smile was warm and featured one gold tooth. She wore a yellow jumpsuit sewn from parachute cloth, with stylish pockets on the shoulders and thighs. Meanwhile, Beth poured inches of red wine into another jam jar and put it at the open place, for Bruno.

"But I don't know our host's name." Even as Bruno settled himself onto the cushion between the two women the Kropotkin's counterman had jumped up and gone into his narrow kitchen, which also mirrored Bruno's. Now he returned, cradling a full bowl of the chunky red soup, which he placed in Bruno's lap.

"I'm Garris. You want some hot sauce?"

"Do you recommend it? I recall you as a goop-eschewer."

"Different context. Soup *is* goop, I suggest you hot it up. I grind my own chipotle."

"I wouldn't miss it for the world."

Garris—the "G. Plybon" from the nameplate at the door—grinned as he shook his concoction into Bruno's bowl. The soup was minestrone, or something even more various, featuring both rice and twists of pasta, chickpeas, red beans, stringy chunks of chicken. With the fiery pepper sauce, it was delicious. Bruno felt it wetting the tight-seamed mouth hole of his mask, but he couldn't pace himself. "You should feature this at the counter of Kropotkin's," he suggested. "The sauce, I mean."

"Not a bad idea. I could call it 'A Dash of Insight.'"

"Who minds the store when you're off duty?"

"There's always someone who can put together a slider, it isn't a prohibitively difficult formula. Fraternity kid named Jed has the night shift at the moment, though I usually take evenings myself—conversation's better."

"I imagine there's a sharp drop-off in philosophical content when you're away."

"The decor has a certain dissident vibe that impacts even the least willing minds."

"I'm sure you're right."

"Beth told me you're an old friend of Keith Stolarsky's," said Alicia, gold-tooth-grinning with conviviality as Bruno slurped. Her tone held both sympathy and implication. "What's that like?"

"Oh, it's not like much of anything, actually. He's never around. I think he's left town for some reason."

"Sure, we all know that," said Garris Plybon, with a trace of aggression Bruno couldn't account for. "We feel it like a black cloud lifted, when he absents himself from this town. Allah be praised for his whoring jaunts."

"Is that what he does?" asked Bruno. "Whoring?"

Plybon shrugged. "No idea," he admitted.

Alicia handed Bruno a section of paper towel, torn from a nearby roll, for a too-late napkin. "So what does your friendship with him . . . consist of? I'd really be interested to know. He's famous for not having friends, not that that's the only reason we're glad to meet you, Alexander."

"It consists of . . . remembering him from high school," said Bruno. "Except mostly Keith does the remembering." *That, and several times nearly fucking his girlfriend,* Bruno thought but didn't say. I don't like him either, he'd add, if that was the ticket for entry into their peculiar club. Though it seemed Bruno was already included. "Do you work for Keith too?" he asked Alicia. How strange, their sycophantic distaste for his old acquaintance, while either drawing his pay or living under his roof.

But no. "I work at the Pacific Film Archive," said Alicia. When Bruno responded with blankness, she added, "It's part of Cal's art museum. I'm a film and video librarian, basically."

"Ah."

"Beth and I met because she's doing a dissertation on Abraham Polonsky."

"I'm in the Rhetoric program," Beth explained, though this hardly made the reference less opaque. "I'm just moonlighting as a shop clerk, to keep from racking up too much student debt."

"Of course." Bruno basked in their sincerity, to drink it in as he did the soup.

"And what do you do, Alexander?"

Ah, the abyss. Bruno's life had been struck open, as much as his face. But there was no mask for his life. Bruno's new companions, however unglamorous, functioned in the petty workaday realm he'd so long ridden above, aloof, and which now had spit him out. The others at least existed in economic relation to Keith Stolarsky, while Bruno relied on handouts: Cheerios, envelopes of twenties, and Beth's offer of fresh T-shirts.

"I'm between things." A mention of backgammon seemed out of the question.

"He's sick, 'Licia," said Beth. She nodded at Bruno's face, acknowledging the mask at last. "He just needs time to get it together."

"Yes, I see that."

"I'm cured, that's the funny thing," said Bruno, wonderingly. "I was sick *before*—as it was explained to me, I may have been sick nearly my whole life. It's the cure I need to get over."

"Western medicine is a motherfucker." Garris Plybon produced this like a worn and familiar maxim.

"Well, you've come to the right place," said Beth. Did she mean Plybon's apartment or the building as a whole?

"I feel that, at the moment." Bruno held his soup bowl with two hands, put aside his spoon, and slurped the dregs.

Plybon clarified with another witticism: "Sure, Telegraph Avenue, the island of lost toys."

Here people reached fame with a trademark costume or spiel, by a hand-printed book of tirades, by nudity or a ritual utterance bellowed at top volume. With mask and hood, Bruno could join their ranks. Yet the soup beggar tried not to take it personally. Open your door under the watchword *Bread for All*—shouldn't it be lost toys who'd wander through?

An egalitarian rabble of burger flippers, shop clerks, and film archivists: Bruno could be their pet. In Monaco once, in the early months under Edgar Falk, Bruno had left the Café de Paris with two women, lovers, elegant as film stars. He'd let them make him their diversion and toy. It was as near as Bruno had ever come to fulfilling Keith Stolarsky's suggestion that he was a gigolo and Falk his pimp, though there'd been no motive for Falk in it and no money changed hands. It wasn't so different from Bruno's dalliances as a nineteen-year-old with Chez Panisse customers, older women with an appetite for Bruno's body and grateful for his seeming disposability. Here, worlds removed, Bruno would be lucky enough to be fed soup and swaddled in T-shirts by these sweet, innocuous humans, at whom he'd never have glanced in his former life.

If Bruno hoped to disguise his new wretchedness, he'd failed. "Do you really have nobody here at all to care for you?" said Alicia.

"Not in Berkeley, no."

"Someone elsewhere?" Bruno needed no further evidence the blot had wrecked his quarantine; Alicia's tenderness made it seem likely he'd translated the contents of his brain into hers.

He'd test it with an outright lie. "My girlfriend is in Germany." The lesbians might like him better with warranty of female approval.

Alicia reached for his chin with her own napkin. Bruno instinctively flinched, then leaned forward. She might as well be Oshiro.

"Your mask is a mess," she said.

"That's okay, I've got another one." A second lie.

"Do you want to take it off?"

"No."

"Why isn't she here?" asked Beth.

"Who?"

"Your girlfriend. Why isn't she taking care of you?" Her tone was tough, an instinctive "bad cop" to complement her partner.

"We . . . couldn't afford the ticket."

"That's fucked up," said Beth. "I thought Keith was, like, giving you a blank check, the royal treatment."

"Not beyond sweatpants and Cheerios," he said. This glossed over a hospital bill that might have mounted into the tens of thousands. But casting aspersions on Stolarsky was the currency in the social economy of the Jack London Apartments. Bruno doubted he could further damage Stolarsky's abysmal reputation.

"Well, shit," said Beth. "I've got access to petty cash dispersal. He lets me sign off on the business account, and nobody's gonna blink, especially when Wells Fargo knows he's out of town."

"You never told me that," said Plybon.

"It was none of your business," said Beth, curtly. "There's a travel agency on Shattuck," she continued, to Bruno. "We can go down there tomorrow."

"She's . . . a German national," said Bruno. "She'll need a visa, I think. I don't even know if she's got a passport."

"Well, find out!"

"She's a sex worker," Bruno blurted. "A dominatrix." She wasn't, so far as he knew, but it sounded more empowered than a half-nude waitress in a torture mask. His whimsical lie blossomed into a wild fictional vehicle, one swerving out of his control.

"Good for her. What's her name?"

"Madchen."

"So, flexible schedule then," said Beth, the pragmatist.

"I bet she's a cutie-pie," said Alicia.

"Yes."

"Has she seen . . . your face?"

"Not yet."

"That's why you're reluctant, isn't it?"

"Maybe."

"You've got to tell her," said Alicia. "Share your fears, let her in."

"I've been ignoring her calls."

"He's right to worry," said Plybon. "You know what Renzo Novatore called *woman*, right? 'The most brutal of enslaved beasts.' "

"Shut up, Garris." Alicia drew herself nearer on the cushions and put her arm around Bruno's back, touching his knee with her free hand.

With that Plybon was shunted to the margins of his own gathering. Bruno didn't think it was worth asking who Renzo Novatore was. Instead he leaned into Alicia's strong, soft shoulder. If Beth joined herself to their embrace from his other side, Bruno wouldn't mind.

Perhaps even Garris Plybon could benefit from a group hug—at the moment, Bruno couldn't begrudge it. But Plybon went into the kitchen and returned with four shot glasses, each painted with the word *Arizona* and a tiny cactus and roadrunner, and a bottle of single-malt scotch, as well as a large irregular chunk of dark chocolate wrapped in butcher paper, as if hacked off a massive block. The Gourmet Ghetto had infiltrated the anarchist bread party, at least a little.

Later, returned to number 25, Bruno removed the mask, to rinse in the bathroom sink. He palpated the fabric with his thumbs, working red soup blotches and smears of chocolate free of the mesh. Then hung it over the shower-curtain rod to dry and put himself to bed, but not before checking his cell, charging at the wall socket. No new calls. Madchen's last attempt dated from before his surgery. But the phone still glowed, ready. Falk, Bruno's distant benefactor, continued to foot the bill.

III

The Phantom of the Jack London slept for ten and twelve hours at a stretch, took pills in a sporadic and careless fashion, and anointed his incisions before bed. His mask, his underwear and socks, he cleaned in the sink and air-dried as required. Copious *ABIDE* shirts and Cal sweatpants had appeared at his door, bundled in a large plastic Zodiac bag, the day after Plybon's soup party. There was no evidence of Tira Harpaz's presence. The Phantom allocated the twenties from the envelope parsimoniously, fed himself at student haunts at random hours, the international grub a thin echo of his expatriate life: Mongolian barbecue, soggy sushi, falafel. On daily strolls he'd roam Shattuck, or College Avenue, unkinking his anesthesia-withered limbs, testing his strength. At café counters he gathered discarded American newspapers and read them in the open air, on a bench at Willard Park, accompanied by the pong of tennis. The papers barely caught his interest. He greeted no one. With his mask, he went unapproached, except by the mad.

He avoided Kropotkin's. It was enough that he might run into Garris Plybon in the building's corridors. On the fifth or sixth day of his solitude he did, meeting the slider cook in the building's lobby.

Bruno thanked him for the soup and the company.

Plybon raised a forbidding finger. "Nothing more than the mutual aid any random human soul ought to transact with any other."

"Well, it made a nice evening. Have you seen Beth and Alicia? I need to thank them for the clothing."

"Those girls are all right," groused Plybon. "They believe radical fucking can alter collective reality. It's a nonviable approach, but I grudgingly admire their spirit."

"That makes two of us."

"I do have a message for you. The ladies were beside themselves hearing about your dominatrix. I guess Beth took it upon herself to confer with the travel agent, some former lover of hers. They booked an open ticket from Berlin, off the Zodiac slush fund, ordinarily used for hiring ringer citizens to create false-flag diversions during public meetings of the Telegraph Avenue Business Owners Association. You only have to call your Kraut and substitute her name for Beth's, from what I hear."

"That's astonishing."

"One shark, many remoras, all swim in the same direction."

"Sorry?"

"Just remember, your old friend Stolarsky makes money faster than his flunkies could possibly redistribute it. All this shit"—Plybon gestured around him, seeming to indicate a conspiracy palace that lay around them, invisible—"is nothing more than rooms in a house that needs burning to the ground. But meantime, I'm sure it'll be a relief to see your girlfriend."

"Yes." Bruno felt wearied by the counterman's baited conundrums. Next time they met, Bruno hoped it was with Beth and Alicia. The odds of that, Bruno couldn't guess.

"I gotta go open the shop."

This ended their exchange.

•

When he found himself craving a hamburger, the Phantom passed through the prohibited doorway into Zombie. The molten-looking building was too present for him to ignore, throbbing with dance beats and bleeding its red lasers into the dark sky. He picked an early hour, hoping to avoid the lines that extended once night fell, then cinched his hood tight to make a small port window, a reversal of the blot, the world condensed to one bright hole. How bad could the burgers be? Bruno was willing to find out.

The line wasn't through the door, but inside it snaked three layers deep before the counter, like an airport security queue, marked with a heavy velvet sash clipped to brass stanchions. The students waited in bunches or alone. In either case their faces were lit, within the deep crimson glow of the building's vaulted ceiling, by the glow of their cell phones. This miasma was punctured by the blazing-white low-cut T-shirts of the Zombie staff, and the glow of tiny *Z* toothpick flags stuck in the burgers, which flared in the black-light bulb as violently as the shirts. Here and there another detail picked up the luminescence: a pair of Converse sneakers, the collar and cuffs of a Lacoste shirt. The servers, as advertised by Tira Harpaz, were zaftig to a fault.

Behind them, deeper in the murk, those not taking their burgers out into the evening sat on long picnic-table benches across from one another, laboring over their sloppy plates, any attempt at conversation surely drowned in the noisy disco. The scene resembled that old story about the cave, spotlit breasts standing in for shadows.

Bruno felt invisible until he reached the head of the line and saw the reaction of the cashier. She pointed and giggled, drawing the attention of one of her fellow workers, who'd just then returned from the tables, bearing trays of detritus.

"That's freaky, man!"

"Sorry?"

"Your face is glowing!"

The mask's mesh was alive to the black light, strongest at the counter to highlight the T-shirts and burger flags. Bruno cinched his hood tighter, restricting his peripheral vision, shrinking the reverse-blot. This might not have been a winning move. Other voices clamored to know what had triggered the outcry. Soon curious faces, both servers and clientele, bobbled past his porthole window, to steal a glimpse of the mask's effect: the full moon trapped in the bottom of a well.

"Could I just order a meal?" he said.

"Sure, Jason!"

"Better make it bloody rare for the man in the mask."

"Treat him right, we don't want a mass-slaying incident!"

The attention was intolerable. Bruno turned away. He had to jostle through the surrounding bodies, less a matter of a mob with pitchforks than of navigating in the gloom. Bruno had no doubt he was forgotten once he plunged in dismay into the open air.

He settled for a bag of tortilla chips and a plastic container of guacamole from an indifferent clerk in a brightly lit grocery. With these spoils Bruno retreated to number 25. Shedding his sweatshirt on the bed, he noticed the cell phone, at the baseboard. He detached it from the charger for the first time since returning from the hospital and hit Call Back.

Her meek "Hallo?" came only after the fifth ring, when he'd become certain the call would bounce to a mailbox.

"Madchen?"

"Ja?"

Her voice was faint, clouded with what he instantly knew must be sleep. Was it ten hours later? Well, so he hadn't diverted her from the action in some all-night leather-masked bottomless dungeon. Bruno knew nothing. His stories were only stories.

"It's me, Alexander. You've been calling my phone."

"So sorry—*bitte*—I was mistaken."

"No, don't be sorry. I'm glad."

She was only silent, the ocean between them roaring in the electronic vacuum as if in a seashell.

"No," he said. "It's meant a great deal to me, in fact."

"Then I am glad too." On the telephone, in the second language, half asleep, Madchen was like a baby bird. He had to keep in mind the forthrightness she'd projected on the Kladow ferry, in her leather mask and bare ass, in her persistent calls to his phone.

"Did I wake you?"

"No," she obviously lied.

"I'm the one who should apologize," he said. "I've ignored your messages. I mean, I haven't ignored them. But I should have called before now."

"I was afraid you had died."

It was still possible the Jack London Apartments were Bruno's franchise in the afterlife. But he said, "No."

"At Charité I could discover nothing."

"I suppose they wanted to protect my privacy." *You should have claimed to be my girlfriend,* he thought. *Seeing as I've taken the same liberty, on my side.*

"Have you been extremely sick?"

"Truthfully, yes."

"You're . . . better now?"

"Better, and worse, both." Could he divert the obvious topic? He wished to keep Madchen from waking, to appear to her as a figure in a dream. "I feel very far away."

"Are you in America?"

"California."

"It's very late, you know—*Gott,* it is nearly morning."

"Is it still dark, Madchen?"

"*Ja.*"

"Don't turn on the light." He lay on the bed, his room lit only by the street, mediocre guacamole warming untouched in a sack on the floor. If the staticky-seashell call made room for all the ocean between them, it was also a nest in which their two voices mingled, a virtual enclosure against that measureless galaxy of rooms unfilled by their two bodies.

"The light is off."

"Good."

"Are you going to ask me if I'm alone?"

"Are you alone?"

"*Ja.*"

You're not anymore, he wanted to say, but didn't.

"Do you want to ask me what I'm wearing?"

"No," said the man in the dark in a mask.

"Okay."

"We don't need to do that."

"*Ja.*"

"Let me tell you a story. There was a man, a man on a ferry once, and he saw a person, another person, a woman, a very beautiful woman. This man and this woman person, their eyes met and something was communicated very quickly, I'm certain you understand. But the man was very stupid, very dense and shortsighted, and when he was given a chance to do something very important for the woman, a short time later, he missed that chance, missed it badly. And this, for whatever reason, this was the end for him. Like in some fairy tale, but this isn't a fairy tale. The very next thing for this man was that he took a sudden fall. He tumbled off a cliff into the underworld. Into a kind of twilight in his life. The woman, of course, was there to see it. She's the only one who has any idea what happened. She's the witness. The woman could no more help the man than he had been willing to help her. But that she was present to see was still his salvation. There's no other word for it."

They were more words than he was accustomed to hearing himself speak. The story was the least he owed her, he felt now, to reward the string of unanswered calls that made a trail of bread crumbs or pomegranate seeds pointing to freedom, from the dungeon of his illness but also of California, of Keith Stolarsky and Tira Harpaz, of Bruno's enslavement to their patronage.

He listened to her breathing. He could think of nothing more sublime than gratifying Madchen in her astonished bedroom in the Berlin dawn. They could have sex on the phone, she'd already more or less suggested it. Given Bruno's ruined looks, it might be all he should want. Yet there was a higher game here, beyond his volition. It was as though the dice had presented numbers dictating a blitzing game. He blitzed.

"The man, he took with him into this underworld a kind of dream of this woman. He was her witness too, you see. She'd entrusted him with her secret, almost accidentally. Through chance, he might know her better than men who'd known her for years, or who thought they knew her. This knowledge was his sustenance in the dark place. It kept him alive. *She* kept him alive, I mean." The clarity necessitated by the tongues dividing them, on the call bounced by satellite across zones and boundaries, purified Bruno's language. This was an advantage, since he spoke of the deeper erotics of fate. "There's something I need from you, Madchen."

"*Ja?*"

"To come and care for me. I'm among enemies."

"To come . . . to where?"

"California."

"Now?"

"Is there a reason you can't?"

"I don't know."

"I have a ticket for you."

"*Nein,* Alexander! Can this be true?"

"It is true."

Without speaking, Madchen sounded more distant. As though she'd exited the seashell. A ticket, a summons to him? He'd lose her now to this improbability.

"Madchen?"

"I have to think."

"Naturally. If it's too much—"

"I could travel in one week, maybe."

"Don't decide now."

"I'll come."

"But Madchen—"

"Ja?"

"I don't look the way you remember me."

"Oh, Alexander, my dear Alexander, do you think this matters to me at all?"

IV

The afternoon before Madchen's arrival, Tira Harpaz reappeared in Alexander Bruno's life. It was six days later, the same day he'd reached the bottom of the stash of twenties, the life support he both resented and denied. Money, like anesthesia, kept you alive and asleep.

Tira's own extrasensory gift might be to reappear precisely as Bruno wondered whether he'd need to go begging for food at Plybon's door or to search out Beth Dennis at the counter of Zodiac. Days before, Beth had taken Madchen's phone number from him; the next day she'd knocked on his door, to grinningly hand him a printout of Madchen's e-ticket confirmation, the ferry woman's full name revealed as Madchen Abplanalp, her age as thirty-two. Since then, Bruno hadn't laid eyes on either Beth or Plybon, though he'd made no special effort to avoid them. Bruno hadn't even put aside the price of a BART ticket in order to go and collect his German visitor from the San Francisco Airport. He had no idea how he'd explain his situation to her when she came.

Tira Harpaz collared him at the Jack London's door. She'd parked in an illegal spot, blocking the alleys where the Dumpsters lay, and wolf-whistled to bring him to the Volvo's open window. There, she sat low and complacent behind the wheel, smoking a joint. Despite all this, and despite how Bruno could easily have walked on, ignoring her, he felt firmly apprehended.

Her first words informed him of the charges. "So you went to Zombie despite my pleas."

"I only heard one plea. Were there more?"

"Okay, wise guy. Wanna go for a drive?"

He entered her car on what he supposed was a voluntary basis. She wore a strangely fluorescent polyester blouse, with lime-colored flowers stretched too tight over her breasts and stomach, and tight white sleeves half covering her surprisingly articulated biceps. It might have fit her once. The long arm of the law, he found himself thinking, continuing to hallucinate Tira Harpaz as a policewoman. Or she and Stolarsky could be a team of detectives, of the disheveled, throwing-you-off-stride variety.

"Were you staking out the entrance here? How long would you have waited for me to come out?"

"I just drove up."

"How long would you have been prepared to wait? I realize you may have no idea."

"About forty-five minutes, then I'd have let myself in."

"I thought you gave me back the extra key."

"Oh, yeah, that's right, you wanted me to pretend there was only one. Sorry."

"What about Zombie Burger? Were you following me personally, or did you hire someone?"

"The manager bundles up the security tapes once a week and sends them to Keith, with the highlights flagged. I usually watch them for kicks before posting the best ones to YouTube. There was a pretty good one just now, this guy with a glowing mask. You should have seen it."

"I can't actually tell which part of all that is meant as a joke."

"That's an improvement on what I was thinking you'd say, which was that you'd never heard of YouTube."

"No, I'm familiar with YouTube. It's one of the places people go to become heroically incompetent at backgammon." Accepting the joint from her, Bruno positioned it through the mouth hole for a drag. Beneath the mask, the muscles of his face steadily strengthened, readying to meet the world.

"Don't you get hot under that thing?"

"All the time." In this light he noticed for the first time that her raven hair was surely dyed. He felt obsessively aware of Tira's physical presence. Likely he'd been mulling over her body in absentia, without

199

noticing he was doing so. For the past days he'd felt an unaffiliated buoyancy to his existence on Telegraph, as if Tira had followed Stolarsky in vanishing from town. Past and future had floated away, leaving only Bruno's gently widening circuit of cappuccinos and sidewalks, at least until the twenties ran out. He'd even wandered as far as the campus of Berkeley High School and begun cutting across People's Park with impunity, as though these carried no intimate associations. Now Tira had come to present her bill of arrears.

She turned and drove him north, on Shattuck. After a couple of tokes he held the joint up to her attention, then nodded at the floor, miming tossing it there, and she said, "Go ahead."

Strangely, though the Volvo had hardly been cleaned, the little haystack of Tira's half-smoked reefers was missing. He tossed this new one instead onto a floor strewn with candy wrappers, balled tissues, a knuckle Band-Aid with a scab-dark stain. "You've been recycling?"

"One of Keith's minions knows I leave my car unlocked. The guy takes my discards for his stash. It's an example of the myriad thankless ways we keep the whole machine humming along around here."

"A personal assistant around the house?"

"Creepier than that. One of his shop dorks. Comes prowling around on his bicycle, doesn't imagine I see him. The revolutionist, your apartment-mate, Plybon. From what I gather, you've been whooping it up with the kids in the rumpus room quite a lot since I saw you last."

"Wait, Garris Plybon works for *Keith*?"

"You kidding? You think Keith wouldn't have a rival burger place under his control? It isn't public information. People like to fantasize that they're putting a thumb in Keith's eye by preferring the anarchist sliders."

"I thought he and Plybon were mortal enemies."

"That's not a mutually exclusive situation. Plenty of people draw a salary from their mortal enemy."

Bruno sat, staring ahead as they crossed into Northside, overturned, feeling his cheeks burn beneath the mask. Meanwhile Tira went on in her garrulous way. "Keith calls it a move from the Stalin playbook. Why bother infiltrating dissident cells, when you can start one yourself, just to see what grows there?"

"Does Plybon know?"

She made a sound like the air going out of a tire. "What do *you* think?"

"Where are you taking me?" he asked, to change the subject. He didn't really believe the destination was a secret interrogation chamber.

"I wondered when you'd ask. I've got a surprise planned out. You're not dressed appropriately, but you're not really dressed appropriately for anything."

"Do I guess, or do you tell me? Should I put a sack over my head?"

"You already have a sack over your head. I got us a table at Chez Panisse."

For the second time in the space of a minute Bruno was rendered dumb.

"What do you think?" Now Tira's voice betrayed the strand of vulnerability that all her chafing repartee was devised to conceal. Or perhaps it was a masterly brushstroke of calculation—why should Bruno abandon his paranoia?

"Just the café," she said, reasoning with him. The central restaurant, with its set menu, would be too ostentatious for a pair like them. The café was looser, a place you could hide, a place you could flee.

"My last meal?" he said.

"Huh?"

Why should she understand his joke? He doubted it would be worth the effort to explain that he'd fantasized her as a policewoman.

"Sure, let's eat."

"Then shoot and leave."

"Sorry?"

"You know, like a panda? Eats shoots and leaves." She grinned. The further they wallowed in bafflement and mutual misunderstanding, the more she appeared to feel at home. Perhaps this derived from her life with Keith Stolarsky, himself so addicted to the gnomic reference.

"I no longer shoot and leave," Bruno said. He touched his T-shirt. "I only abide."

"Cool, then, we'll abide, just lemme find a parking spot."

Bruno knew that even the café was devised to usher a table through a sequence of gastronomic ideas, but Tira derailed the waiter's presentation of the elaborate menu in favor of a series of glasses of pink champagne. He supposed that money, even slovenly money, got what it wanted, was able to carve Chez Panisse into little more than a cocktail bar, just as it had partitioned Singapore into an air-conditioned hotel room and a bag of burgers. Money, in this case, backed with the silencing enigma of a figure in a mask.

Bruno caused a little stir, he felt it. He lowered his hood, to improve his peripheral vision and to dissipate the strangeness—to allow the covert gawkers in the kitchen and at other tables to see his ears and neck, to confirm him as human. For his part, drinking not at Tira's pace but drinking enough, barely listening to her left-field forays while he picked at the rounds that had begun to arrive, trout roe and potato pizzetta, chicken livers and peas crostini, nothing remotely suited to the sparkling rosé with which Tira kept topping his glass, Bruno suffered hallucinations that those who served him, or those breezing past to the upstairs kitchen, were his old company. His dissolute mentor, Konrad, and others, young waiters and bussers and sous chefs with vanished names. But of course those would be aged now, as old as Bruno, older, if not as ruined. These faces were young not because time was stopped but because they had been replaced with newer versions. Who had replaced Bruno?

Tira had ignored the waiter's attempts to describe a special or confirm their satisfaction, seeming intent on broadcasting her crassness. Now, a second bottle almost polished, she captured the waiter's sleeve and pulled him close, a slurring policewoman this time.

"This place used to be good."

"Is there something I can help with?"

"No. It's just it used to be special. Now it's ordinary. You know that, right?"

"I believe it's still special." The waiter's formulation left various exits open.

"How old are you?"

"Twenty-six."

"Well, see? Alexander, tell him."

"Everything's been wonderful," said Bruno.

"He used to work here, you know that? So he's in the cult, same as you. But the ironic thing is he should know better than anyone, better than me. He was *there*. It's just ordinary now."

"I'll clear these," said the waiter smoothly, freeing himself to begin corralling their plates.

"Is there a peach galette?" said Tira.

"Not tonight."

"I want a galette, any galette you got."

Their exit was a blur. They finished with something chocolate and a dessert wine. If Tira paid, Bruno didn't see. She'd palmed a card onto a check, perhaps. Or Stolarsky had an account, if such a thing existed. Dark had fallen and Bruno felt benumbed by the drink and though he ought to have been fearful of her driving he was barely conscious of returning to the Jack London. She was upstairs and at his door without Bruno being party to any decision. At least she waited for him to produce his own key.

The obnoxious overhead he left off, in favor of the kitchen light.

"What've you got?" He heard her shoes, kicked off to tumble on the floor.

"I don't need more to drink, and I doubt you do, either." He fixed them cool tap water, in the single jam jar he'd borrowed from Garris Plybon.

"You're right, I'm shitfaced. Let's smoke and mellow out instead." Before he could protest her fuming up the apartment, there came the click of her lighter. "So, you know that thing you said about YouTube and backgammon?"

"More or less."

"Well, I've been following in Keith's footsteps. Not on YouTube, but this tutorial site called Gammaniacs."

"I don't really know anything about it, you'll have to excuse me if I was rude."

"Rude, crude, lewd, nude, and apt to be misconstrued."

"Sorry?"

"You're, like, the least rude person I ever met, Alexander. It's practically a crippling deficiency." Tira had laid open his backgammon set across the Murphy bed's sheets. As he turned back from the kitchen she was chucking aside his Berlin stone with a complete lack of curiosity. "I got good enough in the last week to lose five thousand dollars on the Ladbrokes site, you should be very proud of me."

"Yes, that's an accomplishment." He shed his sneakers and sweatshirt and joined her on the bed.

"I'm sure you should be able to take me for everything I've got in three or four games."

"We're playing?"

"Yep." She handed him the joint. "I can never remember how to set up these little fuckers, though. I guess that's a classic symptom of playing online, huh?"

"I don't know if I would call it classic." He knelt on the bed, feeling the urge to straighten out her confused placement of the checkers, if nothing else. Having drawn once on the joint, and fearing the effects of more, he tried to return it. She shook her head.

"Do you have a phobia of other people's saliva?" It could explain Plybon's cornucopia, the discarded half joints in her passenger's-side footwell.

"I like other people's saliva fine," she said. "Assuming it's the right person. I have a phobia of my own saliva. I don't dig wet rolling paper."

Bruno extinguished it as before, between his fingers, feeling more accustomed to the spark of pain. If he worked at it, he could regress all the way to high school. Yet his board was before him, rosy with innate glamour, promising, as ever, transportation. The Berlin stone had scuffed the playing surface surprisingly little. "So I have to earn my nest egg of twenties this time?"

"Nope. You're not playing for twenties, you're playing for my clothes."

"Your clothes?"

"To remove them, dummy. Don't be evasive, you were gobbling my stuff with your ghosty eyes all through dinner." She slung one arm beneath her breasts, hoisting them like an infant offered into his embrace. They swarmed together near the strained top button of the sheer polyester blouse, that mystic margin Bruno couldn't doubt he'd rained with glances. "Double me, gammon me, make me bare my tits."

He slurped water from the jam jar, felt it soak the lip of his mask. It was too late to reclaim his hood—anyhow he was hot from the drink. He wouldn't need it. The board arranged, Tira threw both blond dice into the board, drawing double fours.

"It's customary to roll one die to see who'll go first."

"I've never played a human before, so I'm not customary. You can afford to give me the advantage, spookyman."

Bruno shrugged. She shifted the pale checkers into a strong starting position. He rolled a two-three, dropped lazy descenders into his outer board. There should be time enough to play more boldly. First he'd see what lessons she'd absorbed and wait out the blurring effects of the champagne. Whatever his and Tira's involvement, it had commenced some time ago, before the start of this game. She was right: Bruno could afford the amusement. With Tira humiliated in defeat it might be possible to reclaim number 25, though that presumed she had the capacity for humiliation.

She offered to double immediately. Inside the mask he raised an eyebrow. "What's the hurry?"

"We need to make this worth something. Or, you know, resign if you feel you're beat."

He accepted the cube from her, then built a five-prime. She wasn't lucky. He watched her run in panic, then caught and demolished the blot she left behind. The game devolved into a race, and Tira was behind. Rather than double again to make this point, Bruno let her play it out. She grunted in anger at dice that refused her a miracle.

Then, when Bruno parked his last checker, she began balling off her ankle socks, which she threw one after the next at his head. He ducked.

"If I understand the international rules of strip backgammon, socks are a single garment, not two."

"Right—and you won once."

"You doubled the stakes. That's what the cube is for. I'll have your pants as well, thank you."

"If you'd been boning up on the rules of international strip back-gammon, or strip *anything*, you'd know that the loser gets to take off whatever the fuck she wants to take off." Tira unbuttoned her blouse and laid it aside, giving air to the bulkily architectural black brassiere he'd extrapolated from a thousand angles. "You'll appreciate the rules when it comes your turn to lose."

"Based on what I've seen, my turn isn't coming."

"Fuck you. And I'd be insulted if you didn't want to get my shirt off except you're exactly the kind of avoiding-the-obvious person who'd want to go at this thing backward. Because you're going to *love* my tits."

"Self-abnegating, that's what Edgar Falk always called it."

"Your twisted old pansy Gandalf, you mean? I guess he'd be quali-fied to know."

Bruno reset the pieces and took the privilege of rolling first. With a six-three he again seeded his backfield, daring her to hit. He felt the effect of her poor play dragging him down, as much a suppressant as the champagne and marijuana. Yet no blot obtruded between him and the board, or her body, so he studied Tira. She bore down like a teenager over a standardized test, tongue protruding as she shook the dice, then surveyed her options. Playing through a screen had taught her nothing of a player's attitude or comportment. She resembled the sort of computer-bred gaming nerd Bruno had begun to encounter in the clubs in recent years, but her moves betrayed a hopeless deafness to the command of the pips.

This time, Bruno turned the doubling cube. An act of mercy either way—if Tira were smart enough to refuse, she'd economize on shed clothing. If she accepted, a swifter end to the farce. She cast him a shocked look.

"Don't be so surprised," he said. "This is how the game is played."

She made a face, took the cube, and ground on. Bruno nearly gam-moned her, but at the last moment double sixes enabled a stray blond checker to race home to her inner board, and another to bear off.

"Two items again," he reminded her.

She unhooked the bra, then stood on the bed, looming above

him, and wriggled free of her jeans. Her underwear, which hoved into the center of his vision, didn't match the brassiere, was instead pink and cottony, worn. It was also capacious, grandmotherly, though not enough to quarantine a wild black pubic thatch defaulting every boundary at her thigh and stomach, inch-wide on the flesh of her thighs, trailing to tiny hairs at her navel. Bruno caught himself elaborating a comparison between the black bra beneath the sheer blouse and the bush erupting behind the underwear, that which is hidden erupting through its paltry veil. Pubic hair itself a further concealment, a beard for beckoning flesh. But really, it was his distractible mind that formed the true veil. All his foolish comparisons, Bruno's attempt to dissociate from what he wanted and that he wanted it, the startling absolutes of the body before him.

Pants discarded, Tira swayed wonderfully back into place behind the board, crossing her legs. Her underwear stretched, a feeble screen. Oddly, Bruno found himself staring at her sole item of clothing—he supposed this could be the fatal politeness of which she'd accused him, though it also meant he glared at her crotch. Her breasts and stomach deluged his sight anyhow, triple globes triply eyeing Bruno in return. No blot to save him now. Though he leaned in to reorder the checkers and seize the dice, the board would need to be ten times its present size for him to pretend not to see, or to be seen seeing.

"Your roll," he croaked.

Tira's cascade of luck began with sixes. She played them properly— not difficult—and offered Bruno the doubling cube on her next turn. He didn't refuse. He again dropped builders, his play leaden and automatic. This time, her roll placed his two undefended checkers on the bar. By the time he'd danced for three rolls she'd assembled a six-prime. Could her nakedness be warping the action of the dice? No, it was his brain her nakedness addled; dice were impartial to breasts, as to everything. He supposed that by playing in such a deliberate style he'd accidentally schooled Tira in the worth of a blockade, a textbook instance of playing a mediocre opponent up to your level.

Fate, unforgiving of his blunder, rewarded her with doubles twice as she bore off. The gammon cost him nearly everything: socks, sweatpants, *ABIDE*. He felt free of shame. His body might be withered, collapsed on itself from the starvation of recovery, yet the hospital had killed his embarrassment. It was only a body, a poor object hurtling through time, and anyhow what he'd lost weren't his clothes, were hardly clothes at all.

Owing Tira one more, Bruno faced a decision that was no decision at all. He stripped off his underwear, addressed her in nothing but his mask. His cock had flushed, grown rigid without his noticing. Now it trembled in the air. It might be the first erection of a new self-epoch.

"The puppets come onstage at last!"

"Puppets?"

"That's what Keith calls them."

"Calls what, penises?"

"Genitals, both kinds. They're the puppets. All floppy, like scraps of cloth, until the show starts." She reached across the board and held him as if in a handshake. Bruno grunted, the pleasure almost intolerable. Just when he'd managed to exhale, she gripped him harder, tweaking, and let go. Then began shoving checkers into their proper starting places, a fast learner.

"Aren't we done?"

"No way, Jose." She pointed at his mask.

He threw a two-one, split his back men. Tira grazed him again as she gathered her dice to throw.

"Don't."

"You're sticking out." She gave out with her seal bark.

"I can't play if you're touching me."

"Fine." She took her roll, three-one, built a point on her inner board. "I'll touch myself instead." Her hands ran crotchward along her thighs, fingertips passing behind the scrim.

"I can't tell if I'm losing or winning," Bruno said. A whine, not what he'd intended. He threw his dice, could barely read their faces. His checkers seemed of varying size and without gravity, drifting unmoored between points.

"Could be both at once."

"I think I'd like the puppet show." His voice was helplessly diminished, but she heard.

She turned the doubling die and moved it toward him. "Resign and we'll see."

"But you still have . . . a scrap of cloth covering your . . . scraps of cloth."

"So let's double resign." Tira reached across again and caught up the rim of his cockhead with her fingertips. At her encouragement it might float thrillingly free, to the ceiling. With her other hand she threaded her underwear around each hip in turn, and clambered forward, upsetting the board. "Open your mouth," she commanded. He obliged. She jammed the underwear between his teeth, then reached behind to grapple at the mask. "Where's the zipper on this thing?"

"It doesn't—" he mumbled through the gag.

"Never mind." She tore the Velcro fasteners loose, then swept the mask over his skull, bundling it in one hand with the fragrant underwear. Reluctantly, he opened his jaw, and she tossed both aside, their last disguises.

She fingertip-traced the toughening stitchery that framed his eyes. "Gentle."

"I used to have these tan alligator-leather pumps, fabulous shoes, they were in some luggage that was stolen in Costa Rica, I'm still pissed. You feel like you're made of that stuff."

"I'm a work in progress. I tenderize my alligator parts with vitamin E."

"You'll never look the same, Alexander. You're wearing a mask that won't come off."

Had she plucked it from his thoughts? He'd never suspected Tira of such powers. His head uncontainerized, anything was possible now. "As above, so below," he said, and guided her hand from his cock to the time-lost scars nested deep at its root.

"You're still fucking gorgeous," she said.

"Thank you."

"Now feel this." She guided his hand to her crotch, but surprised him, veering left. In the dense hair at the joint of her thigh, his fingers discovered a hard lump, golf-ball size, floating beneath the silken skin.

"A cyst," she said. "It's benign, I've had it for years."

"Oh." He caressed her there, drunk on confusion.

"They told me they could remove it," she said, defiantly. "I said not to bother, it wasn't troubling me."

If this was her test, it was easily passed. "You feel amazing."

The board was elbowed into the jumble with balled socks, his Berlin stone, the empty jam jar. A checker and a die slid into the sheets, clattering gently where Bruno's and Tira's bodies caved a depression in the tired mattress. Her presence was sturdy and watery at once, arms weirdly muscled, nipples like small tongues riding on the mercurial flesh that glided on his surface, thighs smooth to where his fingers plummeted inside, followed by the rest of him. The golf-ball cyst swam too, faintly present against him, a feature, not a bug. Tira, for all her usual chatter, wasn't a screamer or even a moaner. In the silence their breaths fell into concert with the whining Murphy springs. Bruno's mind felt poured into hers as well, at least conveyed a great distance out of his body.

The kitchen's light blocked by his own shadow, he couldn't read her face.

"I feel . . . swallowed," he said.

"Eat or be eaten," she whispered. "Engulf and Devour. That's our motto."

"Our?"

"It's a thing Keith says."

"Could we leave Keith out of it?" Bruno was no longer amused by puppets or anything else bearing Stolarsky's cloying trademark. He fought the suspicion that Stolarsky and Tira were one person, or that they at least assumed only a single attitude toward him. If there was no other reason to have fucked Tira, it would be to plant a definite secret between her and Stolarsky.

"Why bother to try?"

"Perhaps because he *is* out of it."

Unable to contain her hilarity, Tira issued a string of barks. She pushed Bruno off and rolled free, her postcoital transition palpable as steam or frost. "In what sense is Keith out of it?"

"He's left town." Bruno raised his hand, vaguely indicating Telegraph, the commercial row Stolarsky might rule but had mercifully abdicated, in favor of the mice who played. At least to claim number 25, their clandestine cell. "I don't want to presume, but I gathered he might have left *you*."

"I don't know what you're gathering or smoking. Moss maybe? Keith's been back for a couple of days. Actually, he wants to see you in his office tomorrow."

"His office?"

"Yeah." Now Tira was the one to gesture, with a nod of her chin. "Over at Zodiac." She rescued her clothing from the morass of sheets and checkers. Deftly restringing her brassiere over her shoulders, she groped behind to bring it taut. "He said the free ride is over now that you're well. That's what I came over here to tell you in the first place."

BOOK THREE

Sixty-Four

|

Keith Stolarsky's office was hidden at the back of Zodiac's second floor, behind a door layered with Nike posters, its doorknob a negligible detail anyone might overlook. Inside, it featured a long window, mirrored on the side the customers faced, like an archer's slit in a medieval battlement, so Stolarsky could peer out unseen. He might even have been here, spying, the day Alexander Bruno first discovered the *ABIDE* shirts and sweat gear in which he now stood arrayed before Stolarsky's desk—who knew?

The office was worse than ill-furnished and generic. It was like something an unmarried super might throw together at the back of a boiler room, a refuge whose walls investigators would later pry apart in search of hidden bodies. The huge, battered steel desk could have been salvaged from the Department of Motor Vehicles. Files bulged in the opened drawers of a metal cabinet, but also from cardboard boxes, on bracket shelves bolted into the concrete-block rear wall, and on the floor. On the desk before Stolarsky no computer, only a desk lamp, a scattering of paperback books and pornographic magazines, a tan Slimline telephone, a vintage Cal Bears ashtray, paper cups stained with evaporated coffee, a Polaroid camera, and Stolarsky's hands, which twitched and picked and abraded each other as though managing a craving for cigarettes or self-abuse. This was a bunker for firings, a black site for interrogating cornered shoplifters, or headquarters for plotting dark interventions at gatherings of the Telegraph Avenue Business Owners Association. Its existence ratified every worst implication in Garris Plybon's arsenal.

Bruno had come at noon, on Tira's instructions. The store was

215

empty, Telegraph still yawning. He'd been guided to the secret door by an unfamiliar clerk running the upstairs counter. Beth wasn't on the floor, that Bruno could see. Perhaps she slaved over receipts in another hidden room.

Keith Stolarsky didn't rise, or greet Bruno, just said, "Shut the door," then belched, stared, smacked his lips. The trollish face twitched, as if in strain at avoiding some too-obvious thought. Bruno stood, sealed in mask and hood, feeling at once mummified in his apartness from Stolarsky—and from the human species—and utterly naked. The room had one chair, besides Stolarsky's own, but it was a sorry thing, a plastic folding chair leaned against the side wall. To fetch it, in order to sit across from the man behind the desk, seemed a losing move. Bruno stood.

"So," said Stolarsky at last. "More hurt birds on my dime, eh?"

"Hurt birds?"

"Your poor pitiable dominatrix from the Fatherland."

"You know about her?" Either another human being was scanning every part of Bruno's mind, sifting it like sand, or wasn't. Bruno reminded himself this was the permanent situation, whether he troubled to think of it or not.

"Hey, I forked up her plane fare, I should know a thing or two."

"I apologize for that."

"Don't be sorry for me, be sorry for Beth."

"What happened to Beth?"

"Unemployment happened to Beth. She's out on her dyke ass for that horseshit. In fact, I was thinking of giving you her job, but then I got a better idea. Tira showed me that tape of you at Zombie. You made an impression. You're a spook-and-a-half, a legend in the making."

The lowliest European functionary—a border inspector, say— dressed immaculately, and furnished even a cubicle to lend an impression of respectability. A truly wealthy man, like Stolarsky, pronounced his status in paneling, burnished wood, fountain pens, leather volumes. Bruno banished the despondent thought; this baleful room was Europe's nullification.

"What's the matter, I trample on your delicate sensibilities? Look

216

at you, Flashman. You're all nobly damaged now, sealed in your face condom. What're you going to look like when you come out from under there—Jonah Hex?"

"It's a medical mask."

"Oh, sure. Don't worry, you should embrace the tall-dark-and-strange thing. You'll slay the ladies. It's that added layer of tragic mystery, like Bob Dylan or Lawrence of Arabia after the motorcycle accident."

"If I remember correctly, Lawrence of Arabia didn't survive his motorcycle accident."

"Whatever."

"Did you really fire Beth?"

"Let me put it to you this way: Is a high-end Nazi hooker really deplaning at SFO in two hours? One question answers the other."

Bruno didn't speak. Into the silence beats trickled through the tiles, something funky the clerks had cranked loud to salve their retail angst. Bruno glanced again at the chair, his fellow captive, the only thing less free to depart this room than he.

"What, you want to sit?"

"No."

"Should I make this more pleasant for you? Perhaps a drink? Maybe I should lay out some antipasto? Forgive me, it's hard to know how to make a man in a hood comfortable."

"I'm fine."

"You know, Flashman, when we were at Berkeley High, you were the most advanced kid I ever saw. It was thrilling, believe me. Like the girls, I practically came in my pants when you went walking by. Now I look at your life, and I think under the bogus mid-Atlantic accent and world-weary Man of La Mancha shit you probably never matured another inch beyond where I first laid eyes on you. You're stuck, while everyone else kept growing."

"I sip from a fountain of eternal youth." He meant to lampoon Stolarsky's fulminations, but circumstance had spoiled Bruno's tone. His ironies were ghoulish now.

"Yeah, well, contrary to a lot of wishful thinking on this avenue, I do not spend from a wallet of fathomless wealth," said Stolarsky. "You owe me."

Bruno fell silent at what was, after all, incontestable. Did Stolarsky regard Tira Harpaz as a feature of this debt? Bruno didn't want to know.

"I talked with your surgeon, he's wiping his hands of you. I wish I could say the same about the bills from intensive care, or the anesthesiology group—great racket!—or a hundred other fucking invoices coming out of the woodwork. You got an expensive new face, not that I'm noticing any gratitude. Are you in there, Flashman?"

"I'll honor the debt."

"We're not playing backgammon here. I've got businesses to run. Not to mention I could be taking rent out of that unit you're in."

"I can vacate the premises."

"That's how you're planning to greet your warm leatherette? Heil Hitler, and by the way, we're sleeping at the homeless shelter?"

German history, that wound gaping for anyone to poke a stick in; Bruno wouldn't be goaded into a defense. "I wouldn't worry. She should have them up and into boxcars in no time."

"Good one! Now there's the spirit we've been waiting for."

"Honestly, I have no idea where we'll go. It isn't your problem."

"Oh, it is, it is. My money, my problem. You know how it works in Native American lore, right? We all had to take that class at Malcolm X, it was as mandatory as gym or fractions. You save a man's life, he's your responsibility."

"That may not actually have been Native American lore, it might be from *Kung Fu* or *F Troop*. Anyway, I hereby absolve you."

"No dice. I got another one for you, Flash: my money, my problem, but also my *opportunity*. Here." Stolarsky slid open a wooden drawer, not smoothly, and pulled out something, a lump of cloth and rope, and shoved it onto the desktop. His smirk invited Bruno to understand this presentation as significant, a trump card played.

"What is it?"

"You can't serve food in that mask, it's too unsavory. You look like a burn victim, like there's no skin underneath. Nobody'll want to eat.

I got you this instead. It goes perfectly with the Zombie Burger motif. Like I said, you'll be a sensation. All you have to do is stand there, just like you're doing now. Hand the meals across, don't say a word. Here, try it on, I'll turn my back."

Bruno stepped nearer to see. He spread the loose-bunched object on the desk. A burlap hood, with precise, machine-sewn openings for the eyes, nostrils, and mouth. The thick rope hung at the neck, noose-knotted.

"You had this made?"

"Nah, it was lying around at Zodiac, from some Halloween crap we never could sell. Whole box of 'em. Just dumb luck."

The room seemed to incline beneath Bruno's feet. The desolate folded chair now stood uphill.

"It should light up pretty sweet," Stolarsky continued. He seemed abruptly cheery, high on his conceit. "If not, we've got this black-light-sensitive treatment we can douse it with, we keep it around. Sometimes the girls get crazy, use the stuff instead of lipstick."

"I'm not working at Zombie Burger." These words themselves seemed to Bruno to emanate from a zombie region of his anatomy, a howl of last resort.

"The hell you say."

"I can't." Now he pleaded. "I'm too old."

"You're not old, you're a 'totemic figure.' And you'll pull action like nobody's business. Everybody knows, they've been trained by the movies, that the guy in the Elephant Man sack is always gorgeous, it's always Mel fucking Gibson or David Bowie under there."

"I couldn't bear it."

"What, some sort of misguided loyalty to Tira?" It was the first time Stolarsky had mentioned her. So she'd told Stolarsky her request: that Bruno boycott Zombie. Bruno should accept it, he was encircled.

"Loyalty to myself," said Bruno. "Let me work at Kropotkin's instead."

"Shit. You like the little slider joint better?"

"Yes."

"That's fucking great, actually. I think I love it. Horn in on Plybon's scene, eh? You can even keep tabs on the righteous little bastard for me. Of course, it's a lot more work, you realize? You're destined to come home with twenty pounds of cancer smoke in your clothes. That hoodie's gonna soak up the carcinogens like a sponge. You sure it's recommended by your doctor?"

"I didn't have cancer."

"Sure. Cool. You can still wear this." Stolarsky pushed the sack-and-noose to the edge of the desk, near to falling at Bruno's feet. "In fact, that's the deal, from my end. Rent, medical bills"—he waved both hands outward, as if clearing steam from a windshield—"poof, finito. You only have to flip sliders in a noose."

"Thank you," Bruno heard himself say.

"We'll call you, I don't know, *Le Martyre de Anarchie*. Is that a real thing? It *sounds* real." Stolarsky's French accent was surprisingly good, at least for the duration of one phrase.

"Real enough."

"Plybon's gonna shit his pants."

Bruno could think of nothing to say to this. He gathered the Halloween mask and bunched it into one pocket of his sweatshirt, to contemplate later. He felt dizzy with submission. As well as famished at all the talk of burgers. Had he done enough, been served adequate justice, to be excused from detention?

"I don't care if you don't want to try it on. Lemme see your face now."

"Sorry?"

"I paid for it, I want to look."

Bruno loosened the Velcro at the back of the medical mask. If he'd complied in the hope of jolting Stolarsky into decency, he was disappointed. Stolarsky grabbed the Polaroid camera from the junk heaped on his desk and pulled the trigger—a flash, then a mechanical wheeze as the device produced its black, chemical-smelling tongue.

"What's that for?" Bruno replaced his mask.

Stolarsky jerked his thumb at the wall. "Rogue's gallery." Polaroid shots were stuck on a bulletin board in a loose collection, each a surly portrait of a startled subject. "Shoplifters. We bring 'em back here and take a picture, so we'll recognize 'em if they come back. Don't worry, I won't hang yours up."

"Thank you," said Bruno stupidly.

"So, Flashman's returning to his roots," said Stolarsky, expansive again. "Scene of the crime, just like back in the day." He spoke as if envious of some romantic fate Bruno were about to enjoy.

"How so?"

"East Bay, serving grub. Like you never went away."

"I think it's like I went very far away indeed."

"Oh, *indeed, indeed.*" Generous in victory, Stolarsky seemed to believe his taunting could be taken as affectionate. "So what's with the German paramour, how come you didn't mention her? Why wasn't she at your bedside?"

"It's a . . . new thing."

"A leap into the unknown!"

Would he never shut up? "Yes. Excuse me, Keith, I should go. I have to take BART to the airport, to meet her flight." Bruno didn't mention his hunger.

"Are you kidding? That's a hell of a flight, you don't want her to have to ride public transportation after a crossing like that."

"I'm not sure I have another option," said Bruno neutrally. He didn't want a handout, let alone a ride in the Jag.

"Relax, I wouldn't dream of it. Tira got her arrival gate off the receipt, so I sent a car. The Kraut'll be delivered with her luggage right to your door. You can go buy some flowers, air out the sheets, get prettied up, whatever that means in your current condition."

Bruno struggled to find his voice. "You didn't have to do that."

"Well, I did. She's under my wing now—just like you."

II

In a daze that seemed to command him to locomotion, Bruno crossed campus to Northside. There he found a panini, a concession to hunger and a minor gesture of resistance against his burger fate. Strolling clear of the shops, up Euclid Avenue toward the hills, he entertained a modest fantasy of wending into Wildcat Canyon and vanishing from Berkeley altogether. Ironically, now it was Madchen who bound him, his obligation to her arrival that kept him from rupturing his bubble of captivity. Bruno reversed course, out of the eucalyptus-crisp hillside, back to the beer- and clove-tainted avenue, back among the street vendors and runaways. He entered the Jack London fearful of running into Plybon, not knowing how he'd account for himself if he did, but saw no one.

In the stillness of number 25, Bruno waited through the afternoon and until after dark. The previous night he'd rinsed and wrung his mask, hand-washed his dirty clothes, spread all on the shower-curtain rod to dry. Now, defying the sense that he obeyed Stolarsky's command, Bruno neatened his rooms, tightened the sheets on the Murphy bed, folded the towels, swabbed the counters, the little there was to do.

•

Hours later, Madchen knocked. Opening the door, Bruno found her standing, tall and pensive, sallow in the corridor's light, with a single large backpack she'd removed and set beside her like a teenage backpacker on a train platform.

She stared and lifted her hand as if to touch his mask, but stopped short. "Alexander?"

"Yes."

He took the backpack inside. She stepped in wonderingly, taking the measure of the apartment's modesty; a reassurance, it seemed. She smiled shyly and put herself forward, into his embrace. He marveled again at her superb height. They jostled together, chins delicately perched over each other's shoulders, arms mingling with a goofy hesitancy. She unclenched her hand to reveal a ring with two fresh-cut keys.

"I was given this key, by the driver—"

"Yes, I know." He spoke soothingly, not wanting to jar her. "Was your plane late?"

"Only a little—he drove me to a restaurant, this was very strange for me."

"Who drove you?"

"The driver of the car, I don't know the word. I was sent alone inside, to eat. A meal was ordered for me—you know this, *ja?*"

"I didn't, but I can guess. Was the restaurant called Zuni?"

"Alexander, are you a wealthy man?"

"No, the opposite." *You and I are the captives, together, of a wealthy man.* He didn't speak the words. There was time. "So, you ate."

Madchen shook her head firmly. "I was given chicken and seafood, but I can't eat this, I'm a *vegetarierin*, Alexander. A vegetarian." So the avalanche of all he didn't know about this woman would now come loose. Bruno would have to let it come. He rehearsed her peculiar last name silently, Abplanalp, Abplanalp the Vegetarian . . .

"You didn't explain?"

"The food was waiting for me. And the driver, outside. I ate salad."

Bruno offered Madchen water in the jam jar and fixed her Cheerios and milk in his single bowl. She sat on the edge of the bed. He watched. As she chewed Madchen offered the wary grateful glances of a creature lured indoors, a feral pet rescued. Finishing, she put the bowl aside. She must be tired; he'd put her to bed. He reached to smear away a dribble of milk on her chin. She took the gesture, though, as a call to reach out in turn. With the barest of touches, she located not the mask itself but his throat, at the margin above his shirt.

"About your sickness, I don't understand, Alexander."

223

"I'll explain. There's no hurry."

"*Ja.*" Her hand lingered at his throat, with the opposite of urgency. As when she'd entered, half dressed, into Wolf-Dirk Köhler's study, even walking her bike off the ferry, Madchen drew from a reservoir of stillness, as though her movements were dictated by an offstage choreographer whose motifs she rendered dispassionately, though they might stir passion in others. Or was she depressed? She might be traumatized, bullied, in flight not from a choreographer but from a pimp. Or more simply an anemic, jet-lagged vegetarian barely able to lift her arms.

Now she traced the mask's seam at the chin. Bruno felt the awful perplexity of her arrival here, the duty incurred, the bomb dropped into his solitude.

"You should sleep," he said.

"No."

"No?"

"I don't want to sleep. I slept in the airplane."

"Yes."

"May I go now in the bath?"

"Yes, of course." Bruno had never filled the tub, only drawn the curtain to use the shower. He moved into the bathroom and ran it now, first stopping the drain with a clunky metal lever. The porcelain tub was short and steep, half Madchen's length. The taps gushed torrentially.

"Have you candles?"

"No, I'm sorry. I can get some."

"It's okay, Alexander. Just shut the light." Bruno obeyed, also turning the handles to stop the water, which had quickly risen to the level of the gulping overflow drain. He immersed his hand, testing the temperature, swirling to mix the currents of hot and cold. High moonlight leaked in across the courtyard, outlining Madchen as she shed her clothes and pushed past him, to lower herself into the water. Her lithe body seemed to sparkle uncannily, as though she'd captured some radiation from her passage through the lower stratosphere; perhaps it was this layer she wished to sluice off. She hugged her knees and bent her head back against the porcelain, showing her long throat, careless of her hair soaking and drifting on the water's surface. Her eyes were shut, allowing him to inspect her face, to rediscover the discrete net of wrinkles at the corners of her mouth and eyes, the coarser hairs, white hiding among the blond.

"Please, take away your clothes and your mask."

"Are we going to make love?"

"Only I want to see your face, Alexander."

He stripped, lay the mask on the sink, knelt again. She turned enough to see, stretched her hand out again, not quite to touch his chin.

"Oh, baby."

"Yes."

"They hurt you, baby."

"They did their best," he said stupidly, not even knowing what he meant.

"Wash my back."

Gratefully Bruno placed both hands in the water, took up the soap and the thin cloth. She bent forward, gathered her hair to the far shoulder, stretching a sweet dinosaur's spine. As he rinsed foam from her ribs he saw in the moonlight that a portion of Madchen's sparkle, her weird radiation, had transferred to him, was blended in the hair of his forearms. Peering closer, Bruno determined it was glitter, infinitesimal foil stars and hearts and half-moons. Mixing with silt and soap, the stuff was everywhere, had formed a ring on the porcelain, above the waterline.

"From a party," said Madchen unapologetically.

"Okay."

She rose shimmering and allowed him to wrap her in a towel. She gripped her loose hair in both hands and squeezed it like a sponge, trailing drops on the floor and soaking the towel where it made a collar at her neck.

"Now I will wash you."

"It's okay, I showered before." The gray glittered soup wasn't completely appealing.

"Stay with your clothes off, *bitte*."

225

"Yes."

"And no light too."

"Yes."

She took him by the hand to the bed and they lay side by side. Bruno didn't ask again whether they were going to make love. He wasn't against or for it, couldn't locate desire. The moonlight cast planetary shade hollows at her cheek and clavicle and hip bone. Bruno's hand felt made of cheese, something heavy and yellow, left out too long and sweating. He didn't dare lift it.

Then Madchen touched his face, at last, and he began to weep, the first evidence that his ducts lived. Once loosed, he couldn't stop. Her hand moved to his chest, fingers nestled in the hairs, and as if activated by her touch his chest began heaving too, carving out sea-lion or water-buffalo sounds it was an effort to believe he was the source of. He felt the saltwater's course complicated by irregular topography, his map of facial disaster. Madchen lay simply parallel, as though obeying the command of Bruno's discarded T-shirt. After some time her unjudgmental stillness seemed to reach into Bruno and cool his seething. She rolled the other way so he could spoon her, and they both slept. Neither woke, neither heard, when the envelope was slipped beneath his door, to be discovered in daylight. Its contents, another clutch of twenties, three hundred dollars in total, and a note in Garris Plybon's handwriting, which Bruno knew instantly from the conspiratorial scrawlings annotating the printouts and manifestos Scotch-taped to the walls of Kropotkin's: *Come for the night shift, Fuckface. And don't forget the noose.* Bruno pocketed the money and crumpled the note, with the envelope, discreetly into his kitchen trash.

III

Madchen Abplanalp wasn't from Berlin to begin with. Like so many young Germans, she'd had to arrive there. The only child of strict and straitlaced Catholic parents, Madchen came of age in the city of Konstanz, on Bodensee Lake and the Rhine River, a town which had spared itself from Allied bombing—spared its great cathedral, spared its picturesque "old town," spared its historical traces, its medieval bridge pilings—by pretending to be part of Switzerland. Madchen's father, a corporate lawyer working in patents, adored and ignored her, spending more weeknights in Frankfurt, at an apartment he kept there ostensibly for business purposes, than he did at home. Weekends, resplendent at a beach-house camp that stood as compensation for both his absences and for their small, too-formal suburban home, he fished and cooked and doted on his daughter while neglecting his wife. Madchen's mother, in turn, clung to the girl and confided what she had—which was nothing.

This was a childhood of lakes, chocolate, and boredom. At eighteen, when Madchen's escape should have come in the form of entrance to Goethe University Frankfurt, reward for diligence in her studies, her father wrecked it. On the day of his daughter's acceptance to university he announced his demand for a divorce, from the mother and from Konstanz. As soon as possible he sold the beach house and was gone. He seemed to think he'd served his time, done his duty, and that he and Madchen would be fellow escapees, but the result was the opposite: the mother collapsed.

It was their family priest who contacted Madchen, a week into residency in her first-year dormitory room, to say she was needed at home. Madchen's compliance, her return to that house, closed the door on Frankfurt. Madchen was required to mourn with her mother, to hate with her mother, and it was only at twenty-two, still a virgin, at the age she should have been finishing a degree, that she broke away, shifted responsibility to their remaining church friends, and fled the cloistering atmosphere of Konstanz and the mother and former wife so totally unstrung.

Madchen attained entry at the Freie Universität in Berlin, far from Konstanz but also from her father's Frankfurt, though she continued to take his money, the allowance she'd hidden from her mother and had largely squirreled away. There'd been nothing to spend it on in Konstanz; now it purchased an apartment in Neukölln.

But the punishments didn't stop, because life isn't like that. Her mother died three months after Madchen left. This was the blow that sent Madchen reeling, after such dutifulness. Perhaps she'd inherited, after all, her father's sense that familial allegiance could be paid off, as if on account. Now Madchen hated him for her own part, not her mother's. In fresh defiance, she found a way to inflict punishment as well as absorb it: She refused his money and broke contact, but not before alluding to a heroin problem. This last, a sly torpedo to her father's long-range filial vanity, but unfortunately also real. For the second time, she dropped out of university, but not to return to Konstanz. She never did return to Konstanz. Berlin was home.

•

She'd spoken as they walked, this bright cool morning, launching from a breakfast of croissants and lattes at Café Mediterraneum, along College Avenue to the BART overpass at Rockridge. There they found a boutique and spent a couple of Bruno's twenties on candles and incense. Then back, to inhabit a bench in People's Park. Seated here, the paper sack at her feet, she and Bruno dwelled nominally in Berkeley's open-air communal armpit, but her narration made a bubble around them, and no one approached. The German's company had elevated the man in the mask to something invulnerable, perhaps sublime, not to be mistaken for another eccentric denizen here. The park couldn't touch him.

Madchen didn't specify how heroin desolation had led, in the decade that followed, to vegetarianism and bicycles, to serving shrimp sandwiches in a zippered mask on the island of Kladow, or occasions that left her slimy with spangles. Bruno didn't need to read her mind to guess at the corrupting boyfriends, shitty jobs, the solidarity of Berlin's sex workers. The drugs were surely put behind her; Madchen radiated good health, expert dentistry, the Alexander Technique, a vitality that made the sun-beaten dreadlocked urban campers roaming the park resemble by contrast the dazed survivors of a neutron bomb.

At the exact moment Madchen touched his arm and asked about his parents Bruno was startled, even panicked, by the sight of an elderly woman pushing a rusted shopping cart that trailed rattling bags of aluminum cans up Haste Street. The woman made an emblem, a Sisyphean tableau. Of course it wasn't June. June was gone.

"I grew up here." It was more precisely true than she could know. If Madchen had delivered him, with her tale, to Konstanz, he'd walked her into his own unbearable ground zero. But he felt disinclined even to say his mother's name aloud. She felt present, anyhow, evoked somewhere in the distance between the hag now rattling mercifully beyond hearing and the woman on the bench beside him, Madchen with her strange innocent worldliness. Not everything needed to rise to converge: It could just drift together into the indiscernible middle, and bewilder you. All sad bereft girls were prone to fall, and to fall prey. Some pulled themselves up, at least partway. Bruno fooled with such thoughts, then abandoned them. Madchen waited.

"I never knew my father at all," he said at last.

"But your mother?"

Oh, that's her right there. But the woman with the cart was gone from sight.

"Do you know whether your father is still alive?" Bruno asked instead.

She shrugged. "He must be alive. Or some lawyer would be calling me, *ja*? I would be getting his houses, I think."

"Well, if my mother was dead I wouldn't know. No one would." Bruno let this remark sit dry and unadorned. He had no desire to cultivate Madchen's pity. Bruno's self-pity was already so luxuriant he could barely see over the top of it. Tira's scorn, or even Stolarsky's, would make a better tonic to his mood.

But here was Bruno's weakness. He relished the scorn of his enemies. It was one thing when he'd been suavely robbing them at clubs and in their private drawing rooms, then gliding like a knife through their four-star amenities. Now that he was cornered, a baited creature with a devastated face, Bruno couldn't afford their contempt. Tira and Stolarsky meant to destroy him. He grabbed Madchen's arm.

"We have to leave this place."

"You mean the Menschenpark?"

"Yes, but also Berkeley." His mask told her nothing of his panic, restricted her from his thoughts. She merely waited, with a St. Bernard's faithfulness. Bruno was beneficiary of the same implacable patience that had mired the Catholic girl in Konstanz, in a delayed virginity. He didn't need her pity, no, but Madchen's unfathomable faith in him was like a diamond found in a field of mud.

"Don't misunderstand," he said. "I'm glad you came here, all this way. I *needed* you here. But now you have to help me escape."

"Of course, I will do this, Alexander."

"We'll buy a car." He heard himself falling helplessly into jumbled images of a frontier exodus, passage into some road movie. A car was meant to ramble west, and there was no farther west to go. Perhaps Big Sur, though Kerouac fantasies might be out-of-date, overwritten by the Esalen hot tubs of Tira's account. Or Joshua Tree, Sedona. Germans loved the desert and canyonlands, the pure Martian America. "I just need to earn—to *win* us the money, and we'll go."

"Okay." Madchen smiled and touched his hand. "Alexander, when you spoke to me on the phone, of this man who had seen this woman on the Kladow boat, I understood you were my friend, *ja*? And that you had to find your way out. You sounded in a prison, or a tunnel. Maybe it is possible the prison is inside? Sorry, inside your . . . skull? I don't have the better word." Again Madchen employed her magic gesture: to reach for, but not quite to touch, Bruno's mask. Then raised her hand to sketch the picture of where they sat on the bench in the shade of the sick, resigned trees, the park hemmed everywhere by the crooked sidewalks, the parked cars that looked as though they never moved. "Maybe there, not so much *outside.*"

"Maybe both places," he said.

Madchen smiled lightly, as if she'd gained a concession but didn't want to appear to rub it in. "You must need to see your doctors, *ja?*"

"No." In fact, Bruno had ignored the calls from Kate, Noah Behringer's martinet assistant. Bruno's new cell-phone petitioner, to replace Madchen. He'd erased the messages and switched off the ringer.

"But you have your friend."

"He only seems like a friend." Bruno restrained himself. Better not to panic Madchen into flight. She'd need to be comfortable at the Jack London, to hide safe in the trap until they could fully elude it. "You shouldn't have anything to do with him."

"I'm confused, Alexander. Didn't this person paid for your surgery, and also sent my airport car?"

"Yes and no. I mean, it is the same person. He's treated people . . . badly." Bruno felt seasick with an onrush of guilt: He'd barely thought of Beth Dennis. "The girl who arranged your ticket, that's your real friend—he fired her for it."

"Why?"

"Because he could."

"But this is a terrible thing."

"I know." He pulled her to her feet. "Come, let's see her girlfriend, I should have thought of this sooner. She works at the art museum, we passed it, coming here—" They swept from the park, along Bowditch Street, aloft on his urgency. Madchen had a runner's lightness, unlike most who slugged along these piss-soaked sidewalks—in her company, he might not even need a car to vanish.

•

The vast brutalist art museum seemed abandoned. Though the doors were open, the halls lay dark, apart from the café and gift shop, as though in a hideous concession to the fact that no one cared for art exhibits in the first place. But what of the film archive? The only person answerable for the conundrum was another clerk, manning the gift shop's lonely counter, a near-teenager with green hair. Bruno marched up, oblivious to the effect of his mask. Madchen behind him, Alice to his Red Queen.

"What happened to the film archive?"

The green-haired boy opened his mouth soundlessly, both hands rising slightly into the air with surprise or perhaps fear. He might have believed he'd entered a crime story, might be about to break into sweat and mumble pleadingly that he didn't have access to the store's vault. At that moment Madchen leaned in and touched the clerk on the arm, and said, "Don't worry, *bitte*. My friend was in the hospital. He recovers from an injury."

"Oh."

"We're only looking for the film archive that used to be here," said Bruno. "It was part of the museum."

"Ah, yes." The green-haired boy rearranged his expression, landing on one simultaneously bored and placating. "Oh, the screenings are across the street now, on Bancroft. It's a pretty good temporary venue, actually."

"I want to talk to one of the archivists."

"Oh, I'm sorry, the archive won't reopen until the new building's finished."

"A new building?"

"This place isn't earthquake safe, even though it looks like one big piece of concrete." The clerk glanced at the ceiling. "We're under the Sword of Damocles here."

"You're quite brave," said Bruno.

"Heh."

"They didn't fire the archivists, did they?" Had Keith Stolarsky arranged to have a museum condemned in retribution for Beth and Alicia's defiance?

"Fire them? No, the same people will run the new place, sir. At the moment they're busy readying the collection for transfer."

"I'm looking for Alicia—do you know her?"

"Alicia? Oh, yeah. I'm not sure, I think she's on leave."

"Do you know Beth Dennis?"

The green-haired clerk looked at him blankly.

"Thanks anyway," said Bruno.

"Of course. They're screening Rohmer's *Perceval le Gallois* later today, a rare print. I'd go if I were you."

"Thank you," said Madchen.

Outside the museum door, Madchen climbed a low concrete wall, into the grounds of the strange condemned museum, the gated lawns punctuated with forgotten sculpture. Bruno followed. They slid into the shadow of a rusted-steel glyph bolted to a concrete apron. Madchen put her face near Bruno's, as if they were under threat of surveillance beneath the California sunshine. She entered easily into his spirit of persecution; that might be what he loved in her.

"Don't be worried," she breathed. "We'll find your friends."

"I'm not sure how."

"You terrorized the young man, in your mask." She took his hands, their fingers tangling splendidly.

"All I have to do is interrogate all the clerks and waiters in this town, until one admits what he knows." But Bruno's guilt had evaporated into happy helplessness. It wasn't his fault Stolarsky had the power to make people and archives disappear.

"They will give you anything you want."

"No, but it's the two of us that terrorized him. Alone I'm just another Berkeley street nightmare, and so practically invisible. A preposterously tall and elegant German at my side, that's what made the impression."

"*Ja,* thought he met the Rote Armee Fraktion."

"The who?"

"The Baader-Meinhof Gruppe, they are called also."

"Yes." Bruno didn't need to understand exactly. Likely it was some variant of the Nazi culpability Germans tended to confess at the slightest instigation.

"But now, Alexander, you no longer need this." She freed her hand to touch the nape of his neck, then sprung the bottom-most Velcro fastener.

"I—"

She was close to his ear, whispering again. "You will be more beautiful, also maybe more terrifying because more real. It's okay."

"I don't know."

"Try for me, *bitte*. Here in this garden."

Why not? Bruno could shed the mask, and he and Madchen their clothes, to reenact Eden on the condemned museum's grounds, claiming the real estate preemptively against Keith Stolarsky or any other speculator. Lay down and fuck before the bulldozers, a People's Park of two. By the logic of Berkeley it was surprising it hadn't happened already. Bruno only feared the unstoppering of his head's two-way valve. It might be safe here, with the blob of sculpture for a barricade, an external blot against mental radiation. There was nothing to fear from Madchen. She wasn't capable of it. If he read her mind he might only unwittingly unveil the street plan of Konstanz, the faces of those who'd spangled her torso with stars and moons, or the truth about the Baader-Meinhof Gruppe.

She eased her hand up to the next of the Velcro fasteners. Bruno felt the mask slip loose, air circulating to the tender flesh beneath his eyes. She was a genius at undoing clothes one-handed. What that indicated, Bruno didn't need to know. She slipped it loose, bunched it in her hand, and ran the fingers of her other hand through his hair.

"I know what you need," she said.

"What's that?"

"*Haarschnitt.*" She mimed scissors with paired fingers, as if trimming along the curve of his ears.

"The barbers near campus are for swimmers and wrestlers, they only buzz it off." He made a fist, and the sound of an electronic clipper, moved it threateningly toward her long hair. They were like Crusoe and Friday, marooned on the museum's lawn, reinventing human society.

"No, no, we should find scissors."

"The candles."

Her eyes widened.

"We forgot them."

They scurried back to People's Park, Bruno barely noticing the absence of his mask. The white paper sack containing candles and incense was unstolen, safe beneath the splintery bench where they'd sat. On Telegraph, she stopped him in front of Walgreens, put the sack into his hands, a finger to her lips. "I'll come back." He was left to contemplate the sidewalk, full of listless earring vendors ready with their piercing guns. She'd lifted away his mask the way Behringer had lifted away the blot, so that more world could flood in. But it was nothing he'd particularly missed when it was gone. Madchen reappeared and took his arm. Halfway down the block she revealed the plastic-packaged scissors shoved up her sleeve.

"I could have given you some dollars."

"It's not crime to steal from a store like that."

Inside number 25 she stripped him and placed him in front of the mirror, where he studied his own altered face while she clipped and schnitted expertly away. Beautiful and terrifying: He could accept the verdict now. It helped that Madchen cleared the salt-and-pepper scruff, repairing the outlines of his last, too-long-ago haircut, in Berlin. Bruno could permit himself to enter the ranks of the legendary and scarred. Madchen evened his sideburns, then braced one foot on the tub to snip at his crown. As the tiny clipped lengths rained on Bruno's shoulders and nose, she whisked them clear with puffs of her mild sweet breath. Within the narrow symmetry of his temples, the irregularity of his features was like an action painter's gesture immaculately framed, hung on a museum wall. Finished, she stood beside him in the mirror, almost his height. Then she stripped off her own clothes and rotated the taps.

"We wash each other."

They still hadn't made love, or even made out. They didn't now, under the shower. It was less than twenty-four hours since her arrival. Their purification rite could take longer, Bruno wasn't sure. He wouldn't tamper with a sequence that seemed foretold, beyond his control. Clipped hairs and glitter swirled together into the drain. The supply of glitter might be infinite, it might issue from some part of her body, who was he to presume?

Afterward, in a fresh *ABIDE* shirt and sweatpants, he left his mask aside. He switched on the cell, not because he was curious about calls—there were none—but because it was the only timepiece in the apartment. The Kropotkin's night shift began at five. Bruno went into the kitchen and took some pills, though he'd stopped knowing exactly what they were for, nor had he kept to any schedule. He'd finish the bottles, anyway. For now he'd follow orders, lay low, though Madchen had given him new courage. She'd returned Bruno's face to him. It might not be the same face, but he had something he could work with.

"Will you be comfortable staying here alone?" he asked her. She'd helped herself to one of the *ABIDE* shirts as well, sat dressed in only the T-shirt at the joint of the wall and the Murphy bed's mattress. "I have to go out for a few hours."

"You are going to gamble for money?"

He nodded. The lie assembled itself so neatly, it seemed pointless to resist.

"Please be careful, Alexander."

"I'm not doing anything dangerous. I'll simply be relieving some undergraduates of a few of their parents' dollars." This was effectively truthful. Bruno reached for his sweatshirt hoodie.

"Do you need this?" She offered his backgammon set from beside the bed. It was the first she'd remarked on it.

"That won't be needed, thank you."

"Okay."

There was something plaintive beneath her consent. As though the girl from Konstanz had offered up her father's briefcase when he departed for the train to Frankfurt, and been refused. She needed a deeper assurance, but Bruno hadn't much to give.

"I'll be fine."

"You have the keys if you want to go out."

"*Ja.* I might be sleeping."

"You should."

Bruno felt in the pocket of the sweatshirt, confirming Stolarsky's Halloween sack-and-noose was bundled there, where Bruno had left it. He'd don it outside, or maybe stop in the bushes of People's Park. She might have restored his face to him, yes. But Bruno remained, like Madchen in Kladow, a performer designated to appear in a mask.

IV

They weren't burgers. They weren't to be called burgers, nor mini-
burgers, nor burgerettes. They were *sliders,* a whole other species.
This was the first thing to know. Garris Plybon had said before that
assembling the Kropotkin's specialty wasn't a "prohibitively difficult
formula"—but on Alexander Bruno's arrival for the night shift Plybon
bore down like a drill sergeant to be certain Bruno had grasped its
intricacies. The buns were steamed. Actually, news of this particular
fetish had reached Bruno's ears. His Gourmet Ghetto days had left
him alert to such distinctions. But steamed in beef and onion broth,
rather than water? That he couldn't have known. The patties themselves, despite the delectable char wafting up, were principally steamed
as well. The flattop grill was kept at a moderate heat and sprinkled
with the same broth to keep it moist, beads that hopped among the
rivulets of grease which melted free of the fatty ground chuck.

"The patties barely touch the grill, see?"

"I see," said Bruno, the rapt student. Indeed, the patties reclined,
like in *The Princess and the Pea,* on a heavily salted bed of vaporizing
onions.

"White Castle never even flips 'em," said Plybon. "That's why they
punch the little holes, so the beef cooks through from one side. Highly
efficient, cuts down on smoke, but you're basically eating meat loaf.
The Kropotkin's way is to flip. We keep the grill hotter over here"—he
indicated the area nearest the gutter—"for one quick scorch at the end.
You know the word *rime*? Like *frost*?"

"A poetical word." The burlap mask's mouth hole hung loosely,
unlike that of Bruno's medical garment. Still, he could make himself

heard. Despite the burlap's rough outer surface, the interior was satin-smooth and fit comfortably, cinching securely at the nape of his neck. The noose was ballast, its knot bumping annoyingly below his Adam's apple.

"Sure, poetical. Well, we give these puppies a rime of carbon—you read me?"

"I think so."

"Cheese, too, if they want it, goes at the last possible second." Plybon, demonstrating, reversed a quartet of sliders off their pallet of onion, to kiss the greater heat. He flopped on thin squares of orange cheese, peeled from a nearby stack. This the steam flash-dissolved, so the cheese donated its own grease to the reservoir. Then, just as rapidly, Plybon shifted them off, between steamed buns and into the tiny paper wrappers.

Orders flew, for burgers eaten at the counter or taken out in grease-spotted white bags. Plybon, energized in congenial chaos, cooked, waged his tutorial, bagged, and rang the register, like some mad organist operating a Wurlitzer; still, his customers were backed up through the door. At the peak the line went nearly to Bowditch. After the counterman pushed the almighty bladed spatula into Bruno's hands, he only seized it back when the outcome of some patty or batch of onions didn't suit his perfectionism. Then he'd scrape the result into the grill's gutter and slap down new raw ingredients. When Bruno got it right, Plybon merely rang the register and regaled the clientele with non sequitur proclamations: "In times of revolution one can dine contentedly enough on bread and cheese while eagerly discussing events!" he'd shout. Or: "The house was not built by its owner, nor the sandwich by its eater!"

Those who'd gotten through the door, suffering their hunger pangs in the savory fumes, groaned when seemingly perfect sliders went into the bin. This might have been Plybon's desired effect: Let them suffer, force them to dwell on the agitprop taped or stenciled on every available surface. Don't like waiting? There's always Zombie Burger. No one ever surrendered their place in line. They gabbled on devices or among themselves, or tittered in fascination at the show, a tandem act starring the famous geek-revolutionary slider cook and his tall apprentice in burlap and noose. The boldest, usually healthy frat-boy types decorated in extra hair or sleeve tattoos or seashell necklaces, minimal renovations acquired overnight, after disappointing the hopes of the swim coach who'd ratified their scholarship, threw out half-assed provocations of their own.

"Hey, Anonymous! Make me two with extra hacktivism!"

"Oh, yeah, *V for Vendetta*!"

"But look, he's Lebowski. That's the Dude under there!"

"Lost some weight, if so."

"He's a lynched man, can't you see? I think Johnny Depp shot him off a tree branch in *Lone Ranger*."

"*Django Unchained,* you mean."

"Sterling Hayden in *Johnny Guitar*," Garris Plybon corrected in passing. Bruno said nothing until a young woman in bangs and glasses, waiting for her food to come off the grill, asked quietly, "Who *are* you?"

Bruno demurred. "Just the new guy at the shop. A trainee."

"No. What are you meant to *be*?" She spoke as if Bruno's costume was a cipher demanding decryption.

"The Martyr of Anarchy," Bruno replied. The deeper he hid within Stolarsky's charade, the less he'd give away. A holding game: count the pips, obey the dice, and move his trailing checkers to safety.

"Anarchism doesn't produce martyrs," said Plybon. "The state makes martyrs." The slider cook's jaw was clenched, his eyes black and hard inside their magnifying prisms.

"What does anarchism produce?" asked the young woman.

"Anarchism produces humans, thanks for asking. And meals. You want extra onions?" Extra onions remained Plybon's quiet high sign of respect. "Go ahead, I can see you want to say yes. Anyone put off by onion breath isn't who you want to know in the first place."

Plybon refused her money, shifting it back without explanation. Ever mercurial, he was set off again. "An apple a day keeps the doctor away, you've heard that one?" He looked to the slider line for some "yea"s. "Right, it's like the rain in Spain falls mainly on the plain, we're all drilled on this shit in the Fordist factories that pass for primary school. Well, an apple a day keeps the doctor away, right, sure, *but an onion a day keeps the whole world at bay.*" This drew laughs, but Plybon raised his hand for silence. "My colleague here, he can't show his face to the world, in point of fact he's one of the famous disasters of Western medicine. You think I'm kidding, right? But I'm not. Tell them, comrade."

"Tell them . . . what?"

"Who did this to you, the so-called health industry or anarchism?"

"It's true I had a run-in with a neurosurgeon. It seemed necessary at the time."

"You should have stuck to onions." At this, Plybon lost his audience, who'd perhaps found the medical explanation for the Halloween mask unsavory. "I shall continue to be an impossible person," Plybon snarled, turning back to the grill, "so long as those who are now possible remain possible! Bakunin said that, suckers."

At that, Plybon jammed a scuffed compact disc, Sharpie-marked "Sonny Sharrock," into a boom box, let the resultant skronking guitar be his proxy. Bruno had found a reliable rhythm of production at the grill. He'd stopped sizzling up rejects. Moving like an agitated puppet, Plybon bagged the results and worked the register, slapping change into palms, impounding dollar-bill tips for the plastic tip jar on his own prerogative, glaring with his X-Ray Spex to dare anyone to complain.

As suddenly as he and Bruno became a systematic team, the line evaporated. Plybon raised the volume to an intolerable level, scouring the counter seats free of loiterers. For a while the counterman ignored Bruno, scraping at the grill, loading the steaming trays with fat pale buns, and restacking the raw patties and cheese slices. Then he reduced the volume and turned on Bruno, startling him. "Do you know the first fucking thing about the Haymarket Trial?"

"Sorry? No."

" 'The Martyr of Anarchy'? Who came up with that crapola, you or Lord Zodiac?"

"It was Stolarsky," Bruno admitted.

"Eight anarchists in Chicago, 1886, four hanged by the neck after a frame-up and kangaroo trial. They were left dangling, instead of dropped properly through a trapdoor, so they died by slo-mo strangulation. I guess that's your childhood playmate's idea of yuks."

Bruno understood: It was the noose mask that had offended him. "I'm not sure Keith knew the historical reference. It seemed more impulsive, really. If he'd had a mask lying around with a fake butcher's cleaver stuck in the forehead, he'd probably have given me that."

"Don't underestimate Stolarsky. Look at you, for instance. He's fucking slaughtered your pride six ways from Sunday just for . . . what, being handsomer than him on the playground one day in 1978?"

"The surgery saved my life."

"Riiiight, but what's it worth?" The counterman's eyes pinwheeled behind his goggly lenses.

Bruno wasn't certain he understood the question. "My life?"

"Yeah, to Stolarsky. Count up his outlay on the surgery, flying you across the ocean, forgoing rent, et cetera. Because whatever the price tag, Stolarsky never lays a bet with less than a ten-to-one payout. It may appear he's doing charity, but trust me, you're human capital. The Tsar of Telegraph may hang fire awhile. Hell, he bought up vacant lots he'll pay taxes on for a decade just to ensure his competition does business in what looks like Dresden after the war. But he's got something cooking on the back end, he always does. He's got a role for you, O Martyr. You just don't know what it is yet."

"What about Beth? Was she also human capital? Keith seems willing to take a loss there."

"Listen, Stolarsky's been looking to fire Beth for a while now, she was a huge disappointment to him."

"Disappointment how?"

"He was cultivating a lieutenant. Beth was meant to be his set of eyes, his mole in the burrow. Instead she got heavy into workplace solidarity, a syndicalist tendency I'll admit I encouraged. Among other things, she was originally supposed to spy on me, just like he probably asked you."

"Not in so many words."

"Ha!"

"I won't."

"You'll do it despite yourself, comrade. You're a leaky sieve. I don't hold it against you. Listen, you want a taste of what you're up against? The sheer vindictiveness? Stolarsky gave her notice on her apartment."

"Wait, she's in the Jack London?"

"Nah, just some antiseptic cracker-box complex on Bowditch, but Stolarsky owns that, too."

"That's cruel."

"I'm not done yet. He made certain Beth's dissertation committee heard about her so-called white-collar crime spree. She was scheduled to make her defense in six weeks. Now she's run back to Chicago in a vale of tears. Alicia had to take a leave from the archive just to help usher home the tattered remnants of her girlfriend."

Stolarsky's Berkeley was a chessboard, where ignominious pawns evaporated without notice. Bruno had always loathed chess for its iron-clad hierarchies and the bullying invulnerability of its champions, their belief that they stood outside fate.

"He really has the power to make people disappear."

"He's just the local model. 'No revolution can be truly and permanently successful unless it puts its emphatic veto upon *all* tyranny and centralization—the complete reversal of these authoritarian principles will alone serve the revolution.' That's Emma Goldman."

"I beg your pardon, but why doesn't he fire *you*? You were party to Beth's insurrection, for one thing."

"That's an excellent question. I see you're beginning to examine for the strings and levers, it's the first glimmer of awakening."

"Yes, but why?"

"Mainly overconfidence on his part. Plus I'm the face of the franchise. He handed me a script and I made it real and it amuses him, I guess."

"What script?"

"He named the place Kropotkin's. Not that he grasped the implications, I had to school him in that. But the reputation depends on Stolarsky's stake being hidden, right? Plus he wouldn't have the least hope of replacing me." As if in demonstration, Plybon was cooking. Almost without glancing he'd begun sliding buns into the steamer, flapping patties onto slow-broiling onions, ladling out broth to reinvigorate the cloud of steam. New patrons had appeared, and though Plybon made no communication with them—they might be regulars, or Plybon a mind reader—the sliders were bagged and traded for dollars. Perhaps they'd been too buffaloed by Bruno and Plybon's talk even to introduce their wishes for marginal adjustments—cheese? more onions or less?—to the baseline artifact. The slider cook was a mind reader by default, since everyone walked in here wanting the exact same thing. Human life, reduced to a bottom line of animal want, and Plybon an assembly-line machine for supplying bread and meat. Did this support or undermine Plybon's ideological premise? Bruno wasn't qualified to judge.

Now Plybon reversed his previous verdict. "Actually, I shouldn't be so obtuse. Stolarsky might have a scheme for replacing me, one staring me right in the face—you."

"I'm not versed in Kropotkinism."

"Ha! No, this would be a rebranding along the spooky lines of Zombie Burger. 'Elephant Man Sliders, come one come all and buy a sack from the notorious pitiable enigma!'"

In fact, Plybon sounded so much like Stolarsky now, the two antagonists might be one man, split to play a doppelgänger game, with Bruno as the shuttlecock. Before he could reply, Plybon shoved the bladed spatula into Bruno's hands. "Here. You give it a go, a dry run for total usurpation, Hooded One." Another pair of customers had appeared. As Plybon began to snap on his bicycle helmet, he nodded at the newcomers. "My comrade will be helping you, just belly up to the bar."

"Wait," Bruno protested. "I don't know how to run the register."

Plybon shrugged as he went outside. "Then give 'em away."

A restaurant worker's obeisance lurked deep in Bruno's psyche. He set up a new flotilla of sliders, for this couple and the next. The night was young, the earlier rush just the first wave on this shore. Plybon, meanwhile, was visible between the manifestos Scotch-taped to the window. He freed a gigantic chain and padlock from where it bound a partly disassembled bicycle to a lamppost, then lashed it around his shoulder, bike-messenger-style.

The food was safe for now in its onion-steam cloud. "One moment," Bruno said to those waiting. He ducked around the counter and outside to the sidewalk, to catch Plybon before he wheeled off. Bruno still held the spatula, a greased onion snaking slowly down its handle. Plybon reattached his front wheel with a stage magician's ease.

"You can't go." Despite this protest, Bruno found himself thinking that alone at the grill, he'd feel free to wolf a couple of the sliders, in hope of ballasting himself to the earth.

"Sure I can. You're authorized to weaponize the People's caloric bombs. I'll be back to help you close shop, don't worry."

"Where are you going?"

"I've got a hankering for cannabis. Figured I'd take a spin up to the imperial palace and see if they've replenished my stash."

"Your stash?"

"Don't play dumb," said Plybon. His bald, hatchet-shaped head couldn't grin. Instead it seemed to hinge Muppetishly open in a mirthless laugh. "My stash lives in Lady Macbeth's Volvo."

•

With that, the counterman whirred off uphill, toward Stolarsky's unknown demesne. Bruno went inside: Sliders needed flipping. He'd had the clock installed in him, a circadian rhythm of the grill. He prepared the meal, then futzed open the register and collected the cash. For the next hour he left the drawer open, making change not by keying the device's tabs but by doing the math in his head. He finally resorted to shoving a few sliders across free of charge during a rush, when in a clamor of mockery he'd lost count of whom he'd already fed once, twice, or not at all. Plybon had instilled a mood of permanent combativeness in his regulars, who jeered and complained with impunity. For them it was a game with no stakes. A few tourists snapped his picture. One frat boy leaned across to grab at the end of Bruno's noose. Bruno obliged by silently raising the bladed spatula high as if to sever the hand, which was withdrawn to a gratified chorus of shrieks.

When the wave passed, Bruno found Madchen standing in a corner by the agitprop-encrusted mirror, watching. Her expression was as gentle as on the ferry, when she thought Bruno had lost a contact lens. She wore one of his Cal hoodies, zipped and laced. The night outside must have cooled, though Bruno sweated beneath his flocked burlap.

"Did you follow me?"

She didn't hear it as an accusation. "*Nein,* I found you. I *felt* you here, I think. I was only walking."

"Of course."

"It is good you are not gambling, Alexander."

"Yes." Should he correct her assumption? It was as though they'd forged a twelve-step deal to relieve Bruno of his tendency to wager, while preventing Madchen doing precisely whatever it was she'd last been doing in Berlin.

"You have found a job, *ja?*"

"Yes," he admitted. A quiet satisfaction had overtaken him. As a waiter, he'd known it too, the minute but distinct pleasure of freeing another human from hunger, like easing someone's dress jacket from their arms.

"You are alone?"

"For now."

"May I join you?" Madchen asked. "To help?"

"Yes—yes."

And so, with the same frictionless elegance with which she'd immersed in the Jack London bathtub, Madchen tucked herself behind the Kropotkin's counter, and Bruno taught the *Vegetarierin* to compose a perfect slider.

Gammon

―――――――――――

I

In his extreme youth Alexander Bruno had imagined life to have a top side and an underneath. The underneath was embodied by all he saw around him in San Rafael, then in Berkeley, in People's Park and on Telegraph Avenue; it was populated by his mother and by the two plaster-pediment artisans in their sea of white dust, berating his mother; by the landlord evaded in his visits to the apartment on Chestnut Street; by the barely coping public-school teachers who corralled Bruno, and the other children they corralled; by the pitying volunteers filling trays at the soup kitchens to which June too frequently resorted for their meals.

Bruno had at first only clawed his way into a vibrant layer of that underneath: the realm of dishwashers and waiters at Spenger's, then Chez Panisse, their cheap white drugs and horny remarks transacted just out of sight and earshot of those who sat at the tables they serviced. It was at the tables where, as if through a one-way mirror, the top layer was made visible to those below. That zone of privilege and luxury, the only destination worth attaining. Or so Bruno had thought at the time. If this view was one he'd never questioned, now, on return from the near-death of surgery, it dissolved in a new understanding. Keith Stolarsky might be emperor of the plastic facade of Telegraph Avenue—its top layer, which held no allure—but Garris Plybon was king of Telegraph's underneath. It was to this layer that Bruno had sunk, or been reduced, gladly. This wasn't a matter of embracing a past he'd once discarded as if it were something stuck to his shoe. Bruno was done wondering what had become of June, or schoolmates beyond Stolarsky, or other waitstaff, or even Konrad. Bruno didn't need Berkeley to remember him. At Kropotkin's, he felt reinstated in a timeless freakish demimonde to which he'd always belonged.

The restaurant was a theater. On leaving, Bruno shoved the mask and noose into an unused drawer full of potholders. On the street he was anonymous to the same students who'd gleefully addressed him as "dead man" at the counter. He'd retired his medical mask now, too, become one with his scarred face. It still startled him, caught in passing, reflected in a storefront window. Yet his old face would have startled him just as badly. It was startling, to a dead man, to be alive.

•

Beth Dennis returned from Chicago and reappeared at Garris Plybon's. On leave from the Rhetoric Department, shorn of her own retail perch at Zodiac, Beth's slicked-back hair and angry glasses seemed less drolly ironic, more dangerous. Sexier, too, in the manner of a 1950s gang girl, or cellblock boss in a female prison movie. She was like Bruno, another soldier in Plybon's secret cadre. At her first chance, hunkering around Plybon's fathomless soup, Beth latched on to Madchen Abplanalp. They were joined in ironic conspiracy, Madchen the passenger on the airplane ticket whose purchase had gotten Beth canned. And Beth spoke German. The women vanished into talk Bruno couldn't follow even if they hadn't been shrouded in mutual admiration. *"Alexander wäre perfekt für dein Bankautomatenprojekt. Das Blöde ist nur, dass er kein Girokonto hat . . ."*

Bruno, happy to be invisible, dredged material from his bowl, trying to parse the soup's theme. He found carrots and celery, as always, but also miniature tentacles, yellow beardy mussels, caraway seeds. The soup is a picture of my life now, Bruno thought. The soup is *me*. At any moment a baby sea monster . . . yet now, here, a soft lump of potato . . . Plybon, meanwhile, had returned from the kitchen bearing a small Tupperware container loaded with the recycled joints he'd gathered from Tira Harpaz's passenger's-side footwell. Everywhere in his new life Bruno traveled in a fog of pot, the sole drug that had never interested him in the slightest. No matter: He no longer identified with his own preferences but with those of his natural homes in the world, Kropotkin's and the Jack London. The smell of ancient dope lay deep in the boards and millwork of the apartment building—you could probably smoke the moldings if your supply ran out.

"*Er kann meine Karte benutzen, um Geld abzuheben. Es ist völlig egal, wessen Konto das ist.*"

"What the hell are you two on about?" Plybon's tone of maximum irritation made no impression on Beth and Madchen, who sat entwined. Bruno had heard no mention of Alicia, but he wouldn't presume their relationship excluded one behavior or another: Among lesbians, among humans generally, there was always so much you didn't understand. As for Madchen, though his German roommate had transformed number 25 into an intimate shrine of incense and candles, she and Bruno hadn't consummated their nightly spooning. Bruno wasn't jealous. They were all in it together, whatever it was.

Possibly, even, Bruno might *be* a lesbian.

Anyway, in his guilty heart he desired Tira Harpaz. Yet there was no evidence of Tira and Stolarsky anywhere that Bruno could tell. Regular abdication was a feature of Stolarsky's reign over Telegraph, an imperial refusal to appear. Or was Stolarsky a scientist, peering in from a hidden vantage while mice worked his maze?

"I was just getting Madchen up to speed on your ATM action," Beth explained lazily. "She thinks Alexander would be perfect."

"Perfect for what?" said Bruno, caught entranced by the soup.

"Garris is part of the East Bay Countersurveillance Group," said Beth. "They're planning this thing with the banks. I want to film it." She hefted an imaginary palm video recorder, aimed at Bruno. "You explain, Garris."

Plybon concluded a draft on a joint. "A little how-do-you-do to the cameras at the ATMs, that's all . . ." The slider cook detailed the scheme: At noon on May 15, the anniversary of the People's Park Riots, dozens in masks would each withdraw twenty dollars from every automatic teller machine in Berkeley. A coordinated action and totally legal, but calculated to alarm the authorities into an overreaction. "The girls have a point," said Plybon. "You've already got your Lon Chaney thing going." The joint passed to Beth, then Madchen, the room clouding.

"I'm afraid I have no bank account."

"You'll use my card," said Beth. "With your medical thing, you've got full deniability, it'll be a cause célèbre. Plus for the cameras, you're intense. Tall and weird, if you don't mind me saying."

"I don't mind. I am tall and weird." His hand drifted up to fondle the scars parenthesizing his nose. Once, the blot had been something only Bruno could see, forever between him and the world. Now that his disfigurement was visible to others, Bruno often forgot it was there.

"It is brilliant, I think," said Madchen. "I would enjoy to go to one of the bank machines too."

Plybon shook his head. "As a foreign national you'd be assuming too much risk."

"Okay."

"If you want to help, you can cover the shop for me and Bruno."

"*Ja.*" Madchen stretched from her cushions to return what remained of the joint.

Plybon mopped his hands hurriedly on a dish towel, placed the remnant on his tongue, and gulped. "Waste not, want not."

"Tell them about the Million Masked, Garris," said Beth, her tone seductive. Bruno was overtaken by a vision of Plybon as a kind of pimp, his apartment a harem with its cushions and red wine in jam jars.

Plybon flipped his hand. Civilian, he still wielded a phantom spatula. "Just a little concept I was fooling with. Since Seattle they've employed facial recognition tech in protest surveillance, you know."

"I didn't," said Bruno.

"Black bloc and Zengakuren and Anonymous, they all rely on concealment. Sikhs remove their turbans at airports, we persecute black kids in hoodies and women in burkas. So, what about a Million Masked March?"

"Fascinating."

"Sure, but it'll never happen. That committee's all green-flag Bookchinite types. Not a Situationist bone in their bodies." Plybon hovered over Bruno. "You gonna eat that soup or just stare into it?"

"I'm savoring it," said Bruno apologetically.

"I can reheat."

"It's fine."

Plybon made a face and went into the kitchen. The wiry counter-man's dissidence was like an epileptic upwelling within his body, pos-sibly the result of pressure on some lobe. If you were Noah Behringer, the essential fact of anyone might be lopped out, leaving the patient to reconfigure around its absence. Bruno, for instance, had forsaken luxury, possessiveness, wagering, everything that made him himself. Yet he still existed, custodian of a tall, weird body on a rudderless voy-age through time.

"*Wir sollten ihn davon überzeugen, auch am Millionen-Maskierte-Marsch, teilzunehmen.*" The women resumed their conspiracy. Bruno didn't need to understand their words. Whether it was a baseline con-dition of telepathy or the background hum of the pot, he felt embraced in the sanctum of Plybon's soup-scented harem.

"*Ja, verdammt. Er sollte ganz vorne mitmarschieren.*"

Madchen smiled at Bruno. He smiled back, blinked at her. Having crossed to the Kladow landing and kissed across her bicycle, bounced their voices off lonely satellites, flown thousands of miles to lotion each other's scarred and spangled bodies, his and the German's inti-macy was still opaque, inchoate.

"It might be hard to persuade the women in burkas," said Beth, still working on Plybon's march.

"It wouldn't matter who was underneath," said Plybon from the kitchen. "You chicks could volunteer, for instance."

"*Ja,* why not?" said Madchen. Her air suggested she'd been a burka protester many times before. Madchen and Plybon drifted together in Bruno's mind's eye: The lanky, smooth German, with her undemol-ished innocence, her eruptions of glitter. The pale wretched anarchist, his elbows like branches of a diseased tree, eyes blinking like a mole's the moment he laid aside his Coke-bottle spectacles. Impossible and yet not, since all human conjunctions were possible, after all.

The idyll eased Bruno's guilt. He wanted to tumble into the abyss of Tira Harpaz's contemptuous wit and chunky nipples, the magic cyst at her inner thigh. Having retired his backgammon board he mentally shifted the humans before him, like checkers, to favorable positions. Madchen might be a trailing runner, a piece he'd ushered a wild distance against titanic odds. She had to be played safe, for Bruno's own absolution. Bruno himself could be left uncovered, Bruno was the stray, always. He was the blot.

"And you'd be perfect," said Beth. "The Nooseman, at the head of the column."

"I'm perfect for anything," said Bruno. "That's why nobody knows what to do with me."

•

Beth, with the help of Alicia and Madchen, groomed Bruno for a star turn in her video. She armed him with her debit card and password, and a stack of tiny photocopied slips, to be presented to any authority, reading:

> I am a participant in a nonviolent social experiment, with no wish or intention to harm anyone or any institution in any way whatsoever. Thank you for your interest, and have a nice day.

They chose his outfit, too, the tuxedo and dress shoes he'd sidelined in favor of sweatpants and *ABIDE* shirts. His medical mask, in place of the burlap and noose. The action wasn't a comedy, shouldn't fall under the sign of the Hanged Food Worker. Madchen worked on him again with her shears, perfecting the line of his ears and neck, her chaste ministrations not unlike Oshiro's. Then Bruno showered, carefully shaved, and tried on his outfit, dress rehearsal for Beth's camera. Privately, he guessed he'd disappoint their hopes for photogenic catastrophe. The tuxedo made Bruno unapproachable, as unlikely to be arrested as a stage magician in mid-performance. He'd used it to withdraw untaxed income from protectorates and emirates; it was hard to imagine that withdrawing twenty dollars in broad daylight would be the downfall of its Teflon privilege.

Wearing it, though, was agreeable. On Plybon's soup and pilfered sliders Bruno had fleshed out, regained his form, and the tuxedo fit. He was healing, he supposed. He glanced once at his abandoned backgammon set, but there was no one to play. Instead, toes creaking in Italian leather for the first time since he'd bought the cheap sneakers, he reached to pull Madchen to him, hand gently pressuring the small of her back as in a tango. She laughed as he dipped her. He had an erection. He didn't care if the lesbians saw.

He'd wear the mask for their nonviolent social experiment, yes. But it was the last time. Overnight Bruno had become cruelly handsome, more striking than before the opening of his face's door. He wished to hear someone call him Flashman, though there was no way to explain this. When Garris Plybon returned late from his closing shift at Kropotkin's, Bruno changed again, into an *ABIDE* shirt, and removed the shoes. In bare feet he joined the women for an anticipatory celebration in Plybon's apartment, more red wine and salvage pot. By the time he and Madchen tottered back to 25 these new energies were dissipated, and they only slept. But he wouldn't forget.

II

As Beth and Alicia trailed him with their video camera from the Jack London, Telegraph was already like a muddied pond. The People's Park Riot anniversary had roiled the street's psychosis from underneath, mixing the park's population, the righteous aggrieved and forlornly traumatized, the recyclable-gleaners, with the frat boys and tourists, the midmorning vomiters. Someone with a bullhorn recited an ancient speech on the subject of speech, words lying in bunches in this district to be seized up at any moment. No one listened. The words had triumphed and failed entirely, a puzzle impossible to solve. Traffic was halted while someone rolled a wheeled pallet bearing a fifteen-foot-tall puppet down the center of the avenue.

Bruno kept his medical mask in his tuxedo jacket's right pocket, though he passed others with their faces covered, likely sharers in his own conspiracy. Others wore only a mask of pain. In his breast pocket, Bruno carried his cell phone and forty dollars, all that remained; in his pants pocket, for luck, the Berlin paving stone. If he'd taken the backgammon case, too, he might have discharged the apartment to its rightful owner, along with the phone charger and the supply of soiled T-shirts and sweatpants. Another opportunity to keep walking and never return.

Beth backed her way through the swirling confusion on the sidewalks, capturing the tuxedoed man's approach, while Alicia set picks in the crowd, protecting her girlfriend's back. Madchen wasn't with them, instead off on her own small adventure, manning the Kropotkin's counter alone, freeing Plybon to join in the action.

At the point of noon Bruno fell into alignment with the others at the row of seven ATMs facing campus. The other six wore Guy Fawkes masks. Looking to have been drinking all night, they careened and roared and drew hoots from passersby, hardly the ideal of serene provocation Plybon had described. In their company, Bruno's tall overdressed presence was as invisible as he'd predicted. He formed the opposite of a sensation, a blinding outline, a vacancy of light. He Velcro-fitted the medical mask over his face but it added hardly anything, possibly subtracted. He might have done better with the noose but it lay in the drawer at Kropotkin's.

Bruno entered the code, then handed Beth her card and receipt, with the twenty-dollar bill, but she palmed the cash back into his hand.

"It's my dad's account, you might as well keep it."

He and Alicia backed across the street, through more halted traffic. Beth kept her camera trained on the site. Two of the Guy Fawkes had gotten into a shoving match with a Wells Fargo guard, a short Mexican, hardly a strikebreaking Pinkerton type. It was unlikely that this took place near enough to the teller machines' cameras to matter—but it had been explained to Bruno that urban surveillance was omnipresent, as in a casino. The little tableau of unrest might conceivably become a matter of public record and outcry, though rival unscripted disruptions were unfolding close by. Bruno was relieved, in any case, to have completed his assignment. He removed his mask, shoving it into his pocket beside the Berlin stone.

Alicia offered her warmest gold-toothed smile. She stroked Bruno's sleeve. "You did good."

He was a dog taking its treat. "Thank you."

"We're gonna circulate," Alicia said. Beth craned on her toes, trying to point her lens above the milling scene. No one had been arrested at the teller machines, a disappointment. The new energy seemed to be locating a little ways into campus, near Sather Gate. "Soak up some of the vibrations."

"There are a lot to soak up," he agreed.

Now Bruno was alone, to be drawn into and repulsed by the street's air of incipient chaos. His primordial knowledge of Telegraph suggested that what would happen waited for nightfall. He wasn't certain he cared. What mattered was to make his way to Kropotkin's, to discover how Madchen had managed the grill, rescue her if she needed rescue. A roadblock of orange cones had appeared at the mouth of Telegraph, whether official or not, Bruno couldn't tell. He wasn't the only one confused. Someone plopped an amplifier at the barricade of cones, then plugged in an electric guitar.

•

Bruno knew the Kropotkin's regulars by now, but in his tuxedo and scars he moved unseen among them. The scheduled riot had had no dampening effect on the lunchtime rush. If anything, it flushed more slider types from the woodwork. Servicing this demand with his usual panache was Garris Plybon, with Madchen nowhere in sight. Plybon wore a semitransparent Ronald Reagan mask, souvenir of his own turn in the ATM-withdrawal action.

"Well well well, it's Dapper Dan. You eluded the fuzz."

"Where's Madchen? I thought she was helping."

Plybon-Reagan shrugged. "She got a better offer. Happens to me all the time."

"What better offer?"

Plybon rustled thumb and forefinger together, tipping his head knowingly. "When in doubt, follow the money."

"I don't understand."

"Big Chief Come Take Kraut Squaw." Now Plybon jerked his thumb over his shoulder, a gesture familiar from his references to his raids on Tira Harpaz's Volvo. "The Folks That Live on the Hill," he'd once called them. Bruno's heart lurched.

"Do you mean Stolarsky?"

"Yeah. His Jaguar was double-parked when I turned up. The Pharaoh self-soothes by eating his way through a pyramid of sliders from time to time, but he never puts bubkes in the tip jar."

"What happened?"

"They were talking when I came in. He asked if she'd step outside for a word, so I took over. About ten minutes later he comes back in alone, hands me the sack"—Plybon poked with his spatula to point out a to-go bag, crushed whole atop the garbage bin—"and said they were going off to lunch."

"How could you let him?"

"Let him? His Excellency Lord of all the Beasts of Earth and Fishes of the Sea wasn't asking my permission."

"You could at least have warned her."

"Madchen's a grown-up, from what I can see. Anyhow, comrade, do I look like I'm in the business of telling other people what to do?" All the while Plybon flipped, chopped, cheesed, and bunned, managing the line's progress with minute nods and scowls. Plybon's business might be acting as dictator of the tiniest possible nation on earth.

"Do you know where they went?"

Plybon again shrugged. "He's probably pouring a sequence of martinis into her, at the Paragon bar at the Claremont. It's the best place around here for saying, 'Look, baby, someday all this could be yours.'"

"Was he alone?"

"Look at you, the great stone face. Your scars are turning red. Was he alone? He was until he led her out of here like a cat on a leash, yes. Then he was no longer alone."

"No sign of . . . Tira?"

"In my experience those two don't travel together. She's no Kropotkin's devotee, either."

"We have to go get her. Madchen, I mean."

Plybon arched his eyebrows above his glasses, then gestured at the mob of eaters stretching through the door. "Even if I had the first idea where to look, I'm on here until the kid comes in at six. Why don't you just go cool your jets? I bet Stolarsky'll drop her back at the apartments, especially the minute he gets a load of her conversation."

Standing aloof in his tuxedo, Bruno imagined vaulting the counter to strangle Plybon backward against the grill. But this was the impulse of someone wholly other than himself—one of the young men now agitating to the condiment shelf for mustard or ketchup, say—and so it evaporated.

•

He sat alone in number 25, facing not the door but the open windows. Distant bullhorns and the thud of reggae were punctuated by the sporadic crackle of laughter or sirens. The sky darkened slowly, low and orange, as if hills burned somewhere. His thoughts remained opaque. Not so much waiting, since he'd guessed Madchen wouldn't return, or told himself he'd guessed it. She didn't. He waited for Plybon, perhaps. Bruno had accustomed himself to the sound of Plybon's bicycle clanking out of the elevator, through their corridor. Plybon didn't return, either.

He went back to Kropotkin's. Two bicycles were chained to the lamppost now. Plybon had been joined by his fresh-faced protégé, Robin to his Batman. Bruno went inside. The younger counterman did all the work, serving the excitable rabble, the would-be revolutionaries and vicarious lookers-on, while Plybon berated them.

"So this is what passes for the People's Park Riot anniversary nowadays. Like twitches in Freedom's corpse. It boils down to an excuse to break windows and steal bongs and leather and distressed-denim keepsakes. You probably lack the wherewithal to invert even a single police car. Kids these days."

"I waited for you." Bruno stepped in to speak low and close.

"Okay, you waited for me. Here I am."

"Madchen's still . . . kidnapped."

"What do you expect me to do about it?"

"Take me up the hill."

"It seems like I should stick around," said Plybon. "Things look to get a little feisty around here tonight."

"You want me to tell them you work for Stolarsky?"

Plybon made a long, sour face, his eyes like two magnified oysters. Bruno wasn't certain his blackmail amounted to much, but Plybon appeared to reconsider. He smoothed his sweaty dome with both hands, then extended and interwove them to crack his knuckles. He looked to his protégé. "You cool for half an hour or so?"

The kid gave a thumbs-up. "Why not?"

"Can Alexander borrow your bike?" Perhaps it had been Bruno's purposeful tone. Or maybe Plybon's imagination had caught the scent of something, another action he didn't want to miss out on.

"Sure." The young counterman dug in his pocket for the padlock key and tossed it to Plybon. "Look out on the downgrades, the rear brake is shot."

"It's not the downgrades I'm worried about," said Plybon. "You capable of climbing a mile up Euclid? The Sultan's residence is almost up to Lake Anza."

"Sure." Bruno's bluff was double. He had no notion of his capabilities nor of the location of Lake Anza.

"Then what are we waiting for?"

III

The house on The Crescent, stepped into the hillside, had no face. In the darkness it presented as a lip of driveway, beneath which the tails of the Jaguar and the Volvo were just visible, tipped up on a slanted driveway that terminated in a barred garage door and a high wooden gate. The low roof was blurred on one side in dark leaves, the other in pink blossoms glowing in the moonlight; beyond it lay the hint of hills, carving to the canyon below. The two men approached on, or with, bicycles. The first, the rangy bespectacled bald man, wore a bike helmet, and scythed efficiently up the grade to the driveway's lip, where he dismounted. The second, the tall man in the tuxedo, who'd refused a helmet, arrived with shoulders bent, walking his bicycle, heaving it before him like a dogless sled.

Cicadas chirped—either that, or some transformer high on a telephone pole shorted in a circular rhythm in the silence.

The hill-etched homes opened to the rear, with picture windows and sliding doors, with decks and patios; at the street side they presented like bunkers. If the two men had picked their way up from the canyon, like coyotes, they could have gained an element of surprise. Bruno Alexander might have suggested it, if he hadn't been winded and bleeding, his tuxedo both sweated through and torn at the knees. It was enough to have arrived.

Garris Plybon leaned his bike into the springy hedge. Bruno did the same. His knuckles bled, too, from his tumble from the bicycle—fortunately, he'd missed the road, or the parked cars along Euclid, with his bare head. He hardly noticed his knees or knuckles for the tight burning band of his ribs, the effect not of falling but of the climb, before he'd abandoned the pedals and begun pushing the bike uphill. Something, maybe blood, trickled in his lungs.

Bruno gripped the Berlin stone, deep in his pocket. An element of riot, perhaps, in this placid, implacable dominion. But he could see no window through which to toss the stone. Then he spotted it, a small triangle, just above the dark door and beneath the roof's pitch, its glass reflecting blue night and black leaf cover. Another of Stolarsky's one-way mirrors. Bruno hefted the stone, curled his wrist, and heaved. A perfect strike, it dashed the reflection with a thin, tinkling sound. Bruno's Berlin talisman vanished inside. The house was unimpressed.

"What are you doing?" hissed Plybon, who'd just then opened the passenger's-side door of Tira Harpaz's unlocked Volvo.

"Announcing myself," Bruno managed, his breath stolen by pedaling what had seemed miles.

"He's got a doorbell for that, but I admire your style, comrade."

"Thank you." Bruno stood at the top of the drive, peering down at the house. The street behind them was still. The bay, necklace of bridges, distant towers, all they'd glimpsed at the curve of the Rose Garden, lay concealed behind the rise. The Berkeley of the flats, People's Park, as distant from this preserve as Neukölln from Kladow. Bruno had fired his one shot, was bankrupt. Stolarsky's compound had no reason to acknowledge him. Could he release the Jaguar's brake, roll it through the garage door? Not only hadn't Stolarsky left the keys in the ignition—unlikely after all—but the car was locked.

"Plybon, you shit-squirrel, is that you?"

Bruno had missed the click of the door. Stolarsky stood half hidden behind it, in darkness. Plybon didn't speak.

"The fuck you do to my window?"

Again, no reply from Plybon, and Bruno didn't volunteer.

"You brought company?" Perhaps he'd seen the bicycles in the hedge.

"Don't shoot," said Plybon.

"Step into the light, you anarchist motherfuckers."

"There isn't any, Keith." Plybon slid into the Volvo's passenger seat and left the door open, to make himself visible in the car's interior light. He raised his hands.

"Who's that with you? Your radical cohort, shit-squirrel? Is *this* your big play, finally? Two dudes and a rock? Is there a note tied to it reading 'Eat the rich'?"

"It's me." Bruno spoke feebly, his voice shredded. He stepped down the drive, moving around the Volvo's open door.

"Holy shit, look at you, putting on the Ritz, covered in blood and guts and French cuffs. You look like Frankenstein and his own monster, all stitched together."

As Bruno neared, Stolarsky stepped from behind the door. His feet and legs were bare. He held a pistol, loosely, and wore nothing but a thin T-shirt. The darkness beneath its hem revealed as a scribble of genitals and hair, his penis like a second sarcastic nose.

"Why don't you gather your harvest and get lost, shit-squirrel." Stolarsky's voice had turned, grown mossy and insinuating. He twitched his gun to give direction, as casually as if sliding an image from a screen.

Plybon shamelessly loaded his pockets with joints. "I'll be needed down at the shop now."

"I bet."

Plybon turned and mounted his bicycle and was gone.

"Step inside, Flashman."

Bruno followed the half-naked man down a corridor illuminated here and there by the tiny red and blue lights at baseboard sockets, toward an open area lit only by the sky's pale shadows. Bruno heard his own rasping breath. The picture window widened before them as they reached the corridor's end, expected but still startling: dense treetops, rooted beneath the limit of view on the vertiginous pitch of hillside, then the stark rise on the far side of the canyon. There, the dirt and rock was yellow, clung with scrubby growth, sideways trees like cartoon witchy fingers. The three-quarter moon reached in and silvered the room's contents: couch and chairs, low bookshelves, framed prints, free-standing bar littered with bottles, ice bucket, and balled-up napkins, a podlike device that might have been a humidifier or ion generator, Stolarsky's hairy-pudding buttocks, the low modernist coffee table on which he'd carelessly placed the pistol, first rotating it with a flourish as if proposing a round of spin the bottle.

"You need something to drink?"

Bruno wanted water, but wanted more to accept nothing from Stolarsky. He shook his head.

"Band-Aids?"

"No."

"Then what the fuck are you here for?"

"Where's Madchen?"

"Madchen's fine. What are you, her valet?"

"I want to talk to her."

"Ah, sorry, she can't talk, she's in-this-pose at the moment." Stolarsky buckled his knees and grabbed his genitals with both hands, briefly lolled his head and stuck out his tongue. "Get it, *in-this-pose?*" Stolarsky snorted and went to the bar and refilled a glass from a bottle of scotch. "Just pulling your leg, Flash. She's doing great. I think I scored myself a new personal assistant, in fact. These German people are so organized, it's like a compulsion with them. She'll help me get my shit in order. Here, take a load off." Stolarsky, gesturing at the couch, caught Bruno's glance at the gun. He added, "Don't mind that, I guess I must have heard a bird or bat going through the attic window. I got spooked."

Stolarsky's bullshit was a fog, making it hard for Bruno to think. "She's really going to . . . work for you?"

"Sure, why not?" Stolarsky turned his back, moving toward the broad window. "I mean, I said that off the top of my head, but she already does, if you look at it a certain way."

"I don't agree."

"No, you wouldn't—because you've got no sense of gratitude yourself."

"Is Tira here?"

"Nah, she took a powder. She's got this little cottage up in Sonoma, she likes to disappear up there—"

"At a winery in Glen Ellen?"

Stolarsky turned and grinned. "How'd you guess?"

"That's where she told me *you* go." Bruno was strung between them, Tira and Stolarsky and possibly Plybon, in a mad web of untruths. Perhaps Stolarsky had never been out of town—now that Bruno had laid eyes on the compound's interior, it seemed possible Stolarsky had been squatted on this hill as trolls dwelled beneath bridges. Perhaps there was no winery, no such place as Glen Ellen to begin with.

"Why is her car in the driveway, in that case?"

Stolarsky pointed at Bruno. "You got me. She's actually in a trench at the property line, I was just going to the shed for a bag of quicklime." He smacked his forehead theatrically. "The car! Why didn't I think of that, such an obvious fucking clue."

Bruno measured his nearness to the gun against Stolarsky's. The toadlike man stood almost pressed to the window now, to make a black blot against the glinting foliage and pale sky, the moonlight outlining his bandy legs in a halo of coarse hairs. Bruno could reach the weapon. Then Stolarsky beckoned to him, and the opportunity, if it was one, had passed. "Look."

"What is it?"

"You wanted to see she's okay, right? So come see. It's a nice view, anyhow. She hasn't aged too bad."

Bruno stepped forward, and felt as if he were plummeting into the picture window's expanse. The room, which Bruno had taken for the whole house, was a matchbox perched atop a larger structure, impossible to guess from the bungalow visible from the street. He and Stolarsky stood pitched over a house nested half underground, with a long, low wing running down the steep hill, joining there to a smaller house, a guest quarters or studio, far below. The windows of the smaller house were lit.

Between these, in the hive of patios and miniature gardens below, sat a built-in redwood hot tub, steam whispering into the trees, disheveled clothing and flip-flops and empty tumblers scattered on the neighboring planks. Half immersed, leaning dreamily on her elbows, nipple-deep in foam, was Madchen. She didn't look up.

"I'd invite you to join us for a soak, but forgive me, it's a water-recycling system and the introduction of blood and cum and bodily substances generally just wrecks the pH for weeks, I've learned that lesson the hard way."

Bruno had to hand it to Stolarsky: Madchen liked her baths. If it had only been Plybon's soup into which she'd fallen, Bruno could have reached down with his spoon and ladled her out. He wondered if she'd even hear if he shouted her name. He didn't try.

"You want to know the funny thing, though? It handles cocaine just fine, no problem. You could practically use it instead of chlorine, even."

Bruno had quit breathing through his mouth, and the constriction at his ribs had loosened. But he had no voice.

"That lady sure likes her drugs, though. Slowing her down could end up somebody's full-time job."

Bruno wasn't listening, just gazing at the ferry angel he'd found no use for, and who'd found no use for him.

"Lucky thing for me I wasn't in the mood to slow her down."

Stolarsky could say what he liked. It made little difference now.

"Here, I found these in her bag, I think they might belong to you." Stolarsky had reached to grab something off the bar—three blue vials, childproof-capped, which he now pushed into Bruno's hands. Bruno recognized the labels: the prescription painkillers given to him by Oshiro, those he'd failed to exhaust before quitting the regimen. Bruno shoved them into his pocket where the Berlin stone had been.

"Yummy fucking picture, huh?"

But Bruno looked past Madchen in her tub to the windows of the small house below, nearly shrouded in foliage—was it motion there, behind the curtains? Tira Harpaz? If only he'd made that coyote-approach from the canyon below, Bruno would have encountered the little house first, found Tira there. Then—what? Would they have absconded together, never looked back, Bruno junking his naïve gallantry and leaving Madchen behind? Or would Tira have enmeshed him in further bewilderment, claimed to have murdered Stolarsky, or Stolarsky and Madchen both? Bruno's purposes were in tatters, yet he still cared what Tira thought of him, would have been ashamed of his bleeding knees and the nude German cooking in Stolarsky's pot, of his foolish mistakes. Just as well that he'd approached the house from the front.

"*Cocaine Suppe Mit Tittenschnakken,*" said Stolarsky from behind him.

"What?"

"Just thinking what you'd say as you set the dish on the table, Mr. Chez Panisse."

"You read my mind," Bruno blurted.

"Like reading a Bazooka Joe comic," said Stolarsky. "Doesn't take more than a glance, but good for a quick laugh. Then you crumple it up and hope it doesn't get stuck to your shoe . . ." He quit, for a slurp of scotch. Otherwise, Stolarsky surely could have amused himself in this vein indefinitely.

"Did you know?"

"Know what?"

"The surgery, it brought my telepathy back. Did you . . . know this from before?"

"Before what?"

"As a child, I mean. Did I confess it to you? There's a lot I've forgotten."

"Confess you had *telepathy?*" Stolarsky scratched his bulging stomach, under the dirty T-shirt, exposing himself further.

"Yes."

"Flashman, get serious. You might be the least telepathic creature stalking the earth. You think being easy to see through adds up to some kind of superpower, or what?"

"It's unreliable," Bruno admitted. "I've never cultivated the gift. For years I avoided it—that's how I formed this block, this blot in my skull. From the desire not to hear the voices—"

"You're insane."

"No, it's true. When Dr. Behringer removed the growth, he freed the flow of . . . thoughts, back and forth."

"I've just about discharged my fascination with you, Flashman. But tell me, how can somebody so shallow be so deeply fucked up?"

"Don't you see, it might be the *source* of your fascination." Bruno, immune to insult, only wished to break through. "You sensed I was like you. That's why you remembered me all this time—"

"Nah, you and me have nothing in common. Except, I guess . . . you know." Stolarsky winked lewdly and tipped his head at the window, the cottage beyond. "She gave you a feel of her secret cyst, huh?"

"But you *are* a mind reader, yes?" He'd bow to Stolarsky, in exchange for the satisfaction of an answer.

"Hey, compared to you, who isn't?"

"You've misunderstood—"

"Where do we even start? When's the last time you recall being on top of one single human situation, instead of it being on top of you? You had no idea the ding-a-ling was abusing your cancer drugs, did you? And she was sleeping right there in your bed, though apparently unfucked, poor thing. What, was she too wrinkled-up around the edges for you?"

"I don't have cancer."

"Oh yeah, I forgot, I'm supposed to talk in euphemisms around you. What should we call it, your *growth*? Your little friend? The drugs for that thing that was pushing your eyeballs out of your head—that better?"

"Let me talk to her."

"Which one?"

In the interval of Bruno's hesitation, Stolarsky retrieved his gun. He weighed it casually, in both hands. "Trundle onto your Schwinn and roll out of here now. Schadenfreude has its limits, even for me."

"I won't leave without her." It might have been the most hopeless phrase Bruno had ever heard himself utter.

"What are you going to do, break all my windows? It looks to me like you're out of rocks."

"I thought you said it was a bird."

"Grow up. I was watching on the security cameras the minute you and that shit-squirrel crossed the motion detector. Or maybe I used my *telepathy*, who knows?"

"Why do you let him steal from Tira's car?"

Stolarsky shrugged. "I dunno. 'Keep your friends high, keep your enemies higher'?"

"Put the gun down."

"Let's not kid around. If you'd brought one of your own we could duel, ten paces, then *pow,* it's settled. Too bad. I guess we could've played backgammon over her, but you didn't bring your set either, did you?"

"No."

"See, you're not even good for that anymore."

Bruno leaned into the glass and opened his mouth, but nothing came out.

"Go ahead, she'll never hear you over the roar of the bubbles, including the ones in her head. Or don't bother, just take one last look, then find the horse you rode in on."

"What's going to happen?"

"You go help shit-squirrel flip burgers, maybe after getting cleaned up a little."

They're not burgers, they're sliders, Bruno almost said. Instead he asked, "What about Madchen?"

"Here, we'll test your powers. You see if you can read my mind *while I tell you the exact same fucking words with my mouth,* okay? Madchen's gonna practice her craft, since unlike you she didn't forget the one thing she was good at, until she's in the black and I'm bored and then she's gonna get a plane ticket and a nice tip. Beats sitting around eating Cheerios on Haste Street, wouldn't you say? So quit worrying about her and focus on your own situation."

"I don't have a situation."

"Go write a Beckett play on your own time. To the street, Flashman."

Stolarsky shut the door unceremoniously, stranding Bruno with the cars, his borrowed bicycle, the indifferent moon. Bruno supposed even Stolarsky drew the line at raving around his own driveway half dressed. He surely wasn't the only one among his neighbors possessing surveillance apparatus. Bruno's medical mask remained bundled in his pocket, not that it would have disguised him from the cameras he presumably acted for, having bumbled at the proscenium of Stolarsky's curb for so long. Could he pick his way around the back, the coyote raid? But no. Having steeped in Stolarsky's humiliation bath, Bruno couldn't imagine facing Tira Harpaz.

•

Lacking a rear brake, Bruno crashed the bicycle twice more on Euclid's steep grade. He managed to land upright the first time, to clatter to a stop leaning sideways against a parked car the second, so added only scraped palms and a twisted ankle to his woes. Even in this, there was consolation; downhill he could coast, rather than exhaust himself pedaling.

He reentered the barricaded street, vacated of cars and lit by the flares of a police occupation. Telegraph's riot had come as scheduled. The sight stirred a primal and incoherent memory: the tang of a child-hood tear-gas canister; huddling for shelter with June in a feminist bookstore. Now, carousers milled, waiting for something to happen. The crowd was too dense to thread on the bicycle, so Bruno dismounted to push it, as he had up the hill.

Certain shopwindows boasted fitted-plywood shields, a routine, even ritual precaution. Not Stolarsky's, however. Zodiac Media's glass edifice was lit like a beacon, brazening it out. The store might rely on its monolithic aura for a certain inviolability; that, and the security guards. Beyond, Zombie Burger, that meat sculpture, glowed out its obdurate unholy weirdness. It still featured a tail of patrons, mingled into throngs crossing from the pavement into the roadway, a confusion of hungers that might be unimportant to sort out.

"Holy shit, look what the cops did to this guy!"

"It's the Dude, man, I almost didn't recognize you in that monkey suit. Where's your mask? You're looking bad."

"You need us to bust some heads?"

"Thanks, but no. Actually, I took a spill."

Bruno turned off Telegraph, up Durant. Filtering through the crowds to Kropotkin's, he found the shop alive with eaters, some tucked at the narrow counter, some arrayed on the sidewalk, even seated on the curb, all wild-eyed and chomping sliders. Inside, Plybon and his ward appeared to have quit charging for the meals they handed out, making the shop a protein-distribution cell for the larger unrest. Plybon, his back turned, used his spatula to scour carbon detritus from the grill. Bruno went unnoticed. He leaned the bicycle, only scuffed and with a few spokes bent, against the lamppost.

Kropotkin's was safe from rioters, since no one knew the shop belonged to Keith Stolarsky. It struck Bruno that he might owe his presence in Berkeley, the whole joke of his current existence, to Stolarsky's Stalin impulse to arrange for a thorn in his own paw. Garris Plybon might be right, righter than he knew. Bruno was meant to replace him, not at the slider counter, no, but as Stolarsky's antagonist. Stolarsky's local adversaries were too easily vanquished, Plybon included. So Stolarsky had plucked Bruno up from afar, a new enemy to stem his boredom.

Bruno had failed the test. He could have had the gun when Stolarsky first put it down. He could have saved his Berlin stone for the picture window, or smashed the glass with a piece of furniture. But no, the glass would have rained down into the hot tub. On the hill Bruno had been paralyzed by the matter of Madchen, a checker he never ought to have shifted from its place of safety. Here, at street level, he could see more clearly: She'd never been the point. If Bruno had rescued Madchen, Stolarsky would have answered with a shrug. The ugly man had no vanity to destroy. To make Stolarsky regret stirring the Flashman part of him to life, Bruno had to rob him of something that actually counted.

Plybon only had to first be brushed aside. He deserved it for his cowardice on the hill. Bruno stepped swiftly in behind the counter and opened the drawer of potholders in which he'd stashed the burlap mask. A last hurrah for this face, to stir his audience, which might not know him without it. He turned to rinse his bloody knuckles and stinging palms in the small stainless-steel sink. The counter concealed his ragged knees, and the mask took care of the rest, covered the general disaster and despair that was his face, his person now.

"We don't need three cooks," complained Plybon.

"He should chain his bicycle," said Bruno. "And he might be due for a break, don't you think?" He pulled the mask over his face.

"Yeah, well, we hardly need two."

"Deadman!" someone called.

"The Martyr of Anarchism," Bruno corrected quietly. He felt animated by a calm ferocity. "Garris, will you hand me your implement, please?" Plybon's protégé had gone, to protect his bicycle, perhaps also sensing trouble.

"What happened with your girlfriend?"

"The situation is still unresolved. Hand me the spatula."

"I'm just scraping the flattop here," said Garris, puzzled. "Then you can help me put on onions and start a batch."

"I have something else in mind."

"Okay, then, how about you take your cryptic ominous shit out of here and let me do my work?"

"Do you want me to explain who you do your work *for*?"

"Sorry, what?"

"I'll tell them you're Stolarsky's employee," said Bruno in a low voice. "His patsy, is that the word?"

"It's not the night for high jinks, comrade."

"Oh, I think it's very much the night. Here, allow me." Bruno hadn't brought himself to seize Stolarsky's gun from a table but had no trouble wrenching the spatula from Plybon's grip. Perhaps it was the power of the mask. "I'll give you a fighting chance. Do you play backgammon?"

"Board games, opium of the masses? As a lonely child lost in the bourgeois dream, I played 'em all. What's your point?"

"I'll refresh you on the rules." Bruno spilled out the aluminum bin of chopped onions, to blanket the grill. The vegetable matter began its gentle sizzling. With the keen edge of the spatula, Bruno chopped and sluiced, sketching in onions a rudimentary game board, twenty-four points and a central bar. Bruno skipped the broth—too much moisture and the onions would swim, wrecking the playing field.

"You move your pieces in this direction," he explained to Plybon, using the spatula as a pointer. "I pass you, the opposite way." Seizing up a tall stack of raw patties, he laid them into the starting positions on the onion-points. "The goal is to move your men off first."

"Hey, it's too soon for cheese—" Plybon protested as Bruno began laying the orange squares onto one set of meat-checkers.

"It's necessary to tell our men apart. You'll play the bare patties, I'll play the cheesed ones. Is it coming back? A simple, elegant game. Like riding a bicycle, once you've learned you can hardly fail to pick it up again, that is unless the brakes are out of order."

"Sure, I remember." Plybon eyed the slider-board with his grim nerd's intensity. He was drawn, despite himself, to anything cultish. "But what are we supposed to do for dice?"

"The register," Bruno improvised. "We'll hit the keys blind. The first two numbers of the total make up a dice roll—skipping zeroes, of course."

"Zeroes don't occur in the wild, you know, they're abstractions, a step toward the denaturing of human labor."

"Good then, we'll do away with them." Bruno put last touches on the opening positions, the raw pink checkers already starting to singe and brown atop the frying onions. The cheese had relaxed, to drape securely over his own pieces.

"You first," said Bruno.

"Here I come." Plybon punched at the register's keys theatrically. It was true the counterman frequently operated the device without glancing; with rapid enough addition in his head, he might be able to dictate his throws. But no. Bruno saw Plybon had to squint at the total to learn his numbers. A six-two wasn't anyone's idea of an advantageous opening. Plybon plucked up a fork and stuck it in one of his back men, then counted steps, *one-two-three-four-five-six,* no sense of where his man would land, hallmark of a rube. The back man secured on the eighteen-point, Plybon moved his second two spaces, further confession of cluelessness.

Bruno tapped at the register's keys. It was easy to use the register-dice honestly, thanks to the mask's narrowing of his peripheral vision. A six-one. He hit and covered. An innocuous play, yet the three-prime was already advantage enough that Bruno would have doubled, had he a doubling cube. He could mash one together out of the softened buns, but no. Bruno didn't look to win but to play. He sought some deeper outcome from these meat-checkers than Plybon's surrender. The scent rising from the brothless grill was crucially sharp and dangerous, the meat-game a kind of oracular device, a Ouija board or Magic 8 Ball. No rush to see what it unveiled.

"Check it out, they're playing Parcheesi!"

"*Shut* up, nigga, that ain't Parcheesi. It's whatchoocallit."

"Lemme get a couple of those when they're captured—"

Plybon held up a stern hand. "Wait." He worked the register again and drew up a four-three, to bring his man off the bar, then open another random blot in his backfield. He smirked at Bruno, daring critique with the same inverted defensiveness with which he plopped down bowls of his latest soup.

The onion-points at the hot end of the grill began to smolder. Plybon switched the overhead exhaust fan to high, a gentle roar.

Bruno hit Plybon three more times in the next three rolls, a punishing surplus of good fortune. Plybon's men danced on the bar, then trickled onto Bruno's home points in unruly clusters, so many it was nearly annoying—the game might only take an hour to win at this rate.

"You've fallen into my little trap," Plybon crowed with maximum irrelevance.

"The People like a back game, apparently."

"You bet your sweet ass."

They'd gathered a fair crowd, including Plybon's apprentice, who'd taken it as his task to hush the viewers and stall demands for food. The sliders on the grill were carbon-checkers now, inedible. Bruno found it harder to shift his shrunken men with the giant spatula, so he followed Plybon's example, traded for a fork. As the distinguishing cheese had boiled off in rank smoke, Bruno laid fresh orange squares atop the remains. The heat rising off the grill forced him to lay his tuxedo jacket aside—it was nearly spoiled anyhow. He sweated heavily under his burlap but left it on, just tugged the noose upward to momentarily ventilate his neck. Plybon pressed Play on his infernal Sonny Sharrock CD, cranking the volume to drown the roar of the exhaust and the clamor of the gallery.

It was just as Plybon reached in to fork another captured patty off the bar, that two of Bruno's checkers—his prime at the nineteen-point—burst into flame. The counterman only grunted, unimpressed, and smothered the fire with forkfuls of spare onions, enough for the moment.

"Better hurry!" Plybon shouted over the noisy music. "I've got you right where I want you."

They had to lean back against the counter between moves, for oxygen. Bruno, already playing down to Plybon's Cro-Magnon level, now struck at near random, opening blots in his home board simply in order not to have to stretch over the noxious fumes of the backfield. Both players had men on the bar when the captured pieces exploded into blue-hot fire.

"I'd accept your resignation at this point!" shouted Plybon, reaching for the ladle to apply broth to extinguish the flames. "Ow, FUUUCCCK!" The stainless-steel ladle, extended over the silo of heated air drawn upward into the exhaust, was impossible to touch; Plybon shook his scalded hand over his head in a mad dance. All the sliders were on fire now.

"Let it burn," said Bruno. "It wasn't a high-quality contest to begin with."

The watchers had sagged out beyond the doors for air. Bruno rushed to join them. Only Plybon remained inside, barely visible in the smoke. Fumbling under the counter, perhaps for a fire extinguisher, the counterman had come up instead with Bruno's tuxedo jacket, which he flipped out above the flames like a toreador. Too late: the coat exploded. Plybon's protégé rushed inside and dragged his mentor free and to the curb, where the slider cook sat stunned. He removed his glasses, dazedly. The thick lenses had protected his eyes. Around them, a blast pattern of instant sunburn, eyebrows that might crisp off into dust if touched. The tiny shop blazed, black flumes coursing to the roofline and into the night sky, reverse waterfalls.

"Holy hell, Nooseman, you blew up Kropotkin's!"

"It belonged to Keith Stolarsky," Bruno said, to whomever had levied the accusation.

"Darth Vader?"

"Yes."

"Well shit, that's not right!"

"No."

"We gotta blow up the Death Star!"

"Yes, that's what we must do."

"Death to Zodiac!"

•

The loose arrangement of bodies resolved into two parties: those fleeing the arriving sirens and others at Bruno's back, as he drifted through the debris along Durant's car-vacated white center line toward Telegraph. The burlap mask spotlit Bruno's next destination, sparing distraction at what lay behind, either the ruin of the shop—now the theatrical crash and screams as the manifesto-plastered plate glass splintered and gave way—or the number or character of the loose army gathered in thrilled fascination as he marched.

A phalanx of policemen greeted them at Durant and Telegraph, behind roadblocks and flares seemingly meant to steer any rioters southward, away from the sanctuary of campus, back in a loop toward People's Park, the long-conceded ground. Zodiac Media blazed like a lampfish lure behind this defense, made unreachable.

"To Zombie," suggested Bruno. He barely had to speak to lead his followers, whatever sort of rats or children made up his parade.

"Fuck yes! Burn down mo-fo capitalist tittyburger!"

Zombie Burger lay undefended by any official presence. Instead, the tower, like some horrific Dr. Seuss drawing, steamed away at its gross purposes, humans steadily plunging through its cavelike entrance, reemerging handcuffed to giant narcotic sandwiches, a method of crowd control far more effective than plastic shields and batons. Should Bruno elbow past the line to invade the overpopulated kitchen and incinerate the pumpkin palace from within, by its own fire and grease?

Or burn it from the outside? Before he'd settled on an approach, the students who'd trailed him from Kropotkin's were at work, busy shattering a wooden sawhorse with high-flying kicks and idiotic kung fu yells, taking turns as if at a piñata.

"Let me build it, I was a Boy Scout! You need surface area and airflow—"

"Tinder, I mean, like, kindling—"

"Fuck tinder! Fuck kindling!" Another masked body wheeled up, dancing maniacally, and jetted copious lighter fluid from a tin held provocatively low, between his legs. The liquid fell in pissy loops along the Zombie's hammered-metal exterior, and down onto the smashed remnants of the barricade, the splintered blue two-by-fours that had been hurriedly kicked up in a ragged heap against the wall.

Were these forces really under Bruno's command? A pointless question. Another somebody struck a series of matches and tossed them at the cold pyre. One finally sparked the lighter fluid, but the result was less than explosive. The sawhorse began to burn, yes, but Zombie's outer surface was indifferent to the little fire. One of the burger girls appeared in the doorway, apparitional in the nimbus of her black-lit uniform. A massive fire extinguisher on her back—she gave the appearance of an angel or scuba diver—from which she casually blew cascades of chunky white foam on the flames. One of Bruno's foot soldiers, masked with a train-robber's bandanna, ran at her, in chaotic defense of the hard-won, pitiable blaze. She raised the extinguisher's nozzle threateningly in his direction and he sheared off sideways, as if dodging a policeman's Taser.

Zombie's odor of char was nearly unbearable, its upper stories beaming lasers into the void, too much a totem of fire to succumb. The building might have been specially formulated as riot-proof, perhaps even to survive a nuclear war, after which it would remain standing in Berkeley's blasted desert, an ironic emblem of human voraciousness.

"I know another Stolarsky building." Bruno barely had to whisper it. "This way." He started off down Channing Way, circling the block—a longer route, but it put the rising sirens and uncomfortable scrutiny of a fevered crowd likely full of undercover policemen behind him. There was no need to glance, his lieutenants stayed at his heels, an effective cell of four or five, no more than was called for. Plybon, advocate for the value of small audiences, would have been proud. He strolled downhill in the cool and quiet, People's Park at his back. He no longer felt his knees or knuckles. Numbness, always among Bruno's talents. Another chance, perhaps, to wander out of his own wearisome destiny? But no, he turned the corner on Dana Street. Then again, up Haste.

As the door shut behind them, the Jack London's inlaid-wood lobby formed a temple of caramel light and calm. The riot seemed miles and possibly years removed. It was as if Bruno and his followers had snuck off, a posse of Samurai, to invade some European drawing room. Or—what had Madchen called them?—the Baader-Meinhof Gruppe. One member, still in kung fu mode, howled and leaped to kick at one of the foyer's blond panels, which instantly stove in.

"No," said another. "The elevator."

Lighter fluid soaked its graffiti into the raw-surfaced wooden interior, sadly un-refinished for years. The first lit match, touched to each of the car's three walls, took easily too.

"Send it upstairs!"

The doors closed and the elevator rose like a burning paper lamp into the throat of the building.

It was only then that Bruno turned to search out the masked face of the bestower of lighter fluid: another burlap-nooseman like himself. Stolarsky had said he had dozens of the masks, if not hundreds. Bruno had never been out of sight of Stolarsky's operatives, he realized too late. He might even be an operative himself.

IV

Near as he'd come, in so many exotic locales, he'd never spent a night in jail before. It had taken California policemen to bring him to ground. They'd shepherded him the brief and familiar distance to Berkeley's jail, on Martin Luther King Jr. Way—for a moment Bruno imagined they were dragging him back to high school, but they passed it by.

It might be a lesson in the gravity of native places, their ability to demolish pretensions; never mind the interlude between, in which you'd dreamed some weightless escape. What remained of Bruno's jacketless tuxedo—grease-spattered shirt with cuffs rolled up and singed, pants with tatterdemalion knees—held no sway with the authorities, either during his arrest outside the burning apartment building or through the night and morning in various holding pens. There, Bruno blended more or less gratefully into the derelict population, much as he had on the broken sidewalk in the shadow of the Berlin Hauptbanhof. No one had said anything about his face. There were worse faces to be seen.

•

In fogged dawn, he'd suffered a bus ride to Oakland for arraignment and bail hearing. Tira Harpaz had paid his bail and waited at the courthouse door as Bruno stumbled into grainy, headache-inducing daylight, a humbling rescue. Her Volvo's passenger seat was no cleaner, though perhaps more than ever he felt suited to its squalor.

She drove in silence. It wasn't the reunion he'd dreamed of, their puppets traveling aligned but quiescent on the car seats. Bruno's powers were bankrupt, dissolved in Stolarsky's mockery, his energies spent in arson and bicycle spills. He thought *secret cyst,* he thought *eat or be eaten,* he thought *let's double resign,* but the messages floated off like banners untethered from the aircraft that had hoisted them, they furled and tumbled from the sky of his mind.

Bruno didn't ask where they were going. Her route made it obvious. This time there was no pit stop at Zuni for oysters and roast chicken. Tira veered off the bridge southward, over Potrero, to run the gauntlet of billboards, the sun-glinting hills studded with houses like little pink boxes—it was June who'd always called them that. Bruno had spent the night in jail thinking of her—not Tira but June. He'd recalled walks home from Berkeley High while he'd still needed those, up MLK, then past the University Avenue Indian groceries and sari shops, into the flats, to the Chestnut Street apartment before she'd been evicted from it.

Tira surprised him, however, pulling into the airport's cell-phone lot, a desolate sunny asphalt island opposite the ancient United hangar.

"Are we picking someone up?" he half joked. She only glared.

"You can change your clothes. Your stuff's in the trunk, pick out what you like." She groped beneath the steering wheel to pop the trunk's latch.

He bumbled out to see what she meant. A piece of soft luggage lay centered inside, one he didn't recognize.

"Go ahead," she said.

Bruno unzipped it to find the contents of his Charlottenburg hotel-room closet, long since abandoned as ballast in his escape from the unpaid bill. He handled the shirts, the sharp-pressed trousers, in wonder. In the nylon compartment opposite the hanging clothes he found clean tube socks, still-tagged underwear, sweatpants, T-shirts.

"All your favorites." Tira laughed bitterly. She'd gotten out of the car to stand with him at the trunk. Now she gestured at his passenger seat. "Get dressed, I'll avert my eyes, I promise."

He selected a sharkskin two-piece suit, deep mustard brown, an oddity he'd cherished and had believed lost. Underneath it, not a button shirt but *ABIDE.* His two selves spliced into one. Assuming the correct number was two, rather than a hundred, or zero. He changed in the passenger seat, slipping out of the shredded tuxedo pants and shirt, rolled the pants gingerly over his crusted knees, and helped himself into the fresh costume. Tira leaned her back against the car, smoking a joint, her customary two drags before tossing it aside.

"Here, I almost forgot." She opened his door and reached into the glove compartment to hand Bruno two items: his Berlin stone and a neat paper folder, imprinted with the same travel agent's emblem that had decorated the e-ticket paperwork which got Beth Dennis fired. Did everyone in Berkeley use the same travel agency? Or perhaps Beth and Alicia, too, had unwittingly followed a script authored by Stolarsky. Or was it someone else who'd moved the checkers around? Bruno felt the answer lay before him, in the raw circle of understanding from which the blot had been lifted, like a garden stone.

Maybe it wasn't important to know. The ticket inside was in the name Alexander B. Flashman. The stiff new passport tucked into the paper jacket opposite the ticket and receipt featured the same name. The photo showed Bruno's current face—the picture Keith Stolarsky had snapped in his office, that day he'd awarded Bruno the burlap mask.

Bruno put the ticket into his interior breast pocket and balanced the stone in his palm. He looked at Tira.

"Keith claimed that thing was yours," she said.

"Yes."

"He said you could make soup with it, whatever the fuck that's supposed to mean."

"Tira."

"What?"

"I can't leave until I know Madchen is safe."

"Yeah, well, I've got one more surprise for you." She slid back into the driver's seat, checked her phone to confirm a text, then shoved it into her purse.

"Yes?"

She pointed across the lot. Bruno followed the line of her finger and discovered Stolarsky's Jaguar, just now scooting up parallel to their position, aimed at the exit. Madchen peered at him through the passenger window. She raised her hand, looking intact and chastened.

Stolarsky's Toad-in-motorcar shadow was visible at the wheel, but for once he seemed willing to play the silent caddy.

"The German said the same thing as you," said Tira. "She demanded proof you were safe. It's nauseatingly cute."

The arrangement was like a cold war exchange of spies in a neutral zone, or some sulky prom-night-chaperone standoff between aggrieved families. Had Madchen been there waiting, to see him exit the car and browse his luggage at the Volvo's trunk? He supposed she'd had a suitcase packed for her as well, by the same unseen hand.

Now the Jaguar began to move in the direction of the lot's exit.

"Tell them to stop. I want to talk to her."

"There's no time. Her flight leaves before yours, I think."

"He's bored with her already."

"He's bored with everything." Tira's voice was flat. "She made a good alibi, though. Proof he was up the hill when the blaze started. He's wanted the insurance on that firetrap for twenty years—everyone knew except you, apparently."

"What about you?" he asked. "Are you bored, too?"

"I'm bored with seeing him get every fucking thing he wants, if that's what you're asking. I thought you might do better, Alexander."

"You're saying I gave him what he wants?"

"You served a few purposes." She wouldn't meet his eyes. "It came cheap enough."

These were the last words between them.

In the international terminal, once he was checked in and freed of his bag and through security—no one wanted to detain poor A. B. Flashman, a scarred man with a scarred passport photo, and limping slightly besides—Bruno found a Lufthansa nonstop to Frankfurt on the big board. But by the time he'd threaded his way to the distant gate, Madchen had boarded and was gone.

The name on the receipt for Bruno's ticket was Edgar Falk.

Backgammon

I

It was their fifth consecutive night visiting the Smoker's Club, at the top of the hotel beside the casino, and the Brazilian was growing tired of the American asking when he was going to get him into the game with the Mummy. The Brazilian, Tiago Alves, had been playing at the high-stakes table with the American, Dale Thurber (Thurber had an idiotic nickname, which he'd insisted Alves call him; Alves had refused), each of the previous nights. They'd had a run together at a table before, in a private game in Guadalajara. In both instances they'd largely avoided going head-to-head, only skirmished, taken each other's measure and in the process aroused a great deal of suspicion. Here in Singapore the two had each taken money from various men who'd come and stayed just for one evening at the table, Thurber often with hands he'd ostentatiously revealed to Alves as foolish bluffs or cruel beats on hands he ought to have folded, gut-shot straights filled on the river card, last-minute boats on atrocious paper.

Thurber had, in this manner, been steadily feeding Alves the outlines of his game. For Alves, the romance was over. He told himself that tonight he would take Thurber for a great deal of money. Either that or excuse himself from the table and go fuck the American's extremely young and extremely unhappy wife. She'd been petitioning Alves for this courtesy, it seemed to Alves, since Guadalajara. To do so would redeem this pointless waiting, waiting to return to the strange game in the private home of the Singaporean fascist. Alves, who'd played the Mummy months earlier, had told his tale to Thurber in Guadalajara; Thurber's desire to test himself had driven the plan to meet here. In that previous visit Alves had lost against the Mummy, badly, and had

282

no intention of doing it again. But he had thought he might be willing to see the American do it. Now he felt ready to extract the price for such irritation personally.

"You have to wait for the old man," Alves had explained to Thurber more than once. "He takes you there."

Tonight, they'd rehearsed it again. "It's at the home of this *Billy the Kim,* right?" asked Thurber.

"Billy Yik Tho Lim, yes."

"So why don't we just call him direct?"

"It doesn't work like that. When Lim and the Mummy are ready for a game, the old man comes."

"Well, shit. It's really worth all this hoopla? I been at a hundred-thou buy-in game before."

"It is not a game like you've been in before."

"He beat you bad, huh?"

"He will do the same to you. You can acquire a big mountain of Singapore dollars from Director Lim and his comrades, if you are diligent. But if you do not tread lightly you will give it all back, and much more of your own besides, to the Mummy."

"Got into your head, Tiago?" said Thurber.

"Yes," said Alves. "He got into my head."

II

The atmosphere wasn't precisely what Dale "Titanic" Thurber had been anticipating, but it was one he could swing with, and shit, who knew what he'd been expecting to begin with? They'd been driven from the hotel on the docks a short distance to Sentosa Cove, on the water again, still in sight of all the signature skyscrapers, on a rooftop patio with sliding doors that could have been shut, the whole thing refrigerated as it ought to have been, as anything should be in this clime, but instead Billy Lim and his crowd kept them slid open, screened, so the players drowned in the humidity and the chirping of some damn South Asian cricket or shore frog, Titanic wasn't sure which. The patio was jammed to its edges with immense potted ferns, squat palm trees— the chirping could even have been coming from *inside.* The old man, who'd finally consented to summon them from the Smoker's Club, was a horror, could have passed for a mummy himself, and didn't play cards, just lurked around fishily, hairy-eyeballing the game and Billy Lim's servants. But the drinks were fresh and cold and the company, apart from Tiago Alves, who'd the past few evenings gone a bit fishy, too—and seemed to be playing Titanic for keeps, and *fuck* the Brazilian for that, he hadn't more than maybe a thousand of Titanic's dollars in his pocket, counting cumulatively from Guadalajara, and believe it, Titanic *was* counting—the company was jolly. Billy the Lim and his boys, three of them besides Billy, were like a bunch of retired Pentagon types, more or less, and they bet hard and held no grudges, and were full of dirty jokes even if Titanic only understood about a third of what was said in their so-called English. The hands they played were just a warm-up, apparently, which didn't keep Titanic—and Alves too, it didn't escape Titanic's notice—from laying some early waste to the Singaporeans' reserves.

"So where's this Mummy, anyhow?"

"He'll be along," said the old man, smiling like a lizard.

The Mummy did come along. He wasn't precisely what Titanic was expecting, either, from the weird nickname and rep, not a creature in bandages but a tall man in a white linen suit and a pale blue shirt, wearing sunglasses over a soft white mask that was tucked into his shirt like an ascot, and tailored to fit around his ears and to leave room at the top for a shock of sandy hair. He bore himself gracefully though with a slight limp to the empty seat at the table and Billy Lim and his cohort did nothing special to lower the mood to his spooky-ass level, went on chuckling and drinking and shuffling the cards, but the mood was nonetheless drawn down somehow, as though the evening had been organized around the Mummy's presence, his arrival here, and the servant who'd delivered each of their stacks of chips, the hundreds and the five hundreds and the thousands and the ten thousands that so wonderfully quickened your attention, gave you such a blast of goddamn adrenaline each time one was so much as touched, Titanic supposed that it was exactly true that it had been. And Titanic thought: *It's Lawrence of Arabia under there, why didn't they tell me?* It was Titanic's favorite goddamn movie, and now here he was, come all the way to Singapore for the legendary game and facing not a monster at the card table but Lawrence of goddamn Arabia hidden behind a bridal veil. Well, what the fuck?

"You can call me Titanic," he said, and stuck out his hand.

"Pleased to meet you," said the Mummy softly. But he didn't reach across the table for Titanic's hand. Instead he reached into his pocket and withdrew a gray, irregular cube of stone, which he positioned on the table behind his chips.

"What's that?" said Titanic. "Your lucky charm?"

"Yes, that's right." The Mummy's tone was merely pleasant, giving away no embarrassment, nor impatience, nor hostility.

Billy Lim dealt cards. And so it was on.

III

When the sun began to come up across the water you had to admit it was kind of beautiful, it gave the whole Sentosa Cove rooftop-patio thing its reason for being though Titanic was well sick of breathing the humid ocean air laced with the gray biting haze of smoke, the scent of burning that Billy Lim had explained to Titanic when he groused was the fault not of Singapore but of Malaysia, to which Singapore was so unfortunately shackled, and who were burning their rain forests for palm oil, wasn't it a pity? Yes, and it was a pity and really pretty shitty that Titanic at dawn found himself not only a hundred and sixty thousand Singapore dollars in the hole but also sensing that there were not many more hands to be dealt before Billy Lim woke again—he'd been dozing in his seat—and finally asked his guests to excuse him, bringing an end to the game. The warning signs were there. The servants who'd brought at three a.m. the kind of snack men used to fuel play—roast pork sandwiches and black coffee and ice-cold vodka—now came again with elegant little plates of breakfast, eggs and bacon, mini-croissants, and Titanic sensed it was the kiss-off in the making.

"Don't you eat?" he said to the Mummy. "You got a mouth under there?"

"I'm a vegetarian," the Mummy said lightly. He'd been away from the table only once or twice all night, to piss or shoot up heroin or vape or tap a Ouija board, whatever it was that fucking Mummies did on their breaks between ten-thousand-dollar poker hands. Alves, the Brazilian turncoat, was long gone. Alves had only lost a little, to Titanic and to Billy Lim. He'd taken a few hands here and there, too, but for the most part had played tight, folding the instant the

286

Mummy raised on a hand. That, Titanic had noticed, was Billy Lim's practice too, and that of his buddies, a cute little number they were running, boxing Titanic into being the only sucker at the table willing to go into it head-to-head. Which hadn't worked out too wonderfully. Death Valley had come at about three thirty, just after the coffee and meat and vodka had got Titanic brightened up and he'd seen a sweet little flush come together right on the flop and had tried to take back in one big haul what the Mummy had been accumulating from him, and the Mummy had gone for it, called the crazy raises, and then turned over a picayune boat, twos over four for insult's sake. Alves had been right, the Mummy was unbeatable, it was so uncanny it was pretty much even fucking stupid, even fucking boring, except for one thing, the thing Alves hadn't warned him about at all: *The sensation of losing a hand to the Mummy was almost as good as winning.* Titanic was in a trance. Without knowing it he'd waited his whole life to meet the gambler—the ghost? the creature?—who would do this to him, and now that it had happened he felt hypnotized by losing. He felt addicted to it. The old man had asked him politely to convey his bank details after the hand at three thirty, and he hadn't even kicked the old man's face in for it. And now the sun was coming up and he didn't want to leave, not yet.

Alves is with Lisa, you dumb monkey.

The thought came unbidden, one of his hunches, in his own voice as if he was sitting on the shoulder of his own jacket, whispering into his own ear. Titanic knew the voice. It came to him frequently, had come all through the long night of losing with the same urgency: *He's bluffing this time,* or *You'll fill the straight on the river.* The voice had let him down this night, but he still believed it, he felt the facts in the case arrive like an illness in his lungs or stomach. *The audacious fucking Brazilian was fucking his wife.* Alves had gone back to the hotel and straight to her room, or her to his. If he left now he could catch them, it was the true last hand of his night, played not in cards but in bodies.

"I gotta go."

Now, only now, did the Mummy reach across the table. His handshake felt as real as a man's. And then he collected his stone.

IV

"What made him leave so fast?" asked Falk, smoothing his face with cold cream at the sink, removing his foundation and blush. "Is he out of money?"

"Nothing to do with money. He has more than enough, as you well know."

Falk shrugged. "There can be surprises."

"Not this time."

"So what spooked him?"

"I was too tired to continue. I gave him knowledge concerning his wife. Something from the other one—Alves."

"Interesting," said Falk, turning.

"Not really." He'd only been a temporary occupant of the American, but long enough to find the matter putrid, nothing to revisit.

"If you're tired, you should go sleep. May I call you a car?"

"I'll walk."

There was nowhere safer than Singapore in the morning. Yet it was no more dangerous at night. That was what made it Singapore! This permanent marvel amused the tall figure in the white linen suit as he strode across the Sentosa Gateway, past Brani Island, into the city, gripping the stone in his pocket, otherwise unburdened. He needed sleep, yes. But he thought he might first cross along the viaduct and turn into Labrador Villa Road. He wished to see the birds there.

It was reason enough to be content that Edgar Falk had settled here in Singapore, at Sentosa Cove: the birds. The giant cormorants—one, at least, always seemed to be waiting there. His shorebird, the only animal that followed him everywhere he went in the world, begin-

288

ning at Stinson Beach. He could rename himself after the bird, even. Alexander B. Cormorant.

Or he might accept his name at present—the Mummy. Hoary, but conveying a kind of legacy.

In practice, he was a surgeon, delving through faces to what lay underneath, to look out through the eyes. There, to learn the only important thing about most men: what cards they held. He might even call himself Noah Behringer, for amusement's sake. He wondered if Edgar Falk would recognize that name, or whether it would be lost on him . . .

Flashman, Nooseman, Anonymous, Abide.

Ich bin ein Vegetarierin.

We're all Unknown Tragics on this bus.

Or a Vietnam vet, employed as a hydrotherapy attendant at Alta Bates, and looking on as a helpless white kid spunked up a whirlpool, mess you'd be obliged to clean up, damn. If he quested back he might even retrieve the man's name . . .

Anyone, anyone, but "Alexander Bruno"—words for one who no longer existed.

Thanks

Dr. Adam Duhan
Dr. Michael Blumlein
Dr. Marie Warburg
Dr. Laurence Rickels
Dr. Atul Gawande
Dr. Michael Zöllner
Dr. Chris Offutt
Dr. Amy Barrett

About the Author

Jonathan Lethem is the *New York Times* bestselling author of nine novels, including *Dissident Gardens, The Fortress of Solitude,* and *Motherless Brooklyn;* two short-story collections; and two essay collections, including *The Ecstasy of Influence,* which was a National Book Critics Circle Award finalist. Lethem is a recipient of a MacArthur Fellowship and winner of the National Book Critics Circle Award for Fiction, and his work has appeared in *The New Yorker, Harper's Magazine, Rolling Stone, Esquire,* and *The New York Times,* among other publications.